OPERATION KINGFISHER

Totally gripping and emotional WWII historical fiction

HILARY GREEN

Revised edition 2021
Joffe Books, London
www.joffebooks.com

First published by Robert Hale in Great Britain in 2013

Cover art by Jarmila Takač

ISBN: 978-1-80405-032-3

MAP

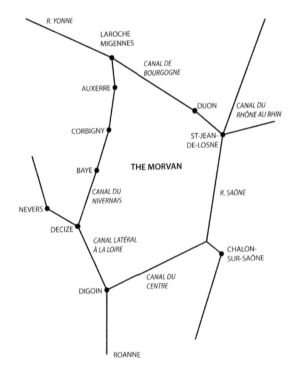

CHAPTER 1

AVIS

SERVICE DE TRAVAIL OBLIGATOIRE

Luke read the notice over the heads of the little group of peasant farmers and petit bourgeois gathered outside the *mairie*. 'Obligatory work service'. He felt a tightening in his stomach, part angry resentment, part fear. The notice was signed by Pierre Laval, head of the nominally 'free' government in Vichy, but everyone knew that it had been issued at the behest of the occupying Nazis; just as they knew that it meant transportation to Germany to work in the armament factories, freeing German workers to join the army. As Luke headed home, a course of action he had been contemplating for some time hardened into a firm resolve.

His mother, Isabelle, was in the low-ceilinged, stone-flagged kitchen preparing the soup for the midday meal. A neighbouring farmer had slaughtered a pig and had agreed to exchange some of the meat for a case of wine, so today the soup would be enriched with stock from the bones. It was illegal, of course, under the rationing regulations, but it made a welcome change from a diet consisting largely of vegetables.

Luke sniffed appreciatively, but the prospect of food could not dispel the tension in his guts.

His mother put down the spoon and turned towards him and, as she registered the expression on his face, he saw her turn pale.

'What is it?'

'The *Boche* have tightened up the regulations for STO. Now they are saying all men between the ages of eighteen and twenty-five. And there are to be no exceptions. All the previous exemptions have been rescinded.'

'*Mon Dieu*! I thought we had a couple of years' grace, when they asked for 20-year-olds. But now . . . When does this take effect?'

'The week after next. We have to report to the station at Clermont-Ferrand. It's organized by the first letter of your surname, so I'd be in the first batch.'

'What shall we do? The local people know that you're not French, but they've accepted us — more or less. The mayor has been prepared to give you and Christine ration cards. But if you have to present your papers to register for this work there will be no way he can conceal the fact that you are a British citizen. And once the Nazis find out, God knows what will happen . . .'

'Don't worry,' Luke assured her. 'It won't come to that. I've been thinking for a long time that I ought to be doing something more useful than helping out in the vineyard. I shall go to the Maquis.'

'No!' Isabelle spoke more forcibly than usual. 'I won't have you mixing with that band of outlaws. Everyone knows that most of them are just common criminals, using the Occupation as an excuse to extort money and goods from hard-working people.'

'That's not true!' Luke protested. 'Some of them may be crooks, but most of them are patriots who just want to strike a blow against the *Boche*.'

'Huh!' his mother responded. 'I've yet to see any evidence of that.' She turned back to stirring the soup with a deep sigh. 'If only I'd let you go back to England with your father when he went to join up! You would both be safe with your other grandparents now.'

'I wish you had let us go,' Luke said. 'Then I could have joined up, like Dad.'

Isabelle sighed. 'Oh, come on. We've been over this so many times. I thought — we both thought — you would be safer here in rural France than you would be in England under the blitz. But that was when this part of France was 'free'. What a fiasco that turned out to be! Two years of that weak-kneed lot in Vichy kowtowing to Hitler's every whim and then, when the *Boche* get the wind up about the Allies invading from the Mediterranean, they let them march in and take over the whole country. And now they want to drag our boys off to work in their filthy factories!'

The kitchen door banged open, letting in a blast of icy air. It was March, but even here in the southern Auvergne there was little sign of spring. With the cold, came Christine, Luke's younger sister, wiping her hands on a piece of oily rag and grinning triumphantly.

'There you are! I told you I could fix it.'

In spite of his worries, Luke found himself grinning back.

'You've got grease on your nose, sis.'

'Have I?' She wiped the back of her hand across her face, spreading the oily mark further. 'Never mind. At least the tractor goes again now.'

'Not for much longer,' her mother said. 'We won't be able to get any more fuel for it when it runs out. I really don't know why I let you persuade me to buy the wretched thing. We managed perfectly well with the horse — and we'll soon have to again.' She regarded her daughter with a look that combined regret and irritation. 'Do go and get yourself cleaned up, Chris. Lunch is ready. And take those oily overalls off. Why you can't put a skirt on like any other girl I don't understand!'

Christine exchanged a look with her brother.

'Because, dearest Maman, I'd look pretty silly on my back under the tractor with my bare legs sticking out so anyone passing could see straight up my skirt.'

'I just wish you would tidy yourself up and do something with your hair,' her mother responded. 'Don't you want to look attractive?'

'Who for? You and Luke? Or Grandad? There's no one else round here I want to attract.'

'There are still some perfectly nice young men in the village.'

'Peasants! Is that the best you think I can do?' Christine returned tartly, as she left the room.

Isabelle sighed again. 'I don't know what is going to become of that girl.'

'Never mind that, Maman,' Luke said. 'We've got more important things to worry about.'

'Yes, I know,' she replied. 'But I need time to think, Luke. Go and fetch your grandfather, will you? And don't say anything at lunch. There's no need to worry him.'

Luke found his grandfather sitting in his wheelchair by the window of his bedroom, with a shawl round his shoulders and a rug over his knees. They had moved him to a room on the ground floor and he liked to sit there, gazing out at his beloved vines, even now when they were nothing but bare stems; as if in his mind's eye he could see them heavy with grapes. The vineyard had been in the family for generations. It was on an early tour of France that Roger Beecham, a buyer for a company of wine merchants in London, had discovered Domaine des Volcans, a small winery in an obscure corner of the country, and fallen in love with its produce — and with the vigneron's only daughter. Then, five years ago, a stroke had incapacitated the old man and brought Isabelle and her husband and children from England to manage the vineyard. That had been in 1938, when peace had still seemed possible.

It was only after the meal, when the old man had fallen asleep as he usually did, that Luke was able to tell Christine about the notice outside the *mairie*. She looked at him with wide eyes.

'But I thought the idea was for people to volunteer, in exchange for French soldiers in POW camps in Germany.'

'How many men do you know who were prepared to volunteer?' her mother asked. 'And how many POWs came home? Very few. Not one for every ten men who went to Germany. The *Boche* soon realized that they were not going to get enough men that way. So then they introduced the STO for men aged 20 to 22 and allowed exceptions for those working in agriculture, or the sons of POWs. And that hasn't produced the numbers they want either; too many claiming exemption, and too many *réfractaires*, who simply disappeared instead of showing up for transportation. So now they want to drag in everyone they can get.'

Christine looked at her brother. 'You can't do it, Luke. You can't work for the Germans.'

'Of course I can't! I wouldn't, even if my papers were in order and I could pass as French. I've told Maman I'm going to the Maquis.'

'And I've told you I won't allow it!' his mother returned. 'We shall have to think of some other way.'

'What other way is there?'

'You may have to go back to England after all.'

'And how am I supposed to do that? Just turn up at Calais and ask the Germans to give me a ticket for the Channel Ferry?'

'There are ways. I've heard rumours. People are smuggled over the border into Spain or Switzerland. Leave it for now, Luke. We've got a little time. I'll make some enquiries.'

'For God's sake, Mother!' he exclaimed. 'Don't you know how dangerous that would be? If the *Milice* get wind of it . . .'

'I'm not a fool, Luke! Now please, say no more for now. There's work to be done in the vegetable patch. Make yourself useful, while you are still here.'

Luke hesitated for a moment, inclined to continue the argument, but his sister touched his arm and shook her head.

He looked at his mother's set face and turned away without another word to put on his working coat.

It seemed that further discussion of the problem was taboo for the rest of the day. That night, Luke slept badly. For months now, he had been dreaming of joining the men who had abandoned home and livelihood to live rough in the forest, preferring that to subjugating themselves to German rule. He knew it was true, as his mother said, that for some of them it was simply a way of escaping the law — whether German or French — but there were plenty of rumours going round of acts of sabotage and defiance and Luke imagined himself ambushing convoys and derailing trains. He had only been fifteen when war broke out, so there had been no question of joining up; but since he turned eighteen he had felt more and more guilty at his failure to play any active part in the conflict.

Mornings in the farmhouse followed a regular routine. While Isabelle attended to her father's needs, Luke fetched in wood and built up the fire in the big kitchen range to brew coffee — or the ersatz substitute made from roasted barley that was all that was available — and Christine cycled into the village for the miserable ration of 100 grams of bread for each of them. That morning, he was gazing gloomily out over the rows of blackened vines when the door crashed open in his sister's usual tempestuous manner.

He swung round irritably.

'*Nom de Dieu*, Chris. Can't you ever . . .' The words died on his lips as he saw the expression on her face. 'What is it? What's wrong?'

'Come outside.' Her voice was hoarse with distress. 'Come and look.'

He followed her out of the door. One side of the long, low, stone house was directly on the road leading to the village. Along it, someone had scrawled in red paint the words: *putain Anglaise* — English whore and below that: *espion* — spy.

'Why?' Christine demanded, on the verge of tears. 'Why would anyone write that?'

'God knows,' Luke said. 'But Maman mustn't see it. We must paint it out, quickly. There's some whitewash down in the cellar. I'll get it . . .'

He turned to go but it was too late. His mother was standing in the doorway, deathly pale and grim faced.

'I'm sorry, Maman,' Luke stammered. 'If I'd known . . .'

'It isn't your fault, *mon cher*,' she answered. 'You couldn't expect this.'

'It must have been done during the night,' Christine said. 'It must have been there when I went out, but I was going the other way. I didn't see it until I got back. But why? Why would anyone do that?'

Isabelle shook her head sadly. 'I think I understand what is behind it. You two don't know how much hostility there was to my marriage to your father. Domaine des Volcans has been in the family for generations — you know that much — but I think there were those in the village who hoped to get their hands on it, either by marrying me or by persuading me to sell. When I married your father and moved to England, people still thought I wouldn't come back, so when Grandpapa had his stroke they thought their chance had come. I'm afraid there is still a lot of resentment, carefully hidden until now, at the idea of the vineyard passing into British hands.'

'But what has that got to do with . . . with this?' Luke waved a hand at the graffiti.

'Since the *Boche* took over, I've heard some terrible stories. Some people have seen this as an opportunity to settle some old scores or grab land they have been trying to get hold of. It's hard to believe, but I have heard of people being denounced to the Germans for all sorts of petty infringements of regulations — like having a wireless set concealed so they can listen to the BBC.'

'And you think someone wants the *Boche* to see this?' Christine said. 'But what's the point? It's so obviously not true.'

'It's true that I am married to an Englishman,' her mother pointed out. 'And that you two are technically British citizens. That is probably enough to . . . Listen! What's coming?'

They all heard the roar of engines and a moment later, a convoy came into sight over the brow of the hill. Two motorcycle outriders led the way, followed by a staff car with two officers in the back. After them, came an armoured car, a helmeted German head protruding from the gun turret, and then several lorries packed with German soldiers. Instinctively, Isabelle and her two children had drawn back against the wall, in an attempt to conceal the words written there. The men were singing and as they passed several of them waved cheerfully, as if they were among their own people, but as far as Luke could see, none of them reacted to the graffiti.

'So! Now we know why the words were written last night,' Isabelle said.

'You mean someone knew that convoy was going to pass here this morning?'

'It looks like it.'

'I don't think they read it,' Christine said.

'They probably wouldn't understand it, anyway,' Luke pointed out.

'I've no doubt someone would have translated it for them,' Isabelle replied. 'But the question is, were they just passing through, or are they staying somewhere near here.'

'I'll find out,' Christine said, grabbing her bike from where she had left it against the wall. 'I'll ride into the village and snoop around. Someone will know if they are going to stay.'

'All right. But be careful,' her mother warned her. 'And we will paint over this . . . this mess. Luke, fetch the white-wash and a couple of brushes.'

Christine was back in half an hour, flushed from riding fast up the hill. Her mother and Luke were sitting at the kitchen table, eating a belated breakfast.

'They're staying. They've taken over the *château*. The officers are billeted in there and the men are camping in the grounds.'

'That settles it,' Isabelle said, and there was a new note of resolution in her voice. 'You must both leave. It's not safe for you here.'

'Leave?' Christine repeated. 'What do you mean? Luke has to go. We said that yesterday. But we can't both go.'

'Yes you can. And you must. It's obvious that there is someone around who wishes us ill. They only have to drop a hint to the officer in charge. I won't see you dragged off to a concentration camp.'

'But what about you?' Luke said. 'You must come with us.'

'How can I? I can't leave your grandfather and it's impossible to take him with us.'

'But we can't leave you to cope on your own,' Christine said.

'Listen. I shall be fine. I can manage your grandfather without help and Robert will have to see to the vines on his own. There isn't much to do at this time of year and, who knows, by the time of the *vendange* the war may be over. Now the Americans are with us, it can't go on much longer.'

'But it isn't safe for you here,' Luke said. 'Suppose this person, whoever it is, who wants the vineyard, tells the *Boche* that you are married to an Englishman . . .'

'That is not a crime. I am French. I have French papers and, whatever anyone says, I am not a spy. But it is a crime to harbour enemy citizens, so the longer you are here, the more danger we are all in. Without you, I shall be safer. So, you see, it is vital for you to go back to England.'

'That's easy to say,' Luke said. 'But how are we supposed to get there? Over the border to Spain?'

'No. I've been thinking. The Spanish border is nearer, granted, but you would need a guide to take you over the Pyrenees. And I have heard that the Spanish will intern any-one they catch. No, you must go north, to Montbéliard and to Marcel Lemaıtre; he is your godfather after all, and one of your father's oldest friends. They used to go mountaineering together before the war. He is a qualified Alpine guide and he knows every path through the mountains round his home. If anyone can get you over the border to Switzerland, he can.'

'That makes sense,' Luke said slowly. 'But how do we get to Montbéliard?'

'I don't see that that should be a problem. The trains are still running.'

'But the Germans check everyone's papers before you get on, don't they?' Christine said.

'They can't have guards at every tiny station, surely,' Luke objected.

'I'll speak to Jacques Dutoit,' Isabelle said. 'As mayor, he has the ability to issue identity papers. He wouldn't do it if you were staying here. There are too many people who know who you are and he must have enemies, like us, who would denounce him. But I'm sure I can persuade him to produce something that will get you onto a train.'

Luke gazed at her in silence for a moment, torn between a sense of guilt at leaving her and a sudden sense of excitement. If they could make it over the border and get back to England, he would be able to join up, like his father. At last there would be an opportunity to prove that he was not a coward.

He said, 'You really mean this, Maman? You really think it's best, for all of us?'

She reached across the table and took his hand. 'I do, my darling. God knows, I shall miss you both. But at least I shan't have to live with the fear that you may be arrested at any moment. Don't let's argue about it. It's decided. You must leave as soon as possible.'

CHAPTER 2

While Luke was tossing and turning in his bed at Domaine des Volcans, on an airfield in Hertfordshire a car with masked headlights drew up outside a hangar and two men got out.

The buildings were in darkness, but the moon was almost full and in its light the outline of a Whitley bomber was just visible on the tarmac. Roger Beecham pulled a small suitcase from the boot of the car and shook hands with the pretty FANY driver. Then, he and his companion went into the hangar. Inside, he was met by the man who had been his conducting officer all through his training and taken through to a small office, made stuffy by the heat of an oil stove. Here, both men were required to turn out their pockets and remove their outer clothing. Every article, down to their underwear was carefully checked; no letters or photographs, no English cigarettes, no souvenirs of home could be carried — a forgotten bus ticket in the corner of a pocket could be fatal. Everything had either been made in France, or produced in England by French tailors and given the label of a French manufacturer. Here, Roger was fortunate; most of the clothes were his own, bought while he was living in the Auvergne. Even his teeth had passed the inspection of the SOE dentist, as the only fillings had been carried out in France.

Once he was dressed again, he was given a packet of Gauloise cigarettes, the wrappers from a couple of French boiled sweets, and a crumpled receipt from a chain of French department stores. His French identity card and ration card were already safely stowed in his pack. As he distributed the items around his pockets, his conducting officer held out a small jewel case. Inside was a pair of gold cuff-links.

'These could come in handy if you find yourself in need of funds,' he said. 'But otherwise they are yours to keep, with the grateful thanks of HM Government. There is one more thing: see, here?' He pressed a tiny catch on one link, which opened to show a small cavity in which rested a little yellow capsule. 'You know about these. Bitten, death occurs within seconds. Swallowed whole, you've got a few hours. There is no obligation to make use of it, of course. That is entirely up to you, depending on the circumstances. Now, is there anything else? Any questions?'

Roger shook his head. At that moment, he felt he was not in total command of his voice.

'Better get your 'chute on, then,' the officer said.

Ten minutes later, swaddled in a thick flying suit and with the parachute banging into the backs of his legs as he walked, Roger followed his companion out to the waiting aircraft. A brief handshake, a wish of 'good luck', and he climbed aboard. The engines roared, the plane taxied onto the runway, gathered speed and took off, circling to gain altitude, and set a course for France.

Isabelle Beecham, or Isabelle Thierry as her neighbours still preferred to call her, sat in the office of Jacques Dutoit, mayor of St Amand. Dutoit was a corpulent man with heavy jowls that made him look like a bloodhound, or so Isabelle thought. And at that moment, the jowls were shaking.

'But, *chère madame*, it is impossible. You don't know what you are asking.'

'I know perfectly well,' Isabelle replied. 'And I know you can do it. We both know the price I paid for you to provide

Luke and Christine with ration cards. Now it is my turn to name my price. Either you produce identity cards for both of them or Jeanne gets to hear all about what we — what you — got up to that evening, here in your office.'

The jowls shook more violently. 'Very well, very well. I will do my best.'

'It had better be better than your best,' Isabelle said. 'If the documents were not to pass muster, Jeanne would not be the only person hearing my story. I have no doubt the *Milice* would be very interested in the various little "favours" you have done for people in the village — at a price of course. Here, I've brought you two recent photographs. Just make sure everything is perfectly correct.'

'Of course, of course. Don't worry. Everything will be in order. When do you need the documents?'

'Tomorrow.'

'Tomorrow? Madame, please . . .'

'Tomorrow.' Isabelle rose. 'I will collect them tomorrow afternoon.'

Later, when the evening meal had been eaten and grandfather had been put to bed, Isabelle sat at the big kitchen table with her two children.

'I have spoken to Dutoit. Your new documents will be ready tomorrow.'

'*Mon Dieu, Maman!*' Luke exclaimed. 'How did you manage that? Old Dutoit would rather see the whole village go up in flames than put himself at risk.'

Isabelle gave him a small, grim smile. 'Oh, I have my ways. Jacques and I have known each other for a long time. Now, listen. I checked on the trains as well. You can catch one from Clermont-Ferrand to Lyons. You change there for Montbéliard.' She shook her head. 'It's a long, roundabout journey and I'm afraid it will take more than 24 hours, the way the trains are these days, but there's no better route.'

Both Luke and Christine were silent for a moment, absorbing all this, then Luke said, 'What do we tell people if they ask why we're going halfway across the country to see Marcel? People don't travel for pleasure these days.'

'I know,' his sister responded. 'We'll say he's been taken ill, like granddad, and we're going to look after him. He's got a shop, hasn't he?'

'Yes, he sells clothes and equipment for mountaineering and skiing — at least he did before the war. He was called up, of course, but I know he went back to Montbéliard when he was demobbed after the capitulation. I haven't heard from him lately but I have no reason to think he's gone anywhere else. Though I don't suppose there's much demand for the stuff he sells these days.'

'Well, he must be earning a living somehow,' Christine said. 'We can say Luke is going to mind the shop and I'm going to look after him.'

'Well done, *chérie*,' her mother said. 'That should be enough to satisfy any enquiries.'

'There's another point,' Luke said. 'How do we get to Clermont? There's no fuel for the car.'

'We could cycle,' Christine suggested, 'but then we'd have to abandon the bikes at the station.'

'I've thought of that,' her mother responded. 'The day after tomorrow, Gaspard Duhamel will be coming to collect the next consignment of wine for Bussy. He can give you a lift on his way back.'

Bussy was the name of the wine merchant in Clermont-Ferrand who sold most of the produce of Cave des Volcans, now that the English market was closed to them.

'The day after tomorrow?' Luke stared at his mother.

'So soon?' Christine said, in the same breath.

They looked at each other, both suddenly aware that their departure, which had seemed a matter of theory and conjecture, had become an imminent reality.

'The sooner the better,' Isabelle said. She reached across the table and took hold of a hand of each of them. 'My darlings, I know it's a terrible wrench. I feel dreadful at the prospect of sending you off into the unknown like this, and

I shall miss you more than words can say. But it is the only way I can keep us all safe. You do see that, don't you?'

Christine squeezed her hand.

'Of course we do, Maman. You don't need to worry about us. Once we get to Montbéliard we shall be fine. Even if Uncle Marcel can't get us over the border, we can stay with him. No one knows us there, so there's no reason for them to doubt what our new identity cards say. What worries us is going away and leaving you on your own.'

'I shan't be on my own. There's your grandfather to look after, and I can rely on Robert and his family. They have worked in the vineyard for generations and they're all old friends.'

Luke said nothing. In all his dreams of joining the Maquis, he had always assumed that his home and his family would still be there, in the background, for him to return to when the battle was won — or when he had need of them. This was different; this meant a complete severance. They would not even be able to telephone or exchange letters. With any luck, he would see his father again, and fulfil his ambition of joining him in the RAF, but he was beginning to have a more realistic view of that, too. The war showed no sign of ending, and there was a good chance that he would not survive. He might never see his mother, or Cave des Volcans, again.

'There's one more thing,' Isabelle said. 'I shall be on tenterhooks until I know you are safe in England. Marcel can write to let me know you have arrived safely in Montbéliard but after that there will be no way of keeping in touch, except for via the BBC. We've listened to the *messages personnels* which are broadcast every evening but they mean nothing unless you understand the code. As soon as you get to England you must apply to the BBC and ask them to broadcast a message for me, but we need to decide on the wording. It needs to be something that could only come from you, but not so specific that the *Boche* could trace it back to me. Any ideas?'

They wrestled with the problem in silence for a moment. Then Luke said, 'You mean something like "The ducklings are safely back in the pond?"'

'Too vague,' his sister objected. 'That could come from anyone.'

'True.' He pondered again. 'I know! Remember our old dog, Michou? How about "Michou's pups are safe in the kennel?"'

'Excellent!' his mother exclaimed. 'Don't forget it, will you? I shall be listening to every broadcast.'

'Be careful,' Luke said. 'You know what the penalties are for having a clandestine radio.'

'Don't worry. I shall take all the usual precautions. Now, let us be practical. You must pack. One suitcase only. You don't want to burden yourself with too much. But it must look as though you really intend to stay in Montbéliard, in case your cases are searched, so put in what you would expect to need for a couple of weeks, at least. But nothing to suggest that you don't expect to be back — in the short term, I mean.'

By the following evening, their new identity cards were ready, as promised, bearing the names of Luc and Christine Beauchamps. As they compared the photographs on them, Christine remarked, 'The trouble is, you don't even look French. You take after Dad — tall, fair-haired, blue eyes. You'd pass for a German any day. I'm much more like Maman, little and dark.'

'*Petite chérie*,' Isabelle said. 'Don't make us sound like gnomes. Anyway, you've shot up in the last few months. You could look quite elegant if you took the trouble to dress properly.'

'Oh, don't start that again, please!' her daughter responded wearily. 'Just be glad I'm not like the girls in the village, constantly complaining about clothes rationing and re-making old dresses to try to make them look new and painting their lips with beetroot juice. Anyway, think of it this way: no one is likely to try to seduce me on the journey tomorrow.'

Isabelle sighed. 'Perhaps you're right, under the circumstances.'

Duhamel arrived the following morning, as expected. He was a small man with a surprisingly chubby face and two little dark eyes that looked as if they had been pushed into its folds like currants in a bun. As usual, when the wine had been loaded into his van, Isabelle gave him lunch. She knew from experience that he was fond of a drink and that day, instead of the *vin ordinaire* which she usually gave him, she opened a bottle of one of the vineyard's better vintages.

When he was halfway down it, she said, 'Monsieur Duhamel, I want to ask you a favour.'

The little eyes swivelled from his glass to her face suspiciously. 'And what might that be, Madame?'

'Luke and Christine are going to visit their godfather. He has been taken ill and needs their help. Could you give them a lift into Clermont? It will hardly be out of your way to drop them at the station.'

The eyes dodged hers as if seeking a hiding place.

'Madame, I regret, there is very little room in the van. That horrible gazogène burner I have had to put in to get round the petrol shortage takes up so much space . . .'

'Oh, I'm sure you could squeeze them in somewhere,' Isabelle persisted. 'After all, it's not a long journey.'

'But I am not going back directly.' He looked delighted to have found a way of escape. 'I have to go first to Vic-le-Comte to pick up some wine from a *cave* near there.'

'Well, they can come for the round trip, then.'

'But, Madame!' He was beginning to sweat. 'Suppose we are stopped at a checkpoint? I came through one on my way here. They searched the van.'

'So what? It's not a crime to give a couple of people a lift.'

The little eyes were almost revolving in their sockets in terror. 'But everyone knows that your children are not French. It is a crime to assist enemy nationals.'

Isabelle smiled at him and refilled his glass.

'You don't need to worry. They have new papers. If you should happen to be stopped there is no reason for the *Boche* to suspect anything.'

'But suppose there are *miliciens* there? They are local men. They know everyone.'

'The chances of there being a member of the *Milice* who knows my family at a German checkpoint kilometres away are so remote, that I think we can safely discount them.' Isabelle reached out and removed the bottle from Duhamel's reach. 'The fact is, Gaspard, that I really need this favour. I don't know anyone else with transport and a good reason for going between here and Clermont. I'm not asking you to take any real risks. And if you oblige me, a couple of cases of the vintage you are drinking now might find their way into your van, without M. Bussy being any the wiser. I'm sure there are plenty of people who are prepared to pay over the odds on the black market to get hold of some decent wine.'

Greed and fear wrestled in Duhamel's fat face for a moment. At length he muttered, 'Very well, Madame. I have only tried to point out to you the possible risks involved . . . but if you insist . . .'

Isabelle pushed the bottle back to him. 'I do. Now, finish your wine and get ready. The two cases are just inside the cellar door.'

Luke and Christine had listened silently to all this. Their mother turned to them.

'It's time, my dears. Fetch your suitcases.'

When they returned to the kitchen, Duhamel was absent. Isabelle handed each of them a package containing the next day's bread ration, split and filled with a few grams of cheese, and an apple, wrinkled from long storage since the previous harvest.

'And take this,' she said, holding out an envelope to each of them. 'There's money for your train tickets and a little over for emergencies. I would give you more, but you know how hard times are at the moment.'

Christine threw her arms round her. 'I wish we didn't have to take it. I can't bear to think of you all alone. Let me stay with you.'

'No, *chérie*, it's impossible, you know it is. We've been through it all so many times. Don't make it any harder, please.'

Christine drew back, sniffing. She prided herself on never crying, but now she could not hold back the tears. Luke embraced his mother. His throat was dry and he could feel himself shaking but he knew he must not let go. If he wept, Duhamel would guess that this was more than a brief parting.

'We shall be together again soon!' Isabelle said, looking into his eyes. 'The war must end before long.' She reached out her free hand to Christine. 'Give my love to papa when you see him, and to your other grandparents — and don't forget the message!'

'Michou's pups are safe,' Christine responded, forcing a smile. 'We won't forget.'

From outside, Duhamel shouted, 'Let's go! I've got a schedule to keep to.'

Luke picked up his sister's overcoat to help her on with it and exclaimed. 'Chris, this weighs a ton! Whatever have you got in the pockets?'

'Just a few odds and ends I thought might come in useful,' she answered. 'A torch, a screwdriver, a compass, a penknife — that sort of thing.'

In spite of the situation, he found himself laughing. 'Honestly, you are extraordinary. We're going on a train journey, not a camping expedition.'

Christine shoved the envelope of money into one of her pockets and picked up the packet of food. 'I don't know where to put this. My case is full.'

Luke held up an old leather satchel, which he had once used to carry his books to school. 'I'm taking this. You can put it in there with mine.'

'Where are your papers?' Isabelle asked. 'Have you got them safe?'

'In my pocket,' Christine said, and Luke patted the satchel. 'In here. I think they will be safer there. Pockets can be picked.'

Duhamel shouted again from outside and Isabelle urged them towards the door.

'Go, go! He won't wait.'

Luke went out, but as Christine made to follow her mother caught her arm. 'Chris, I know this sounds silly, as you are the younger and the girl, but try to look after Luke. He's strong and brave and I know he would do anything to protect you, but he can be a bit of a dreamer. He has these romantic ideals . . . you know what I mean. Don't let him rush into any foolish adventure.'

A brief smile flitted across her daughter's face. 'I know what you mean. I'll do my best.'

Outside, Duhamel gestured to them to get into the rear of the van.

'Why can't we ride up front with you?' Luke asked.

'Better not. If no one sees you they won't ask questions, will they.'

'But if they open the van and find us, it will look suspicious . . .'

'It's that or nothing. Are you coming or not?'

Luke gave his mother a final hug and climbed in and Christine followed. They had a last view of Isabelle waving and biting her lip and then the van doors were slammed and they were left in darkness.

CHAPTER 3

As the van bounced and swayed out onto the road, Luke grumbled, 'It's crazy making us hide in here. If we are stopped it's going to give the game away at once.'

'Duhamel's a coward,' his sister responded. 'He's in a flat panic and he's not thinking straight. We'll just have to hope we're not stopped.'

It was an uncomfortable ride, sharing the small space with crates of wine and the fumes from the gazogène burner. They sensed from the change in speed and the smoother ride that the van had turned onto the main highway heading south, but then they came to sudden halt.

'This can't be Vic-le-Comte,' Christine said.

Luke shook his head tensely, knowing that the same thought was in both their minds. The rear doors were flung open. Duhamel stood there.

'Out!'

'Why?' Luke demanded. 'What's wrong?'

'Out!' the man repeated.

Unwillingly, they both scrambled out of the van and looked around them. They were not, as they had feared, at a road block. The van was stopped at the side of the road on the hill going down to the River Allier, but their view ahead was blocked.

'What's the problem?' Luke made to move round the van to see.

'Stay here!' Duhamel hissed. 'There's a German patrol down by the bridge where the road goes off to Vic. They are checking everyone's papers. I don't want them to see you.'

'But it doesn't matter!' Christine exclaimed. 'Our papers are in order. All you have to do is let us ride up front like ordinary passengers and tell the *Boche* that you are giving us a lift. There's no problem.'

'It's all very well for you to say that,' the little man muttered, 'but I'm not taking the risk. See here. If you walk back a hundred metres, there's a small path that goes down to the river and a footbridge across. I know, because I lived here when I was a kid. You go that way and you will find you can get back up to the road that goes to Vic-le-Comte, well past the roadblock. I'll wait for you there.' He slammed the doors of the van. 'Go on! Get moving. I can't hang around all day.'

Before either of them could argue further he scuttled away and climbed into the driving seat. A second later, the van was moving away downhill.

Luke and Christine looked at each other helplessly.

'Well, there's nothing for it. We'll have to do as he says,' Luke said. 'Come on, we'd better not make him wait too long.'

The path was as Duhamel had described it, and they made their way down through a vineyard to the river bank and across the footbridge. Rain, which had been threatening all day, came on in earnest as they climbed up the far side, making the heavy tweed coats which they both wore heavier still and clogging their feet with mud. They were out of breath when they finally scrambled up the bank onto the lane. For a moment they both stood still, looking to right and left; there was no sign of Duhamel's van.

'Perhaps he meant further on,' Christine said.

They trudged up the road until they could see round the next bend. There was still no sign of the van. Luke put into words what they were both fearing.

'The bastard's gone and left us.'

'*Cochon! Lâche!*' Christine shouted into the distance. 'I knew we couldn't trust him. I reckon he always meant to ditch us at the first opportunity.' A new thought struck her. 'Oh, Luke! Our cases were in the van. He's gone off with them. Everything we needed for the journey.'

'*Merde!*' Luke exclaimed. He thought for a moment, frowning. 'It could be worse. Once we get to Montbéliard, Uncle Marcel will be able to fix us up with what we need. I'm sure he's got friends who would lend us some old clothes. And once we get home to England—'

He was cut short by a cry from his sister.

'Luke! Your satchel! You didn't leave that in the van, did you?'

Luke struck his forehead with the back of his hand.

'Oh God! I did. What a fool!'

'And your papers?'

'They are all in the satchel.'

'Oh no! Luke, what on earth possessed you? What are we going to do without them?'

'I don't know,' he groaned. 'But we'd better move. We can't stand here in the middle of nowhere getting soaked.'

'Just a minute!' Christine caught his arm. 'He said he had wine to collect in Vic. It must be either Perrault's place or the Cave de Veyres. If we hurry we might be able to catch him.'

'Well done, Chris!' Luke squeezed her arm. 'Come on. It's worth a try. We can't be far from Vic.'

It took them half an hour to reach the little town, but the first vineyard they tried had never heard of Duhamel and when they reached the second, it was to learn that he had left ten minutes earlier.

They beat a hasty retreat, but once out of sight they stopped and looked at each other bleakly.

'So he has just left us stranded, the bastard,' Luke said.

Neither of them spoke for a moment.

Then Christine said, 'Well, it's done now. The question is, what do we do next?'

Luke ran his hand through his wet hair. 'I don't know. Try to get home? We might be able to thumb a lift if we go back to the main road.'

'We can't!' his sister said. 'You know what Maman said, the longer we are there the more danger she is in. And I honestly don't think I could bear to go through saying good-bye all over again.'

'You're right. We'll have to find our way to Montbéliard somehow. Do you still have your money and papers safe?'

Christine felt in her pocket and produced a wallet containing the money and her new identity card.

'I might have enough to pay for train tickets for both of us — and perhaps you won't be asked to show your papers. The *Boche* can't check everyone at every station. It's a risk, but I don't see what else we can do. Where's the nearest station?'

Luke screwed up his face. 'Martres-de-Veyres, I'm afraid. It's about eight kilometres from here. Come on. We'll just have to walk.'

They plodded on for a time in silence.

Then Luke said, 'God, I hate this!'

'Trudging along in the rain? I'm not so keen on it myself, especially in these shoes.'

He shook his head angrily. 'That's not what I mean! I hate this whole business. I hate running away.'

His sister stopped and looked at him. 'We're not running away.'

'Yes, we are. Well, I am. I should stay here and fight.'

'Don't be silly. If you stay here, you'll end up working for the Germans. You won't have any choice.'

'Not if I go to the Maquis.'

She took a deep breath. 'Listen to me. The Maquis are all very well, but they are not going to win the war. You are going home to enlist, remember? Don't you think you'll

26

be more of a danger to the Nazis flying a Spitfire, or dropping bombs on their factories, than you could ever be in the Maquis?'

He frowned at her, rain dripping down his face. Then he gave her a crooked grin. 'OK, you win. You're right, as usual. Let's press on.'

They had dressed for the train journey, not for a long tramp in the rain, and by the time they reached the little station, they were both soaked and footsore. It was a relief to discover that there were no German guards or members of the *Milice* checking papers, but the platform was empty and it was clear that they were in for a long wait. The ticket clerk sold them tickets without expressing any curiosity about the purpose of their journey and told them the next train was due in just over an hour.

By the time it arrived, they were both shivering and there was little comfort to be had in the unheated carriages. At Clermont-Ferrand, they were able to change trains without encountering any checks. The train was packed with businessmen in suits and farmers in blue overalls, with an occasional smartly dressed woman, and they were lucky to find seats. As they settled down Christine felt that at last the worst was over. They still had to change trains again at Lyons, but with any luck by tomorrow morning they would be in Montbéliard.

It was warmer here, largely due to the press of bodies; outside it was growing dark and, soothed by the regular rhythm of the wheels, she began to doze. They had been going for about an hour when Luke nudged her.

'Going for a pee!'

He left the compartment and she settled back in her corner. A few minutes later, the door slid open and Luke stood in the doorway. He made no attempt to enter and from the expression on his face, Christine knew at once that they were in trouble. He jerked his head, indicating that she should join him in the corridor, and she stumbled out over the feet of the other passengers.

'What's wrong?'

'There are *Milice* on the train. They are going into every compartment demanding to see people's papers. They're in there now, three compartments up from ours.'

Christine's brain was racing.

'I'll be OK. Can't you hide in the toilet until they've gone past?'

'No, it won't work. A man went in just as I came out and I heard one of them banging on the door and demanding his papers. He was obviously going to wait until the chap came out.'

At that moment the train slowed and tilted as it negotiated a bend.

'Where are we? What's the next stop?' Christine asked.

'I'm not sure. Roanne, I suppose.'

'Let's move down the train. If we keep going back, we might get to the station before the *Milice* reach us.'

'It's an idea, but I've got a feeling we're quite near the back already. Still, let's try it.'

They made their way along the swaying corridor, squeezing past passengers who had been unable to find seats, until they came to the end of the carriage. Luke tried the door that should have given access to the next one, but it was locked.

'Damn! This must be the last carriage. We can't go back any further.'

As he spoke, a door further up the train was slid open and the two *milicien* came out. They went straight to the next compartment and Christine heard them roughly demanding to see everyone's identity documents. She felt the train slowing down more.

'Perhaps we're coming into the station now,' she said. 'Can you see?'

Luke went to the door leading to the outside and lowered the window so that he could lean out.

'We're on some kind of embankment. I can't see any sign of a station, but there's a bridge up ahead. We're definitely slowing up.'

The two *miliciens* came out of the compartment and one began checking the papers of passengers standing in the corridor. The second one went into the compartment nearest to where Luke and Christine were standing.

Luke said, 'There's only one thing for it: I'll have to jump. It's now or never. Once we're on the bridge it will be impossible. You get off at the next stop and wait for me. It can't be far ahead.'

'Not on your life!' Christine responded. 'I'm not risking us being separated. I'll jump with you.'

'No!' her brother exclaimed. 'It's too dangerous!'

The man checking the standing passengers finished with one and moved to the next. For the moment, they were hidden from him in the recess beside the door but Christine saw that if he came any closer he must see them.

She grabbed the door handle and forced it open. The wind whipped into her face and, beyond the rails, the ground dropped away into the darkness. She looked at her brother.

'See you at the bottom!'

The next second, she was falling through space. There was a bone-jarring impact and then she was rolling, over and over, the branches of low-growing bushes tearing her face and legs. She grasped at them; the first one or two ripped through her fingers, but at last she got a grip on one and it brought her headlong progress to a standstill.

For a few minutes she lay panting, becoming aware of stinging pain in various parts of her body. Then she sat up cautiously and discovered that all her limbs seemed to be intact and under her command. She was clinging to the side of a steep embankment, and below her she could make out the gleam of water. Looking up, she realized that the train had gone. She could hear it rattling away in the distance. Apparently, she thought, the *miliciens* had not seen them jump, or they would have pulled the communication cord. Maybe one of the other passengers had noticed the open door and shut it?

She peered round her in the gloom.

'Luke? Are you all right?'

There was no response. She called again, with the same result. She lowered herself cautiously to the bottom of the slope and found herself on a footpath running alongside either a river or a canal.

She called Luke's name again, but only silence answered her. For a terrible moment, she considered the possibility that he might not have jumped. Had he lost courage at the last minute? Or, worse still, had her movement alerted the *miliciens*, and had they caught him before he could follow? If that was the case, what should she do now? If he had stayed on the train and managed somehow to avoid capture, he would be waiting for her at the next station. Should she try to walk there and look for him? Or would it be more sensible to try to get to Montbéliard on her own? The thought of going on without knowing what had happened to her brother was unbearable.

Then she saw a dark, crumpled figure lying on the path a few yards from where she stood. She felt her heart thump once and then it seemed to stop altogether. If he was dead . . .

Luke was lying in a heap, his face half hidden, and he was not moving. Christine dropped on her knees beside him and put her hand on his shoulder.

'Luke! Can you hear me? Luke, it's me. Speak to me, please!' She was weeping in spite of herself. With an effort, she pulled herself together and tried to remember what she knew about first aid. She put her hand on his throat and gave a sob of relief as she felt a pulse.

He gave a low moan and stirred slightly. She gripped his shoulder and pulled him over onto his back. His eyes were half closed and there was a gash above his left eye, around which the flesh was already swollen and discoloured.

'Oh, thank God! Luke, wake up! You must wake up!'

He mumbled something indistinct and she laid her hand on his cheek.

'It's all right. You'll be all right. I'm here.'

'What?' he muttered. 'What's happened? Where am I?'

'We had to jump out of the train, remember? You must have hit your head.'

'Train?' He struggled to sit up. 'Fetch Maman, will you? I think I'm going to be sick.'

He twisted away from her and vomited onto the ground.

She choked back a moan of despair. She recognized the symptoms of concussion; she drew him towards her and cradled his head on her lap.

'I can't fetch Maman, *chéri*. We're on our way to Montbéliard, to see Uncle Marcel. You lost your papers and we had to jump off the train. Try to remember.'

He squinted up at her and she saw him struggling to clear his mind. After a moment, he nodded faintly and mumbled something that sounded like assent. It was still raining and she could feel that he was beginning to shiver. One thing was abundantly clear: somehow they must find shelter.

She peered along the towpath but with the blackout there was no way of telling if there was any kind of habitation ahead. She bent her head to Luke's.

'Are you hurt anywhere else, except your head? Do you think you can walk?'

'Don't know,' he mumbled.

'You have to try,' she said. 'We have to get out of this rain somewhere. Come on, I'll help you.'

With difficulty, she dragged him to his feet. He swayed, but it seemed he could stand, with her help. She pulled his arm across her shoulders and they began to stagger along the path.

After a couple of hundred yards, Christine was exhausted and Luke was hanging ever more heavily on her shoulders. She began to despair of ever finding shelter; but then, a dark shape loomed up ahead. Some kind of boat was moored against the bank.

She lowered Luke onto one of the bollards to which it was tied, and felt in her pocket for her torch. A brief examination showed her that it was a barge with a long cargo hold covered with a tarpaulin and a cabin aft. The cabin windows showed no crack of light and when she leaned her head close, she could hear no sound from inside, but a gang plank led up from the bank. She reasoned that the owners had probably gone into the nearest town, which must therefore be fairly close; but one look at Luke slumped on the bollard assured her that however near it was, there was no chance that he could walk that far.

She climbed the gang plank and knocked on the door of the cabin. There was no response and, with her heart in her mouth, she tried the door. It was locked.

Christine turned her attention to the hold. If they could find space under the tarpaulin, they would, at least, be out of the rain. It was lashed down securely and the knots had swollen with the rain and refused to give. She heard herself whimper with frustration and weariness and gritted her teeth. She had always thought of herself as brave and resourceful and now was the moment to prove it. She delved into her pocket again and found her most prized possession: a penknife with multiple attachments. She opened the screwdriver and used it to prize the knots loose, until she was able to lift an edge of the tarpaulin and peer underneath. A smell rose from the cargo that swamped her with a sudden wave of homesickness. The barge was loaded with casks of wine.

Christine wriggled her head and shoulders under the cover and shone her torch into the space; most of it was taken up by the barrels, but she reckoned that there was just enough room for her and Luke to lie down between them. She climbed down and, with difficulty, persuaded her brother to make a final effort. It was a struggle, but at last they were both inside and she pulled the tarpaulin closed over their heads.

It was pitch dark, and the smell of the wine was almost overpowering, but at least it was dry. She struggled out of her coat and rolled it up to make a pillow for Luke, who was still only semiconscious, and shivering violently. She remembered something her father had told her on one of the expeditions into the mountains he used to take them on before the war:

'If you are ever caught out in the open in bad weather, hypothermia is your worst enemy. Use your body heat to keep each other warm.'

She undid Luke's coat and snuggled against him, with her head on his shoulder. It felt strange at first. When they were small she often used to climb into bed with him and he would tell her stories until she fell asleep, but that had stopped years ago. She had forgotten how comforting the closeness of another body could feel. As if he felt it too, he muttered something and put his arm round her. Slowly she became aware of their mutual warmth spreading through her body.

Luke stopped shivering and began to snore faintly. Christine's stomach rumbled and she remembered regretfully the bread and cheese her mother had given them, and which had disappeared along with Luke's satchel. Damn Duhamel! They had had nothing to eat since an early lunch and now it was almost midnight. But that, she reflected, was the least of their troubles. She closed her eyes and let the exhaustion of the day wash over her.

CHAPTER 4

Christine woke with a start.

A man's voice called something, a woman's answered; there were heavy footsteps and then the unmistakable thud of a diesel engine. The barge was moving!

For a moment she lay paralysed with the shock. How could she have let herself sleep so long? And what was she going to do now? She rolled over and looked at Luke in the faint light that now filtered in around the edges of the tarpaulin. He was still asleep but his face was deadly pale and the left side of it was discoloured by a dark bruise and so swollen that his left eye was almost invisible. She touched his cheek; it felt cold and slightly clammy — so cold that she laid her cheek against his chest and was relieved to hear his heart beating. She tried to sit up and was prevented by the tarpaulin. Crouched uncomfortably, she tried to think what to do next.

Her first instinct was to stay hidden and hope that, before too long, the barge would moor up again and the owners would go away, so that she and Luke could sneak out. That idea was dismissed as soon as it entered her head. It was quite likely, she reasoned, that the boat would not stop again until nightfall and there was no possibility of waiting until then. Luke needed dry clothes and a proper bed, and probably the attention of a doctor. Even if that could be delayed, there were other more urgent requirements. Apart from anything else, she was painfully aware that very soon she would have to pass water and the thought of doing so in this confined space was abhorrent. Equally pressing, was the need to drink; her throat was parched and she knew that even though they could survive a long time without food, they must have water. Staying hidden was not an option.

So the next question was, what should she say to the boat owners to explain their presence and how would they react to the discovery of two stowaways?

She considered making up a story about running away from home, with details of ill-treatment to explain their motives; but she sensed that, in spite of Luke's current condition, they both looked too well fed and healthy to make such a tale credible. Besides which, the likelihood was that their unsuspecting hosts would feel it their duty to hand them over to the police.

After a long internal debate she decided that on balance the best thing to do would be to tell the truth and appeal to the owners' sense of patriotism. To hand two runaways to the police was one thing; but surely, to hand two fugitives over to the Nazis would be unthinkable? To do so would make them collaborators with the hated enemy, and what could they hope to gain? Anyway, there seemed to be no alternative.

Luke stirred and groaned. She leaned over him and murmured, 'It's all right, *chéri*. I'm here.'

'Water!' he mumbled. 'Water, please!'

'Yes, soon. Lie still. I'll get you some as soon as I can.'

She sat up and pushed at the tarpaulin cover, only to discover to her horror that the ropes that held it down had been lashed tight again. For a moment she had to fight down a wave of claustrophobia. Then she began to bang her hands against the stiff fabric and shout.

'Help, please! I'm in here! Let me out! Please let me out!'

There was no response for what felt like a long time. Then she heard footsteps, and the man's voice said, '*Mon Dieu*! There's someone in here!'

She heard the ropes being tugged and then the tarpaulin was folded back, letting in a flood of sunlight. A man with a broad, weather-beaten face stared down at her.

'Mother of God, what are you doing in there?'

'Please, Monsieur, we don't mean any harm. My brother is hurt and we had to find shelter somewhere. Can you help him, please?'

'Hurt?' The man leaned closer and peered at Luke. 'What happened to him?'

'He fell and hit his head. I think he needs a doctor.'

The man looked from Luke to her and seemed to make up his mind.

'Come on, let's have you out of there. Give me your hand.'

A strong arm hauled her up and she saw that the rain had stopped and instead it was a morning of spring sunshine and light wind. The boatman pulled the cover back further, climbed down into the hold, and lifted Luke bodily and laid him gently on the deck.

'Well, that's a nasty bump all right,' he commented. 'When did it happen?'

'Last night.'

The woman's voice called, 'What's going on? Who are they, Bernard?'

Looking aft into the wheelhouse, Christine saw a small woman, with a brightly coloured shawl around her shoulders crossed over at her chest, gripping the wheel with surprisingly muscular arms.

'Give me chance!' the man called back. 'I haven't had time to ask yet.' He turned his gaze to Christine. 'So, I am Bernard. And your name, Mademoiselle?'

'I'm Christine,' she responded. Surnames seemed unnecessary. 'And this is my brother, Luke.'

'Ah yes. Your brother?' He gave her a searching look and she realized that he had jumped to a completely wrong interpretation of the situation.

'Yes, really. I know we don't look alike. He takes after our father and I take after mother.'

He accepted the explanation with a grunt.

'Right. Let's get him somewhere more comfortable.'

He lifted Luke again, with no more effort than if he had been a child, and carried him into the spotlessly neat cabin and through to the sleeping area at the stern, where he laid him on a bed. Then he opened a door leading to the wheelhouse.

'This is my wife, Marie. Marie, this young lady is Christine and this is her brother, Luke. You'd better come down and have a look at his head. You're better at this sort of thing than I am. I'll take over the steering.'

The two exchanged places and Marie bent over Luke and examined his head.

'It's a nasty gash, but not as bad as it looks. It should heal without stitches.'

'I think he's been concussed,' Christine said.

'Very likely,' the woman agreed. 'But if we keep him warm and let him rest he should be all right.'

She opened a cupboard and produced a tin containing lint and bandages, poured water from a jug and cleaned the wound, then covered it with a bandage.

Luke opened his eyes and gazed up at her.

'Where are we?'

'On board the *Bourdon*. Don't worry. You're going to be fine.'

'Water?' he begged.

Marie looked at Christine.

'In the other cabin. You'll find a bottle of Badoit in the cupboard above the stove and mugs next to it.'

Christine filled two mugs and carried one through to Luke, who drank thirstily and seemed to revive.

'Let's get you out of those damp clothes,' Marie said. 'Can you sit up?'

Christine drank some water and was reminded of her other most pressing need.

'Madame, I need . . . I have to . . .'

Marie, busy pulling Luke's shirt over his head, as if stripping a strange young man was no more unusual than plucking a chicken, nodded towards the bed.

'Under the bunk. Empty it into the canal when you've finished.'

Christine pulled the chamber pot out and took it through to the outer cabin. When she had relieved herself and emptied the pot as instructed, she found Luke tucked up under a bright patchwork quilt and wearing what looked like an old-fashioned nightshirt.

'I'll hang these up on deck to dry,' Marie said. 'With a good brush they should come clean.' She looked at Christine. 'You'd better get out of those damp clothes, too. But anything of mine will be far too big. I should think two like you could fit into one of my skirts.' She opened a locker. 'Here, it's just an old overall but it'll keep you decent until your own stuff dries. Now, when did you last eat?'

'Yesterday, midday.'

'Right! We haven't had breakfast yet. How do you fancy an omelette? Friend in Roanne who keeps chickens gave me some eggs, off the ration.'

'That would be wonderful!'

While Marie cooked, Bernard drew the barge alongside the canal bank and moored it. Very soon they were sitting down to omelettes and ersatz coffee. Marie sliced bread into four pieces and shared it round. Christine handed hers back.

'We can't eat your rations, Madame. The omelette on its own will be enough.'

'Eat it!' the woman said. 'God knows, it doesn't taste like bread should. I don't know what they are mixing with the flour these days. But you are more than welcome to share.'

Christine did not argue further. She took a plate to Luke and, to her relief, he heaved himself into a sitting position and cleared it.

It was not until the meal was over that Bernard said, 'Now, tell us how you came to be hiding among our cargo. What are you running away from?'

Christine took a deep breath. She had felt from the start that she had nothing to fear from these kind strangers, but this was the crucial test. In as few words as possible she explained the situation, concluding with their final jump from the train.

Marie clicked her tongue. '*Bon Dieu*! It's a miracle you weren't both killed.'

'You were lucky to get away without broken legs, at least,' Bernard agreed. 'So, what are your plans now?'

'I don't know,' Christine said and felt the sting of tears behind her eyelids. She had been so caught up in the needs of the moment that she had not thought ahead.

Bernard looked at her thoughtfully. 'You say your father is English. What is his name?'

'Beecham — Roger Beecham.'

'And you were born — where? In England or in France?'

'In England.'

'So what brought you to live in France?'

'My grandfather, my mother's father, owns a vineyard. He had a stroke and can't do anything for himself, so we came here to look after him, and the vineyard.'

'A vineyard, you say.' Marie leaned towards her. 'What is the name?'

'It's called Cave des Volcans.'

'And your mother's maiden name was Thierry, no?'

'Yes! How did you know?'

Marie sat back and exchanged looks with her husband.

'You forget, we have connections in the wine trade. You have seen our cargo. And when we moor for the night and go to the local *estaminet*, we meet others in the same line and people talk — gossip perhaps I should say. It was a good many years ago now, but I still remember the scandal when your mother decided to marry an Englishman. People were horrified at the idea of the Cave des Volcans going out of French hands.'

'Yes, I know,' Christine said. 'But you understand now? You believe me?'

Marie smiled. 'Yes, I believe you. So, Bernard, what can we do to help these two youngsters?'

'You need to get to Montbéliard, you say?'

39

'Well, somewhere near there.'

'Have you considered the possibility of travelling by boat, instead of on the train?'

'By boat?' she repeated.

He reached into a drawer and spread a map out on the table.

'Look. We are heading for Digoin. That is the junction with the Canal du Centre, which joins the Saône at Chalon-sur-Saône. From there, it is a short distance up the Saône to Saint-Jean-de-Losne, where it links with the Canal du Rhône au Rhin, which goes to Montbéliard and on to Mulhouse on the border, where it joins the Rhine. It would take longer, of course, but there is less chance of being stopped and asked for papers.'

Christine gazed from the map to his face.

'And that would be possible? Can you take us that far?'

He shook his head.

'I'm afraid not. We are bound for Nevers on the Canal Latéral à la Loire.'

'Oh,' Christine felt the hope that had sprung up dissipating again.

'Wait.'

She saw Bernard and Marie look at each other and the woman nodded as if in silent agreement.

'We may still be able to help you. You see, there are ways — people who are willing to take a risk to help people like you — though usually they are heading the other way.'

'I don't understand.'

'You don't need to know the details. It won't surprise you to know that there are people who need to be got out of the country, so they can continue the fight.'

'You mean POWs, people like that?'

'And airmen who have crash landed or been forced to bale out.'

'And you help them?'

'When we can. We're not the only ones.'

'Who are the others?'

'I couldn't tell you that, even if I wanted to. All I know is that the code name for the *réseau* is "The Kingfisher Line". Sometimes there are "packages" left for us to collect, in certain places, and we pass them on to the next collection point. That's why we were away from the boat last night. We had a "parcel" to deliver in Roanne.'

'How wonderful!' Christine exclaimed. 'But it must be very dangerous. I think you're very brave.'

Bernard shrugged.

'We do what we can. Others risk their lives every day, for our benefit.'

Christine pondered for a moment. 'So, do you mean there might be someone else who would take us on to Montbéliard?'

'I don't know about that. Our *réseau*, the chain of people we work with, brings men from the north or the centre of the country. But I'm sure there must be others who do the same from the east. At least we can get you to Digoin and then we can make some enquiries.'

'We should be so grateful!' Christine said. 'I don't know how to thank you.'

Marie smiled at her. 'We're glad to help. We have good reason to hate the *Boche*, so anything we can do . . .' She left the sentence unfinished and added, 'Now, all you need to do for now is take it easy. You've been through a bad time. We shan't get to Digoin, where the canals divide, before tomorrow at the earliest, so you can relax. Why don't you go and lie down on the other bed?'

Gratefully, Christine accepted the suggestion. Luke was sleeping, his breathing regular and natural, and soon she dozed off too. When she woke, the sun was high and she could hear Marie clattering plates in the kitchen. She got up stiffly and went to see if she could help. A few minutes later Luke appeared in the doorway.

'I'm feeling a lot better. Can I have my clothes, please?'

'They won't be dry yet,' Marie said. 'I'm afraid you'll have to wait a while.'

Bernard was halfway out of the cabin. He looked back. 'Marie, perhaps . . . Philippe's things . . . ?'

In the pause that followed, Christine sensed an unspoken tension.

Then Marie said, 'Yes, you're right, of course. Excuse me . . .'

Luke moved aside and she passed him, and went into the sleeping cabin, where she opened a locker and lifted out some carefully folded garments.

'These belong . . . belonged to our son, Philippe. He was called up at the beginning of the war and we haven't heard anything from him since the capitulation. We can only presume that he was killed when the Germans attacked. I don't know why I've kept them, really, but they might just fit you.'

Luke said uncomfortably, 'It's very good of you, Madame, but I don't want to . . . to presume on your kindness. Your son may come back, after all. He could be a prisoner . . . or he could even have escaped to England. I know a lot of French troops were evacuated from Dunkirk, along with our own . . . I mean, the British.'

She gave him a small smile.

'It's possible, but if he was alive, I'm sure he would have found a way to contact us. Anyway, he doesn't need these things now. I'm sure he would want you to make use of them. They're not smart, like your own clothes, but perhaps they are more suitable. After all, it may be necessary for you to pass as a *batelier*, like us.'

'You mean, the Nazis do carry out checks, sometimes?' Christine said.

'It's very rare, on this section of the canal. But when we go through locks, someone might see you, and it would be obvious that you don't belong. The lock-keepers are our friends, but you never know who else is hanging around.'

Christine watched her brother sort through the pile and select a well-worn pair of trousers and a sweater. She was uncomfortable in the baggy overall and longed for the slacks she had always worn at home.

'Don't you think that applies to me, too, Madame?' she queried. 'I don't suppose there is anything of your son's that would fit me, is there?'

'You? But these are men's clothes.'

Luke grinned.

'Oh, she won't mind that. She's always preferred trousers to skirts.'

Marie looked doubtful.

'I don't know . . . There are one or two things Philippe had grown out of. If you really would feel more comfortable, you're welcome to see if there is anything that would fit. He was a skinny lad as a youngster.'

Christine hunted through the pile and discovered a pair of overalls. With the bottoms turned up and a belt round the waist, they were wearable and a loose sweater covered the top. In ten minutes, they were both dressed and, when they went up on deck, Bernard greeted them with a loud laugh.

'So, I have two new crew members! Welcome aboard!'

All day, the *Bourdon* chugged peacefully through the countryside. They saw no German uniforms and the only aircraft passed high overhead, as unthreatening as the birds. From time to time, they passed other boats and the crews exchanged cheerful greetings. Christine was aware of curious glances, particularly when they passed through locks, but no one asked who she was or why she was on board.

As the day went on, she was increasingly aware that they had been extremely lucky to take shelter in this particular barge. That night she and Luke slept in the main cabin, on the benches which served as seats during the day, lulled by the slap of water against the hull.

Around noon the next day, they came to a junction between two canals. Bernard came up from the engine room.

'Normally we would turn left here and go straight up the Canal Latéral. But we'll make a diversion and go through the lock and over the aqueduct into Digoin. It will give Marie a chance to stock up on supplies and I'll have a chat to the other skippers and find out if anyone is going up the other way. But it might be a good idea for you two to stay out of sight in the cabin while we're in port.'

Sitting side by side in the cabin, they heard the sounds of the barge passing through a lock and glimpsed through the windows the rails of the aqueduct and the river Loire below. They listened tensely to the noises of voices calling from the barge to the quayside and felt the gentle jolt as they moored. The engine stopped and for a while, they could not tell what was happening outside. Then Bernard came into the cabin.

'I'm going to have a nose round. I'll see what boats are in and if any are loading cargo to go up to Chalon. If they are, I'll put out some feelers to see if anyone might be willing to take you.'

'Please don't take any risks for our sake,' Luke said.

Bernard smiled. 'Don't worry. There may be some who don't want to get involved but no one would shop us to the *Boche*. Their lives wouldn't be worth living if they did. We stick together, we *bateliers*.'

Shortly after that, Marie looked in to say she was going to market.

'Do you have a ration card, Christine? I know Luke has lost his.'

Christine handed over her card and Luke said unhappily, 'Look, it's not fair for you to go short because of me. I feel such a fool for losing my papers.'

'Don't worry about it,' Marie told him. 'I know lots of people in the market here. There's always a bit extra on the side for friends.'

When she had gone, the brother and sister looked at each other. Tied up here with the distant noises of the town, they felt less secure but neither wanted to voice their fears. From time to time, they heard voices close by on the quayside and they both tensed in the anticipation of the thud of boots on deck as the barge was boarded.

Christine said, 'Maman must be worried about us. She will assume that we've got to Montbéliard by now and she must be wondering why she hasn't heard from Uncle Marcel.'

Luke ran his hand through his hair.

'*Mon Dieu*! I haven't even thought about that! We must let her know we're all right.'

'How?' his sister asked. 'Can we risk trying to find a telephone and calling her?'

He shook his head. 'No. Bernard told us to stay hidden. But there's nothing to stop us writing a letter. Marie would post it for us. We needn't say where we are or how we are travelling. Just a few lines to let her know we're OK.'

'Of course! We should have thought of it before. Do you think there's anything here we could write on?'

'I don't like to go rifling through drawers. We'd better wait till Marie gets back.'

'No, wait! I've just remembered something.' Christine found her coat and rifled through the pockets, to produce a crumpled sheet of lined paper and a pencil. 'It's a bit creased, but it's better than nothing.'

Luke looked at her, laughing.

'You're incredible! Is there anything you can't produce from those pockets?'

'Well, you never know when you might need to leave a note for someone,' she said. 'Now, what shall we say?'

CHAPTER 5

Bernard returned in the late afternoon. Luke took in the expression on his face.

'No luck?'

Bernard shook his head.

'It seems there is no organized escape line coming from the Chalon area. It's not surprising, of course. Anyone trying to get out of France from there would be heading for the Swiss border, not the Pyrenees. There are three boats in the docks at the moment, all loading cargo for that area, but I'm afraid none of the skippers are willing to take the risk of carrying escapers. Don't worry! I didn't tell them I had a couple on board the *Bourdon*. I made out I was sounding them out with a view to establishing another *réseau* to pick up downed aircrew. They won't blab; they're not collaborators; just too lily-livered to take the chance.'

Luke looked from him to his sister.

'Well, it seems as though we'll have to risk the train after all.'

'Wait a minute,' Marie put in. 'Bernard, suppose they went to Auxerre . . . ?'

Her husband frowned.

'Well, it's a thought. But it's a very long way round to get to Montbéliard.'

'But the junction with the Canal de Bourgogne is only twenty kilometres or so north of Auxerre, and that canal connects with the Rhône au Rhin at St Jean. That would get them to Montbéliard eventually.'

'True,' Bernard agreed. 'But eventually would be the word. And we have no idea whether the *réseau* extends in that direction. All we know is that some of our "packages" have been sent on from Auxerre.'

'It's worth a try though, isn't it?' his wife said. 'Better than letting them risk the trains without proper papers.'

'Does that mean we could stay on board the *Bourdon* with you?' Christine said eagerly.

Marie shook her head.

'Not all the way, I'm afraid. As we told you, we're headed for Nevers.'

'Look,' Bernard unrolled the map on the table between them. 'Let me explain. To get to Auxerre you need to go down the Canal du Nivernais. We can take you as far as Decize, which is another two or three days from here. That's the junction with the Nivernais, but the locks that lead into it are too small to take a barge like this, a *péniche*. The only boats that can use those locks are the *berrichons*, which are much smaller. As far as I know, there are no boats like that which are part of the *réseau*.'

'So how do your "packages" get to you?' Luke asked. 'You said they come from Auxerre.'

'Yes, that much we know, but nothing else. The *réseau* works on the strict basis that each member only knows the next link in the chain. That way, if the worst happened, we couldn't reveal any other details. All I can do is introduce you to our contact in Decize and hope that she will be able to send you on your way.'

'I'm sure Eloise will help,' Marie said.

'So, what do you think?' Bernard asked. 'Do you want to take your chance with us?'

Luke and Christine looked at each other and saw, without the need for words, that they were in agreement.

'Yes, please,' Luke said. 'I'm sure that's our best plan.'

Next morning, having taken on fresh supplies and refuelled, the *Bourdon* chugged on her way towards Decize. It seemed spring had arrived quite suddenly, and the trees along the bank were hazed with green. In the pastures beside the river, cream Charolais cattle grazed contentedly. Ducks paddled out of their way, quacking protests, and occasionally a kingfisher darted across their path in a flash of iridescent blue.

Sitting in the sun beside Luke, Christine said, 'It's almost like being on holiday, isn't it?'

'Don't get too complacent,' he responded. 'We need to stay alert. There's no knowing what's around the next corner.'

The force of his warning was sharply brought home to them not long afterwards. They had passed through a lock some ten minutes earlier when they were overtaken by the lock-keeper's young son on a bicycle.

'My father sent me with a message,' he explained breathlessly to Bernard. 'He just had a phone call from Jacques Periot at the next lock. The *Boche* are checking every boat that passes through. He thought you should know.'

Bernard thanked the boy, who jumped on his bike and set off back in the direction he had come from. Christine drew closer to Luke, her heart thumping.

'What do we do now?'

Bernard spoke calmly. 'You have papers, Christine?'

'Yes, but Luke doesn't.'

'It's all right,' Luke said. 'Let me go ashore. I'll find a way round and meet you further on.'

'No. There is a better way. Come with me.' Bernard led them into the aft cabin and stooped to roll back the piece of worn carpet on the floor. 'There's a screwdriver in that locker just above your head, Christine. Pass it to me, please.'

He slid the tool into a small crack in the planking of the floor and, using it as a lever, lifted a trapdoor to reveal a dark space.

'You will be quite safe down there until we get through the lock, as long as you keep quiet.'

Luke stared down into the hole and shuddered. He had a horror of dark confined spaces. Once, as a child staying with his English grandparents, he had hidden in a wardrobe during a game of hide and seek, only to discover that it was impossible to open it from inside. His terrified banging had brought his grandmother to the rescue very quickly, but he had never forgotten the panic-inducing claustrophobia. He stepped back, shaking his head.

'No, really. I'd rather take my chance on land.'

'If the *Boche* are carrying out a search for someone, there may be road blocks as well. You'll be much safer here,' Bernard said. 'It's perfectly dry down there and well ventilated, and look, there is even a box for you to sit on.'

Christine knew what was going through her brother's mind. She went into the other cabin where her coat was hanging, and felt in the pocket.

'Here, take my torch, so you won't have to sit in the dark.'

'All right,' Bernard said, 'but don't use it while the boat is in the lock. We don't want any light showing through cracks in the planking. Now, in you go. We'll be there very soon.'

Reluctantly, Luke lowered himself into the space and squatted down on the box. Christine leaned down and gave him a thumbs up.

'See you in a few minutes.'

Then Bernard replaced the trapdoor and Luke heard the carpet being rolled back over it. He switched on the torch and discovered that the space was not as small as he had imagined. It stretched the full width of the barge, to the ribs that formed the hull, and was cut off fore and aft by wooden partitions. He realized that it had been specially constructed to conceal fugitives being passed down the escape line in case of emergency, and it gave him some comfort to reflect that none of them had been discovered. If they had been, Bernard and Marie would be in a German prison, or worse. He switched the torch off and made himself breathe slowly and deeply. With any luck he would not be down here for long.

Up on deck Bernard turned to Christine.

'Right. Your mother is a distant cousin of Marie's. You are travelling with us because you've been ill and you are convalescing. No, perhaps not. You don't look as if you have ever had a day's illness in your life. Perhaps your mother is ill?'

'Then why aren't I looking after her?'

'Perhaps,' Marie suggested, 'you and she are not seeing eye to eye about something. Maybe there is a boy she doesn't approve of? She thought a change of scene would be good for you. Will that do?'

'Excellent!' Bernard said. 'As long as we all stick to that, we shouldn't have any trouble.'

The barge rounded a bend in the canal and the next lock came into sight. The gates were open on the side from which they were approaching, and a barge similar to the *Bourdon* was tied up inside. Two German soldiers were in the hold, throwing the cargo, which seemed to consist of sacks of cement, out onto the lock side; while a third stood guard over a man and a woman, presumably the boat's owners.

'It's Jean and Louise,' Marie said. 'Poor things! What a mess!'

'Well, whatever the *Boche* are looking for, they won't find anything on that boat,' Bernard remarked. 'I've never known Jean take the smallest risk. He's too intent on saving his own skin.'

Christine felt her bowels turning to water. 'If they search us like that . . . We should have let Luke go overland like he wanted to.'

'He'll be fine,' Marie said firmly. 'All we have to do is behave naturally. Now, grab that stern line and tie us up. We'll have to wait out here until they've finished.'

The barge bumped gently against the side of the canal, and Christine did as she had been told. A fourth soldier, with a sergeant's stripes on his sleeve, came out of the cabin on the other boat and said something in German to the two in the hold. They left the remainder of the cargo and climbed out and, when the sergeant gestured towards the *Bourdon*, they headed in their direction.

'Oi!' The man identified as Jean yelled after them. 'What about this lot? It'll take me all day to reload.'

'Better get started then,' the sergeant shouted over his shoulder as he followed his men.

Bernard had joined Marie and Christine on the small afterdeck and the German balanced on the gunwale and looked down at them.

'Papers?'

Bernard handed over his identity card and Marie's. The German glanced at them, looked from face to face to check that they matched the photographs, and handed them back. He looked at Christine.

'You?'

Heart pounding, she offered her card. He looked it over and then returned his gaze to her. 'St Amant? Where's that?' He spoke French with a heavy German accent.

'Auvergne.' Her voice came out as a croak and she had to swallow hard to clear her throat.

'What are you doing on this barge?'

Words deserted her and she could only stare at him mutely.

Marie filled the silence. 'Her mother is a distant cousin of mine. She felt it would be good for Christine to have a break — you know, a change of scene.'

The German looked Christine over and gave a half smile. 'She doesn't have much to say for herself.'

Marie shrugged and smiled in return.

'Oh well, you know — teenagers! You must have been one yourself not so long ago.'

He grunted. 'I had better manners. No wonder her mother needed a break.' He looked around. 'Anyone else on board?'

'No, just the three of us,' Bernard replied.

'I'll just make sure of that.'

He stepped down and went into the cabin. Christine could hardly breathe. He went through into the sleeping compartment and she tried desperately to send a message by telepathy to Luke. '*Don't move! Don't make a sound!*' Then she remembered with a shock of anguish that she had left his good clothes, now dry and brushed clean, lying folded on the end of the bed. A moment later the German sergeant appeared at the door leading to the afterdeck, with the clothes in his arms.

'No one else, eh? I don't think these would fit you, Monsieur.'

Christine saw that Bernard was at a loss, but Marie spoke up at once. 'Those belong . . . belonged to my son. He was killed in the fighting at the beginning of the war. I got them out to give to the lock-keeper's wife. She has a boy they might fit. But now . . .' her voice broke, 'I don't think I can bear to part with them after all. I expect you have a mother back in Germany, Sergeant, who would feel the same if anything happened to you.'

Watching the German's face, Christine saw the military mask slip for a moment to reveal the young man beneath. He cleared his throat and returned the clothes to their place without further comment.

Bernard was instructed to pull back the tarpaulin covering the hold and the German made a cursory inspection of the cargo, then climbed back onto the bank, where his subordinates were sitting on bollards enjoying the sunshine.

'All right, you can go.'

'We can't go anywhere until the lock is empty,' Bernard pointed out.

In the lock, the owner of the other barge was still heaving sacks of cement back on board. The sergeant shouted at his men in German and they scrambled to their feet and trotted back to help.

'I'll give them a hand,' Bernard said, and followed.

Crouched in the dark beneath the floor of the cabin, Luke had no means of knowing what was going on. He felt the gentle bump as the barge came alongside but, although he strained his ears, he could hear nothing except the slap of water against the hull. The time stretched out and still there was no sign of movement. The thought crossed his mind that Bernard and Marie and Christine might have been arrested, or taken away for questioning. In that case, no one would know he was down here. He could stay here for hours, days even. He was not sure whether he could lift the hatch from underneath. He wondered if he should risk trying.

Then suddenly there were footsteps above his head and his heart pounded with alarm. He imagined the hatch being raised, a German face looking down at him, a German gun pointed at his head. Then the footsteps went away and the silence enveloped him again.

At length, after what felt like an hour, the engine restarted and he felt the barge moving forward and then coming to a standstill again. The sound of the water against the hull changed and he felt himself sinking. For a moment he panicked, then logic took over; the lock was emptying. They must be ready to leave.

At last he heard the engine start and felt that they were moving, but it still seemed a long time before he heard the carpet being rolled back and the hatch was raised. Bernard leaned in and held out a hand to pull him up and, as soon as he was on his feet, Christine threw her arms around him in an uncharacteristic display of emotion.

'Thank God! You're safe. I was terrified he was going to find you.'

He hugged her.

'So was I! But you're the one I should have been worried about. Did he ask any awkward questions?'

'He wanted to know what I was doing on the boat, but Marie said I was her cousin's daughter.' She looked around. 'She was wonderful. The German found your clothes and she pretended they belonged to her son. You should have been an actress, Marie!'

Marie shrugged dismissively.

'Chance would have been a fine thing! Now, how about you taking the wheel while I get some food on the table?'

Towards evening next day, they rounded a bend and saw the rocky outcrop on which stood the town of Decize, the ruined walls of its castle golden in the setting sun. The *Bourdon* eased her way through the lock and into a large pool, where a few other boats were tied up.

'Where is everybody?' Marie said. 'This place used to be crowded with barges.'

'Sign of the times,' Bernard said. 'Trade has practically dried up. Right, you two,' he added. 'Better get back in the cabin until we're tied up and I can be sure there are no *Boche* nosing around.'

There followed another tense wait, while they listened to the sounds of mooring and then a long pause. At last Bernard came in, accompanied by a tiny, middle-aged woman with very bright eyes.

'This is Madame Delahaie,' he said. 'She is our contact in the *réseau*. I have explained to her where you are trying to go, and why you need our help. She is prepared to send you up the line. Eloise, this is Luke and his sister Christine.'

The little woman clicked her tongue. 'But they are so young! It's all wrong for them to have to hide like this.'

'I'm old enough to fight,' Luke said. 'I want to get back to England so I can join up.'

She sighed. 'It is right that you should, of course. We must all do what we can to free ourselves from these dirty *Boche*. But I hate to see more young lives consumed by this terrible war.'

'But you will help us, Madame?' he said eagerly.

'It won't be easy. Nothing much is going up and down the Nivernais these days. Most of the factories in Decize have closed down, or been bombed, so there's no need for goods either coming in or going out. But if you can get to Blaye, by Lake Vaux, the lock-keeper there may be able to find someone who will take you down the flight of locks to Sardy-les-Epiry. His name is Pierre Simon. That is the last of the short locks. From there, there will be more traffic going up towards Auxerre. The lock-keeper at the bottom lock is the next link in the chain. He will introduce you to a *batelier* who belongs to the *réseau*. But you may have to wait some time, until a suitable barge comes along.'

'How do we get to Blaye?' Christine asked.

'On bicycles. I take it you can both ride a bike?'

'Yes, of course. But we don't have bikes . . .' Luke said doubtfully.

'I shall lend you one each. That is not a problem.'

'But, Madame,' Christine said. 'If we take your bikes and leave them at Blaye, how will you ever get them back?'

Eloise Delahaie smiled.

'Don't worry about that. They belong to the *réseau*. They are registered to a company in Auxerre which rents them out. The owner is sympathetic to our work. Sometimes, if there is no boat available, the men we are trying to help have to cycle from there. The owner's daughter comes with them as a guide and to speak for them if they are challenged. The bicycles need to be returned, so you will be helping, but it is more risky than travelling by boat. If you find a boat to take you, go that way. You can put the bikes on board.'

'How far is it to Blaye?' Luke asked.

'About fifty kilometres. You can do it in a day, easily.'

Bernard spread another map on the table.

'Look, here. You can follow the towpath. It will be safer than the road and it has the advantage for cyclists that it is more or less level. Each lock will take you higher, but in between it's flat.'

'But you will have to avoid Châtillon-en-Bazois,' Madame Delahaie put in quickly. 'There is a German garrison there and they are controlling the main road from Nevers to Château-Chinon. The canal goes right through the middle of the town, which would be risky for you. I suggest you leave the canal at Biches and take the road to Alluy and then Bazolles. You can rejoin the canal there. But take care when you cross the main road.'

'First they have to cross Decize to get to the Nivernais,' Bernard said. 'I thought we might take the *Bourdon* across to the quay below the old city.'

'No chance of that,' Mme Delahaie responded. 'The Loire is in spate. You would never get a barge this size across without being swept downstream.'

'What about the *toueur*?' he said. 'The whole idea of that is to help barges across the river.'

She shook her head. 'The *toueur* is laid up for the duration. There isn't enough demand for it as things stand.'

'What is a *toueur*?' Christine asked.

'It's a kind of electric tug. A chain has been laid across the bed of the river, which passes through the *toueur* from bow to stern. Inside, there is an electric motor which pulls the chain across a series of cogwheels, dragging the boat across the river.'

'How fascinating! I wish I could see it working!'

'I'm afraid you will have to come back after the war for that,' Mme Delahaie said with a smile. 'But for the present you will have to use the bridge.'

'Is that safe?' Marie asked.

'Yes, the *Boche* don't worry too much about people coming and going from one side to the other. There is usually a sentry on guard, but he very rarely asks to see papers.'

Christine looked at Bernard and Marie.

'When do we leave?'

Marie understood her reluctance.

'Tomorrow, I'm afraid, my dear. We have to be on our way, too. I'm sorry we can't take you farther, but I'm sure we are leaving you in good hands.'

'I know you are,' Christine said hastily. 'It's just that we've enjoyed being with you so much. We'll never forget your kindness.'

'Yes, that goes for me, too,' Luke added. 'We shall be really sorry to say goodbye.'

Marie extended a hand to each of them.

'And we shall be sorry, too. But we shall think of you, and pray that you will reach your destination safely. Maybe, when this wretched war is over, you will come and find us and you can cruise the canals with us as long as you please.'

'Oh, I should love that!' Christine said. 'I shall pray for you, too, and that one day we shall all meet again.'

'Amen!' Bernard laid a hand on her shoulder. 'But now, we must eat and then you need to get a good night's sleep. You have a long ride tomorrow.'

CHAPTER 6

Isabelle Beecham was in the cellar at Caves des Volcans, but she was not testing the latest vintage. It was evening and all the workers had gone home. The cellar was lined with huge casks lying on their sides, each labelled with the year of that vintage. At the far end, was one that stood a little further from the wall than the others. Isabelle slipped behind it and tugged at the base, which came away to reveal a small compartment. The cask had been closed off further in, so that if anyone opened the spigot at the other end wine would still flow out, but the space concealed a small radio set, tuned to the BBC.

She carried it up to the kitchen and set it on the table. Then, she poured herself a glass of wine and sat down to listen. Her father was in bed and there was no one else in the house, but she kept the volume so low that she had to lean close to hear the announcer's voice. The news bulletin told of Allied advances in North Africa but she paid only scant attention. What she was waiting for were the *messages personnels*, which were broadcast every evening after the news.

It was almost a week since she had said goodbye to her two children and every day she had expected to hear from Marcel Dutoit that they had arrived safely. Yesterday, in

58

desperation, she had risked using the public telephone to call Gaspard Duhamel, who assured her that he had delivered them both safely to the railway station in Clermont-Ferrand. She called Marcel's number but there had been no reply. Perhaps, she told herself, he was away from home even now, conducting Luke and Christine across the border into Switzerland. That hope was immediately replaced by a terrible fear; maybe he had been arrested in the act and they were all in German custody? She calmed herself by clinging to another thought: it was possible that they had reached him within 24 hours of setting out, and been taken to safety immediately; so they could be back in England by now. That was why she was crouching over the radio, hoping to hear that 'Michou's pups' were safe.

She was so intent on making out the indistinct words of the announcer over the crackle of static that she almost failed to hear the banging on the front door. When the sound penetrated her consciousness, she jumped up, her heart pounding. Neighbours rarely called at this time of night, except in an emergency. Had a German detector van picked up the fact that there was a radio receiving the English broadcast? Was that possible? Had someone betrayed her? She grabbed the set and shoved it into the oven in the old, black range; then, forcing herself to behave as naturally as possible, she went to open the door.

A German officer stood on the doorstep. Isabelle's hand went to her throat. Either she was about to be arrested, or he had come to tell her that her children were in German hands.

'Madame Beauchamp?' he asked, using the French version of her surname.

'Yes?'

He saluted and clicked his heels. 'I am Oberleutnant Gruber. I am the billeting officer for this area. How many people live in this house?'

'Just myself and my father.' Isabelle's breath was coming in short gasps and she fought to control it. 'He is disabled and confined to a wheelchair.'

'According to records held by your mayor, you have two children who are not living with you at present.'

'Not just now, no. They have gone to visit their godfather. He's been taken ill.'

'Then you will have spare rooms. You are required to accommodate an officer and his batman. They will arrive tomorrow morning. Please make sure the rooms are ready for them. They will take all their meals in the mess, so you will not be required to feed them. That is all. Good evening.'

He saluted once more, turned on his heel and went back to his jeep. Isabelle closed the door and leaned against it. Her legs were trembling and for a moment she felt dizzy. Then her head cleared.

Neither she nor the children were in immediate danger. It would be inconvenient and distasteful to have Germans living in the house and it would make it hard to listen to the BBC broadcasts, but at least her immediate fears had not been realized. She straightened up and went back to the kitchen, but by the time she had extracted the radio from the oven, the *messages personnels* were finished and she could only hope that she had not missed the one she was so desperate to hear.

The two Germans arrived early the next day. Isabelle expected to hate them on sight but one look at the face of the young lieutenant who stood on her doorstep overlaid her hostility with a concern that was almost maternal. He looked hardly older than Luke, but whereas her son was well-built, with broad shoulders and a healthy tan, this boy was thin and his face had a sickly yellow tint. His batman, who followed with his bags, was middle-aged, small, and wiry, with a face so lined and creased that it reminded her of a bulldog.

The officer saluted and introduced himself in surprisingly good French.

'Leutnant Hoffmann, Madame. I hope we are not inconveniencing you.'

The words recalled Isabelle to the consciousness that these were the enemy, however unthreatening they appeared.

'It is not as though I have any choice in the matter,' she responded stiffly. 'Come in, please. I'll show you your rooms.'

She had put the lieutenant in Luke's room. There was only one spare room in the house, a small, rather bare space, and she had allocated that to the batman, rather than putting him in Christine's, but that left nowhere else for the officer. Hoffmann looked around and turned to her with a smile that touched her heart.

'This reminds me of my own room at home. Thank you, Madame.'

They dumped their belongings and left almost immediately, explaining that the lieutenant had to go on duty. By the time they returned, it was late and he went straight to his room. Soon afterwards, Isabelle heard him coughing; a harsh, racking cough that went on and on. She was about to go to his room to ask if he needed anything when the batman appeared in her kitchen.

'Madame, would it be possible to make the lieutenant a warm drink? Sometimes it eases the cough.'

'Of course,' Isabelle responded immediately. 'Would he like some warm milk?'

'If you can spare it, Madame.'

While she was waiting for the milk to heat, Isabelle asked, 'What is your name?'

'Schulz, Madame. Fritz Schulz.'

'You are worried about Leutnant Hoffmann.'

'Yes, Madame. He is not strong. He has a weak chest. We were on the Russian Front and he got very ill. That is why we were transferred here, so he could recuperate.'

She looked at him. His face was creased with genuine concern.

'Have you been with him for long?'

'Since the beginning.'

'Really? He doesn't look old enough . . .' She checked herself. 'I'm sorry. It's not my business.'

Schulz shook his head.

'Please, it is kind of you to concern yourself. He is older than he looks, but he was always a sickly child.'

'You knew him, before the war?'

'I worked for the family. We joined up together.'

'You both speak good French. How is that?'

'The lieutenant's mother is from Alsace, Madame. She always spoke French.'

'From Alsace? So he is half French? That must make things very difficult.'

'Yes.' The little man sighed. 'It is not a happy situation for any of us.'

The milk was hot. Isabelle poured it into a mug and reached for a bottle of brandy on the shelf above the range. 'Perhaps a little of this will help him sleep?'

'You are very kind, Madame.'

After Schulz had left, Isabelle wondered at herself. How could she behave like this to members of the enemy force that was occupying her country? She heard Hoffmann coughing again and sighed. Enemy or not, she had a sick boy under her roof. German he might be, but first and foremost he was a human being. That was something to hold on to.

Next morning, she came face to face with her unwanted guests in the hallway. Hoffmann clicked his heels and gave a little bow.

'Good morning, Madame Beauchamps. I want to thank you for the hot drink. It was most helpful.'

Isabelle restrained an impulse to smile and replied coolly, 'I'm glad to hear it. Did you sleep well?'

'Excellently. It was the best night's sleep I have had for a long time.'

To Isabelle's relief the need for further conversation was dispelled by the sound of the postman's van drawing up outside. She took the envelope he handed her and was unable to suppress a gasp of mingled shock and relief as she recognized the handwriting.

Hoffmann was watching her with a smile.

'Good news, I hope, Madame?'

'A letter from my son.' She shrugged in what she hoped was a suitably casual manner. 'I wasn't expecting to hear from him so soon.'

'Ah, we young men!' he responded. 'We are not good at writing letters. My own mother often rebukes me for being so lazy about it.'

'Well, I expect you have other things on your mind,' she said. 'I'm sure your mother understands.'

He looked at his watch.

'I must be on my way, or I shall be late for duty.' He drew himself up, clicked his heels again and saluted. 'Until this evening, Madame.'

'Until then,' she replied, and narrowly prevented herself from wishing him a pleasant day.

Hoffmann left, with Schulz following, and Isabelle slit open the envelope, her mind a whirl of anxious speculation. The postmark said 'Digoin'. What on earth was Luke doing in Digoin? It was nowhere near the route he should have been taking. Dear God! Had he gone and joined the Maquis after all? She unfolded the letter and read:

Chère Maman,

I know you will be wondering why we have not been in touch before, but please don't worry. We are both safe and well. It was not possible to reach our destination by the route we planned, because we were badly let down by the so-called friend who gave us a lift. But we have found another way to get there. It may take quite a lot longer than we expected, so don't be alarmed if you don't hear from us for a few days. I'll write again as soon as I can.

With love from us both,
Luke.

She carried the letter into the kitchen and sat at the table. Her legs were shaking. The letter raised more questions than it answered. How had they been let down? The 'so-called friend' must be Duhamel, but he had assured her that he had delivered them safely to the station. She gritted her teeth. That little snake! He had lied to her.

'Just you wait!' she muttered. 'I'll make sure you live to regret this.'

But what were Luke and Christine doing in Digoin? It wasn't even in the right direction. Why should it take them so long to get to Montbéliard? But at least they were safe. That was all that mattered.

Her father's voice, enquiring querulously what had happened to his breakfast, recalled her to the present. There were chores to be done, and the men who worked in the vineyard would arrive any minute. She put the letter in the pocket of her apron, then on second thoughts took it out and threw it into the fire under the kitchen range. Her children were safe. She must be calm and patient and get on with her work.

Luke and Christine were woken early by Bernard.

'Get ready to leave. It will be best if you mingle with the crowds on their way to work. There is less chance of being stopped and questioned then.'

Marie hurried up the gangplank carrying her shopping basket.

'*Mon Dieu*! The queues! And look at this apology for a loaf. I'm sure they are mixing sawdust with the flour. Still, it will have to do. I still have some of the cheese we got from that farmer at the market in Digoin. I'll make you a sandwich to take with you. Here, Christine, take your ration book. You mustn't go without it.'

Bernard unearthed two old knapsacks from the bottom of a cupboard.

'This was given me when I served in the army in the last war, and the other belonged to Philippe. You can stow your good clothes in them; they're not suitable for a long cycle ride.'

Christine looked at Marie. 'Are you sure you don't mind us keeping these things? I was thinking about what you said to that German sergeant . . .'

'Forget it! I just made that up on the spur of the moment. You're welcome to anything of Philippe's if it helps.' She pursed her lips ironically. 'Not that those overalls do you any favours, chérie!'

'Never mind. They're comfortable.' Christine reached out and took Marie's hands. 'I don't know how we can ever thank you, and Bernard.'

Marie squeezed her hands.

'There is no need. Now, have you got everything? Take a bottle of water each. You'll need it on that ride.'

When the last items were packed, Bernard went up on deck. A moment later, he ducked back into the cabin.

'All clear. Come along.'

Marie kissed them both on both cheeks.

'*Adieu, mes chères*. I shall pray to the blessed virgin to keep you safe.'

'And we shall pray for you, too,' Christine told her.

They crossed the gangplank and paused to take a last look at the barge that had come to feel almost like a second home, in the short time they had sailed on it. Bernard was already moving away, beckoning them to follow, and they turned away and hurried after him. He led them to a small shop at the end of the quay, which sold ropes and anchors and paraffin and other necessities. Madame Delahaie was waiting for them.

'I have the bicycles ready for you. What will you say if anyone asks what you are doing?'

'We decided to say we're on holiday, doing a cycle tour of the area,' Luke told her. 'It is Easter, after all.'

'That should be as good as anything,' the little woman agreed. 'And remember, you hired the bikes from Rameau et Cie in Auxerre.'

'We won't forget,' he promised.

'One more thing. When you get to Blaye, you must ask the lock-keeper this question: "Do you see many king-fishers around here?" That way he will know that you come from me and can be trusted. If he says: "Yes, I saw three just yesterday", you will know that the coast is clear and you can tell him what you want. But if he says: "No. They don't nest around here anymore", you will know that there is a problem and you will have to keep out of the way until he has dealt with it. Do you understand?'

'Yes.' They both answered with a breathless sense of danger and excitement.

She led them outside to where two bicycles stood in a small yard beside the shop. They strapped the haversacks Bernard had given them on the back of the saddles, and shook hands with Madame Delahaie.

'*Merci, Madame! Merci.*'

'*De rien, mes amis! Bonne chance!*'

Bernard said, 'This way.' He led them across the lock gates and along a tree-lined path that skirted the pool to a narrow road that followed the bank of the Loire. On the far side of the river, the old town rose up to the ruined castle crowning the crag, and ahead they could see the bridge and people on foot and on bicycles crossing in both directions. At the end of the road Bernard stopped.

'There is a *milicien* on duty at the end of the bridge. Just join the crowd and act naturally. There's no reason for him to stop you.'

Christine's heart was thumping as they pushed their bikes across the bridge. Random checks requiring identity papers were quite frequent in all towns, particularly if there had been any Resistance activity in the area. She found herself praying that the members of the Resistance, if there were any locally, had been keeping a low profile of late.

On the far side, Bernard stopped again.

'I'll go ahead. Follow me at a small distance. If I stop and light a cigarette that means I have seen a checkpoint ahead. Wait where you are and I will try to find a way around. Understood?'

'Understood,' they both said at once.

Once, as they followed him through the narrow streets, Christine saw soldiers in the hated grey uniforms standing on a corner, but Bernard went forward without pausing. They crossed a second bridge, over a narrower arm of the river, and then a third. Finally, as they reached yet another one, Bernard stopped and turned to them, his broad face unusually solemn.

'This is where we say goodbye. There's the Nivernais below us. Take the slope down and you'll find yourselves on the towpath.'

Christine reached up and kissed him on both cheeks.

'Goodbye, dear Bernard. We'll never forget what you and Marie have done for us.'

He hugged her briefly and embraced Luke.

'Take care. God go with you!' His voice was husky with emotion. 'Now go! Go quickly!'

They wheeled their bikes down the steep path to the edge of the canal. At the bottom, Christine looked back but Bernard had already disappeared.

'Come on,' Luke said. 'We'd better get going. It's going to be a long day.'

CHAPTER 7

Once clear of the town, they both began to relax. The path was lined with fruit trees just coming into blossom and there were cattle in the fields, but they saw few people and on this canal there were no large barges as there were on the Canal Latéral. Spring had finally arrived and it was typical April weather, with warm sunshine tempered by a brisk breeze and sudden heavy downpours of rain. Several times they had to take shelter under trees or bridges where country lanes crossed the canal, but the going was easy and they both agreed that they could almost believe that they really were on holiday.

They passed through the pretty village of Cercy-la-Tour without incident, and then the canal began to climb, lock by lock, into the hills. At Biches, remembering Mme Delahaie's warning, they reluctantly abandoned the towpath and took to the road. Around midday, they found themselves on a plateau with open country spreading out on either side. The sky had darkened again and the clouds looked very threatening.

'It looks as though we're in for soaking,' Luke said. 'I wish we had some kind of waterproofs.'

Christine scanned the fields on either side of the road.

'What's that, over there? It looks like a barn of some kind.'

'Where? Oh, I see. Yes, you're right. I wonder if we can get to it before the rain comes down.'

A short distance further on, they found a rough track leading to the barn and reached it just as the heavens opened. It was a Dutch barn, with open sides, half filled with hay. They propped their bikes against one of the pillars supporting the roof, and flopped down among the loose, dry hay that had fallen from the main stack.

'Just in time!' Christine said. 'It's raining cats and dogs out there.'

'And the roads are full of poodles,' Luke added with a grin. It was an old joke and one they had often enjoyed as children and out of long habit they had both reverted to English.

Christine clapped her hand to her mouth.

'*Zut alors!* Luke, do you realize what we just did?'

'What? Oh, my God! Were we speaking English?'

'Yes. We must be more careful. Thank God there was no one around to hear us.' She looked at her watch. 'It's lunchtime. We may as well eat while we wait for the weather to clear.'

Luke fetched the haversacks and pulled out the two chunks of bread and two bottles of water, and for a few moments they both munched contentedly. Suddenly, there was a rustling in the hay above their heads. Christine jumped to her feet.

'*Mon Dieu*! What's that?'

Luke stood up too and peered upwards.

'There must be an animal of some sort up there. Perhaps it's a cat.'

'Cat's don't make that much noise.'

'A dog, then. Or a sheep?

'Don't be daft! How would a sheep get up there?'

The rustling noise was growing stronger. Luke looked around him and saw a pitchfork leaning against the side of the barn. He grabbed it and poked into the hay stack.

'Come on out. Let's have a look at you.'

His action provoked an unexpected response.

'Stop! Stop! It's all right. I'm coming down.'

Christine gasped. Images of German Stormtroopers flashed through her mind. But the language had been French. Perhaps it was just a tramp, sheltering like them from the weather?

The haystack shook and a man slithered down in a shower of straw, then fell back with a cry of pain as his feet hit the ground. He was in civilian clothes, but he certainly did not look like a tramp. He was quite young, around thirty she guessed, slim and athletic looking, and though his dark hair was rumpled as if he had just got out of bed, and he had a couple of days' growth of beard, he was wearing respectable grey flannels and a tweed jacket.

'Don't be afraid!' he said. 'I don't mean you any harm. I was asleep until I heard your voices.'

'Are you hurt?' Luke asked.

'Yes, yes. I seem to have sprained my ankle — or it may be broken, I don't know.'

Christine looked at his feet. On one, he was wearing an ordinary town shoe; the other was bare and the ankle was visibly swollen.

'How did you do it?' she asked.

'It was just a stupid accident. I was out walking and I tried to take a short cut and tripped over some barbed wire.'

'How long have you been here?' Luke enquired.

'Since yesterday morning.'

'All that time? And hasn't anyone been along who could help you?'

'Not a soul.' He looked at Luke's bottle of water. 'You couldn't spare me a drink, could you? I'm absolutely parched.'

'Of course. Here.' Luke handed him the bottle and he drank thirstily.

'You've been here since yesterday without anything to eat or drink?' Christine said.

'Well, I had a bit of food with me, but that soon went.'

'You can have the rest of my sandwich if you like,' she offered. 'I'm afraid I've bitten it, but you're welcome to it if you don't mind.'

'Are you sure?'

'Yes, go ahead.'

He took the baguette and bit into it, then said with his mouth full, 'I'm sorry. I'm forgetting my manners. I should introduce myself. My name is Cyrano.'

'I'm Luke,' he responded with automatic courtesy. 'And this is my sister, Christine.'

'Pleased to meet you.' He chewed and swallowed. 'Are you from round here?'

'No.' Brother and sister exchanged glances and he went on, 'We're on holiday — a cycling holiday. Do you live locally?'

'In Corbigny.'

Christine remembered the map Bernard had shown them.

'Corbigny? That's quite a way from here, isn't it?'

'Not all that far.'

'It must be fifteen kilometres. That's quite a long walk, in those shoes.'

He glanced down.

'I agree. Silly of me. I should have worn something more suitable.'

'You don't sound like a local — your accent, I mean.'

'Chris . . .' Luke frowned at her, with a look that said: 'don't ask so many personal questions'.

Cyrano smiled.

'That's probably because I'm not from here originally. I grew up in Paris. Look, I hate to be a burden, but do you think you could help me get to a telephone? I really need to contact someone to come and collect me.'

'We could go to the nearest farm and ask them to call an ambulance,' Luke suggested.

Cyrano shook his head. 'No! No, don't do that. I don't want to bother the ambulance people. It's only a sprain. If I can just get to a phone and a road, someone will pick me up.'

'Well,' Luke said dubiously, 'maybe you could ride one of our bikes. I could push you . . .'

'Oh yes! That sounds like an excellent idea.'

Christine plucked at her brother's sleeve. 'Luke!'

'What?'

'Come outside a minute. I want to speak to you.'

'Why? What's the matter?'

She almost dragged him out of the barn and, once they were outside, she lowered her voice almost to a whisper.

'What are you thinking of? We don't know anything about him. He could be anyone.'

'So what? He looks pretty harmless. And he needs help.'

'But doesn't it strike you that there's something funny about him? You don't go country walking in that suit and those shoes. And that accent. He says it's Parisian, but we know what that sounds like. It's almost right, but not quite.'

'Do you mean he's not French at all?'

'Maybe. I don't know.'

'Oh, come on, Chris! What do you imagine he is? A German spy?'

She considered.

'No, I suppose not. Why would a German hide in a barn for two days? Unless . . . unless he's a deserter. That would make sense.'

'Well, if that's the case, I don't see why we need to worry. He's not going to shop us to the authorities.'

'I suppose not.' She caught her breath suddenly. 'Luke, you don't think he's English, do you? A POW trying to escape. Or a downed pilot?'

'It's possible. But we can't very well ask him, can we?'

'Not without telling him who we are,' she agreed doubtfully. 'And if it turned out he is just what he says he is, he might decide to hand us over.'

'We can't just leave him here,' Luke said. 'I've got an idea. Why don't we take him as far as Baye and tell the lock-keeper what we suspect? We know he's involved in helping escapers. They must have ways of checking if someone is genuine. Let him deal with it.'

Her face cleared.

'Luke, that's brilliant! OK, let's do that.'

When they returned to the barn, Cyrano had hauled himself into a standing position. His expression was tense and one hand was deep in a trouser pocket.

'It's OK,' Luke said. 'We've just been discussing the best thing to do. We're heading towards the village of Baye. We can take you there on my bike, like I suggested. I'm sure someone there will have a telephone.'

Cyrano visibly relaxed.

'Oh, that would be very kind. Thank you.'

'I'll get my bike,' Luke said, and went out.

Cyrano was groping around in the hay.

'What are you looking for?' Christine asked.

'My suitcase. I had a case with some clothes and stuff in, in case I decided to stay away for a day or two. It must be here somewhere.'

Christine shifted some hay and revealed a small attaché case.

'Here it is.' She picked it up and almost dropped it. 'What on earth have you got in it? Gold bars? It weighs a ton!'

He reached out with more urgency than seemed necessary and took it from her.

'No, no. It's my flute. I'm a musician, and a teacher. There's quite a lot of sheet music in the case. That's what makes it heavy.'

Christine's suspicions grew. She wondered why anyone out for a walk should burden themselves like that; but before she could ask any more questions, Luke returned with his bike and between them they manoeuvred the injured man onto the saddle. It was clearly impossible for him to hold onto the case at the same time, so Christine took it back.

'Don't worry. I'll take care of it.'

'Hang onto me,' Luke instructed. 'The ground is pretty rough until we get to the road.'

The two of them wobbled away across the field and Christine called after them, 'I'll be with you in a tick! I just need to spend a penny.'

When she rejoined them, carrying the case, her expression was different. She gave Cyrano a broad smile and said in English, 'It's all right, you can stop pretending. I know who you are, and you needn't worry. We're all on the same side.'

'Chris!' her brother exclaimed in dismay.

'What is she saying?' Cyrano asked in French.

'I looked in the case. You've got a radio set in there. You're a British agent, aren't you?' Her face was alight with excitement. 'And you can trust us, because we're English too.'

'Chris, for God's sake!' Luke broke in. Then, to Cyrano, 'Take no notice of her. She's joking.'

'English?' Cyrano looked from one of them to the other. 'Then I wasn't dreaming. I thought I heard English voices back there, but I'd been dozing and I thought it was a dream. Is it true?'

'Yes! Yes!' she said impatiently. 'Tell him, Luke.'

Luke hesitated and Cyrano said suspiciously, 'Just a minute. What the hell would two English kids be doing having a cycling holiday in France in the middle of a war?'

'We're not having a holiday. That was just an excuse. We're trying to get back to England.'

'On bicycles?' He gave a brief sceptical laugh.

'No, of course not. We . . . we're hoping to meet up with some friends who will help us.'

He looked from her to Luke again.

'So what are you doing in France in the first place?'

'We live here. Our mother is French and our father is English, so technically we're British. That's why we have to get out.'

Cyrano's eyes were still on Luke's face. 'Is she telling the truth?'

Luke nodded unwillingly. 'And is she right, about you?' he countered.

Cyrano leaned heavily on the handlebars of the bicycle, his head drooping. He spoke in English for the first time.

'OK. I'm going to trust you. Yes, she's right. I'm a British agent and I was dropped by parachute two nights ago.

I should have been met but I was dropped in the wrong place. I landed badly and, as you can see, I'm more or less helpless. I'm going to have to rely on you to get me somewhere where I can contact friends.'

'You see?' Christine exclaimed triumphantly.

'We'll do our best,' Luke said. 'There's someone in Baye who may be able to help. We'll get you there, at any rate.'

'Thank you.' Cyrano lifted his head and gave them a weary smile. 'What an incredible stroke of luck that you happened to come along.'

'Do you think you can ride?' Luke asked.

'I'll have to try.'

Cyrano pushed off with his good foot and steered an erratic course for a few hundred yards along the road, with Luke and Christine following. It was obvious at once that pedalling the bike with only one foot was not as simple as it sounded. On the downward thrust there was no problem but as the pedal rose, the momentum faltered and he had to hook it up with his instep. Added to which, the other pedal tended to catch his bad ankle and even to rest his foot on it was painful. They covered a short distance but then he came to a stop.

'I'll have to take a breather.' He was sweating and his face was pale.

'Tell you what,' Luke said. 'Lean on my shoulder and I'll push you.'

They made better progress like that but by the time they rejoined the canal, beyond the village of Bazolles, it was obvious that Cyrano was in a lot of pain.

Christine looked at the swollen ankle.

'You could do with a cold compress on that.'

'Good idea,' he agreed. 'But I don't have anything to make a bandage with.'

'Tell you what,' she said. 'Why don't you sit on the bank and dangle your foot in the water for a bit, and I'll see if I can find anything suitable.'

Cyrano slid off the saddle.

'That sounds like a wonderful idea.'

Luke helped him to the edge of the canal, and he lowered his foot into the cold water and gave a small cry of mingled pain and relief. Meanwhile, Christine was rummaging in the haversack containing their clothes. She had dragged out the cotton petticoat she had been wearing under her skirt when she left home. Her coat was too bulky to fit in the haversack and she had rolled it up and tied it to the back of her saddle. Now she undid it, and felt in the pocket for her penknife. A sharp nick opened a seam in the petticoat and she was able to tear off a long strip of material.

Luke watched her with amused admiration.

'Clever old you! But I don't know what Maman would say.'

'She'll never know,' Christine responded.

She took the strip to the canal bank and dipped it in the water. Then she turned to Cyrano.

'Can you swivel around so I can get at your foot?'

He did as she asked and she bound the wet fabric tightly round his ankle and under his instep, then dug into a pocket and produced a safety pin to fasten it. When she looked up, he was watching her with a smile and she was suddenly aware of how blue his eyes were and how they creased up at the corners when he smiled.

'You're a remarkably resourceful young lady,' he said.

'Oh, Chris can fix anything,' her brother said. 'You'd be amazed what she can produce from her pockets.'

'Oh, shut up, Luke!' For some reason she felt the colour rising in her cheeks. She finished the bandage as quickly as she could and stood up. 'See how that feels.'

Luke helped Cyrano to his feet and he attempted to stand, but gave up with a wince.

'I still can't put any weight on it, but it is less painful, so thanks. Let's try the bicycle again, shall we?'

At last, the first houses of the little village of Blaye, and the broad expanse of the lake beyond it, came into sight and Cyrano called a halt.

'Who are you planning to contact here?'

'The lock-keeper.'

'Are you sure he can be trusted?'

Christine and Luke exchanged glances.

'We've been told that he often helps people . . . people like us who need to travel without having to show their papers,' Luke said cautiously. 'Look, why don't you wait here with Chris and I'll go ahead and see who is around. Just in case the lock-keeper's got visitors or something.'

Cyrano nodded. 'Good idea.'

'Sit here, in the shade,' Luke said, pushing the bike close to a tree. He helped him to lower himself onto the grass and Christine propped her bike against the trunk and sat beside him. 'I'll be back as soon as I can,' he promised.

She was suddenly gripped by the fear that was never far from her mind.

'Luke, be careful!'

'I will.' He forced a smile and then mounted his bike and rode away towards the cottage.

Cyrano said, 'You know, I'm really grateful to you and your brother. I hope I'm not being too much of a nuisance.'

She shook her head. 'You're not. Not at all. We're very glad to be able to help.'

She looked in the direction of the lock-keeper's cottage. Luke had disappeared from view, and she suddenly found herself beset by gloomy forebodings. Suppose the lock-keeper refused to help them, or there were no boats that would take them on their way? Suppose he had been arrested by the Nazis and his place taken by someone else, a collaborator; or perhaps the lock might now be in the hands of the Germans . . . Luke could be walking straight into a trap. What should she do if he failed to return? How long should she wait?

Luke leaned his bicycle against the wall of the cottage and stood still, watching and listening. There were no boats going through the lock and the door of the cottage was closed, so there was no way of knowing who, or how many people, might be inside. He waited, steeling himself, but in the absence of any clue about the occupants, there was nothing for it but to go ahead and hope for the best. He walked up to the door and knocked.

There was a pause, then the sound of shuffling and disgruntled muttering from inside and the door was opened by a small man with a shock of grey hair that stood up from his head like a brush. He looked past Luke, obviously expecting to see a boat waiting to enter the lock, then returned his gaze to his visitor.

'Yes?'

'Excuse me, monsieur. I'm sorry to disturb you. I was asked by Madame Delahaie to return this bicycle to you.'

'Ah!' The man narrowed his eyes. 'Madame Jeanne Delahaie.'

'I understood her name was Eloise,' Luke said.

The man nodded. 'Eloise, to be sure.'

Luke drew a breath. 'She told me to ask you if you see many kingfishers around here.'

The man's look of suspicion was replaced by one of alert recognition.

'Yes, I saw three only yesterday.' He stepped forward and examined the number plate attached to the saddle and for the first time, Luke was glad that all bicycles had to be registered, by order of the occupying forces. Obviously the lock-keeper recognized it, because he grunted a form of assent. 'Are you just returning the bicycle?'

'No. She asks for your help to deliver a package.'

'A package?' His eyes narrowed. 'Where is it?'

'Can I come in and explain?'

The man stood aside and indicated with a jerk of his head that Luke should go in. In the low-ceilinged room, which seemed to serve as kitchen and living room, he motioned him to a chair and put a bottle of wine and two glasses on the scrubbed wooden table.

'So, what's your name?'

'Luc Beauchamps. And you are M. Simon?'

'That's right.' He poured two glasses of wine so dark it was almost black. '*Santé!*'

'*A la vôtre,*' Luke responded and drank. The wine, he reckoned, was not a patch on even the most ordinary vintage of Cave des Volcans.

'So, we haven't met before. What's your connection with Eloise Delahaie?'

'I was introduced to her . . . by a friend. The fact is, Monsieur, we need your help.'

'We?'

'My sister and I. We need to get to Auxerre.'

The lock-keeper's small dark eyes narrowed. 'What's wrong with the train?'

'On the train the Nazis check your papers. I don't have the right ones.'

Simon looked him over with a frown.

'You look too young to be an airman, or POW. What are you, a spy?'

'No, nothing like that.' As succinctly as possible, Luke explained his dual nationality and the loss of his identity papers. 'So we need to get out of France, you see. I want to go back to England to join up. Mme Delahaie said you sometimes help people to escape.'

'But, my friend, you are heading in the wrong direction. You should go south, to the Pyrenees and Spain.'

'I know that is what most people do. But our godfather lives near Montbéliard. He is a mountain guide. If we can reach him he will get us across the border to Switzerland.'

'Hmm. I see.' The lock-keeper rasped his hand across his unshaven chin. 'And your sister is with you, you say? How old is she?'

'Sixteen.'

'And the two of you are hoping to cross France on your own, without papers?'

'With your help, Monsieur — and your friends'.'

Simon continued to rub his chin broodingly and Luke began to fear that he was going to refuse.

Eventually the older man said, 'I can get you down to the bottom of the staircase. My brother has a boat. If anyone asks, he can say he is going to collect stone from the quarry at Picampoix. Jacques Molan, at the bottom lock, can be trusted. He may know of someone who is heading north and might be prepared to take you.'

Luke let out a breath he had been unconsciously holding.

'Thank you, Monsieur. If you can speak to him for us, we shall be forever in your debt.' He hesitated. 'There is one other thing. We are not alone.'

'Now you are going to tell me your sister has a child with her!'

'No, nothing like that.'

'Your pet dog, then? No, no. No animals!'

'No, that's not what I mean. We met a man, a few kilometres back. He was hiding in a barn. He has a sprained ankle, or it may be broken for all I know. He says his name is Cyrano.'

The lock-keeper almost shot out of his chair.

'You have Cyrano with you?'

'You know about him?'

'A man was here yesterday, asking if I had heard any-thing — one of the *Maquis* from up there in the Morvan. Well, come along! What are you waiting for? Show me where you left him.'

He was out of the door almost before Luke could get to his feet and striding away up the towpath, as fast as his short legs could carry him. As they reached the tree where the others were waiting, Luke saw Cyrano drag himself to his feet and his hand went once again to his trouser pocket.

Simon stopped a few feet away and spread his hands in a gesture of reassurance.

'You are Cyrano?'

'Yes,' was the cautious response.

Simon stepped forward and embraced him.

'Welcome to France! Your friend Gregoire was here only yesterday asking if I had any news of you.'

Cyrano submitted to being kissed on both cheeks, and then said, 'You know Gregoire?'

'Of course. Don't worry. We are all friends of the *Maquis* here. He is worried because you did not arrive at the time and place he expected. Come, you need to get the weight off that foot.'

Before long, all four of them were sitting around the kitchen table and the rough *vin ordinaire* had been replaced by something much more palatable. Cyrano's ankle was encased in a proper bandage and he had his foot up on a chair.

'What happened?' Simon asked. 'According to Gregoire, you should have been dropped two nights ago, close to the Lac du Settons.'

'That was the plan,' Cyrano said. 'But if you remember, it was very misty two nights ago. It was as clear as a bell when we left England, but once we got here it was impossible to see any landmarks. I knew we were looking for a lake, so when I saw this one through the mist I assumed it was the right one. The pilot tooled around for a while, looking for the signal lights, but in the end he was getting short of fuel so I had to make a decision: either jump and hope we were somewhere near the target, or go back home. I was fed up with waiting, so I chose to jump. Unfortunately,' he indicated his bandaged ankle, 'I landed badly, with the result you can see. I managed to drag myself as far as the barn where these two found me, and then I lay up, hoping it would get better. But no luck. I was beginning to get desperate when they happened along.' He smiled at Luke and his sister, then turned to the lock-keeper. 'Can you help me to get to Corbigny? I have a contact there who will pass a message to Gregoire.'

'*Pas de problème, mon cher!*' their host exclaimed. 'Tomorrow my brother will take you down to Jacques Molan. He will know someone who will take you on from there. Now young lady, you can help me get some dinner on the table and then we'll have to think about where you are all going to sleep.'

CHAPTER 8

Soon after dawn next morning, a small barge appeared out of the mist that lay over the surface of the lake and moored beside the lock. A slightly younger version of Pierre Simon stepped onto the quay, where the three travellers were waiting.

'My name is Jean,' he said, shaking hands with Cyrano. 'Welcome to France.'

'Thank you,' Cyrano responded. 'It's good of you to agree to help us.'

'I am a patriot, Monsieur,' the man replied. 'I am too old to fight but I am happy to do anything I can for those who are prepared to help drive the *Boche* out of our country.' He turned to Luke and Christine and offered his hand to each of them in turn. 'And you, my brother tells me, are going to England to join the fight.'

'That is our plan,' Luke agreed.

'Then you too, are welcome to any help I can give. So come, let us be on our way.'

After brief farewells to the elder Simon, the three boarded the barge. Although Cyrano's ankle had benefited from a night's rest, he was still unable to walk so Pierre had given him a stout stick and with the help of that and Luke's steadying hand, he managed to hop up the gangplank. Pierre heaved their bicycles on after them. Jean cast off and the barge moved out into the mist. Luke shivered suddenly.

'Cold?' his sister asked.

He shook his head. 'Not really. It's all this — the lake and the mist. It reminded me of Tennyson's *Morte d'Arthur*, where the barge with the three queens comes out of the mist to carry him off to Avalon.'

'That's the trouble with poetry,' Christine said brusquely. 'It puts ideas in your head.'

Before long, the canal veered away from the lake and entered a deep cutting. Here, Christine found that the surroundings worked on her own imagination, in spite of her scornful dismissal of her brother's poetic reaction. The wooded banks rose steeply on each side so that only a narrow strip of sky was visible. Wraiths of mist lingered among the trees and overhanging branches mirrored themselves in the still water. Even Cyrano seemed uneasy.

'What a place for an ambush,' he murmured.

'No fear of that,' Jean replied, overhearing him. 'The Germans never come anywhere near here. Why would they?'

Nevertheless, Christine wrapped her arms around herself and huddled a little closer to her brother. Worse was to come. Ahead of them loomed the mouth of a tunnel so narrow it hardly seemed wide enough to take the barge. A small, grey vessel was tied up just outside it and they all jumped as Jean sounded a short blast on his horn. In response, a door banged somewhere above them and a man appeared, scrambling down a flight of steep steps cut into the bank.

Jean cut the engine.

'Gilbert will tow us through the tunnels. It would be dangerous to use the engine, because of the fumes.'

The man jumped aboard the grey barge and threw a line to Jean, which he made fast to the bows. There was a whine from some kind of motor and a clanking of chain and they began to move forward.

'Oh, it's a *toueur*, like the one Bernard described at Decize,' Christine exclaimed.

Her delight was short lived. The tunnel was unlit, except for the headlight on the towing vessel, which showed them the dank walls closing about them, and cold drips fell from the roof, which was only feet above their heads. It seemed a long time before the pinprick of light, which marked the tunnel's end, grew to the size of an orange, and then a pumpkin and finally allowed them out into the daylight. Even that was only a brief interlude. There were three tunnels to negotiate in all and they breathed a sigh of relief when they came to the end of the last one and found themselves at last in the open. Here, the hills fell back on either side to form a wide valley and the morning mists had evaporated. It was good to feel the sun's warmth on their shoulders.

Close by, there was a small village.

'Port Brulé,' Jean announced. 'Don't worry. No one will bother us.' He cast off the line from the *toueur* and they waved goodbye to the man who operated it. 'Now,' he went on, 'comes the hard work. This lock is the top of the staircase and there are sixteen in all.'

'We'll help,' Christine said eagerly. 'We know about locks.'

There were times when she almost regretted her offer. It took them nearly four hours to negotiate the sixteen locks. Each had, as a matter of course, its own lock-keeper, who operated the sluices and whose job it was to open and close the heavy gates; but they were all more than happy to allow Luke and Christine to help. They soon found it easier to walk from one lock to the next instead of jumping on and off the barge, and that was a pleasure after the darkness of the tunnels. It was a beautiful spring morning and the canal descended step by step through a sylvan landscape. Each lock had its tiny lock-keeper's cottage, with its little vegetable garden and pots of spring bulbs, and the canal was bordered with apple and pear and walnut trees, which would provide extra sustenance in season. Wild cyclamen and primroses bloomed in the grassy banks and every now and then, they heard the plop as a fish rose to the surface of the canal to feed.

'Not a bad life these chaps have,' Luke commented.

'You'd be bored to death in a week,' his sister told him tartly.

The keepers greeted Jean as an old friend, but none of them seemed at all interested in the three passengers on his barge.

Once Cyrano asked doubtfully, 'Are you sure they can all be trusted?'

'What could they possibly gain from talking to the Germans?' Jean asked. 'Everyone else would know at once who had done it, and from then on he wouldn't be able to sleep in peace. He would have to move away and take his family with him. Why would anyone want to give up his home and his livelihood for the sake of a pat on the back from a *Boche*?'

It was past midday when they reached the bottom lock, and Jean introduced them to Jacques Molin, a big, red-faced man who greeted them all with handshakes that made them wince. His wife invited them to join them for a meal, but Luke and Christine tried to refuse, hungry as they were by this time. There had been no opportunity to buy food since they left Decize and they both felt guilty about sharing their hosts' sparse rations. Jacques Molin would brook no argument, declaring that as they kept chickens and grew their own vegetables, they never went hungry. Very soon. they were sitting down to onion soup and omelettes and boiled potatoes. Over the meal, they discussed their next move.

'Georges Pasquier is loading stone down at Picampoix to go north,' Molin said. 'He has been known to bring escapers down with him, but he's a cussed character. There's no knowing how he'll react to the idea of taking you three in the opposite direction. Still, we can ask. I'll cycle down when we've eaten and have a word with him.'

Jean Simon got up.

'I'd best be on my way. I'll go down to the quarry and pick up some stone. There's always a need for it and it will look odd if I go back empty. But if I don't get on it'll be dark before I get home.' He shook hands with all three of them and wished them luck and they all tried once again to thank him for his help. Cyrano offered him money, but the boat-man refused. 'Free my country from these accursed Nazis,' he responded. 'That's all the recompense I want.'

'But they are children! Just kids! What did Eloise think she was doing, giving us away to them?'

Georges Pasquier was shaking with fury. He was a tall, thin man with hollow cheeks and muscles like whipcord and his manner had been truculent, even before Luke had explained what he and Christine were asking him to do.

'We're not kids . . . !' Luke began hotly but Pasquier overrode him.

'The *réseau* was set up to get fighting men back to Britain so they could continue the struggle. Not to help snotty kids to run away from home.'

'We're not running away. We want to get back to England so we can fight, too,' Luke said.

'And suppose you are caught, on my boat — or after-wards, for that matter? How long will it take the Gestapo to get the names of everyone in the *réseau* out of you?'

'We wouldn't tell them anything,' Christine protested.

'You think not? What makes you so much braver than thousands of others?'

'You wouldn't tell them anything, would you?' she asked. 'What makes you think we can't be as brave as you?'

'Me? I'd sing like a canary if I was caught — give you all away, the whole lot of you. You don't know what these swine can do to you.' He looked across the room at Cyrano. 'I'll take him. He's here to do a useful job, and he's been properly trained. And anyway Corbigny is only half a day's voyage away. You two will have to find your own way home.'

'We're not going home,' Luke said. 'Not to our home in France, anyway. If I go back, I'll have to register for STO.'

'So? Thousands of others like you have already had to go. What makes you so special?'

'He doesn't have the right papers,' Christine said. 'If the Nazis find out he's British, he'll be shot, or sent to a prison camp. So will I.'

Pasquier shrugged. 'It's not my problem. It's too much of a risk. I'm not risking my skin, and my son's, and the boat — to say nothing of the rest of the *réseau* — just so you can scuttle off to your cosy bolt-hole.'

'We're not scuttling!' Luke was white with anger. 'I'm going to join up. And England's not "cosy". People there are being bombed out of their houses every night, which is more than has happened to you French, since you surrendered and left us to fight your battles.'

'Right! That's it!' Pasquier growled. 'I don't care where you're going. You'll have to find your own way there.'

'Just a minute.' Cyrano had said nothing but now his voice cut across the argument with quiet authority. 'Of course it's up to you, Monsieur, to decide who you will take on your boat. But I would ask you to consider two points. One is this: you say your purpose is to return fighting men to their units. Luke here is old enough to join up, and he wants to volunteer for the RAF. God knows, they need all the extra pilots they can get, so if you help him to get home that will be one more nail in Hitler's coffin. The second consideration is this: I've only known these two for a few hours, but they've proved to me that they can be trusted. They are brave and resourceful and if it wasn't for them I would still be stuck in that barn, desperate for food and water — or perhaps in the hands of the Gestapo by now. So I owe them something. The local *Maquis* are waiting for me, and when I get to them I'll be able to organize arms drops so when the Allies get here, the *Maquis* will be in a position to prepare the ground by disrupting German communications and blowing up fuel dumps and railway lines. Once the area is liberated, the *Maquis* will know the names of all those who helped them, and those who didn't.' He paused and Christine saw that Pasquier's face had lost its high colour. 'You are worried that Luke and Christine might betray you if they were caught.' Cyrano went on. 'And I agree that it's unlikely that any of us would be able to withstand Gestapo interrogation techniques for long, however brave we were. But doesn't it occur to you that they already know your identity, and Jacques' here, and presumably other people further down the chain, like the Eloise you mentioned earlier. Don't you think it would be safer all round if you helped them to get out of the country? You would be safeguarding the secrets of the *réseau* and helping the war effort at the same time.'

There was a silence. Pasquier looked from Cyrano to Luke and Christine, his mouth working as if he was chewing something.

At length he said, 'Very well. Since you ask it, Monsieur, and as a favour to you and out of respect for the organization you represent, I agree.' He glared at the two young people. 'But you'll have to work your passage. You're a well-built young chap. You can help with loading and unloading and save my back. And you, Mademoiselle, will take over the cooking. But I don't want you boarding at the quarry. The whole place is crawling with *Milice*. I'll pick you up at the pool below this lock. I'll have to come up that far to turn round. We cast off first thing tomorrow morning. If you aren't there I shan't hang about waiting for you. Understand?'

'We understand,' Luke said, his voice tight with the effort of controlling his temper. 'Thank you, Monsieur.'

Pasquier looked around at them all once more, nodded briefly at Jacques Molin, and left the room. There was a collective sigh of relief and Christine said, 'Thank you so much, Cyrano. You were brilliant.'

'Least I could do,' he responded. 'You got me out of a hole, after all.'

Luke suddenly began to laugh. 'Oh dear! Pasquier doesn't know what he's let himself in for.'

'What do you mean?'

'He's told Christine to take charge of the cooking!'

As instructed, they set off the next morning at first light. After another night's rest, Cyrano's ankle was improving. He was still unable to put his full weight on it, but at least he could manage better on the bicycle, though either Luke or

Christine had to stay close by to help him on and off. It was another chilly morning, with mist lying low over the fields and along the canal, and when they came to the appointed place it was impossible to see far in any direction. The canal and the road that ran alongside it were eerily quiet.

'You don't think he's already gone, do you?' Christine asked.

Luke shrugged. 'We couldn't have left any earlier. It would be rotten luck if he has.'

'Those boats don't move very fast, do they?' Cyrano said. 'I'd be surprised if he's beaten us to it. Anyway, there's nothing we can do but wait and hope.'

'Listen!' Luke said.

From somewhere down the canal, they all heard the faint chugging of a diesel engine and surprisingly quickly, the outline of a *péniche* came into view. The engine note changed as it approached and the bows swung in towards the bank. A boy of about Luke's age was standing on the foredeck with a rope in his hand. Luke was helping Cyrano to his feet, so the boy focussed his gaze on Christine.

'Oi, kid! Catch hold of this.'

'I'm not a kid!' she called back, catching the rope and hauling the boat to the bank.

'*Mon Dieu*! It's a girl!' He jumped ashore, grinning broadly. '*Salut, mon amie*! My name is Roland. Call me Rollo.'

Pasquier emerged from the engine room.

'Forget the introductions. Get them on board. I'm not hanging about here all day.'

Between them, Luke and Roland got Cyrano on board and went back for the bikes, which they lashed to the front of the wheelhouse. Christine cast off the mooring line and followed. As soon as they were all aboard, the engine note changed and Roland pushed them off with a long pole. When the tricky manoeuvre of turning the barge around had been completed, he came into the cabin and repeated his introduction, shaking hands with all of them. He was tall and lean, like his father, with sandy hair cut *en brosse* and a wide mouth in a face marked by the scars of a spectacular attack of acne. There was something in his smile as he shook hands with Christine that made her feel vaguely uncomfortable.

'OK. I'll show you where you can stow your gear. It's going to be a bit cramped with five of us on board, but at least you will have a cabin to yourself, Monsieur. Let me show you.'

He opened a cupboard built against the bulkhead, which divided the cabin from the hold, and pushed aside some clothes hanging there. With a tug, he removed the back to reveal a dark space and a short flight of steps. He took a torch from a shelf and directed it into the space.

'*Voilà!*'

In the torchlight they saw a small compartment, which had been constructed in the area normally used for cargo. It contained a bed, a bucket, and an upturned box which served as a table.

'It's hidden by the cargo,' Roland said proudly. 'The *Boche* will never suspect it's there. You won't have to sleep there, of course. We'll get to Chitry-les-Mines this afternoon. That's as close to Corbigny as we go. But you might need it when we go through locks. The *Boche* have put guards on some of them because the bloody *Maquis* have tried to blow them up once or twice.' He turned to Luke and Christine. 'I'm afraid you two will have to make do with the benches in here — unless,' with a grin at her, 'you fancy sharing with me in the other cabin. We could kick the old man out?'

Luke said sharply, 'You can cut that out!'

Rollo shrugged and turned away.

Cyrano said, 'Christine can have my bed. I won't need it after this afternoon.'

'What did you mean by the "bloody *Maquis*"?' Luke said. 'We're all on the same side, aren't we?'

'You think so? If that was the case, they might give some thought to poor sods like us who are trying to make a living — to say nothing of getting escapees out of the country.'

'Have you brought many down the line?' Cyrano asked.

'Four, no five, so far. One soldier who got left behind in the evacuation right at the start, one POW, a Polish pilot, and two bomber crew.'

'You're doing a fantastic job.'

Pasquier called down from the wheelhouse. 'Rollo, get up here and give me a break.'

His son rolled his eyes and left the cabin and a moment later, Pasquier put his head through the doorway. 'And you Mademoiselle, had better get into the galley and see what you can find for lunch. I didn't have your ration cards, so you'll have to make do with what I could scrounge.'

Christine sighed and exchanged a wry smile with her brother.

'Want some help?' he offered.

'From you? You're a worse cook than I am. No, I'll manage somehow.'

The sight of the little galley almost caused her to regret her words. It was filthy, with every surface thick with grease, and the dust from the cargo of stone. She found a bucket and scooped water from the canal, then set it on the oil-fired stove to boil. Meanwhile she searched the shelves and cupboards and found half a dozen eggs, a loaf, a small piece of butter, and some very overripe *Bleu d'Auvergne* cheese. Not much to feed five hungry people; she cringed at the thought of Gregoire Pasquier's reaction. Then, in a basket, she discovered some potatoes, two onions and some carrots and was immediately reminded of the dish her mother fell back on when rations were short: *Potage Bonne Femme*. Tasty and filling. She could serve an omelette afterwards and finish with bread and cheese. When the water boiled, she scrubbed the small work surface as clean as she could get it and found a saucepan and scoured out the remains of whatever had been cooked in it last. Then, she melted the butter and fried the onions. Soon the galley was filled with savoury smells.

Cyrano decided to lie down and rest his ankle so, at a loose end, Luke went up to the wheelhouse to talk to Rollo. Pasquier was sitting up in the bows, smoking and Rollo was perched on a high stool, holding the wheel loosely in one hand.

'*Eh bien, mon ami*', he said cheerfully. '*Ça va?*'

'*Oui, ça va*,' Luke agreed. He looked around, seeking a topic of conversation.

'Where is the cargo bound for?'

Rollo's smile faded and he looked almost defensive. 'The *Boche* are building a new airfield outside Auxerre. It's for that. They commandeered all the barges. We had to do as we were told or they would just have requisitioned the boat and put their own crew on board. This way, we still have a living.'

'And you make up for what you have to do by helping Allied airmen to escape. And right under the Germans' noses! That takes some guts.'

'We do what we can.' Rollo visibly relaxed. 'Smoke?' He produced a crumpled packet of Gauloises.

'No, thanks. I don't.'

'Don't smoke?' Rollo looked at him as if he had said he never slept. Then he shrugged. '*Tant pis.*' He lit his own cigarette, drew on it and said, '*Alors*, tell me about your girlfriend.'

'What girlfriend?'

'You must have a girlfriend — good-looking chap like you. I bet the girls are falling over themselves. Come on, describe her to me.'

Luke procrastinated. 'Which one?'

'Aha! There are so many? You are like me. I have a girl in every town up and down this canal, from Auxerre to Corbigny. And each one thinks she is the only one! Not likely! No one is going to have exclusive rights to what I've got here!' He pointed to his groin and grinned. 'So tell me. Which one is your favourite?' Then, as Luke searched for a reply, he went on, 'For my part, I can't decide between Suzanne and Jeanette. Jeanette has these fantastic tits,' he cupped his free hand as if weighing something round and heavy, 'but Suzanne . . . ah, Suzanne will do anything! I mean, anything!' He rolled his eyes and licked his lips. 'So, now tell me. Do you have a girl who will do that for you?'

For a moment Luke could think of no response.

Then he said, 'I don't think it's something a decent man should talk about.'

Rollo crowed with laughter. 'A decent man!' he repeated, imitating Luke's prim tone. '*Mon Dieu!* You're not a virgin, are you?'

'It's none of your business!' Luke responded curtly. 'I think I'll go and see how my sister is getting on in the kitchen.'

Rollo was looking at him with amused contempt.

'*Merde alors!* He *is* a virgin!'

In the cabin, Luke stood silently, his hands thrust deep in his pockets, breathing hard through his nose. Cyrano, thank God, seemed to be asleep and Christine was clattering pans in the galley. It was true. He was a virgin. The secret knowledge chafed at him, but he had never felt so humiliated by it before. There were reasons, but not ones he felt Rollo would understand.

When he and his family had returned to France, he had found himself very popular with the local girls. They had flirted with him, even girls several years older than he was, and he had been made welcome in their houses.

One evening, his mother had taken him aside and said gently, 'Listen, my darling, I don't want to spoil your fun, but there is something you should bear in mind. There are a lot of families round here who hoped that one day Cave des Volcans would belong to them. Then, when I married your father, they thought they had lost the chance. But now, they see a new one. If you were to marry one of their daughters, sooner or later the vineyard would pass to their grandchildren. Of course, if that was what you wanted, that would be fine. But you should be careful. If you were to give one of those girls the wrong idea it could put us all in a compromising position. You're a good-looking boy. It's not surprising that they are attracted to you. Just be aware that it may not only be for the sake of *tes beaux yeux*.'

He had never forgotten the warning. He knew that ideas about relations between men and women were still strict, almost

Victorian, among the local bourgeoisie and it would be all too easy to find himself trapped into a marriage. It had put him very much on his guard in his dealings with the opposite sex.

He took a deep breath and told himself that it was stupid to let himself be upset by a boy who was obsessed with sex — and whose conquests, he had enough experience to guess, were probably largely a matter of fantasy.

Christine's lunch was a great success, to her relief and Luke's barely concealed amazement. The soup should have been garnished with cream and fresh parsley, neither of which was available, but it did not seem to matter. The omelettes were rather small and there was a definite tang of ammonia about the cheese, but when the meal was over, Gregoire Pasquier leaned back in his seat and said grudgingly, 'Well, Mademoiselle Christine, it looks as though you may earn your keep after all.'

Christine suppressed an angry rejoinder and replied meekly, 'I'll do my best, Monsieur.'

After the meal, Roland offered to show Luke how to steer the boat and Christine found herself sitting with Cyrano in the well behind the wheelhouse. The day had turned warm, and it was pleasant to sit in the sun while the banks of the canal drifted slowly past. She had been longing to ask Cyrano more about himself and she seized the chance.

'Are you really a music teacher?'

He smiled. 'Yes, that bit was true.'

'So are you going to be working at a school in Corbigny?'

'No. The idea is I am supposed to teach privately, going round to people's houses to give lessons. It gives me a reason to travel around the area.'

'I suppose your name isn't really Cyrano. What is it?'

He shook his head. 'I'm not allowed to tell anyone that. I'm afraid you'll have to make do with Cyrano.'

'That's all right. I rather like it. It's quite romantic. Like Cyrano de Bergerac.'

He laughed. 'That's how I came to choose it. I read the play at school.' They were silent for a moment. Then he said, 'Why didn't you go back to England with your father?'

'We stayed to help our mother run the vineyard. It belongs to grandfather but he had a stroke a few years ago and needs to be looked after. That's why we came to live here, about a year before the war started.'

'Where did you live before that?'

Christine was beginning to be irritated by this interrogation. It seemed unfair that he could ask her questions while she was not allowed to reciprocate.

'In a village called Fetcham, close to Leatherhead in Surrey.'

Cyrano's gaze seemed to become sharper.

'What did your father do, before the war?'

'He was a buyer for a firm of wine merchants.'

For a moment he frowned, as if trying to recall a memory. Then the expression faded and he said, 'Right! Sorry to be so nosy but I have to be careful.'

'That's OK,' she said. 'I understand.'

'What will you do, when you get home?' he asked.

'I don't know. I'd like to join up too, but I know they won't have me until I'm seventeen.'

'When will that be?'

'October. I thought I might be able to sign up for some war work until then — in a munitions factory or something.'

'Where will you live?'

'With our grandparents, I suppose.' She wrinkled her nose. 'They will probably want me to go back to school.'

He was looking at her differently, with a thoughtful expression, as if he was trying to make up his mind about something.

Then he said, 'I think I know an organization that would be very glad to have someone like you. It's a Women's Corps but not attached to any of the regular services. I know they are always on the look-out for practical, sensible girls with a bit of guts. And specially if they are fluent in another language. If I give you a name and an address to go to, can you memorize it?'

She stared at him, wide-eyed, feeling her pulse quicken. She was sure that this organization must be in some way connected to his own activities.

'Yes!' she said breathlessly. 'Of course I can.'

'OK. When you get back to London, go to 64 Baker Street and ask for Mrs Bingham, and tell them Cyrano sent you. They won't take you till you are seventeen, either. But there's no harm in getting your name on the list. Can you remember that?'

'64 Baker Street, ask for Mrs Bingham.'

'Again!'

'64 Baker Street, ask for Mrs Bingham and say you sent me.'

'Good! I think you will fit in to that crowd very well.'

'I hope so! Thank you! I'm really, really grateful.'

He gave her a wry smile. 'I hope you'll still feel that way once you're in. It'll be tough, you know.'

'I don't care. As long as I'm doing something useful.'

They reached Chitry-les-Mines in the late afternoon, and moored in a wide basin.

'Corbigny is up that way, about a kilometre and a half,' Pasquier said. 'How are you going to get there?'

'I don't know,' Cyrano responded. 'I was hoping by now I'd be able to walk, but I still can't put any weight on this ankle. I did think about borrowing one of the bikes, but you'll need to hang on to them and there's no way you'd get it back.'

'I'll come with you,' Luke said. 'You can ride and I'll bring the bike back.'

Cyrano looked unhappy with the idea, but after a moment he nodded. 'Yes, it's the only answer.'

'Don't take the main road,' Pasqier said. 'Take the old Roman road that runs just north of it. You're less likely to encounter any checkpoints there.'

Christine watched as one of the bikes was unlashed from its position on the deck, and Cyrano collected the case with his radio and shook hands with Pasquier and Rollo. She felt an unfamiliar tightness in her throat at the thought that in a few minutes he would be gone and they would probably never meet again. As a talisman against that probability, she repeated to herself the address he had given her. Maybe if she was accepted by this mysterious organization they would bump into each other, somewhere. Meanwhile, he was about to vanish from her life and she found the prospect unexpectedly painful.

'I'll come with you, to Corbigny,' she said.

He smiled at her and shook his head. 'Better not. It's like the *réseau*. The fewer people who know the next link in the chain, the better.'

She wanted to assure him that no power on earth would force her to betray his secret, but she remembered what Pasquier had said and knew that it would be an empty assertion. She tugged her brother's sleeve.

'Don't leave me here alone with these two!'

'You heard Cyrano,' he replied. 'Besides, one of us needs to stay behind. What's to stop Pasquier shoving off and leaving us stranded if we both go?'

She bit back tears. 'I don't like it. I don't trust either of them, especially not that creep Rollo.'

'You'll be all right. There are plenty of people around. Just stay on the deck where you can be seen and don't let him get you alone.' He squeezed her arm. 'I'll be back as soon as I can.'

Cyrano finished strapping his case onto the bicycle rack and turned to them.

'Time to go. Take care of yourself, Chris. And thanks again for your help.'

She took a deep breath and held out her hand.

'Goodbye. And good luck!'

'Thank you.' He kept her hand in his a moment longer than a formal handshake required. 'Don't forget that address.'

'I won't!'

Luke had lifted the bike onto the towpath and returned to help. He and Rollo half lifted the injured man off the barge and perched him on the saddle and then, with a final salute, he pushed off and wobbled uncertainly along the dock, Luke trotting at his side.

They found the old road without difficulty and Luke found the chance to say something he had been mentally preparing.

97

'You know, if it wasn't for Christine I'd have told Pasquier not to wait. I'd stay with you and join the *Maquis*.'

Cyrano glanced sideways at him. 'But, as you say, your first duty is to make sure your sister gets home safely. That's the most important thing.'

'I know,' Luke said regretfully. He had put aside his romantic notion of joining the *Maquis* in favour of his mother's plan for a return to England, but the encounter with Cyrano had revived it as an all-too-present possibility. 'The thing is, I really want to do my bit, make a contribution towards getting rid of the Nazis . . .'

'And you will,' Cyrano assured him. 'Believe me, you will be far more use as a pilot with the RAF than you would be hiding out in the forest with a bunch of amateurs.'

'But it's what you're going to do,' Luke objected.

Cyrano gave a brief laugh.

'*Touché*! But I'm only following orders — and I do have a definite contribution to make.' He jerked his head to indicate the suitcase strapped to the rear carrier. 'Hopefully, I can help to turn this lot into something more useful than amateurs. But I still say you will be more use as a pilot. You'll be up there, dropping bombs or fighting off the Luftwaffe, while I'm still lurking in the woods hoping the Gestapo aren't picking up my transmissions.'

They had reached the top of the hill and found themselves by the railway line. From here, there was no option but to join the main road where it passed over a level crossing. A German sentry leaned in the doorway of a small cabin, yawning, and took no notice of them as they passed.

Luke asked, 'Where do we have to go?'

'There is a pharmacist's shop, in the Rue du Vézelay. That's where I should be able to make contact.'

'How do we find it?'

Cyrano tapped his forehead.

'I was shown it on a map. I just hope I've memorized it correctly.'

There were people about in the streets of the little town, shopping, or making their way home from work, but Luke knew they could not risk asking their way. After all, Cyrano was supposed to be a resident.

The swastika flew outside the town hall, and a German motorcycle patrol overtook them as they reached the main crossroads, but no one queried their presence. On the far side, a green-cross hung outside a small shop.

'There?' Luke said.

'Looks like it,' Cyrano agreed.

They stopped outside and Luke helped his companion off the bike and into the doorway. He was about to push the door open, when the pressure of Cyrano's hand on his shoulder stopped him.

'I think this is where we say goodbye, *mon ami*. I'm more than grateful for your help. But the fewer people you can recognize and identify the better. You understand?'

'Yes, I understand,' Luke said unwillingly. He had been imagining being introduced to other members of the *Maquis*, perhaps being congratulated and thanked, even invited to join them. He would have to have refused the offer of course, but even so . . . 'Yes, you're right, of course. But are you sure you can manage on your own?'

'I can hop inside, and after that I'm sure someone will give me a hand.' He squeezed Luke's shoulder. 'Good luck! Take care of that sister of yours. She's a great kid. You're both great. You will be a real asset to the Allied war effort when you get back. Take care.'

'You too,' Luke said, feeling a sudden constriction in his throat. 'I'm really glad we were able to help.'

Cyrano let go of his shoulder and gripped the door handle.

'Bye now.'

The door swung open and Luke had a brief glimpse of the interior, with its flasks of coloured liquid on the shelves. Then it closed and he turned away, oppressed by the thought that this was probably the closest he would ever come to joining the *Maquis*.

CHAPTER 9

As soon as Luke and Cyrano were out of sight, Pasquier thrust two ration cards into Christine's hand.

'You'd better go and see what you can find for dinner.'

Christine hesitated for a moment; Luke had told her to stay close to the boat, in case Pasquier and his son decided to leave without them. Then it occurred to her that she had both their ration cards; as long as she held them, they could go nowhere.

She collected her own card and set off into the village. It was a tiny place. She wondered how it had earned the soubriquet 'les mines'; it certainly didn't look like a mining village. At first, she felt nervous knowing that the locals must recognize her as a stranger, and afraid of being stopped and questioned. But before long she realized that this was a place used to transient characters, moving up and down the canal, so no one queried her presence. She relaxed and began to enjoy the sense of normality. Shopping for food was something she had always done with her mother and some of her earliest memories were of Isabelle's instructions about how to choose the freshest produce or the best value as they wandered through the local market.

Since the capitulation of France, it had become an exercise in eking out the scant supplies provided by the rations.

She had complained about being made to go along at the time, but now she recognized the value of the experience. There was little choice in the few small shops but she returned to the *Madeleine* with a shopping basket stocked with items she knew she could turn into simple but palatable meals.

By the time Luke got back, the lock-keeper had gone off duty for the day, so they had no option but to moor up for the night and Rollo had taken the opportunity to do some fishing. They ate a meal of salad followed by freshly caught carp and finished with a small piece of Camembert cheese. Afterwards, Pasquier went off to a local bar and she and Luke sat with Rollo in the open cockpit, while he told them tales of close brushes with the Germans while they had escapees hidden on board — the dangers of which, they both guessed, had become more acute in the telling.

'I've just remembered something I wanted to ask,' Christine said. 'Why is this place called Chitry-les-Mines?'

'It's not coal mines, if that's what you're thinking. They used to mine silver round here, once upon a time.'

Later, as she settled to sleep in the tiny cabin concealed in the hold, Christine called softly to her brother, 'Luke?'

'What?'

'I bet you wanted to go with Cyrano, didn't you?'

'Don't be daft. I had to come back to you, didn't I?'

'Yes, but I bet you wished you could stay.'

'Well, I wouldn't have minded — if things had been different.'

'I'd have come with you — but I don't think he'd have let me.'

'He wouldn't have let either of us.'

'I'll miss him.'

'So will I. Now go to sleep!'

The day had been hot and waking next morning in the stuffy little cabin, Christine was more aware than ever that she had not had a bath since leaving home. She wriggled back into her overalls and went up to the cabin, keeping a wary eye out for Pasquier and Rollo. She had not been uneasy on the *Bourdon*, reassured by Marie's presence, but in the close confines of the *Madeleine*, she felt awkward at being the only female on board. Pasquier was shaving in the stern cockpit and Rollo was sitting on deck smoking, so Luke was alone in the main cabin.

'Luke, I need a bath — or at least a good wash. Do you think there's any chance?'

'I could do with one, too,' he agreed. 'But somehow I get the impression it's not something that our hosts put a high priority on.'

She wrinkled her nose.

'I know what you mean.'

'I'll have a word with Rollo and see if he can suggest anything.'

Rollo, approached with the problem, laughed. 'No problem, *mon ami*. Wait until we moor up for lunch and we'll have a dip in the canal.'

'I don't have bathing trunks.'

'Who needs them?'

'There's something else. It's a bit delicate . . . What about Christine?'

'Tell her to turn her back, if you're shy.'

'No. I mean, she'd like a dip too.'

'Well, that's OK. Tell her we'll turn our backs. We'll send the old man off to the café.'

This seemed the only solution, so he relayed the idea to Christine. She grimaced and shrugged. 'Well, I suppose it'll have to do.'

They moored just below a lock for lunch and when the meal was over, Pasquier, as predicted, took himself off with the lock-keeper to the nearby café. With the lock closed for the lunch hour, there was no danger of other boats passing, and any locals who might have been about were closeted in their houses for the sacred *midi*. Christine sat on deck with her eyes carefully averted, while the two boys stripped and jumped into the water. They splashed about happily for a

102

while and then Luke shouted, 'We're coming out. Turn your back!'

When they were dressed he said, 'OK. Your turn.'

Rollo sniggered. 'You should have come in with us. What is there to be shy about?'

Christine ignored him and made her way to the stern cockpit. The boys sat on the roof of the wheelhouse with their backs to her and she undressed quickly, with frequent glances over her shoulder to make sure they were still looking the other way. Then she lowered herself over the side and gasped with pleasure as the cool water enveloped her. She swam around for a few minutes, feeling the sweat washing off her body, but she worried that Pasquier might return from the café, or that Rollo would get fed up with sitting with his back to her, so she soon hauled herself out. She dried herself as quickly as she could, and pulled on her only set of clean underwear. It was then that she noticed that Luke was alone.

'Where's Rollo?' she demanded anxiously.

'It's OK. He's down below, tinkering with the engine.'

'Why? There's nothing wrong with the engine.'

'He said it wasn't ticking over properly.'

'Rubbish.'

'Well, anyway, he's not anywhere where he could see you. So you don't need to worry.'

Later, while Christine was preparing the evening meal and Pasquier was steering, Luke and Rollo sat in the bows sipping a pre-prandial *pastis*.

'Tell me something,' Rollo said. 'Why does your sister dress like a boy?'

Luke looked at him, taken slightly by surprise.

'Well, those overalls are borrowed from the people who owned the first boat we were on. We had lost all our luggage, and the clothes we were wearing weren't really suitable for jumping on and off boats — especially for Chris. I mean, a skirt wouldn't be very practical, would it? So we had to borrow things their son had left behind.' He paused, then added with a grin, 'But actually, she's always preferred boy's clothes. When she was a kid, she used to read these books by an English author called Enid Blyton. One of the main characters was a girl who really wanted to be a boy. Her name was Georgina but she insisted on being called George. I think Chris has always modelled herself on her.'

Rollo gave him one of the sly, sideways looks that he was beginning to recognize.

'Pity. She's got a nice little figure, under those dungarees.'

'How would you. . .' Luke began. Then he understood. 'You little shit! You watched her, didn't you? You told me you were going to do something to the engine.'

Rollo shrugged and winked.

'So I did. But when I finished . . . well, where's the harm? I've seen it all before . . .'

It was the wink that did it. Luke felt anger and embarrassment rise up like a hot tide and Rollo's sentence came to an abrupt end as Luke's fist made contact with his nose. He staggered back, staring at Luke wide-eyed for a fraction of a second. Then, he launched himself and the two of them crashed to the deck in a whirl of fists and feet. Rollo was solid muscle, but Luke was bigger and heavier, and back in England he had studied judo. By the time Christine came panting up from the galley, demanding 'What on earth is going on?', he had Rollo face down on the deck with one arm twisted painfully behind him.

Putting his lips close to his adversary's ear he muttered, 'Don't say a word! Understand?'

Rollo groaned and nodded and Luke let him get up.

'What was that all about?' his sister asked.

'Nothing much,' he replied, trying to be casual. Then, seeing he couldn't get away with that as an explanation, he added. 'He said something insulting.'

Christine met his gaze and his eyes said plainly, '*Don't ask*!' So she shrugged and turned away with a muttered, 'Boys!'

Luke looked around at Rollo and was surprised to be met with a shamefaced grin and a two-handed gesture, which he took to indicate an apology.

Isabelle was in the cellar, about to remove the radio from its hiding place. She could not take it into the house with the two Germans liable to come in at any minute, but they never came near the cellar and all the workers had gone home long ago. She no longer bothered much with the *messages personnels*, knowing that there was no chance that her children could have found their way back to England in the short time since that letter had been written; but just listening to the BBC bulletin was a comfort. The Germans were in retreat in North Africa, and Allied air forces controlled the skies over the Mediterranean. At last, the war was turning in their favour.

As she reached into the barrel where the set was hidden, she heard someone come into the cellar behind her. She swung around to see a young man she recognized, through a mass of unkempt hair and beard, as the son of the village cobbler. She had heard rumours that he had gone to the *Maquis*, so she was not surprised at his appearance; but his presence in her cellar set alarm bells ringing.

'It's Louis, isn't it? Louis Beaupaire? What do you want?'

He came down the cellar steps.

'I'm sorry if I have given you a fright, Madame. But I have been sent with a message.'

'A message? Who from?'

'That doesn't matter. I have to tell you that tomorrow you will receive a delivery of wine casks. Do not ask where they have come from. Just let the men store them safely in here until we need them.'

'And what is in these casks?'

'Ammunition, explosives. Stuff we liberated from a *Milice* post two days ago. We need somewhere to keep it until the time is ripe to use it.'

'Are you mad?' Isabelle's heart was pounding. 'Don't you know I've got Germans billeted on me?'

'Why should they suspect anything? You have purchased some new casks to replace old ones.'

'And suppose the Germans search? They must be looking for the stuff you stole.'

'Not stole, Madame! We are not thieves. It is the spoils of war, *n'est-ce pas*? And if they were to search — two or three barrels, among so many? And as you say, you have soldiers living here. It is the last place they would suspect.' He glanced over his shoulder and edged towards the door. 'I have to go. The barrels will arrive tomorrow afternoon. You will be doing your duty as a patriot, Madame.'

With that, he slipped outside. Isabelle followed him to the door and watched as he loped away into the darkness. When she turned back to the cellar, her hands were shaking, but it was clear that she had no option but to comply; the casks would arrive, whether she wanted them or not.

That evening, Hoffmann had returned, grey-faced and wheezing.

'His chest is worse,' Schulz confided to Isabelle in the kitchen. 'He should be in hospital but the Colonel thinks he is swinging the lead and refuses to allow him to go sick.'

'Why would he be so inhuman?' Isabelle asked.

'I think it is an old family dispute. I don't know the origins of it.'

All night, she could hear the young lieutenant coughing and in the morning it was obvious that he could not report for duty. Schulz went to the *château* with a message and later on, the medical officer came to visit and signed a note to say that Hoffmann was excused from duties for at least a week. Isabelle was torn between contrary emotions; her maternal instinct responded with relief that this poor boy, enemy or not, was no longer at the mercy of a cruel commander. But she could not forget that later that day, the casks containing the ammunition would be delivered and there was no way she could stop them.

To make matters worse, Hoffmann chose to sit by the open window instead of staying in bed.

'He finds it easier to breathe sitting up,' Schulz explained.

In the late afternoon, a horse-drawn wagon rumbled into the yard and two young men Isabelle did not know began to off-load several large casks, and roll them into the cellar. She had managed to send her foreman into Clermont on a spurious errand and the other workers were down among the vines well away from the house, so there was no one to question the reasons for the delivery. But Hoffmann was looking out of the window and raised a hand in salute as she went out to greet the men.

Later that day, Schulz returned from the *château* carrying a basket, which he proudly emptied on the kitchen table. It contained a *gigot* of lamb and half a kilo of sausages.

'I told the cook that the lieutenant was too ill to come to the mess, so I persuaded him to send these. I thought perhaps you could cook them, Madame? And then perhaps you and your father would care to share them with us?'

It was a long time since Isabelle had seen a whole leg of lamb. Roasted and accompanied by potatoes from her vegetable patch, and the first broad beans of the season, it made a delicious meal. She set places for herself, her father and Schulz at the table in the kitchen, but when she took a tray into Hoffmann's room he begged to be allowed to join them.

'I am feeling so much stronger, and I should appreciate having some company.'

So they all ate together and Isabelle opened a bottle of one of her better wines. She asked herself why she was doing this for two men who were not there by invitation, but by the orders of an occupying power; but she was finding it increasingly hard to think of them as the enemy — and besides, it would be a shame not to complement such a generous gift with an equally generous wine.

Her comfortable mood was roughly disrupted when Hoffmann said casually, 'Those casks I saw being delivered. Do they contain wine? I was under the impression that everything you produce came from your own vines.'

Isabelle remembered what the cobbler's son had said.

'No, no. They are empty casks. You are quite right. All our wine is grown here. But you have to remember that this vineyard has been going for many years — hundreds of years, in fact. Some of our casks are very old and one or two are beginning to leak. I heard that one of our neighbours had some casks he no longer wanted, so I bought them to replace the leaky ones.'

Hoffmann seemed satisfied with the explanation, but her father, sitting in his wheelchair at the head of the table, gave a sudden grunt and looked as if he was about to query it. She forestalled him by clearing the plates and setting the last of the previous season's apples on the table.

But later, when Hoffmann had retired to bed and Schulz was outside smoking, the old man demanded, 'What was all that about leaking casks? You've never mentioned a problem before. Who did you buy them from, anyway?'

She hesitated, then decided there was nothing for it but to lie.

'They came from the Corbusiers. Apparently the old man bought them some time ago and they've never been used. He asked if I wanted them, so I took them to help him out. His vines haven't done well over the last few seasons.'

'So what was all that about ours leaking?'

She gritted her teeth. Because her father was immobile and his speech was slurred, it was easy to think that he was not taking everything in, but she knew that in reality very little escaped him.

'Well, some of them are getting very old,' she temporized.

He reached out a shaky hand and laid it on her wrist.

'What are you hiding, Isabelle? What have you got yourself into?'

'Nothing, papa! We're just . . . just storing them for some . . . some friends. It's only temporary.'

He gave her a long look, then he turned his head away with a grunt and she knew he had guessed who the 'friends' were, and decided it was better not to ask any more questions.

CHAPTER 10

The *Madeleine* proceeded on her way without further incident. Luke found that Rollo's attitude of worldly condescension had been replaced with something which might even be interpreted as respect, and in Christine's presence he became almost bashful. It dawned on him that Rollo was lonely, trailing up and down the canals with only his father for company, and all his bragging had simply been a ploy to impress someone slightly older and, in his eyes, more sophisticated than himself. Now that a pecking order had been established, he really wanted to be friends. Even Georges Pasquier had mellowed, largely due to Christine's efforts in the galley. They chugged through peaceful countryside, the hills of the Morvan rising to their right and rich farmland to their left, and the sun shone.

Late that afternoon, they were approaching yet another lock.

'With any luck,' Pasquier said, 'we'll get through before the keeper goes off duty. Then we can cover another five or six kilometres before we moor up for the night.'

The gates were shut, but a barge had recently passed them in the opposite direction, so they knew the lock must be full. Pasquier sounded his horn as they approached, and the lock-keeper appeared. But instead of opening the gates, he shook his head and pantomimed looking at his watch, implying that they were too late.

Pasquier yelled back, 'Don't give me that, you lazy bugger! You've got another twenty minutes before you can pack up for the night.'

With bad grace, the keeper opened the gates and the *Madeleine* slipped into the lock. By now well versed in the routine, Luke and Rollo threw lines around the mooring bollards and wound them around the iron bars, which Luke had learned to call 'bitts', to hold her steady while it emptied. Rollo greeted the man cheerfully, but he only growled at them and muttered something about hurrying as he headed for the gates astern.

'Come on,' Rollo said. 'We'd better give him a hand to close the gates.'

'What's up with him?' Luke asked. 'He seems to be in a bad mood.'

'Probably got a hot date!' Rollo said, with a characteristic snigger.

As soon as the gates were shut, the keeper hurried to open the sluices ahead of them. Water surged out of the lock and the *Madeleine* began to sink with it. Suddenly there was a shout from somewhere to their right, and an almost simultaneous crackle of rifle fire.

The lock-keeper yelled, 'Get down! Get down!' and Luke and Rollo leapt from the quayside onto the descending deck and threw themselves flat.

The rifle fire was answered by the rattle of a machine gun from the opposite side of the canal, and they heard shouts and screams in French and German. Christine appeared white-faced from the cabin, and Luke shouted to her to stay inside, while Pasquier crouched on the floor of the wheelhouse.

The firefight went on over their heads for several minutes, then stopped as suddenly as it had started.

Luke raised his head and looked at Rollo.

'What was all that?'

'Must be the bloody *Maquis*. Why can't they leave us alone? I suppose they were planning to blow up the lock but the Germans must have known they were coming somehow.'

'I wonder what's happened to the lock-keeper.'

'Bought it, must have, poor bastard,' Rollo replied.

Cautiously, Luke got to his feet and grasped the slimy rungs of the ladder on the side of the lock. He climbed slowly, until his head was just above the level of the quay and looked around. To his amazement, the lock-keeper was busy at the wheels which operated the sluices. At his side stood a German officer, laughing and lighting a cigarette.

'The bastard!' Rollo had climbed a parallel ladder to take in the scene. 'Look at him! I bet the *Maquis* warned him what they were planning and he's betrayed them to the *Boche*. Swine!'

'What can we do?' Luke asked.

Pasquier was standing on the deck.

'Nothing. We mind our own business, that's what we do.'

'Well, come on! Let's get these gates opened, or are you planning to sit there all night?' the lock-keeper shouted.

Luke and Rollo climbed out onto the quay and went to help him. Looking around, Luke was shaken to see several bodies lying at the edge of a field of maize, a short distance from the bank. Two German soldiers were dragging one of them towards the lock; on the opposite side, more soldiers were dismantling a machine gun.

The German officer strolled along the quay and looked down at the *Madeleine* and Luke froze in terror. In the excitement of the moment, he had forgotten that he had no papers and now there was every likelihood that they would all be asked to produce them.

'What cargo are you carrying?' the officer enquired.

'Stone. For your new airfield outside Auxerre,' Pasquier replied in surly tones.

'Ah well, then we had better not detain you,' the officer said. 'On your way.'

The gates were open. Luke lowered himself back onto the deck, hardly daring to breathe in case he was called back at the last moment. Rollo followed and the barge glided slowly out into the open water. Nobody spoke until they were well away from the lock. Then Christine came out of the cabin and accosted her brother.

'What were you thinking of, you idiot, standing up there in full view? You should have been down in the secret cabin.'

'I know,' he mumbled. 'I just forgot for a moment.'

She met his eyes and saw that he was as scared as she had been.

'Idiot!' she repeated, and left it at that.

Further on, the scenery changed, with chalk cliffs rising above the canal to the east until they reached the ancient town of Clamecy, with its winding narrow streets. As they passed under a bridge, Christine noticed a statue of an old man in baggy trousers and a peaked cap, carrying a long staff with a hook at the end.

'Who is that?' she asked Rollo.

'Him? He's a *flotteur*. In the old days, they used to bring logs out of the forests in the Morvan and float them all the way to Paris in huge rafts. They clogged up the canal so that barges couldn't move, until it was made illegal. Good thing it was!'

From here, the canal snaked around in a huge curve until they passed below the heights of Mailly-le-Château. Now the banks were bordered by vine-covered slopes, until the canal merged with the waters of the River Yonne, whose course it had followed all the way from Sardy. On the morning of the sixth day since they boarded the *Madeleine*, Pasquier said, 'We'll be in Auxerre by midday. What are your plans?'

Luke and Christine looked at each other and she felt a sudden hollowness in her chest.

'I'm not sure,' Luke responded. 'We need to find a boat going up the Rhône au Rhin, but I suppose we will have to go to Laroche Migennes before we can do that.' He hesitated.

'It's a pity we can't use the bikes. But I suppose they have to be handed back to the company that lent them.'

Pasquier shrugged. 'Not necessarily. They were lent for the purpose of helping people to escape, so they would still be being used for that purpose. But don't be too hasty to make a decision. Once we've delivered this load, we shall have to wait and see if the *Boche* want us to go back for another or if there is anything going in your direction. If we can get a cargo for Dijon, or somewhere along the Doubs, we might be able to take you further.'

'Would you do that?' Christine asked in surprise. 'It would be wonderful if you could, but we don't expect you to change your plans to suit us.'

'Oh, we go where the cargo takes us,' Pasquier said. 'I wouldn't mind a change of scene — and I quite like the idea of keeping my resident cook!'

Christine looked at her brother and felt a small flush of pride, which was rapidly displaced by a nagging anxiety; Pasquier had spoken confidently but she found it hard to believe that he would really go out of his way to help them.

Here, the broad current was busy with river traffic of various sorts. They moored up for lunch within sight of the towers of Auxerre cathedral, and there was a valedictory mood which seemed to have settled on all of them. When the meal was over, the barge chugged on towards Auxerre until, upon rounding a curve in the river, they found that the way ahead was jammed with stationary boats.

Pasquier edged the *Madeleine* up to another barge and shouted across, 'Hey, Jacques! What's going on?'

'Search me,' was the reply. 'The *Boche* have closed the canal ahead for some reason. I've heard it's only temporary, but who knows?'

'I'll walk up and see if I can find out,' Rollo offered.

'I'll come with you,' Luke said.

'You will not!' Christine and Pasquier spoke simultaneously.

'Do you want to get us all arrested?' Pasquier asked. 'The place will be swarming with Gestapo and *Milice*. You go nosing around and someone is bound to want to see your papers.'

Luke stepped back with a sigh. 'Damn papers! Why was I such a fool?'

'I'll go with Rollo,' Christine said. 'I've got the right papers, if anyone asks.'

They jumped across to the other barge, and from there to the bank. Men and women from other boats were already making their way along the towpath towards the city, and they mingled with the crowd.

Finally, they found their way blocked again by a solid wall of backs, while those in front of them craned their necks to see what was going on ahead.

'Good God! It's incredible!'

'What on earth are they playing at?'

'What fools! Trust the *Boche*!'

Comments like these only served to increase Christine's frustration. Even standing on tiptoe, she could not see over the heads of those in front of her.

'Here!' Rollo grasped her arm, and pulled her to one side where a fence bordered the path. By climbing onto it, they could finally see what was happening and it was easy to understand the incredulity of the people in the crowd. On the side of the river opposite the cathedral there was a slipway, and at that moment a huge, grey-painted vessel was being slowly hauled up it.

'*Mon Dieu*! It's some kind of warship!' Rollo exclaimed.

'But what are they doing with it?' Christine asked. 'Do you think it's being hauled out for repairs?'

'They'd take it to a naval base for work like that,' he replied. 'Anyway, what's it doing here? That's a sea-going vessel. It must have come all the way up the Yonne from the Atlantic. But where are they trying to take it now?'

'The Saône,' said a voice from the other side of the fence.

Looking over, Christine saw a boy a few years younger than herself whose face had the satisfied expression of one 'in the know' and eager to communicate the information.

'You're joking!' said Rollo.

'No, I'm not. Everyone round here is talking about it. The *Boche* have been knocking down houses and rebuilding roads for weeks, right the way from here to Avallon and beyond. No one knew why of course, until this lot started arriving.'

'This lot?' Rollo queried. 'You mean there's more than one?'

'Oh yes. I've seen six and there are still more queuing up in the river.'

'But why are they hauling them out?' Christine asked.

'I can guess the answer to that,' Rollo responded. 'They must have thought initially they could take them through the Canal de Bourgogne, but they are far too big. That thing must be sixty metres long at least. It would never fit into the locks on the Bourgogne.'

'But imagine hauling it across country!' she said. 'How on earth do they do it?'

'They've got two huge wheeled bogeys under it. Look, you can see now it's clear of the water. And there is a tractor lorry pulling it.'

'Not one lorry,' the boy said. 'It takes three of them in line, with four behind to stop it if it runs away on the hills. I've watched them going by.'

'*Mon Dieu!*' Rollo repeated with a whistle. 'But I still don't get it. Why do they want to get them into the Saône?'

'Because the Saône runs into the Mediterranean,' Christine said. 'The Germans obviously wanted to move them from the Atlantic to the Med for some reason, and this must have seemed the best way to do it.'

The huge vessel was now clear of the water and inching its way up the slipway to the road. Rollo jumped down from the fence.

'It looks as though things might start moving now. We'd better get back.'

Reaching the *Madeleine*, they found Pasquier and Luke waiting impatiently for news. When Rollo told them what they had seen, his father's face took on an expression of scornful incredulity.

'Someone's been pulling your leg. Even the *Boche* wouldn't be that crazy.'

'No, it's true!' Christine said. 'We saw the ship with our own eyes. It's a gunboat of some sort and they are obviously taking it across country somewhere. So I don't think the boy was lying. It's the only explanation that makes sense.'

'And you reckon it's heading for the Mediterranean?'

'Where else could it be going?'

'But why?' Luke asked.

'I think I can guess,' Pasquier said. 'The Yanks are in control in North Africa now. I reckon the Germans are afraid of an invasion on the south coast. They are reinforcing their defences.'

'And there are several of these boats being moved?' Luke said.

'The boy said he'd seen six himself, and there were others waiting up river,' Rollo told him.

'If only the RAF knew what was going on,' Luke murmured. 'They'd be sitting targets.'

'If someone could get a message to London. . .' Christine said, and stopped short, looking at her brother.

For a moment, neither of them spoke but both knew what was in the other's mind.

'How long will you be in Auxerre?' Luke asked, turning to Pasquier.

'Hard to say. A day to unload cargo, then we have to find out where the *Boche* want us to go next. Another day to load. Could be as short as three days, or we could be hanging around here for a week or more. Why?'

'How long would it take us to cycle back to Corbigny?'

'It must be about seventy kilometres by road. You could do it in a day. What are you thinking?'

'If we could get a message to Cyrano, he could tell London what we've seen.'

'He's probably up in the Morvan hills by now. You won't find him in Corbigny.'

'But I know where I left him. That was where his contact was. They must be able to get in touch with him.'

'Luke,' Christine interrupted, 'it's not safe for you to go. Suppose you were stopped on the way?'

'It's the only chance.'

'No. I could go. It's different for me.'

'You can't go alone.'

'I don't see why not.'

'I won't let you.'

'You can't stop me.'

'But suppose . . . suppose something happened and we . . . we were separated. We have to stick together, Sis.'

'I could go with her,' Rollo said.

'No!' Luke spoke more sharply than he intended, and both Rollo and his sister looked surprised.

'You are not going anywhere,' Pasquier growled. 'I need you here.'

'Chris, we have to do this,' Luke said. 'It's a chance to help the Allies. We can't just ignore what we've seen. And after all, we cycled from Decize to Blaye without any problems.'

She looked at him, biting her lips in indecision. Her mother had asked her not to let Luke go off on some romantic escapade, and she knew that she should try to dissuade him. But on the other hand, she could not dismiss the thought that Cyrano would approve. He would certainly be told who had brought the message and he was bound to be impressed. He might even pass the information to the woman she was supposed to report to when she got back to England, and that must enhance her chances of being accepted into the mysterious organization to which he belonged. Better still, and this was the prospect that clinched the matter, they might be taken to meet him, to tell him in person what they had seen.

She caught her breath and nodded. 'OK, you're right. We'll do it.'

Luke looked at Pasquier.

'We'll need a day each way and probably one in between. Will you wait for us?'

'There's no chance I'll be ready to move in less than three days,' was the curt answer. 'And there's no guarantee that I'll be going in the right direction for you when I do, but provided you are not longer than that, we'll be here.'

'Right!' Luke said. 'That's decided then.'

CHAPTER 11

Next morning, Luke and Christine untied their bikes from where they had been lashed to the wall of the wheelhouse, and wheeled them down the gangplank and onto the wharf. The traffic jam on the river outside the town had cleared eventually and the *Madeleine* had been able to tie up in the appointed place.

Christine had already been ashore to buy bread, and breakfast had been a hasty, rather tense occasion. Now, as at Decize, they had waited until the morning rush hour when the quaysides and the roads were crowded with people, many of them on bicycles, either heading out to work in the fields or going to the various factories and workshops along the river frontage. Rollo came ashore with them. He was more subdued that usual and when they shook hands, Luke saw that he was genuinely reluctant to see them go.

'I'd come with you, if the old man would let me,' he said.

'We'll be back in three days,' Luke promised. 'Even if it's only to say goodbye.'

There were German soldiers patrolling the quay, but there were too many people heading in both directions for them to check everyone and Luke and his sister were just two more faces in the crowd as they pedalled away along the towpath. Nevertheless, they both let out a breath of relief when they were safely out of sight.

The going was easy for the first thirty kilometres, as they retraced the route they had just followed along the canal, and they were both amazed at how quickly they were able to cover a distance that had taken more than a day in the boat. At Mailly-la-Ville, with the castle towering above them on the far bank, they paused to draw breath and drink from the water bottles they had brought with them. Here, the canal veered away to the west so they left the towpath and took a minor road that climbed through thick forest, until Christine's legs were aching.

'Phew! I haven't had as much exercise as this since . . . I can't remember when,' she said when they stopped again to eat their sandwiches.

'Cheer up,' her brother answered. 'It'll be downhill all the way now, until we reach the canal again.'

They approached the main road between Clamecy and Vézelay with caution, having been warned that it often carried German convoys, but it was clear in both directions and once they were clear of the little village of Clamoux, they felt the worst danger was past. Shortly afterwards, they came to a corner and saw the road ahead of them dropping away through the trees in a series of tight bends.

'What did I tell you?' Luke pushed off, pedalling to pick up speed and then freewheeling. 'Tallyho . . . !'

Christine raced after him until her front wheel was level with his rear wheel, both of them laughing with the exhilaration of their speed.

The German roadblock was so close to the bend, that they were on it before they had time to react. They were at the entrance to a small village, where a bridge crossed a little stream, and a temporary barrier had been erected across half the width of the road. A battered *gazogène*-powered van was drawn up, facing in the opposite direction, while its driver was being questioned by a soldier in German field-grey. A second man stepped forward and raised a hand as they skidded to a stop.

'Papers!'

Luke was panting, dizzy with shock, but he tried to sound casual.

'What's going on? Why are you stopping us?'

'Papers,' the soldier repeated, as if it was the only word of French he knew.

Christine was already digging in her pocket. She held out her identity card and gave the man what she hoped was a seductive smile.

'Here you are. My name's Christine Beauchamps. We're not from round here. We're on a cycling holiday.'

Luke was making a show of searching his pockets. The soldier scrutinized Christine's card, glanced up at her face to check that it tallied with the photograph, and handed it back with a grunt.

She chattered on, 'Isn't it a lovely day? Do you like·it here? It's very pretty, isn't it? But it's prettier where we live. We come from the Auvergne. My family own a vineyard. Perhaps you've tasted some of our wine? It's called Caves des Volcans . . .'

'Papers! *Schnell*! Quickly!' The soldier was not to be diverted.

'I . . . I can't find them,' Luke said breathlessly. 'I think I must have left them behind in the last place we stayed . . .'

'Oh, he's so forgetful!' Christine forced a laugh. 'Honestly, he'd forget his head . . .'

There seemed to be some kind of dispute going on around the stationary van. The guard was trying to open the rear doors and the driver was trying to stop him.

'Come!' The German reached out and gripped Luke's arm, pulling him towards a small hut where a third man was lolling on a stool beside a motorbike.

Luke instinctively resisted, and the man's free hand went to the rifle that hung from his shoulder.

'Luke, don't!' Christine shouted.

At that instant, the other guard succeeded in tugging open the van doors. There was a cacophony of shouts and squeals as a dozen piglets spilled out into the road, running between the legs of the driver and the two guards. The soldier who had hold of Luke let go, and made a dive at one of them, while another ran under his feet and tripped him so that he measured his length on the road. The second guard and the driver of the van were engaged in a futile attempt to grab the others.

'Come on!' Luke jumped onto his bike and tore across the bridge and into the village street, with Christine close behind.

As they pedalled frantically down the street, which was mercifully empty as it was *le midi*, they heard the motorbike being kicked into life behind them. The village was tiny and within a minute or two, they were out on the open road again and among the trees. The way was still downhill and they picked up speed, but they could both hear the motorbike gaining on them. They rounded a bend and Christine skidded to a stop.

'In here! Hide in the trees.'

They heaved their bikes over a small ditch and dragged them behind some bushes, then lay panting as the sound of the bike came closer.

'He can't see round the next bend,' Christine breathed. 'He'll think we're still ahead of him.'

She was right. The bike rounded the bend, one of the guards riding pillion behind the driver, and sped past them without stopping.

'Oh, thank God!' Christine gasped.

'Wait. It can't be long before he gets to the bottom of the hill and realizes he's missed us,' Luke said.

'What do we do now?'

'Lie low and hope they don't search too thoroughly. Pray they haven't got dogs with them.'

Very soon, they heard the sound of the bike returning. It passed their hiding place and they heard the engine die away and then cut out.

'He's gone back to the guard post to report,' Luke said. 'Come on. Let's see how far we can get before they start looking again.'

They dragged their bikes back onto the road and pedalled away as fast as they could. Outside the next village, they veered off to the left along a tiny lane which led them deeper into the forest and finally petered out into an unmetalled forestry track.

'I can't hear any sound of the motorbike,' Christine said breathlessly. 'What do we do now?'

Luke studied the map.

'If we're where I think we are, this track will bring us down to the road again at Nuars. From there, it's a maze of minor roads until Corbigny. Unless they've got road blocks on all of them, they haven't a chance of catching us.'

He spoke with more confidence than he felt and for a moment they looked at each other, reading the same thought in each other's eyes.

What fools we were to abandon the Madeleine for this crazy adventure!

Christine peered over her brother's shoulder at the map.

'First we have to get through Nuars. I don't see any way around.'

'We'll just have to go very carefully and hope for the best,' he said.

They rode on, bumping along the rutted track until they came out of the trees and saw the village ahead of them. It was mid-afternoon by now, but the place seemed to be only just recovering from its lunchtime siesta. A few elderly women were sitting outside their front doors, gossiping with neighbours; some men were drinking outside the café in the square; a horse-drawn wagon loaded with timber rumbled out of a side road.

Luke and Christine dismounted and wheeled their bikes behind it, until they crossed a bridge and found themselves once again in open country.

'No sign of the *Boche* there,' Christine said. 'Perhaps they've given up looking for us.'

'Well, we won't take any chances,' her brother responded. 'Let's take this road. It goes across country.'

It was early evening by the time they reached Corbigny and they were both weary, hot, and hungry. Luke found the street where the pharmacy was located without difficulty, but as they parked their bikes outside Christine said, 'Who do we need to speak to?'

'I don't know,' Luke replied. 'Cyrano wouldn't let me go into the shop. He said it was a matter of security — better if I couldn't recognize anyone.'

'So you've no idea whether we have to ask the owner or one of the assistants?' She stared at him in dismay. 'We can't just walk in and say "anyone here know Cyrano?"'

'Perhaps there's only one person in there,' Luke suggested lamely.

She sighed.

'Well, we're here now. I suppose we had better try.'

There was only one person behind the counter, a slight, earnest-looking young man with glasses. Luke was about to speak when the door opened behind him and an elderly lady came in. He stood back and gestured to her to take his place.

'After you, Madame.'

She gave him a suspicious look, but walked past him to the counter, where she engaged the pharmacist in a long, low-voiced discussion and eventually left with her bottle of medicine. The young man turned to Luke, 'Yes?'

Luke took a deep breath. 'We're looking for Cyrano.'

'Who?'

'Cyrano. We've got a message for him.'

'I'm sorry. I don't know anyone of that name. It's a character in a play isn't it?'

'Yes, but it's a man as well.' Luke was beginning to feel desperate. 'I brought him here, a few days ago. He had to meet someone. He'd hurt his ankle and I brought him on my bike.' He saw the man's eyes narrow, as if the description meant something to him. 'He's a music teacher, here in Corbigny.'

There was a pause. The pharmacist studied him for a moment.

'A music teacher, you say? I think I might know who you mean. What did you want him for?'

'We have an urgent message for him. It's . . . it's to do with his job.'

Another silence. Then the pharmacist appeared to come to a decision.

'You'll have to wait until I close the shop. Come through here. You can wait in the back room.'

He raised the flap in the counter and led them through into a small, stuffy room that doubled as a store cupboard.

'Wait here. I shall be closing in just over half an hour.'

He shut the door and left them alone.

'I think we're on the right lines,' Luke said with relief. 'He must know what I'm talking about.'

'I hope so,' Christine said. 'For all we know, he could be phoning the nearest German camp.'

'Don't! Why would he do that? If Cyrano came here, he must be OK.'

'Well, I wish he'd offered us a drink,' she said. 'I'm parched.'

The minutes dragged by and the room became stuffier. Luke went to the door and tried it.

'He's locked us in!'

'Why? He wouldn't hand us over to the *Boche*, would he? Not really?'

'I don't know.' Luke sat down on a stool and ran his hands through his hair. 'No, surely not. Perhaps he just doesn't want us coming back into the shop, in case there's a customer there who would ask awkward questions.'

They heard footsteps outside and the door was opened. The pharmacist stood there.

'Come!'

'Why did you lock us in?' Christine demanded. 'We don't mean any harm.'

'This way,' was the only response.

He led them down a passage and opened a door at the rear of the shop. Darkness had fallen, complete because of the blackout, and it was hard to make out where they were. Luke reached for his sister's hand and they stumbled forward, following the shadowy figure of the pharmacist.

Suddenly he was grabbed from behind, a hand was clamped over his mouth and something that smelt of old sacking was thrown over his head. He kicked out blindly and heard a grunt of pain but then his legs were seized and he was lifted bodily off the ground. He felt himself being carried and then swung and dumped roughly, face down, onto a hard surface. He tried to speak, to protest or explain, but the sack was pulled up and a piece of cloth was forced between his teeth and tied behind his head. At the same time, somebody else bound his hands and feet. Seconds later, he heard doors slam and then an engine started and the vehicle he was in, whatever it was, lurched off over uneven ground.

He lay still, struggling not to gag on the cloth in his mouth, his mind whirling. No one had spoken, so there was nothing to give him a clue about the nationality of his captors, but it seemed to him that the Germans would have been more open. They would have marched into the room with their guns at the ready and handcuffed them. So if these were not Germans, who were they? What was more important, where was his sister? He had not heard her cry out, but then, he had not had time to cry out either.

A movement close beside him told him that she had suffered the same fate. He wriggled across the floor until his shoulder touched hers. She made an inarticulate noise of mingled fear and pain and he nudged her and made what he hoped was a reassuring noise in return. She wriggled closer and they lay against each other, drawing what comfort they could from the contact. The engine note of the vehicle changed and Luke realized that they were climbing, going back up into the forest. Was it possible, he asked himself, that they were the captives of the *Maquis*? If so, what did that portend? Clearly, the man in the pharmacy had not trusted them. He must have thought that they were spies or collaborators. How could they convince their captors otherwise?

Similar thoughts were going through Christine's mind, but one predominated; if they were in the hands of the *Maquis* they were presumably being taken to their camp. And that was where Cyrano would be. Cyrano would vouch for them and they would be set free. She clung to that thought as the truck bumped and swayed. Face down and unable to steady themselves, their heads were banged against the metal floor every time the vehicle hit a bump and before long, the pain in Christine's bound arms became almost unbearable. Luke groaned as they hit a deep pothole and she could hear herself whimpering. She bit down on the filthy rag in her mouth and forced herself to be silent.

At last, the truck swung round in a tight curve and came to a standstill. There was another agonising wait, and then the sound of the rear doors being opened. Hands grabbed them and dragged them out, their feet were untied and they were shoved roughly forwards, stumbling on numbed legs. Christine was dimly aware that the ground she trod on was soft; grass or leaf mould, not paving stones, and something about the quality of the sounds around her indicated that they were in the open air.

Hands reached under the sack that still covered her head and the gag was untied and a voice demanded in French, 'Who are you?'

Her mouth was so parched that she was unable to speak, but she heard Luke croak, 'We're friends of Cyrano's. We've come with a very important message.'

'Name?' the voice snapped.

'Luke Beauchamps — and my sister is Christine.'

'Let's have a look at them.'

Hands pulled the sack off her head and she saw that they were standing in a forest clearing. In the centre, a fire was burning and dark figures stood between her and its light. One of them stepped forward and grabbed her arm, pulling her nearer to the fire.

'Sister, eh?'

'Yes,' she managed to whisper. Then, her voice coming back to her, 'Luke's my brother. Please, where is Cyrano? He will tell you that we're on your side. We just want to help.'

'On our side, eh? And whose side is that?'

She was beginning to make out his features in the dim light. He was very dark, with a mop of curly hair and a beard trimmed close to his chin; tall and broad-shouldered with powerful fingers that held her arm in a vice-like grip.

'Your side,' she replied, confused. 'You're with the *Maquis*, aren't you?'

'And what do you know about the *Maquis*?'

'I know you are fighting the *Boche*. And Cyrano has been sent to help you. Please, is he here?'

'This Cyrano you keep talking about, who is he?'

'He's . . .' she stopped suddenly. If these were not the people to whom Cyrano had been sent, then she must not give away the fact that he was a British agent. She remembered that the *Maquis* was not a single organized body; they were simply men who had escaped to the forest for various reasons and, according to popular myth, many of them were nothing more than bandits. It was quite possible that they had fallen into the hands of a different group.

'He's what?' her captor demanded. 'What were you going to say?'

'It's a nickname, that's all.'

'A nickname for whom? Come on, you say you have an important message. Who is it for?'

From behind her, Luke said, 'He's a music teacher, in Corbigny. We heard he was with the *Maquis*. Maybe we got it wrong.'

'So what is this important message, that you have to give to a music teacher? You want to tell him that Mozart is dead, huh?'

He chuckled at his own wit and some of the men standing around the fire joined in.

'I can't tell you,' Christine said.

'Oh yes, you can. If this message concerns the *Maquis*, you can tell it to me — and you will. I assure you of that.'

'Look, it's not to do with the *Maquis*,' Luke said and Christine could tell that he was improvising desperately. She prayed that it was not so obvious to the man holding her arm. 'It's just a personal matter . . . to do with his family.'

Their captor seemed to find this very amusing.

'Personal, eh? And you have come all the way from — where? — to give him this news. Where have you come from? Show me your papers.'

'I can't. I lost them. That's why we . . .' he tailed off into silence.

'Why you what?' Getting no answer he jerked his head towards one of his men. 'Search them.'

Rough hands delved into her pockets, pulling out her penknife, her torch, the small first aid kit, the stub of pencil and the rest of the bits and pieces that she had put there in case of emergencies.

Inevitably, they found her identity card and ration card and handed them to their chief.

'Nothing on him,' the man who was searching Luke reported. 'Maybe he's telling the truth?'

'Or maybe he just doesn't want us to know who he is. Bring him here, closer to the fire. Handsome fellow, eh? Blonde, blue eyes, just like a German.' He gave Christine's arm a rough shake. 'So, who is he? Your boyfriend? You've been consorting with the enemy, you little whore! And they've sent you to infiltrate our group.'

'No! It's not true. He's my brother. We're both French. That is . . .'

The man was examining her papers.

'You're from the Auvergne. What are you doing in these parts? How did you get here? Did the *Boche* send you?'

'No!'

'So tell me, how did you get here?'

'I can't!'

129

'Oh yes, you can.' His voice had softened. 'You'll be surprised how much you can tell me when . . . when you are in the right mood. Come here, nearer to the fire.' He jerked her arm, forcing her forwards and made a gesture to one of his men, who reached out and pulled a branch from the flames, the end still glowing. He handed it to his chief and Christine shrank back as she felt the heat from it approaching her face.

'Now,' the soft voice went on, 'what were you going to tell me?'

'Leave her alone!' Luke shouted. 'You've got it all wrong. You don't know what you are doing.'

'Then you can explain it all to me,' the chief said. 'Tell me truthfully, who you are and what you are doing here.'

'We have told you. It's the truth.'

'You'll have to do better than that if you don't want your girlfriend's face scarred for life,' the man snarled. 'Come on. I give you thirty seconds.'

'What can I say? There's nothing else to tell.' He was almost sobbing.

'Twenty . . .'

Christine forced back a scream as the red-hot brand came closer to her face.

'Ten . . .'

The noise of a motorbike engine approaching at speed shattered the silence. Christine's captor turned towards the sound.

'About time!'

The bike skidded to a stop and a dark figure dismounted from the pillion and came towards them; and Christine gave a cry of relief when she saw that he walked with the aid of a stick.

'Cyrano! It is you, isn't it? Oh, thank God! Please, tell these men who we are. Tell them we don't mean any harm.'

'What the hell is going on here?' Cyrano demanded. 'Xavier, what are you playing at? Let her go, for pity's sake.'

'Just a joke,' the big man said, releasing Christine's arm. 'I wouldn't have gone through with it. But I had to be sure they are telling the truth.'

Cyrano limped closer.

'What on earth are you doing here? You should be in Auxerre by now, at least.'

'We were.' Her voice was shaking. 'But we saw something, something you have to know about, so we came . . .'

He touched her arm.

'OK. Tell me later. Xavier, tell your men to untie them. They are quite harmless, I promise you. If it wasn't for them, I probably wouldn't be here.'

'If you insist. As long as you can vouch for them. But I hope you know what you're doing.' Xavier sounded sulky and Christine had the impression that he did not like being given orders by Cyrano.

Cyrano said, 'I'm sorry, Xavier. I'm not trying to question your authority, but I'm quite sure they are trustworthy and I do owe them a lot.' He took Christine's arm. 'You poor kid. You look just about done in. Come over here and sit down.'

While he was speaking, their hands had been untied and they were led closer to the fire, where several tree trunks had been carved into rough seats. Christine sank down on one, thankful to sit before her shaking legs gave way under her.

Xavier was saying, 'No harm done. But it's a good job you arrived when you did. We don't want strangers turning up uninvited.' He raised his voice. 'Bring some warm wine for our guests.'

'Water!' Christine croaked. 'I'd rather have water.'

A tin mug was pressed into her hand, but she was shaking so much that it rattled against her teeth and spilled down her chin. To her shame, she found she was crying. Cyrano put his arm across her shoulders and murmured gently, 'It's OK. You're quite safe now. Let me help you.'

He guided her hand and the cool water flooded her mouth, but her throat was so parched, that it was hard to swallow. She choked and he said, 'Take it easy. Just a sip to begin with. There, that's better.'

She managed to swallow a trickle of water, then a little more, until finally she was able to drain the mug.

'Thank you,' she whispered huskily, and he patted her shoulder in response and turned away to ask, 'Luke? Are you all right?'

'Just about,' Luke responded shakily. 'Thank God you arrived when you did.'

'I was up a tree, sending a message,' Cyrano said. 'It's the only place where I can get decent reception. Luckily, Xavier sent one of his men to fetch me.'

'He knew who you were all the time!'

'Yes, of course. But you can understand that he had to be cautious. I'm sorry you were manhandled like that.'

'It wasn't your fault. I suppose I can see Xavier's point of view. We must have looked suspicious.'

'I don't understand what you are doing here,' Cyrano said. 'What on earth could be so important that you came back?'

As briefly as he could, Luke explained what they had seen at Auxerre.

'We thought that, if the Allies knew what was happening, the boats would be sitting targets for bombs. Then it occurred to us that you could probably get word to the people who need to know. You could, couldn't you?'

'Certainly! And it will be very useful information.' Cyrano clapped him on the shoulder. 'Well done, both of you! You took a big risk coming back, and you've had a pretty rotten time for your trouble. But I'll make sure the powers that be know where the information came from and the courage it required to bring it to me.' He looked at his watch. 'I don't have another sked — a scheduled transmission — until tomorrow morning. But I don't think a delay of a few hours will matter, do you? Those boats aren't going to get anywhere very quickly. Now,' he got up, 'let's try to make up for what you've been through. Where's that warm wine, Xavier? And when did you last eat?'

The rest of the evening passed in a haze for Christine. The wine went to her head and then there was a delicious smell of roasting meat, as chunks of lamb were barbecued over the fire. Cyrano put a blanket around her shoulders, and she looked up at him and knew that the fear and the danger had been worth it. Then someone handed her a plate and by the time she had finished eating, she was almost asleep. Her last memory was of being helped across the clearing to a small tent, where a straw-filled paillasse was laid out for her. She looked for Luke and saw that he was settling down beside her, then she pulled the blanket over her head and slept instantly.

CHAPTER 12

Christine woke to the smell of wood smoke and the sound of an axe. Beside her, Luke was sitting up, rubbing his face drowsily. Hearing her groan, he looked around and grinned.

'Sore head?'

'Sore everywhere,' she mumbled.

'Not surprised. You were sozzled last night.'

'No I wasn't! I was just tired. And I suppose you're good as new and full of beans.'

He ran his hands ruefully through his hair. 'No, to be honest. I feel as if I'd gone ten rounds with a heavyweight boxer. I'm stiff from the cycle ride and bruised all over after being thrown about in that van.'

She struggled into a sitting position.

'Me, too. Still, here we are — and it was worth it, wasn't it?' Cyrano's warm words came back to her, soothing the pain in her head.

'Definitely,' Luke agreed. 'Who'd have thought it? We're actually with the *Maquis*.'

'Only temporarily,' she reminded him.

She peered out and saw the *Maquis* camp properly for the first time; hidden among the trees around the clearing, were an assortment of shelters. Some were tents, others rough constructions of logs and branches with tarpaulins for roofs. The camp was already awake. The fire was alight and a fat man was stirring a large pot hung over it. Someone just out of her vision was chopping wood and as she watched, two men came out of the forest carrying buckets of water. It reminded her of a pressing need.

'I wonder what they do about . . . you know . . . toilet facilities.'

'Good point,' he responded. 'I'll go and enquire, shall I?'

She watched him cross the clearing to speak to the man by the fire. Further off, Xavier was talking to two others but there was no sign of Cyrano. Then she remembered, he had a 'sked' that morning (she stored the term away in her memory as part of a new life that was just beginning to open up for her).

Luke came back.

'There are some latrines somewhere down that track. Come on. I'll keep watch for you.'

The latrines were no more than a trench with a rough plank seat above it and a tarpaulin hung between two branches as a screen. It was smelly and she had to suppress a feeling of nausea, but she told herself that she might have to put up with worse than this in the future.

When they had both done what was necessary, Luke said, 'There's a spring somewhere a bit further up the hill. That's where they get their water from.'

They found it, bubbling out of some rocks and splashing into a clear pool. They rinsed their hands and faces and then drank from their cupped hands.

'Better?' Luke said, and Christine nodded.

'Much better.'

Back at the camp, Xavier hailed them. 'Aha, our two young heroes! Come and have some breakfast.'

To their surprise, there was fresh bread and creamy goat's cheese to go with the ersatz coffee.

'Jacques is a baker by trade,' Xavier explained, indicating the burly figure by the fire. 'He puts the loaves in the hot ashes overnight and we have bread in the morning — even if it does have a flavour of charcoal sometimes. And Jean-Luc has brought some of his goats with him, so we have milk and cheese.'

'How do you manage about the flour?' Luke asked. 'I thought the Nazis were requisitioning it all.'

'To hell with that! We've distributed leaflets all round the area, telling people to barter among themselves rather than hand their produce over to the enemy. French food for French people! That's our slogan. Jacques has a mate who owns one of the local mills. He sees we're all right for flour. For everything else . . . well, the local villagers are happy to oblige.'

Looking at his piratical grin, Christine wondered just how accurate that last remark was.

They had just finished eating, when they heard the sound of a motorbike approaching along the forest track and a moment later, Cyrano appeared, riding pillion as before. He dismounted, gave his driver a pat on the shoulder and came over to sit facing them on a tree trunk.

'Good morning. How are you feeling? Recovered from yesterday?'

'More or less,' Luke said.

'I'm fine,' Christine declared, untruthfully.

'Well, I sent the information you gave me and it has been acknowledged, but of course we won't know how it is being dealt with for some time. We may never hear any more about it, but I think you can be sure that it will be acted upon. So, now what? What are your plans?'

Sister and brother exchanged looks and each read in the other's face an unspoken reluctance.

'I suppose we must get back to Auxerre and see if M. Pasquier has got a new cargo for the *Madeleine*,' Luke said.

'Is there any chance that he can take you further?'

'It all depends. If he can find a cargo going towards Montbéliard, he says he will take us and if he can't he has promised to ask around and see if there is anyone else who would be prepared to help.'

'And if he can't?'

Luke shrugged. 'I don't know. Perhaps we could cycle, if we are allowed to keep hold of the bikes. Do you know what happened to them? We left them at the pharmacy.'

'I'll make enquiries. I expect they are safe. But it's a hell of a long way to cycle.'

'I know. But the only alternative is to thumb lifts, unless we risk the train again.'

Cyrano pursed his lips.

'I don't like to think of you doing any of those things. Let's hope Pasquier is able to sort something out. But do you need to start back today? You both look pretty exhausted to me, and it's no wonder after yesterday. Why don't you wait until tomorrow?'

'Pasquier said he would wait three days,' Christine put in quickly. 'Tomorrow would be all right, wouldn't it?'

'Yes, it should be,' Luke agreed.

'You'll need transport back into Corbigny,' Cyrano said. 'I'll see what I can arrange. I'm glad you can hang on for today. There's someone I want you to meet.'

'Who?' Christine asked.

'You'll see. He'll be here shortly.' He rose. 'I must get on. I've got some decoding to do.'

'Can I help?' Christine asked eagerly.

Cyrano shook his head with a smile.

'Sorry, no. It's something I have to do on my own and it requires complete concentration. Just relax. Rest while you can.'

He walked away, to where an open-sided tent sheltered a table and a couple of folding chairs. There, he sat down with his back to the rest of the camp and remained hunched over his papers, apparently oblivious to everything else. Around them men were sitting in small groups, chatting, while some of them cleaned an assortment of shotguns and old rifles.

Christine slid off the log she was sitting on and leaned her back against it, closing her eyes. The sun shone through the canopy of leaves and the only sounds were the murmur of voices and the cooing of wood pigeons. It was hard to believe they were sitting in the middle of an outlaws' camp.

'I wish we could do something useful,' Luke said restlessly.

She opened her eyes. 'Nobody seems to be doing anything much. It isn't quite what you imagined, is it?'

He shrugged.

'I suppose they have to have rest days, like us.'

The sound of someone trying to start a car engine shattered the peace. Again and again, the starter motor whined and the engine coughed and then subsided into silence. Christine sat up irritably.

'He's going to flatten the battery if he goes on like that.'

Luke looked at her with a grin. 'Perhaps you ought to go and sort him out, Sis.'

Then his mischievous expression changed as she rose to her feet, saying, 'Perhaps I'd better.'

'No, really, I don't think . . .' he called after her, but she ignored him.

The source of the noise was the van they had been brought to the camp in the night before, which was parked to one side under the trees. As Christine approached, a young man she recognized as one of their captors climbed down from the driving seat and kicked one of the wheels, swearing under his breath.

Seeing her, he blushed and muttered, 'Sorry, Mademoiselle.'

'Having trouble?' she asked.

'You could say that. This pig of an engine's been playing up for days. Now it's finally died on me.'

'Have you checked the spark plugs?'

'What?'

'The spark plugs may need cleaning. Have you looked?'

'How the hell am I supposed to do that? I'm not a *garagiste*.'

'But you drive the car.'

'That's different. My old boss taught me to drive so I could do deliveries. He didn't expect me to mend the damn thing if it went wrong.'

Christine shook her head in exasperation.

'No one should drive if they don't know what's going on under the bonnet. Now you see what happens? OK. Let me have a look.'

He tried to suppress a grin of disbelief and failed.

'You, Mademoiselle?'

'Yes, me! Mind out of the way.'

He stood aside and she opened the bonnet. As she expected, the spark plugs were thick with soot.

'Are there any tools?'

'I dunno. There's something wrapped up an old rag under the dashboard.'

'Let's have a look.'

The roll of cloth contained various tools and Christine pounced on one triumphantly.

'Plug spanner! This is what I need.'

He watched as she removed the plugs, his air of supercilious amusement vanishing.

'*Merde alors*! Where did you learn to do that?'

'From my father. Hold on to these for a minute.' She delved in the pocket of her overalls and found her penknife, then took the plugs and carefully scraped away the deposit. A final polish with the rag and they were ready to replace. She straightened up and turned to the young man.

'Try her now.'

He climbed into the driving seat and pressed the starter, and the engine burst into life. He leaned out of the window.

'Mademoiselle . . . I don't know your name. I'm Jean-Claude, by the way.'

'Christine.'

'Mademoiselle Christine, you are a miracle worker! *Mercie mille fois*!'

'*Ça ne fait rien*,' she responded, and turned away to conceal a grin of satisfaction.

As she rejoined her brother, the sound of another vehicle approaching attracted her attention. An elderly Mercedes bounced along the track with two armed men balancing on the running boards. It stopped in the centre of the camp and a tall, fair, man got out. Cyrano had heard the car too, and hurried from the tent to greet him and they were soon joined by Xavier.

There was a rapid exchange of handshakes and she saw that Cyrano was showing the other two what he had just been writing. Something about his body language suggested excitement and the impression was confirmed when Xavier gave a shout of triumph. The newcomer laid a hand on his arm, apparently enjoining restraint, and then all three moved away to the tent, where they sat with their heads together poring over what looked like a map.

Luke had been watching too.

'Well, I don't know what's going on, but it's obviously pleased Xavier.'

'It must be something to do with the radio message Cyrano was decoding,' Christine said.

'I see you got the van started,' Luke said. 'Well done.'

She shrugged.

'Really, no one should be allowed to drive when they haven't got the remotest idea how to maintain an engine.'

'Well, I haven't,' he admitted.

'No, I know you haven't. I'd better teach you when we get home.' She stopped abruptly, and they were both aware of the unspoken 'if'.

Eventually, the conference in the tent came to an end and Cyrano led the stranger over to where they were sitting.

'This is Luke, and his sister Christine. They are the two who were responsible for getting me out of that barn and safely to Corbigny. This is Gregoire, my boss.'

Gregoire shook hands with both of them.

'I'm very grateful to you. But for you, I should have been without a radio operator . . . again.' He exchanged a look with Cyrano. 'And I'm told you have just brought us some very useful intelligence.'

'We were lucky to be in Auxerre at the right time,' Luke said. 'But we thought someone should know what was going on.'

'Quite right, and I hear you took a considerable risk getting to us. I'll try to make sure that is noted in the right quarters. Cyrano tells me your father is English.'

'Yes. Well, so are we,' Luke pointed out. 'That's the problem.'

Gregoire seated himself on the log.

'Relax. There's no need to stand on ceremony.' Then, when they were sitting opposite him, 'So, your family owns a vineyard. Is that right?'

'Yes. It's been in the French side of the family for generations, but Father and Mother were running it together until the war broke out.'

'And your father is currently serving in the RAF?'

'As far as we know.'

'Tell me, what does he look like?'

Luke looked at Christine, apparently at a loss.

'He's very much like Luke,' she said, puzzled. 'The same build, same hair, same eyes — but he has a moustache.'

Gregoire nodded, his eyes narrowing.

'I think I may have come across him. At least, I met someone answering that description, who was obviously a bit of an expert in the wine business.'

'You've met him?' Christine exclaimed. 'Where?'

Gregoire looked vague. 'Oh, on some course or other. I can't put my finger on it precisely.'

'You didn't ask his name?'

'No. It wasn't . . . appropriate at that juncture.'

'Just a minute,' Luke said. 'Cyrano said you're his boss. Does that mean you are . . . ?'

Gregoire nodded quietly, 'English, like you. We're here to liaise with the *Maquis*, in the hope that when the time comes, they may be able to play a useful part.'

'You mean when the Allies invade? When will that happen?'

Gregoire shook his head. 'I'm afraid on that point your guess is as good as mine.'

Luke looked around the clearing.

'How much help can they be? There aren't very many of them and they don't seem to be doing much right now.'

'Well, they are not the only ones. There's another group about six miles away, led by a man called Vincent. He's got nearly forty men with him. That's where I'm based at the moment.'

'Why don't they join forces?' Christine asked. 'It doesn't seem to make sense to have two separate camps.'

'Because Vincent is a communist, and this lot don't trust the communists. The fact is, his group are better organized and better disciplined. He's an intelligent man, well-educated. He was a schoolteacher until he joined the *Maquis*. Xavier's men are mostly peasants. They're good fighters but strategy is not their strong point. However, with good leadership and better arms, they could make a nuisance of themselves behind the German lines when the time comes.' He got to his feet.

'Are you two going to be around for a while?'

'Only until tomorrow,' Luke said regretfully. 'We have promised to meet up with the boat people who brought us up from Decize.'

'Well, in that case we probably won't meet again.' Gregoire held out his hand. 'Goodbye, and good luck. I hope you get home OK.'

'Thanks,' they murmured in chorus and Gregoire turned away with Cyrano and crossed the clearing to where his car was waiting.

For a moment neither Luke nor Christine spoke.

Then she said slowly, 'So, Gregoire and Cyrano are British secret agents — and Gregoire's met Dad. He and Cyrano speak perfect French, and so does Dad. Do you think . . . ?'

'That Dad has been recruited for the same job? The same thought occurred to me. But then, surely, if he had been, he'd have been sent back to our area, where he has contacts? And in that case, he would have got in touch with us. Even if he couldn't actually visit us, he would have got a message through, don't you think?'

'I suppose so. Unless . . .' she left the sentence unfinished. Something Gregoire had said lurked at the back of her mind: '*I'd be without a radio operator — again.*' What had happened to his first radio operator?

The next hours passed slowly. Cyrano had gone back to his table in the tent and Xavier was in intense conversation with the two men who appeared to be his lieutenants. The van returned and two men unloaded several sacks and dumped them in the back of an old truck which, from the fact that two wheels were missing, was obviously no longer any use as a means of transport but offered the only weatherproof storage in the camp. Another sack, which proved to be full of vegetables, was handed to Jacques, who it seemed doubled as head cook as well as baker.

'Looks like they've been on a foraging expedition,' Luke said.

'More contributions from the willing villagers,' his sister agreed sardonically.

'They ought to be glad to help out!' Luke said, with an edge of indignation to his voice. 'After all, these men have given up their comfortable homes and families to fight for their country.'

'I can't see much evidence of that,' Christine said. 'If you ask me, they're just avoiding the STO and enjoying themselves playing Robin Hood in the forest.'

'Don't be such a cynic!' Luke said irritably.

Before long, an appetising smell wafted to them from the big pot hanging over the fire and Christine's stomach rumbled audibly, which made Luke chuckle and broke the angry silence. Men began drifting towards the fire in the centre of the camp and Cyrano packed away his papers and came over to them.

'I've been neglecting you. I'm sorry. But something has come up which needs immediate attention.'

'Xavier looks pleased,' Luke said. 'Is something going to happen?'

'Yes, hopefully.' Cyrano's eyes gave away his own excitement.

143

'What is it? Do tell us!' Christine begged.

He shook his head.

'I'm sorry. It's top secret. After all, you're leaving tomorrow and after that . . . I mean, I know you wouldn't accidentally let something drop but . . .'

They both understood what he meant. There was no guarantee that they would not be arrested and questioned by the Gestapo, so the less they knew, the better.

'Come on, let's eat,' he said. 'Jacques usually manages to produce something quite tasty.'

The company was settling down on logs arranged around the fire and tin plates of soup were being passed around. As they joined the circle, Xavier came across to them.

'Hey, this is the young lady who mends engines! Jean-Claude has been telling me you made the van go.'

Christine ducked her head and replied in the offhand manner that was her habitual response to compliments, 'I just cleaned the spark plugs. Anyone could have done it.'

'But no one here knows what a spark plug looks like,' he replied. 'Without you, there would have been no soup for our lunch.'

Cyrano grinned at Luke. 'You were right! She can fix anything.'

'Most things,' Luke agreed, giving her elbow a squeeze.

When lunch was over, Xavier insisted that Christine should teach him and as many of the others as were interested how to maintain an engine. He led her to what he laughingly termed 'the garage', which was no more than another clearing in the forest where a number of vehicles were parked, carefully camouflaged under leafy branches.

'*Mon Dieu*! What a collection!' Luke said. 'Where did they all come from?'

They were indeed, a motley assortment. There were two fairly modern Renault saloons, which looked as if they might have belonged to a prosperous bourgeois family, though they were now covered in mud and scratches; three tradesmen's vans, two of which had been adapted to run on gazogène and two ancient Citroens.

Xavier shrugged and grinned.

'The vans came with the men who drive them, when they decided to join us. That one there,' pointing to one of the Citroens, 'was given to us by the *curé* of St Marc's in Dun-les-Places, as a gesture of support. The two Renaults we "borrowed" from families who were being a bit too helpful to the *Boche*. Now, Mademoiselle Christine, where shall we start?'

For the rest of the afternoon, Christine demonstrated how to clean spark plugs and adjust points and fan belts, as well as how to check oil and water and brake fluid and tyre pressures.

'Air filters should be changed from time to time and you should top up the batteries with distilled water, but you won't be able to get hold of that unless you go to a garage. Failing all else, you could use the water from the spring if you filter it through a piece of cloth.' She straightened up and wiped her greasy hands. 'That's about it. Anything more complicated will need a proper mechanic with the right equipment.'

'Mademoiselle, we are in your debt,' Xavier said. 'If only you were not leaving us tomorrow. I should appoint you chief engineer, in charge of all these.'

Christine looked at her brother and sighed.

'I'm sorry. We have to go. But I'm sure you'll manage quite well without me.'

As they returned to the main camp, the boy on the motorcycle rode in and spoke urgently to Xavier and a few minutes later, the van Christine had repaired that morning drove away with three of his men inside.

'What's up now, I wonder,' Luke said, but no explanation was forthcoming.

The evening meal was over, and Cyrano had returned from his scheduled radio transmission when the van came bumping back along the track and pulled up in the centre of the clearing. The three men jumped out and one called out, 'We've got another one!'

Luke and Christine joined the men who were converging on the van, in time to see the rear doors opened and a slight figure dragged out, bound and with his head covered by a sack, reviving painful memories of their own arrival the day before.

'Pierre sent a message to say he'd caught him snooping round the pharmacy,' the man said. 'Told Pierre he was looking for some friends but wouldn't say who.'

'Bring him over here. Let's have a look at him,' Xavier said.

The captive was shoved forward into the firelight. The sack was pulled off and Xavier grabbed him by the shoulder.

'Now, it's no use lying, if you know what's good for you. What were you doing?'

Luke sprang forward. 'Xavier, it's all right! We know him. He's a friend.' He caught hold of the newcomer's arm. 'Rollo! What in the name of God are you doing here?'

CHAPTER 13

'Luke! Thank God! Tell these goons to untie me!'

The words were defiant, but Rollo presented a very different appearance from the cocky youth they had got to know on board the *Madeleine*. He had a black eye and there was dried blood around his nostrils, and his voice shook. Luke put an arm around his shoulders and could feel that he was trembling.

'It's OK, Rollo. You're safe now. These people are on our side.' He looked at the *Maquis* leader. 'Xavier, please let him go. He's the son of the boatman we were travelling with.'

'What is he doing here, that's what I want to know,' Xavier growled, but he signed to one of the men to cut the ropes around Rollo's wrists.

Luke led him over to a log by the fire.

'Sit down. I'm sorry you've had a rough time, but the same happened to us yesterday.'

'I had to come. There's an important message . . .' Rollo's voice was still hoarse and uncertain.

'It's OK. Take your time. Xavier, can he have a cup of wine?'

Christine knelt by them with a tin mug in her hand.

'Here, give him this. Water was what I wanted more than anything.'

Rollo gulped the water, sniffed hard and muttered his thanks.

Xavier handed Luke a second mug.

'Give him a swig of this. It's *marc*.'

The boy sipped, coughed, drank some more and sat back, straightening his shoulders.

Xavier said, 'Now then. What's all this about?'

Rollo looked at Luke. 'You can't come back to the *Madeleine*. She's been requisitioned by the *Boche*.'

'Requisitioned!' Luke and Christine spoke together.

'They came on board yesterday afternoon and searched the boat from bow to stern. Thank God they didn't find the secret compartment! Then they said she was needed to carry equipment. They wouldn't say what, or where to, except that we would be going north. So that means up the Yonne, maybe along the Seine to Paris or the Channel. So it's no good to you, and anyway they've put a permanent guard on board to make sure we do as we're told.'

Luke and Christine looked at each other.

'Now what?' he said.

She shook her head helplessly.

'Rollo, it's very good of you to come all this way to tell us. I'm so sorry you've been so badly treated.'

He shrugged, 'I didn't want to tell this lot who I was looking for. I didn't know if they could be trusted.'

'How did you know about the pharmacy?' Cyrano had been listening to the conversation.

'Luke said he'd taken you to a pharmacy in Corbigny. I didn't know which one, so I tried them all. When I got to the third one, the pharmacist told me to wait. Then he locked me in a room until these thugs came to fetch me.'

'It's exactly what happened to us,' Christine told him.

Luke looked at Cyrano apologetically.

'I'm sorry. I suppose I shouldn't have said anything.'

'Well, it's just as well you did, under the circumstances,' Cyrano responded. 'Rollo, the Germans didn't try to stop you leaving the boat?'

'I told them I was going to visit my girlfriend in Jonches. I said I'd be staying the night.'

'And you're sure you weren't followed?'

'Yes. Anyway, Jonches is in the opposite direction. I started off that way and then doubled back.'

'You've done very well.' He looked at Luke and Christine. 'The question is, what are you two going to do now?'

'I suppose,' Luke said slowly, 'we could go back to Auxerre and see if there are any boats going our way who would be prepared to take us.'

'No! You mustn't!' Rollo said. 'Auxerre is swarming with *Boche*. It wasn't just our boat that was searched. The rumour is that there's been a big break out of POWs from somewhere and the Gestapo think some of them may have stowed away on barges.'

'That's bad news,' Cyrano said. 'If they are looking for escaped POWs, it means there will be extra vigilance on the trains as well.'

'We're stuck, then,' Luke said.

'It seems to me, 'Cyrano said, 'that you are probably safer staying here than trying to go on — at least until things settle down.'

Brother and sister exchanged looks.

'Could we stay, really?' Christine asked. 'Would Xavier let us?'

'And keep my resident garage mechanic?' Xavier responded with a grin. 'Why not?'

'That's a point,' Luke said. 'If we do stay, I don't want to be just an extra mouth to feed. I want to join in, be part of what you are doing.'

'You mean you want to fight with us? Of course! You are a big, strong young man. Can you use a gun?'

'Yes. I used to go pigeon shooting with my father before the war.'

'Wait a minute,' Cyrano said. 'I suggested you might hang on here for a bit because you'd be safer. I didn't mean you to risk your life in the fighting.'

'But why not?' Luke said passionately. 'I'm old enough. If . . . when I get back to England, I'll join up. I'll be risking just as much then.'

'Maybe,' Cyrano agreed. 'But at least there you will be properly trained.'

'How much training does it need to use a rifle? Anyway, from what I've seen there isn't all that much fighting going on here.'

'That may be about to change,' Cyrano said.

'Then Xavier will need all the men he can find. Cyrano, I can't stay here as a . . . a passenger. If I'm staying, it has got to be as a member of the *Maquis*.'

Cyrano lifted his hands in a gesture of surrender.

'It's not my decision. It's between you and Xavier.'

'And I say he's welcome,' Xavier said. 'You are both welcome.' He looked at Rollo. 'What about you, my friend?'

Rollo shook his head. 'I have to go back. My father needs me to help manage the boat — and I don't want the *Boche* to come looking for me if I don't turn up.'

'How will you get back?'

'The same way I got to Corbigny; I borrowed a bike. Can you take me back there tomorrow?'

'Of course.' Xavier stood up. 'So, now it is time to eat, and to celebrate the addition of two new members. Come!'

'There's just one thing, Cyrano,' Christine said quietly as the others moved away. 'Our mother will be worried out of her mind. We agreed that when we got back to England, we would ask the BBC to put something in their *messages personnels* — coded of course — to let her know we were safe. We managed to send a letter from Digoin, but that was more than a week ago and she will be wondering what has happened to us since. Is there any chance you could contact someone back at home and arrange for a message to be broadcast, to let her know we're safe?'

'I'm sure that could be done,' he said. 'You concoct a suitable coded message and I'll put it in my next transmission and ask for it to be passed on to the BBC.'

She thanked him with a smile that expressed more than simple gratitude.

That evening, as darkness fell, one of the men produced an accordion and began to play a popular love song. Then, Cyrano got out his flute and joined in. Sitting in the glow of the campfire, Christine felt happier than she had for days.

Isabelle stepped back from the big kitchen range and ran her hand over her forehead. These days, she seemed to have a perpetual headache and the unseasonably warm weather was not helping. One anxiety seemed to be piled on another, until she no longer knew which was the most oppressive. The constant nagging uncertainty about the whereabouts of her children and the safety of her husband would have been enough to worry about, without a load of explosives hidden in her wine cellar and two German soldiers living in the house; and on top of everything, her father was becoming increasingly querulous and demanding. He resented the presence of the Germans and seemed unable to understand that she had no option but to accommodate them; but his real anger was directed at the fact that she gave Hoffmann warm milk laced with brandy every evening to help him sleep.

'You should be putting poison in his milk, not brandy!' he complained. He had even gone so far as to accuse her of being a collaborator.

Schulz came in carrying a load of wood for the stove and, as she thanked him, Isabelle was forced to acknowledge guiltily that his presence in the house was a boon rather than a burden. He had taken over most of the jobs Luke had done when he was at home, fetching and carrying wood and water and seeing to the fire in the range. What was more, he often brought back little luxuries begged from his friend the cook in the officers' mess, which were a very welcome addition to the meagre rations. And he was company; they both were, in their different ways. Schulz was a cheerful character, with a fund of amusing anecdotes about army life; while with Hoffmann, she had discovered a mutual interest in literature.

He borrowed books from the small library she had accumulated and it was pleasant to have someone to discuss them with. He was well-educated and sensitive, a far cry from the popular image of a German soldier, and she knew from Schulz that he was bullied by his commanding officer, who regarded him as a coward. She found herself developing an almost maternal concern about his health. The problem, she now understood, was that he was asthmatic and any undue stress, or exposure to things he was allergic to, could bring on a paroxysm of wheezing.

The positive aspects of the situation were almost outweighed by one great drawback: with the two men in the house most evenings, it was almost impossible to listen to the evening news bulletins from the BBC. Isabelle had no idea whether her children had reached England, but she was terrified that she might miss the one broadcast which carried the message she so longed to hear, so she risked slipping out to the wine cellar every evening to listen. She had tried telephoning Marcel again but as before there was no reply. The suspense ate away at her until she felt prepared to do anything to bring it to an end.

She gave her father his supper and forced herself to eat something, then cleared away the dishes. As she finished the washing up, she glanced at the clock above the dresser and saw that it was 8.50 pm. Hoffmann was in his own room as usual, and Schulz had gone into the village to join his friends in the café on the square.

Isabelle took off her apron and pinned up a stray lock of hair.

'I'm just going out for a breath of air,' she told her father.

'As usual,' the old man muttered. 'It's the same every night. What's so important out there that you have to go out every night?'

'There's nothing important,' she said, keeping her tone light with an effort. 'It's a warm evening and I fancy a little stroll, that's all.'

'Yesterday it was raining, but you still went out,' he said. 'You're not going out there to smoke cigarettes, are you?'

'No, Papa! You know I don't smoke.' She knew from many exchanges in the past that, although he had no objection to men smoking, her father had a rooted disapproval of the habit for women. 'Anyway, where would I get cigarettes from? There's no cigarette ration for women.'

'From your German pals, I shouldn't wonder,' he replied.

'They are not my pals! They are billeted here and we treat each other with as much courtesy and consideration as the situation permits. That's all there is to it. Now, I've got a headache and I need some fresh air. I'll be back in half an hour.'

'Oh, don't mind me! Don't hurry back for my sake. I can sit here on my own, like always.'

For a moment, she was tempted to explain why she needed to go out, but she was unsure how far she could trust the old man to be discreet. He often said things in the presence of the two Germans that were intended to provoke, and she could imagine him dropping hints that he was privy to some secret. It was not a risk she could afford to take, so she shook her head in silence and went out into the dusk.

It was a beautiful spring evening. The sun had just gone down and the sky was pale duck-egg blue, with the evening star hanging low above the western horizon. For a moment she stood still, inhaling the perfume of the Gloire de Dijon rose that grew around the door. Then, she hurried to the cellar. A rapid glance around reassured her that no one was watching and she unlocked the door and was about to slip inside, when a movement nearby caused her to give a cry of alarm, quickly stifled, as a hoarse whisper came from the shadows.

'Don't be frightened, Madame. It's me, Louis. I need to speak to you.'

Isabelle opened the door and gestured for him to go in. She followed and pulled it to behind her, before feeling for the candle and matches that she kept on top of a barrel just inside. Louis was even more dishevelled and unkempt then before.

'I'm sorry, Madame,' he went on. 'I know it was a shock to find me here, but I didn't want anyone to see me hanging around outside.'

'What is it?' she asked, more curtly than she intended. 'Why are you here?'

'To tell you that we shall be collecting the stuff you are hiding for us, the day after tomorrow. The same men who delivered the barrels will collect them. If anyone asks, you can say you have sold a consignment of wine.'

'But everyone knows that all my wine goes to Bussy in Clermont, and it is collected in a van, not by horse and cart.'

'Perhaps there is no fuel for the van?' he suggested, 'so they must use the horses instead.'

'Very well,' Isabelle drew a deep breath. At least this meant that she would be relieved of one anxiety. Then, impelled by curiosity she could not deny, she added, 'Why do you need it?'

The boy's eyes gleamed.

'We have received intelligence that a large contingent of the enemy forces is due to move from here to Saint-Nectaire. They will pass through the Gorges de la Monne. Where the road crosses the river is a perfect place for an ambush. We need the explosives to blow the bridge.'

'I see.' Isabelle had a momentary vision of the explosion, of men and vehicles plunging into the river, of the survivors being mown down by enfilading fire from the slopes above. She knew that as a patriot she should rejoice in the prospect, but she could only feel a deep sense of revulsion.

Louis moved towards the door.

'I must go now. Remember, tomorrow afternoon.'

He opened the door, stood for a moment peering out into the gathering darkness, and then was gone. Isabelle hesitated, gathering her thoughts, then she moved quickly to the rear of the cellar and extracted her radio from its hiding place.

The main news broadcast had already started, but she listened to the rest, crouching over the set and straining her ears to catch the words through the crackle of static. Then came the part she was waiting for, the *messages personnels*, a stream of apparently unintelligible announcements that meant nothing except to the one person they were intended for. Her attention began to waver. It was going to be another wasted evening. Then, incredibly, there it was:

'*Michou's pups are safe, but in a different kennel.*'

She almost failed to take it in the first time but, as always, the message was repeated:

'*Michou's pups are safe, but in a different kennel.*'

Almost weeping with surprise and relief, Isabelle switched the set off and returned it to its hiding place. *Safe!* That was the important point. Only Luke or Christine could have known to send that message and it had said 'pups' in the plural. But 'in a different kennel'. What could that mean? If they were not back in England, how could they have got that message to the BBC? So why say a different kennel? Not with their grandparents, perhaps. If so, why not? Perhaps the grandparents had been bombed out, or had been evacuated? That seemed a likely explanation. Anyway, they were safe. That was all that mattered. She closed the cellar door behind her and went back to the house.

Her father had wheeled his chair close to the window and as she entered he greeted her with a growl in which triumph and fury were equally mixed.

'So, now I understand. Who is he? Who is this man you go to meet every night?'

'I don't know what you're talking about,' Isabelle said, flustered. 'What man?'

'I saw him. Don't try to lie to me. Hanging about in the shadows, like a criminal. Who is it? Why is he ashamed to be seen? You're not having an affair with a *Boche*, are you?'

'Of course not! What do you take me for?'

'You're far too pally with them. I thought it might be your officer friend, but I can hear him coughing in his room. It's not that other one, is it? That Schulz?'

'Of course it isn't!' She hesitated, then moved to crouch by his chair. 'Papa, I can't believe you think so badly of me, but I see I have got to tell you the truth. The man you saw is Louis Beaupaire, the cobbler's son. He's with the *Maquis*. He came . . . he came to ask if I could spare some wine for him and his comrades. Of course, I said yes. They will send someone to collect it tomorrow.'

Her father leaned back in his chair and blew a long breath through his nose.

'Well, why didn't you say so to start with? The *Maquis*, eh? Brave fellows. Pity you wouldn't let Luke join them, instead of sending him off to Montbéliard. Come the end of the war, young Beaupaire will be able to hold up his head with pride. I doubt if Luke will be able to do the same.'

Isabelle stood up. She had not wanted to trouble her father with her own anxieties about the children, so she had let him think that they were safely in Montbéliard with their godfather.

'I think you'll find Luke will have done his bit by the end of the war, Father. Just wait and see.'

CHAPTER 14

Rollo left the camp early the following morning, travelling in the same van in which he had arrived. Luke and Christine saw him off and he shook hands with both of them.

'I'm sorry we can't help you get any further. Father was asking around for a cargo going in the right direction when the *Boche* came and took over the barge.'

'It's not your fault,' Luke said. 'You were very good to come here and warn us. I'm sorry you got such a rough welcome.'

'We might have walked straight into a trap if you hadn't come,' Christine agreed. 'And it was a risk for you, too. You were very brave.'

Rollo shrugged and grinned, but the colour rising in his cheeks gave away his pleasure in the compliment.

'It was nothing. What are friends for, after all? But I'm afraid we shall not meet again.'

'It seems that way,' Luke agreed. 'Good luck with the Germans. I hope they won't keep your boat too long.'

'Who knows?' Rollo responded and Christine saw that underneath his casual manner he was afraid.

'Come on, let's go!' the driver of the van called.

'*Adieu! Bonne chance!*' Rollo turned away and climbed into the back of the vehicle.

'And you! Good luck! Take care!' they called in return.

As the van bumped away, Luke said, 'You know, I really didn't like him when we first met. He struck me as being much too cocksure. But he's turned out OK in the end.'

'He tried to kiss me once,' Christine said.

'He what? Why didn't you tell me?'

'Why should I?'

'What did you do?'

'I kicked him in the shin and told him if he tried it again, I'd kick him where it really hurt. I feel bad about it now.'

Luke grinned at her. 'I shouldn't. He deserved it.' He put his hand on her shoulder and turned her back towards the camp. 'Anyway, it's just you and me now, Sis.'

'You and me and about twenty *Maquis*,' she responded. 'You've got your wish, haven't you?'

'I had the impression you weren't so averse to staying on,' he retorted. 'I can't think what the attraction is for you. Oh, talk of the devil, isn't that Cyrano coming back from his morning sked?'

She kicked him quite hard in the shin in his turn.

'Shut up, idiot! I don't know what you're talking about.'

An hour later, Gregoire reappeared, with his usual armed escort. After a brief conference with Xavier and Cyrano, he beckoned them over.

'I gather you two are staying with us for a while longer.'

'It seemed the best thing to do,' Luke said. 'Provided it's all right with you.'

'It's not up to me. This is Xavier's show. But I understand he's agreeable and you've volunteered for active service, Luke.'

'Yes. I want to do my bit.'

'You realize how dangerous it could be? Things won't always be as quiet as this.'

'I know that. I'm ready to fight. And Xavier has promised to teach me how to use a gun.'

Gergoire and Cyrano exchanged glances.

Then Gregoire said, 'Very well. I have no authority to refuse you. But if you join us, you will be under orders and you must promise to obey them without question. Is that understood?'

'Your orders?'

'Mine, Cyrano's or Xavier's. OK?'

'Yes, of course. You have my word.'

'What about me?' Christine said.

'You?' Gregoire looked puzzled.

'I want to do my bit too.'

He smiled. 'Well, I gather you are to be in charge of motor maintenance.'

'That won't take much of my time.'

'Well, I'm sure Xavier will be able to find other ways you can be useful. I daresay Jacques can do with some help with the cooking . . .'

'But . . .' Christine began furiously, but Gregoire had already turned away.

He raised his voice. 'We have some important information to announce. Xavier, call your men together, please. Luke, you'd better join us.'

The men assembled and there was a general air of excited anticipation. Since yesterday it seemed the whole camp had guessed that something was about to happen. Luke found a place on a log among the rest and Christine pushed her way in to sit beside him.

Xavier said, 'My friends, this is a great day. At last, our appeals have been heard. Gregoire will explain.'

'I know,' the tall Englishman began, 'that ever since I came here, you have been asking for one thing above all others, and that is better weapons to fight with. I'm now able to tell you that your request has been granted. Tonight there will be a parachute drop of arms and ammunition.' He paused until the shouts of triumph subsided. 'A suitable dropping zone has been located, but it is some distance from here. All of you will be required to make it ready and then to carry back the supplies when they have been dropped. Each man should carry enough food and water for 24 hours. It will be dawn at least before we get back to camp. Prepare yourselves. We leave in one hour.'

The men dispersed amid excited chatter, some heading for the spring to fill their water bottles, others lining up outside the lorry/store where Jacques dispensed the rations. He must have been forewarned, because he had baked extra bread and each man was handed a baguette, a sausage and a piece of cheese. Christine queued up with Luke, but when their turn came, Jacques handed Luke his ration and turned to the next man in the line.

'Hey, what about me?' she demanded.

The cook looked surprised. 'You, Mademoiselle? There is no need. I am staying in camp and we can share something tastier for lunch.'

'But I'm not staying,' she protested. 'I'm going with the rest.'

He raised his shoulders.

'That is not what I understood. You must speak to Xavier.'

'Right!' She swung on her heel and headed towards the tent where Xavier was poring over a map with Gregoire and Cyrano.

Luke hurried after her.

'Chris, hold on a minute! Don't . . .'

She turned to face him.

'Don't what?'

'Well, you know . . . Gregoire said we have to take orders if we want to stay.'

'He said that to you, not to me.'

'But . . .' his words fell on deaf ears, as his sister marched on towards the tent.

'Gregoire?'

He looked up, frowning. 'Yes?'

'Please tell Jacques to give me my rations. I'm coming with you.'

Gregoire straightened up. 'I'm sorry. I don't think that would be suitable.'

'Why not?'

'For one thing, it is going to be a long hike. The DZ is a good ten kilometres from here and it's steep going most of the way. Then there will be work to do and finally we have to walk the ten kilometres back.'

'Twenty kilometres? That's nothing! I can do that easily. Before the war, Father used to take us both hiking in the mountains and we often walked further than that. I can walk just as far as Luke. Tell them, Luke!'

'It's true,' her brother admitted. 'She can do it OK.'

'That's all very well, but this is not a joyride. Everyone will have to pull their weight.'

'I have a thought,' Cyrano said. 'When I was in real pain with my ankle, Chris bandaged me up very efficiently. Couldn't you do with someone who can offer first aid if it's needed?'

Gregoire looked at her.

'Can you do that? Have you had any training in that area?'

'A bit,' she said, recalling her few months as a Girl Guide. 'I can certainly bandage people up, or make a sling and that sort of thing.'

He scrutinized her for a moment longer. 'OK. You can come. But be aware that if you can't keep up, or you get tired, no one is going to drop out to help you. No one!' he fixed his gaze on Luke. 'Understood?'

'I won't need any help,' she said firmly.

'All right. Tell Jacques to give you your rations and then get together whatever you can find in the way of first aid equipment. You've got less than an hour to do it.'

'Thank you! I promise you won't regret it.' She turned to Cyrano with glowing eyes. 'Thank you, Cyrano! You're a . . . you're a pal!'

He looked at once amused and slightly embarrassed.

'That's all right. I owe you a favour.'

As she turned away she was aware of her brother looking at her.

'What?'

He grimaced. 'You've got your own way this time. But . . .'

'But what?'

'You can't keep pretending you're one of the lads. When it comes to the real stuff — the fighting etc. — you can't expect to get involved with that.'

'I don't see why not.'

'Because it's not right. Chris, you're a girl! Isn't it time you grew up and accepted that?'

She turned away, feeling herself flush.

'Oh, shut up, Luke! Leave me alone.' She walked away and he did not follow her.

Christine spent the next hour scouring the camp for anything that could be pressed into use for first aid. She persuaded Jacques to hand over an apron which had got scorched in the fire and tore it into strips for bandages. It should be boiled to sterilize it, she knew, but there was no time for that. One of the men contributed a scarf, which could be converted into a sling. There was no such thing as antiseptic, but she recalled that alcohol had antiseptic properties and asked Jacques for a small bottle of *marc*, which he handed over somewhat reluctantly. There remained the problem of splints, in case someone broke a leg. She searched everywhere, but there did not seem to be a straight piece of wood of the right dimensions anywhere. She had almost given up and decided that in an emergency she would have to improvise with whatever fallen branches she could find, when she noticed the table on which Cyrano was accustomed to work. The tent was empty. Gregoire was talking to some of the men on the far side of the camp and Cyrano had disappeared. The table was made up of a series of laths laid across two trestles. One less, she reasoned, would make very little difference. She sidled over and lifted one lath from the rear edge and walked away with it as nonchalantly as she could manage.

Most of the men were used to working in the forest and it was easy to get one of them to saw it in half, giving her two flat pieces about half a metre long. She packed everything into her rucksack, added her rations and her water bottle, and strapped the two laths on top. Then, she joined the men who were assembling ready to leave.

'What on earth have you got there,' her brother demanded.

'Splints,' she responded succinctly, and to her relief he left it at that.

They set off, walking in single file along the forest track, with Gregoire at the head and Xavier bringing up the rear. Jacques, who maintained that he was too fat for strenuous exercise, remained behind to guard the camp with a boy who had a twisted leg as a result of a childhood accident and Cyrano, who was still limping badly. It occurred to Christine, too late, that she could have stayed behind to keep him company. She banished the thought and concentrated on keeping up with the rest.

It was, as Gregoire had said, a steep climb, and towards the end there was no proper path. They scrambled up, pushing aside low branches and tripping over roots, where the ground was so treacherous that Christine thought her services might well be needed to deal with a sprained ankle, if nothing worse.

It was mid-afternoon when they finally emerged onto a rocky plateau, which thrust itself up clear of the surrounding forest. After a brief rest and a chance to eat some of the supplies they had carried with them, Gregoire set the men to gathering firewood.

'We need five bonfires, good big ones, to guide the plane in. I'll mark out the places for them to go. Make sure the wood is good and dry. We also need a pit to bury the parachutes and containers. There mustn't be any trace left that might be spotted by enemy reconnaissance aircraft. Xavier, can you divide the men into six teams, five to collect wood and one to dig?'

As they dispersed he called Christine to him.

'We need torches to set fire to the wood when I give the signal. We don't want to be messing about with matches. Can you find small, dry twigs and bind them to five long branches that will reach right into the heart of the fire? Then fill in the gaps with anything easily combustible you can get hold of — dry leaves, moss. Do you get the idea?'

'Yes. I'll do my best.'

By the time the fires had been built, she had her five torches ready. She had sacrificed two of her improvised bandages to bind the twigs and, as a final touch, she had soaked the material with *marc*.

'They should catch light pretty easily,' she said, handing them over.

'Very neat,' Gregoire approved. 'Well done.'

When all the men had reassembled, he addressed them.

'The plane is due at 01.00 hours but that is only approximate. It could easily be twenty minutes either side of that time, depending on weather conditions and other factors. When we hear the plane, I shall give a signal in Morse code with this flashlight and, all being well, the plane will respond in the same manner. At that point, I will give the signal for the fires to be lit — but not before. I don't want anyone going off at half cock and setting light to one before that. Understood?' He paused for the murmured response. 'When the pilot sees the fires, he will make a run in over the site. He may decide to drop the cargo straight away or he may want to come round for a second pass, so don't worry if nothing happens the first time. When the 'chutes do come down, it is up to all of you to track where they fall. Grab the 'chute and roll it up, then bring it and the container here. I want you to designate one man in each team to put out the fire as soon as the drop is over. And before we leave not only must we bury the evidence, we must erase all signs of the fires. If the *Boche* spot them, we could get some very unwelcome visitors. Now, we have several hours to wait so I suggest you all get some rest. There won't be much chance later.'

The men settled down, each team by their unlit fire. Luke found his sister and sat down beside her.

'You OK?'

'Yes. Why shouldn't I be?'

'I was just asking. Look, I'm sorry if I was rotten to you earlier. I think you're terrific, really. I don't know how I'd cope if you were a girly sort of girl, frightened of spiders and crying because you'd broken a fingernail.'

'Oh, come off it! Not all girls are that feeble,' she said, but she smiled at him and nudged his arm in a gesture of affection.

The time passed slowly. Darkness fell, but the sky was clear and the moon was just past full.

Perfect conditions, according to Gregoire.

Christine lay down, pillowing her head on her arm, and Luke stretched out beside her. A low murmur came from the groups around the unlit fires, but apart from that, the only sound was the wind in the trees and a distant owl hooting. She was very tired but she knew there was no chance of sleep; she was too keyed-up for that. However, she must have dozed, for she was suddenly aware that Gregoire was on his feet, his flashlight ready in his hand.

'Is it time?' she asked.

'Ssh! Listen!'

She strained her ears and became aware of a low, distant drone. Others had heard it too, and all round the area, men scrambled to their feet exchanging brief, tense snatches of conversation. The sound came closer.

'Ours, or theirs?' Luke asked.

'Ours,' Gregoire replied.

The plane appeared quite suddenly, seeming to rise up from behind the surrounding trees, and the low hum became a roar as it swept overhead. Gregoire was clicking his flashlight on and off, sending a repeated letter in Morse, and for a moment it seemed there was no response. Then, the plane banked and a light blinked from the cockpit.

Gregoire struck a match and his torch flamed into life. He waved it and all round the area, other flames pricked the darkness. Then, Gregoire thrust his torch into the heart of the nearest fire and almost simultaneously four others burst into life.

The plane's engine had faded into the distance and Christine had to suppress a cry of, 'Too late. He's gone!' Then the sound swelled again, as the aircraft circled and swooped once more over the plateau.

Suddenly shapes like dark flowers blossomed against the stars and floated down towards them. The plane circled once more, then, with a waggle of its wing tips, set course for home.

Gregoire was counting, 'Two, three, five — six! Terrific! Grab them, boys!'

The men scattered, chasing down the falling parachutes. Three dropped neatly into the clearing, but the others fell among the trees and had to be dragged out. One caught in the upper branches of an oak and one of the men had to scramble up to cut it loose; but within minutes, all six containers were laid out close to the only fire which still burned.

'OK,' said Gregoire. 'Let's see what Santa Claus has brought us.'

Xavier and his men clustered round eagerly as he opened the first one. As the contents were revealed, a sound went up which combined fury and disappointment.

Xavier grabbed something and held it up.

'Boots! What do they want me to do? Kick the *Boche* to death?'

'Some of your men might be glad of them when the weather gets worse,' Gregoire said reasonably, but it was clear from his face that he was disappointed too. 'Let's see what's in the others.'

The contents of the second container were greeted with similar dismay and this time it was Gregoire's turn to give vent to his feelings:

'Chocolate and cigarettes! What do they think I am doing here, running a NAAFI?'

The third container made up for the first two.

'Rifles!' Xavier exclaimed. 'That's more like it!'

Gregoire extracted one and examined it.

'Lee Enfield Mark III. Not the latest model, but a good serviceable weapon. Excellent.'

Containers four and five held more welcome supplies; there was ammunition for the rifles, new batteries for Cyrano's radio set, grenades and something wrapped in oilskin which Gregoire pounced on with delight.

'An S-phone. Great!'

'What's an S-phone?' Luke asked.

'It's a radio transceiver. This is the ground set. The airborne end is carried in a plane so I can actually talk to the pilot. It has a range of up to thirty miles. Now, what else have we got?' He unwrapped another package. '*Plastique*! Now this is something we can do real damage with.'

'Plastic what?' Luke asked, wrinkling his nose. 'It smells like marzipan.'

'It does, doesn't it?' Gregoire agreed. 'That's one of the drawbacks. It's a giveaway for anyone who has handled it. But it's useful stuff just the same. Plastic explosive. There should be detonators in here somewhere. Ah yes! Time pencils. Good.'

'What do we need pencils for?' Xavier said dismissively.

'You'll see. I'll teach everyone how to use this stuff over the next few days. Now, what's in the last box?'

It seemed fate had kept the best to the last. Xavier unpacked the contents with a cry of triumph.

'A Bren gun! I have been begging for one of these for months.'

Gregoire straightened up.

'Right. Let's get this lot out of sight. Somebody douse that fire. The rest of you, scatter the ashes and cover the burned areas with dead leaves or whatever you can find.'

It was dawn by the time the parachutes and containers had been buried and all traces of the fires obliterated. Then, the new equipment was distributed among the men to carry back to the camp.

Gregoire called Christine over and handed her a parcel.

'This is personal stuff for Cyrano — letters from home and such like. Can you make sure he gets it?'

'Yes, of course.'

He dug into his own pack.

'Here, have a piece of chocolate.'

'Oh,' she hesitated, her mouth-watering. 'What about the others?'

'They'll get their share in due course. Go on. You deserve it.'

She took the proffered bar, unwrapped it and took a bite. Chocolate had never tasted so good. She had finished all her rations the night before and her stomach was rumbling. She stowed the parcel in her rucksack, glad that she had not been given anything heavier to carry.

The walk back to camp seemed very long and she began to regret her airy 'twenty kilometres? That's nothing!' She looked at Luke, plodding ahead with a rifle on his shoulder and a bulging rucksack, and had to admit that she would have been hard pressed to carry that sort of weight after the exertions of the last 24 hours.

Cyrano and the other two who had remained behind greeted them eagerly as they tramped wearily into camp.

'Well, was it a success?' Cyrano demanded. 'What have we got?'

Gregoire opened his rucksack to show him. Christine touched Cyrano's arm shyly.

'This came for you.'

He took the package. 'Oh, great! Letters from home. Thanks.' Then he turned back to Gregoire.

Jacques had fresh bread and coffee ready for them — or the concoction of roasted barley that passed for coffee — but before they could eat, Gregoire insisted that all the equipment was safely locked away in the truck that served as a storeroom.

'Now, eat and then get some rest,' he said when he was satisfied. 'Later we'll have some rifle practice.'

Christine swallowed her coffee, ate half her bread and fell asleep.

CHAPTER 15

Christine woke abruptly to the sound of gunfire, and was on her feet almost before her eyes were open. Gazing round, she saw that the camp was almost deserted and the sound of firing was coming from somewhere beyond the trees.

For a moment, she imagined a German attack, then she remembered that Gregoire had promised rifle practice later in the day. She looked for Luke and realized that he had gone with the rest. Her first impulse was to head in the direction of the noise and ask to join in, but she remembered her brother's irritation when she had insisted on going with him for the parachute drop and it occurred to her for the first time that he might find a kid sister an embarrassment when he was with the other men. Gloomily, she sat down again and wondered what to do next.

The only people remaining in camp were Jacques, who was stirring his everlasting soup over the fire, and Cyrano who was at his table poring over his code-books — encoding a message for his next transmission, she guessed. As if he sensed her eyes on him, he looked up, then stretched and got up and came over to where she was sitting.

'Had a good sleep?'

'Yes, thanks. Everyone else seems to be awake before me.'

'Oh, well. Gregoire kicked most of them awake half an hour ago, to show them how to use the rifles.'

'Yes, so I hear.'

'How do you feel after last night? It was a pretty tough trek from what I gather.'

'I'm OK. Except I'd do anything for a bath and a chance to wash my clothes.'

'Ah,' he nodded. 'I can see the difficulty. You can't very well strip off and take a dip in the stream like the rest of us.'

'Not very easily.'

He tilted his head and gave her a teasing smile. 'I think I might have a solution.'

'Oh, what?'

'You'll have to wait. I've got to OK it with Gregoire when he's free. But I'm sure something can be arranged.'

'Well, thanks. I'd really appreciate it.'

They were silent for a moment. Then he said, 'You look as if you're at a bit of a loose end. How do you fancy learning how to use the radio?'

'Could I?' she jumped to her feet. 'Could I really?'

'Well, it occurs to me that if anything . . . anything untoward . . . were to happen to me, it would be very useful if someone else knew how to send a message. Do you want to try?'

'Yes, please!'

'Right, come over here.'

She followed him to the tent where his table was.

He tidied away some papers and said, 'It's a funny thing, but my table seems to have got smaller. You wouldn't know anything about that, would you?'

'Me? Why should I?'

'Just a thought.' He took a fresh sheet of paper and sat down. 'The first thing you need to do is learn the Morse alphabet. Or do you know it already?'

'Only dot dot dot, dash dash dash, dot dot dot,' she said.

'Well, it's a start. SOS could come in useful one day. Now, I'll write out the whole alphabet for you. When you

170

have it by heart, so that it's as natural as breathing, I'll show you how to operate a Morse key. OK?'

'OK. How soon do you want me to learn it by?'

'That's up to you. There's no great hurry.'

His words recalled to Chris something he had said earlier.

'You mentioned the possibility of something — untoward — happening to you.'

'Oh, that was just a manner of speaking.'

She drew a breath. 'Cyrano, Gregoire had another radio operator before you came, didn't he? What happened to him?' She saw his face change.

'Look, if you're worried about the security aspect, you don't have to do this if you don't want to.'

'That's not what I meant!' She could feel herself flushing. 'I'm not thinking of myself. I just wondered, that's all.'

He hesitated. Then he said, 'Well, you've a right to know. He was caught by the *Boche* in the middle of a transmission and arrested. We don't know any more than that.'

'So that's what you meant by "something untoward".'

'No! No, really. I don't think there's any chance of that happening to me. My predecessor was transmitting from an old mill quite close to the town. The German detector vans were able to triangulate his position. They aren't likely to have detector vans up here, and if one did venture into the forest, we should soon get warning of it. And soon I shall make a point of not transmitting from the same place twice running. That's the virtue of my cover story; I am working on developing a practice as a music teacher, so soon I shall have contacts in a number of houses around the area — all places where they know who I am working for and what I am really doing. And I have arranged to practise the organ in two local churches. Church towers make excellent places to transmit from. All I am really waiting for, is for this ankle to heal sufficiently for me to drive. At the moment, I'm far more likely to be thrown off the back of that motorbike, the way Fernand tears around these tracks. That's all I meant. And

I'm not suggesting that you should actually transmit, except in an emergency. But if you'd rather not . . .'

'No! I want to. Really. I'll start learning these now.'

'OK, if you're sure. And don't give up hope about that bath. You deserve a treat.'

Christine retired to her favourite log and started to commit the Morse letters to memory. At school, she had hated learning things by heart, but now she was determined to show how quickly she could do it. Too soon, in her new mood, Luke reappeared and dropped down on the grass beside her. His eyes were glowing.

'At last, I feel I'm actually doing something useful. Gregoire says I've got the makings of a good shot.'

'Good,' she said. 'Well done.'

'What have you got there?'

'Oh nothing.' She folded the paper and pushed it into the pocket of her dungarees. 'Just doodling.' She didn't know why she was unwilling to tell him, but she felt she wanted it to be something private between herself and Cyrano. 'Where's Gregoire?'

'Gone to the other camp. He said he'd be back later.'

He stretched out on the grass and fell asleep. Christine made an effort to concentrate on the Morse letters, but her eyelids began to droop and before long, she slid off the log and lay down beside her brother.

They woke to the sound of Jacques banging a spoon against a tin plate, the usual summons to eat. They were just finishing the meal when Gregoire returned and Cyrano went over to talk to him. Christine, watching, saw Gregoire look in her direction; then he smiled and nodded and Cyrano beckoned to her.

'What does he want?' asked Luke, following her.

'Don't know.'

Gregoire said, 'Cyrano has suggested a little trip. Hop in, both of you. I think we all deserve a bit of what our American friends call R&R. Xavier, are you coming?'

They piled into the old Mercedes and Christine found herself sandwiched between Luke and Cyrano on the back seat. The pressure of Cyrano's shoulder against her own gave her a strange feeling in the pit of her stomach. With the two regular bodyguards perched on the running boards, the car bounced along the forest track until they came out on a proper road beside a large lake.

Gregoire swung the car through an open gateway and pulled up. Peering through the window, Christine saw that they were outside a hotel called the *Beau Rivage*.

'Is this safe?' Luke asked nervously.

'Don't worry,' Gregoire responded. 'The proprietress is a supporter — or at least, shall we say she knows which side her bread will be buttered after the war is over. We come here quite often.'

The hotel lounge was elegantly furnished, in a somewhat old-fashioned style, and several tables were already occupied by well-dressed men and women. It was a scene more suited to the pre-war era than the present day.

'Who are all these people?' Christine whispered to Cyrano.

'Refugees from Paris mainly. This used to be a popular holiday spot before the war and some people have seen it as a good place to sit it out until peace comes again.'

Gregoire led them over to the bar, where a well-upholstered lady presided.

'Madame, we have two new recruits. May I present Luke Beauchamps and his sister Christine?'

'*Enchantée*,' she responded. Then, 'His sister you say? *Zut alors*! You poor child! What has happened to you?'

Christine felt herself blushing furiously.

'Nothing's happened to me, Madame. I've just been travelling for quite a long time.'

Cyrano said, 'Madame, this is a very brave young lady, but she is much in need of a bath and a change of clothes. Can you help?'

'But of course!' The woman turned to a door behind the bar and called, 'Jeanette! Come here, *chérie*.'

A girl appeared at her summons. She was, Christine guessed, about her own age, but there any resemblance ended. Jeanette was taller and full-figured; buxom was the word that came to mind, with dark auburn hair swept back in a fashionable wave. She was wearing a pale-green spotted dress with a sash and a low-cut 'sweetheart' neckline. What was more, she was wearing lipstick and, Christine was almost sure, face powder.

'Yes, Maman?'

'This young lady is Christine. Take her upstairs and show her where she can have a bath, and find her something nice to wear.'

The expression on Jeanette's face left no doubt about her reaction, but she lifted the section of the bar that gave access to the area beyond and said, 'Come with me.'

Cheeks burning, Christine followed.

Jeanette led her into the residential part of the hotel and opened a door. 'I'll run you a bath. There's a clean towel on the rail.' She looked her up and down doubtfully. 'I don't know about clothes. I'm much taller than you. I might be able to find a skirt I've grown out of.'

'No, thanks,' Christine responded. 'I'll stick to my dungarees. A skirt wouldn't be really suitable where I'm staying at the moment.'

'You're living up there in the woods, with the *Maquisards*?'

'Yes.'

Jeanette nodded judiciously. 'I can see it wouldn't be a good idea to make yourself look too attractive.'

There was some sense in what she said, but the words stung nevertheless.

'What about undies?'

'I've got a change in my rucksack, thanks. I'll just wash out the ones I'm wearing.' She hesitated a moment, unwilling to ask anything from this girl, but common sense prevailed. She had only expected to spend a couple of nights with the

Maquis and her 'good' clothes were still on the *Madeleine*. 'If you've got a shirt you can spare, I'd be grateful. I don't have another one with me.'

'I'll see what I can find.'

Christine was in the bath when she came back, with a navy blue blouse over her arm.

'I don't know if this will look right under dungarees, but it's the best I can do.'

'Thanks. I'm sure it will be fine.' She sat with her knees modestly drawn up to her chest until the other girl left. Then she stretched out luxuriously in the hot water. Jeanette had thrown in a handful of lavender scented bath salts and for the first time she understood fully how unsavoury she must have smelt before. She found some shampoo on a shelf above the bath and washed her hair and pulled her discarded underwear into the water with her to wash that too. It was tempting to go on lying in the scented water, but she was aware of the men downstairs and was not sure if they were waiting for her.

She hauled herself out unwillingly and dried herself, but there was no way she could dry her clothes. She rolled them in the towel to squeeze out as much of the water as possible and shoved them back into her rucksack. Then, she pulled on clean underwear and the navy shirt, which fitted her quite well. Picking up the dungarees, she wrinkled her nose. They were patched with mud from last night's scramble, and oil from her session instructing the men in the rudiments of motor maintenance and they smelt of sweat. But there was nothing else for it. The only alternative was to eat humble pie and ask Jeanette for some of her cast-offs, and she was not even sure where the other girl had gone. She put on the dungarees, combed her hair, and went down to the bar.

The men were sitting round a table on the far side of the bar from the residents, drinking beer. It was clear that they were determined to ignore each other. Cyrano pulled out a chair for her.

'Feeling better? What would you like to drink? A glass of wine, lemonade?'

'I'd like a beer, please.'

'Excellent! Madame, a *blonde* for the young lady.'

Luke leaned closer to her. 'Sorry, Sis. I should have thought. You OK?'

'Yes, I'm fine. Just wish I had my other slacks.'

Jeanette brought over the beers, all demurely downcast eyes and fluttering eyelashes, and Christine was shocked to see how all the men responded with little pleasantries that made her blush and giggle. Even Cyrano joined in!

At that moment, a door opened on the far side of the room and a woman came in; all the men at the table stopped looking at Jeanette and fell silent. The newcomer was probably in her late twenties, Christine guessed, tall and slender with shining blonde hair framing perfectly regular features. She was exquisitely made-up and she was dressed in a full-length crimson evening gown. She greeted the other residents with easy familiarity and Christine was amused by their reactions. The men all got up and two of them kissed her hand. The women's reception was distinctly less welcoming. She looked around to share her observation with her brother, but he was staring at the new arrival like a man hypnotised.

'Who is that?' she whispered to Cyrano.

'Madame de Montfort — Adrienne,' he murmured. 'Though I suspect that is not her real name. A widow, by her own account, and before that an actress. The ex-mistress of some minor aristocrat, according to others.'

The lady turned away from her admirers and came across the room to where they sat and all the men rose.

'Our gallant *Maquisards*! Good evening, gentlemen. I'm delighted to see you all well.'

She offered her hand to each of them in turn. Xavier kissed it, murmuring some fulsome flattery; Gregoire and Cyrano contented themselves with shaking it, though they both gave a little formal bow as they did so. 'And who is this young Adonis?'

Luke was blushing.

'Luke Beauchamps, Madame.'

'*Enchantée*. A new recruit?'

'Just a temporary one, I'm afraid.'

'What a pity. And you,' she looked at Christine, 'you are . . . ?'

'Christine Beauchamps, Madame.'

'Ah! You are *en masquerade, n'est-ce pas?* Playing the breeches part. How droll!'

One of the men from the other side of the room called, 'Adrienne, your drink is here.'

She made a little grimace. 'Such a bore! But one must be polite. *Au revoir, mes amis.*'

As she drifted away, Christine muttered fiercely, 'Ghastly woman!'

Luke responded, 'Oh, I don't know. I thought she was rather . . . attractive.'

'Oh, really!' She wanted to kick him, but realized this was not the time or the place.

Isabelle felt almost light-hearted as she walked back towards the house. She had been tasting the new vintage with her head vigneron and it promised to be good. The men had come as promised and removed the barrels of stolen explosives and, though she preferred not to think about what they intended to do with them, it was a relief not to have them on her premises.

Best of all, she knew that her children were safe, even if their whereabouts was a mystery. She hummed to herself as she entered the kitchen. She was about to start preparing the evening meal when she heard a car draw up outside and then the voices of her two German lodgers. They were back earlier than usual.

Hoffmann came into the kitchen and she saw at once that his breathing was laboured.

She pulled out a chair at the kitchen table.

'Sit down, Leutnant. Is something wrong?'

'No, no,' he replied. 'Not exactly. That is, I fear the time has come for me to say goodbye. I have to leave early tomorrow.'

'Leave?' To her surprise, the news was unwelcome.

'Yes, my company is being redeployed. I shall be very sorry to go. You have been most kind. But I expect you will be glad to see the back of us.'

'Not at all,' she said. 'I can't pretend that you were welcome guests, when we first met. But in the event, we have been good company. Don't you agree?'

'I do, Madame, most heartily. I shall miss our conversations — and your hot milk!'

'So, where are you going? Or am I not supposed to ask?'

'We are being sent to a place called Saint-Nectaire.'

'Saint-Nectaire!' Isabelle turned away to the stove, so that he could not see her face.

'It seems there has been some Resistance activity in the area and we are charged with rooting it out.' He sighed deeply. 'I know we are supposed to be enemies, but I think if the roles were reversed and your people were occupying my country, I should admire these brave young men.'

'Which way will you go?' She had to struggle to keep the tremor out of her voice.

'By the shortest route. It is cross-country, but my captain thinks that is where the *Maquis* are hiding out. He wants to make a reconnaissance.'

'You should stick to the main roads,' she said quickly. 'That other route is very hard to follow. You could easily get lost.'

He shrugged. 'It is not for me to decide, Madame. I go where the captain orders.' He got to his feet. 'I think I will sit outside for a little while. Schulz is packing my things and I feel better in the fresh air.'

When he had gone, Isabelle dropped into a chair and put her head in her hands. The mental image she had had when Louis told her what the *Maquis* intended, of twisted metal and broken bodies, came back even more vividly. To imagine it happening to some unknown enemy soldiers was bad enough, but to let it happen to the gentle soul who had come into her care was unthinkable. But what was the solution? To warn him would immediately expose her as an associate, however unwilling, of the *Maquis* and he might feel it his duty to report the fact to his superiors. What was more, if the Germans became aware of the ambush that was being prepared, they would be able to surround the *Maquisards*, who would become the victims rather than the aggressors. This would result in the death of many and the arrest of the others. She could not be responsible for doing that to her countrymen. There was only one solution: somehow Hoffmann must be prevented from joining that convoy.

As she racked her brains, she heard him cough outside the window and the germ of an idea came to her; if he were to become too ill to report for duty, the convoy would leave without him. She knew that he was allergic to certain things and exposure to them would bring on an asthma attack. What were the things he had mentioned? Horses! He had said that he had been forced to join the infantry because being with horses made him ill. She had a horse, an old cob which had provided motive power for various appliances until the advent of the tractor, and which had now been called into service again. But she could hardly invite Hoffmann into the stable. Whatever pretext she gave, he would refuse knowing the consequences. Would it be sufficient to walk the horse past him, perhaps to stop with it and chat? He would certainly avoid being anywhere close to it. Then she had an inspiration; there was an old blanket in the stable, which they used to throw across the horse's back when the weather was cold. It was thoroughly impregnated with horsehair. If she could somehow smuggle that into his room, even replace the blanket on his bed with it, that might do the trick.

She paused, wondering. How severe might the effects be? Did she have any right to inflict more suffering on her unfortunate guest? But would that not be better than letting him go to almost certain death?

She got up and took a carrot from the vegetable rack as colour for her actions, then strolled across the yard to the stable, where the old horse accepted her offering with alacrity.

The blanket was on the hook where it was kept. She took it down and rolled it into as small a bundle as she could manage. Now, how to get it back to the house without him seeing? To her relief, he was writing something, his head bent over a pad on his knee, and he did not look up as she passed.

The next problem was Schulz. Hoffmann had said he was packing for him. She left the blanket just inside the door of Christine's room, which was opposite the one now occupied by Hoffmann, and tapped on his door. Schulz was stuffing clothes into a kitbag. He looked around as she entered.

'Madame?'

'Fritz, could you do something for me?' (She had abandoned the formal Herr Schulz long ago.)

'Of course, Madame. I have almost finished here, then I am at your service.'

'Thank you so much. I've run out of water. Could you bring another bucket from the well?'

'Certainly. Give me one minute.'

Isabelle returned to the kitchen and took the bucket from under the sink. It was still half full so she poured the contents round the rose that grew by the door. When Schulz appeared she handed it to him, saying, 'The lieutenant tells me you are leaving tomorrow. I shall miss having you to help with jobs like this.'

'I shall be sorry to go, Madame. We both will. But I will bring up the firewood and fill the water bucket again before we leave.'

She thanked him and watched him go off towards the well. Then she hurried back to Hoffmann's room. She retrieved the blanket, stripped back the quilt, tucked the blanket in place and covered it with the quilt. It was too much for a warm evening, but Hoffmann seemed to need warmth, so she hoped he would not notice the difference. Then, torn between relief and guilt, she returned to the kitchen and got on with preparing the evening meal.

Isabelle slept badly. Her room was at the other end of the house so she could not hear anything that went on in

Hoffmann's, but suddenly she was woken from a light doze by the sound of someone moving around in the kitchen. Schulz was stoking up the fire in the range, and he had pulled the big iron kettle onto the hotplate.

He looked around as she entered.

'Madame, forgive me for waking you. The lieutenant is very poorly. His asthma is worse than I have seen it for a long time. Sometimes it helps to inhale the steam.'

'You must do whatever is necessary,' she said. 'Can I help?'

'There is very little we can do,' he replied. 'Sometimes the attack passes off. Otherwise we shall have to get the doctor to give him an injection. Can I bring him in here so he can sit close to the kettle?'

'Yes, yes, of course. Let me help.'

Hoffmann was propped up on his pillows, and Isabelle was horrified by the sight of what she had brought about. His lips were blue and he was breathing in short gasps, as if every breath was a struggle. Between them, Isabelle and Schulz half carried him to the kitchen and sat him by the steaming kettle, but there seemed to be very little improvement; she was terrified that her actions were going to result in his death.

'Fritz, you must go for the doctor straight away. Leutnant Hoffmann needs help.'

The batman looked at his officer and Hoffmann gave the faintest of nods.

'I'll be as quick as I can.'

For Isabelle, the next half hour was one of the longest of her life. She sat by the young German, rubbing his back in a vain effort to relieve the symptoms, and refilling the kettle so that there was a continuous supply of steam. At last, she heard a vehicle draw up outside and a uniformed officer came in, followed by Schulz.

He clicked his heels formally.

'Kapitan Doctor Muller, Madame. I am the medical officer for the battalion.'

Isabelle got up. 'I'm so relieved to see you, doctor. Please, can you do something for this poor young man?'

The doctor bent over Hoffmann, listened briefly to his chest, then opened his bag and took out a syringe. 'Fortunately, the condition responds well to an injection of adrenalin.'

He inserted the needle into Hoffmann's arm and slowly depressed the plunger. The result, to Isabelle, was almost miraculous. Even before the whole contents of the syringe had been delivered, the young man's breathing began to ease and she saw the tension go out of his shoulders. Abruptly, she remembered that the offending blanket was still on his bed. She excused herself and hurried back to his room. She had just had time to extract the blanket and throw it into Christine's room when Hoffmann came back, supported on each side by Schulz and the doctor.

When he was propped up once again on his pillows the doctor said, 'There should be no recurrence of the problem tonight. But he will need to rest. I will sign a certificate releasing him from duty for the next three days. Then we will see how he is.'

'But I understood he was supposed to leave tomorrow,' Isabelle said. 'He told me his unit was being redeployed.'

'So they are,' the doctor agreed. 'But he will not be with them.' He looked at Hoffmann. 'Don't worry, boy. You'll be able to rejoin your men in a day or two.'

When the doctor had gone Hoffmann said weakly, 'It seems you will have to put up with us a little longer, Madame.'

She smiled at him, relief flooding through her.

'I'm very glad you are staying. You must rest and take all the time you need to get well.'

The following evening, Schulz returned from duty, the habitual creases in his face deeper than ever.

'Terrible news, Madame! The company being redeployed to Saint-Nectaire was ambushed by the bandits who call themselves Resistance fighters. Hardly any of them escaped.'

Isabelle put her hand to her mouth. 'Oh, how awful!'

'Yes, indeed,' he agreed. He met her eyes, and for a moment she saw a wild speculation in them. Then he shook his head in wonder. 'And to think, the lieutenant and I should have been with them'.

CHAPTER 16

The next two days at the *Maquis* camp were spent in training with the new equipment. Luke spent long hours at the improvised firing range and Christine swotted away at the Morse code. By the second afternoon, she was able to convince Cyrano that she had a good grasp of it and he unpacked his radio set and showed her how to use the Morse key to transmit the dots and dashes.

'Don't worry, you won't actually transmit anything,' he assured her. 'This is just practice.'

It was more difficult than she had imagined and while she was still struggling with it, Gregoire arrived in camp. He called Xavier and half a dozen other men, including Luke, and they hunkered down in a circle while he opened the pack he was carrying.

'What are they doing?' she asked Cyrano.

'It looks as though he's teaching them how to use the plastic explosive,' he replied.

'Could I watch?' she asked eagerly.

He hesitated a moment, then grinned. 'I don't see why not.'

Gregoire glanced up as she joined the group, craning to see over the shoulders of the men around him, but he made no comment.

'I want you all to listen very carefully to what I am about to say. This stuff is perfectly safe if you treat it properly but it can be lethal if you don't.' He unwrapped a package to expose a lump of material that reminded Christine of green plasticine. The smell of almonds wafted through the clearing. 'Its proper name is Nobel 808 but it's called *plastique* because that is what it is. When it is warm, you can mould it to any shape you want, so it is ideal for fixing to parts of machinery, for example, or metal supports. The best temperature is about body heat, so the most convenient way to carry it is here.' He opened his shirt and lifted his arm to show a chunk of the explosive nestling in his armpit. He removed it and handed it to one of the men. 'See how easy it is to mould it to any shape you want.'

The man took it gingerly and bent it, then gaining confidence he rolled it into a sausage and joined the two ends.

'That's the way,' Gregoire approved. 'Pass it round so everyone can have a try. The only snag with this is, as you will have noticed, the smell. The *Boche* are perfectly familiar with it, so if you happen to be stopped while carrying it, they will know exactly what your intentions are. And it clings. It takes a lot of washing to get rid of the smell. Now,' he reached into his pack, 'in order to detonate it, you need one of these. You can't detonate it by setting fire to it; it will just burn. Even a rifle shot won't do it. You have to have a proper detonator. This is what we call a time pencil. You can see why: it's just about the same shape and size as an ordinary pencil.' He held up a brass tube. 'Inside this end, there is a glass capsule containing acid. Running alongside it is a wire, which is connected to a spring holding back the striker. To activate the device, crush the end of the tube with a hammer or under the heel of your boot so that the glass capsule breaks. The acid then eats away the wire, which releases the spring and the striker then hits the percussion cap at the other end of the pencil, which you have pushed into the plastique. The thickness of the wire determines how long that process takes, so different time pencils give different delays between breaking the glass and the detonation. You can have pencils with a ten minute delay or up to 24 hours. They are accurate to within a couple of minutes with a ten minute delay, and an hour if set for twelve hours or more. Any questions?'

'Yes,' Xavier said. 'What's our first target and when do we start?'

'That's something we need to discuss,' Gregoire said. 'I have identified several possible targets. The main objective is to disrupt the enemy's lines of communication or hamper his ability to rearm or reinforce. So, railways will be a prime target, but also factories, fuel dumps, electricity supplies and so on.'

'What about the canals?' someone said. 'The *Boche* use them to transport materials.'

'We could blow the lock gates at Marigny,' another voice joined in.

'No chance!' Xavier said. 'The *Maquis Serge* tried that outside Tannay a few days back and the *Boche* were waiting for them. They lost four men. The *Boche* must be guarding all the locks.'

'No!' Luke said. 'Not all of them. The *Boche* knew something was going to happen there and they were waiting.'

'What do you know about it?' the first speaker enquired irritably.

'We were there,' Luke said. 'We had just gone into the lock, when the firing started. Luckily for us, the lock was emptying so we were able to shelter at the bottom until it was over. But it was obvious that the lock-keeper had tipped the Germans off.'

'What makes you say that?' Gregoire asked.

'After it was all over, we saw him chatting to the officer in charge. They were obviously on good terms.'

'The swine!' Xavier exclaimed. 'The filthy collaborator!'

'Let's give him a taste of his own medicine,' someone shouted. 'We'll blow up his lock and kill the bastard.'

There was a general yell of agreement and Xavier grinned broadly. 'OK. That's our first target settled.'

'Oh no!' Christine had kept silent with difficulty but she could hold back no longer. 'Please don't do that!'

'What's the matter?' someone jeered. 'Don't like loud bangs? Don't worry, you won't be able to hear it from here.'

'It's not that!' she shouted back. 'I just don't think it's a good idea to attack the canals.'

'Why not, Chris?' Gregoire asked.

'Well, what about the boat people who earn their living there? It's not fair on them. And they help to move refugees, like us, and downed airmen, so they can get back to carry on with the fight. If you blow up the locks they won't be able to do that.'

Gregoire shook his head, not unsympathetically.

'I understand your point, but it is true that the canals are used to transport vital construction materials for enemy bases and airfields. I'm afraid we can't let the possible rescue of one or two airmen weigh against that. And as for the men and women who work on the canals, what about the people who work on the railways, or in the factories that we want to target? We shall do our best to avoid civilian casualties, but I'm afraid they have to accept a certain amount of disruption in the fight for freedom. The canals are a legitimate target.'

'Then we go tonight!' Xavier said and his men cheered.

'There's just one thing,' Gregoire put in. 'I appreciate how you feel about the lock-keeper, but you can't go shooting him out of hand. We are not bandits. We have to abide by some kind of law. Everyone is entitled to a fair hearing. Capture him and bring him back here and you can try him, and if he's found guilty then it is in your hands to punish him as you think fit. Besides, he may have some useful information for us.'

Xavier grunted. 'OK. We'll bring him back and you can see what you can get out of him. But it'll come to the same thing in the end.'

'That's up to you,' Gregoire responded. 'But bear in mind, you are fighting for freedom — and that includes the freedom to be given a fair trial. Now, let's have a look at the map and I'll show you the other targets I have in mind.'

The two men retired to the tent where Cyrano worked, and Xavier summoned the two others who seemed to be accepted as his lieutenants. Soon all their heads were bent over the maps. The rest broke up into groups, eagerly discussing their own suggestions.

Christine caught Luke's sleeve as he was about to join one of the groups.

'Luke, do you think he's right? Are the canals legitimate targets?'

'Of course they are,' he said crossly. 'I do wish you'd stop putting your oar in. It's not up to us. We're just hangers-on as far as the *Maquisards* are concerned.'

'You put your oar in, as you put it,' she said. 'You told them about the fight at the lock.'

'That's different,' he insisted. 'That was useful intelligence. And besides . . .' He trailed off.

'Besides what?' she demanded.

'It's different, that's all,' he mumbled lamely.

'You mean it's different because I'm a girl and you're one of the chaps now.'

'No! Well, yes, sort of. I mean, I wish you'd behave more like a girl. Some of the men . . . I've heard them making jokes. It's embarrassing.'

She looked at him, swallowing back tears. Then anger came to her rescue.

'Well, I'm sorry if I embarrass you! I'll keep out of your way in future.' She turned away and walked off to the far side of the camp, wishing there was somewhere she could go to be alone. He did not come after her.

By sunset, all the preparations had been made and the men were ready to leave. Luke had asked for and been given permission to join them. Christine had not even bothered to ask. The whole party assembled at the 'garage' and piled into the assorted vehicles parked there.

She had been tempted to stay in the camp, but she realized that it would look as if she was sulking, so she went along to wish them luck. The two gazogène vans had been started some time before, as they needed a long time to warm up; the rest burst into life with gratifying promptness, except for one of the elderly Citroens.

Jean-Claude hailed her. 'Mademoiselle Christine! Come here, please. We need your expert help.'

Christine peered under the bonnet. A quick check showed her that no leads had come loose and she had cleaned the plugs herself. She pulled out one of the points.

'This is the problem. They are so badly pitted, it's no wonder the car won't start.'

'Can you mend them?'

'Not a chance, I'm afraid. They need replacing.'

'*Merde!*' exclaimed the would-be driver of the car. 'We'll have to leave it. Come on, lads! We'll just have to squeeze in with the others.'

They hurried away and Christine looked around for her brother. He was just about to swing himself over the tailboard of one of the trucks. It suddenly came to her that he was about to set out on a dangerous mission. She called his name and he paused and waited until she reached him.

'You will be careful, won't you? I mean, I don't know what I'd do if anything happened to you.'

His face, which had expressed barely controlled impatience, softened and he touched her arm.

'Don't worry, Sis. I won't take any risks. You'll see. I'll be back in an hour or two.'

He climbed aboard and she watched as the whole convoy drove away down the forest track and disappeared from sight. Then she wandered back to the almost deserted camp. Cyrano had just returned from his nightly 'sked' and was at work decoding the messages. She was tempted to join him, but she had learned that he hated to be distracted from a job that required total concentration. So she sat by the camp fire, gloomily contemplating her lot. After a while, he came to sit beside her.

'Penny for them?'

She shrugged. 'Not worth it.' To her annoyance, her voice sounded husky.

'Hey, come on! What's the matter? You're not worrying about Luke, are you? He'll be all right, you know. Gregoire knows he's inexperienced. He'll make sure he's kept well out of the firing line.'

'I suppose,' she muttered and added, 'I keep thinking about the Pasquiers, and Bernard and Marie who helped us before. How will they earn a living if the canals are closed?'

'Oh,' he chuckled softly, 'you needn't trouble yourself about that. The Germans can't afford to have them closed for long. Xavier and his men may blow the lock tonight, but by tomorrow the *Boche* will have a working party out there repairing it. In a few days, it'll be fixed.'

'It's a bit of a waste of time, then, isn't it?'

'No, because while the *Boche* are putting right any damage we do, they can't be using the same resources to build new airstrips or other infrastructure. The busier we can keep them, the more men and materials we tie up.'

'I see.' She made an effort to smile. 'That makes sense.'

He looked at her closely. 'There's something else, isn't there. What is it?'

She turned her face away. 'Nothing. Just . . .'

'Just what?'

'Oh, I'm fed up with being a girl. Everybody thinks I'm useless, just because I'm not a man.'

'That's not true!' he exclaimed. 'You serviced all the cars, didn't you? None of the men had any idea how to do it. And you pulled your weight on the *parachutage*. Gregoire was very impressed.'

'Was he?'

'Certainly. And if it's any help, as far as I'm concerned, you're an honorary chap.' He put his arm round her shoulders and gave them a squeeze. 'There. Feeling better?'

She glanced into his face, then inched a little further away.

'Yes, thanks. Much better.' And for the life of her she could not understand why that was not true.

The sabotage party arrived back just after midnight and she could hear them singing as they parked the vehicles.

They trooped back into the clearing, bringing in their midst a pathetic figure whom she recognized as the lock-keeper. He was visibly shaking and begging for mercy. Luke came to find her, his face flushed and his eyes glowing.

'Success?' she asked, unnecessarily.

'Oh yes. Piece of cake, really.' His casual tone belied his expression. 'Not a shot fired. Xavier and three of the others just knocked at the door of the lock-keeper's cottage and when he opened it they shoved the muzzle of a rifle in his gut and marched him back to where the rest of us were waiting. Then we fixed the explosive charges with a ten minute fuse and got well away before it went up.'

'So, you didn't actually see what happened?'

'Yes we did. We parked up on the edge of the forest, where we had a good view down to the canal. There was a bit of a delay and then boom! A big flash and terrific noise. I bet it shook the locals, and any German patrols that were around.'

'But you couldn't tell how much damage it had done from there, could you?' She queried.

'Oh, it blew the lock gates off all right. We could see the water flooding the banks of the canal downstream. The moonlight reflected off it.'

She looked across the clearing to where the lock-keeper was being tied to a tree.

'What do you think will happen to him?'

'There will be a trial. Gregoire will insist on that. But there's no doubt about his guilt. I imagine he'll be shot.'

'Luke, has it occurred to you that the only evidence against him comes from us?'

He glanced at her and then away.

'Well, there's no doubt in my mind. He deserves whatever is coming to him.'

The trial took place immediately after breakfast the following morning. Chairs were set out for Xavier and Gregoire and the rest of the men gathered round squatting on logs. A third chair was offered to Cyrano but he declined, so one of the older members of the *Maquis*, a man called Alphonse, was co-opted as the third judge. The lock-keeper was untied from the tree, where he had spent the night under guard, and dragged into the centre of the circle.

'You are charged with collaboration with the enemy,' Xavier said solemnly. 'You knew there was going to be an attack on the lock and you warned the Germans, so that they were lying in wait. A firefight followed, in which four patriots were killed. How do you plead? Guilty or not guilty?'

'It wasn't my fault,' the man babbled. 'How did I know there was going to be an attack? The German patrol just happened to be there.'

'Guilty or not guilty,' Xavier persisted.

'Not guilty.'

'I call the first witness. M. Serge, please step forward.'

A man whom Christine had not previously noticed stood up. He was a little older than most of the others and his upright bearing suggested a military background.

'I am the leader of the *Maquis* Serge. On the fifteenth of May, my men and I planned to attack the lock at Tannay. We did not wish to cause any civilian casualties, so we warned the lock-keeper, the accused, to keep out of the way. When we arrived, we were immediately confronted by an armed German patrol, which was obviously lying in wait for us. In the ensuing fight, four of my men were killed.'

'Thank you, Monsieur. So, that disposes of the excuse that you did not know what was going to happen. What do you have to say?'

'The *Boche* just happened to be there. What else could I do? They threatened to shoot me if I didn't keep quiet.'

'That is another lie. We have a witness who saw you fraternising with the enemy after the attack. I call M. Luke to give evidence.'

Luke stumbled to his feet, his face first red and then pale.

'Tell us what happened when you were passing through the lock.'

'We had to lie low at the bottom of the lock while the fight was going on. But after it was all over we saw him — the accused — talking to the German officer.'

'Did it seem as though he had been forced to cooperate with them?'

'No, they seemed very friendly. They were sharing cigarettes and laughing.'

'Thank you. That is all.' Xavier conferred briefly with his fellow judges, then continued. 'You have been found guilty. The verdict of this court is that you be shot as a traitor to France.'

There was a growl of general approbation and the two men guarding the prisoner grabbed him by the arms and marched him off into the woods. Xavier called several names and the men chosen picked up their rifles and followed him.

Christine, numb with shock, saw one of them thrust a spade into the lock-keeper's hands. She looked at Gregoire and saw that he was already heading in the opposite direction, towards his car; while Cyrano had returned to his table in the tent. She looked at her brother.

'This is horrible!'

'It's called justice,' he replied brusquely, but she saw that he had gone pale.

There was a pause in which the sound of digging could be heard. The whole *Maquis* waited and no one spoke. Then came the sound of shots and there was a collective exhalation, as if they had all been holding their breath, and the group dispersed about their normal tasks. Xavier returned, grim faced, and in the forest, spades could be heard at work again. Christine looked at Luke.

He got to his feet. 'That's over. I'm going to the range to practise.'

Once again, Christine found herself at a loose end. She decided on an impulse to go exploring. A walk in the woods would be good exercise; it would keep her mind off what had just happened. She wondered briefly if she should tell someone what she intended, but decided against it on the grounds that she would probably be forbidden to go. She set off along the track that led past the 'garage'. As she reached it a voice hailed her.

'Mademoiselle Christine!' Jean-Claude ran across to meet her. 'You remember what you said about replacing the points in the Citroen?'

'Yes.'

'I have a friend, an old school friend, who works in a garage in Montsauche. He might be able to help.'

'I don't see what good that is,' she responded. 'How would we get in touch with him?'

'That's easy! We can drive down there now in the van.'

'Drive into a town? Can we do that?'

'Of course. How do you think we get our supplies?'

'But what about the Germans. Suppose we get stopped.'

He grinned. 'There aren't any Germans in the Morvan.'

'None at all? Are you sure?'

'Oh yes. There are German garrisons in Nevers and Château-Chinon and from time to time they send patrols through this area, but they stick to the main roads. They know we are in control everywhere else. They don't risk venturing into the forest. And all the local people are on our side, so we soon get to know if there are any about.'

'Well, if you're sure about that, I suppose it's worth a try.'

'Let's go, then.'

She hesitated a moment. Luke would wonder where she was. But then he was occupied on the rifle range and wasn't bothered about her, and Gregoire had vanished as he so often did and Cyrano was busy.

'OK. Let's go!'

As they bumped down the forest track, she said, 'Who was that man who said his group had been betrayed by the lock-keeper?'

Jean-Claude looked puzzled. 'Serge? He's the head of the *Maquis Serge*, obviously.'

'You mean there are other groups in the area? I thought there was just Xavier's and the *Maquis Vincent*.'

'Oh no. There are groups scattered all over the Morvan: *Maquis Serge, Maquis Jean, Maquis Bernard, Maquis Socrate*. There may be others but those are the ones I know of. Of course, those aren't their real names, any more than Xavier is really called Xavier.'

'What is his real name, then?'

'I've no idea. Does it matter?'

'Why don't you all amalgamate and make one big force? Surely that would make you more effective.'

'Move everyone together into one big camp? Then if the *Boche* decided to attack they could wipe us all out. This way, if they manage to locate one group, the others are still safe and the *Boche* have no idea where we are hiding or where the next attack is coming from.'

Christine nodded. 'Yes, that makes sense. I see now.'

They came out of the forest onto a road and she said, 'So you are really able to drive around without worrying about running into a German patrol?'

'I told you, there are no Germans in the Morvan.' The van rounded a bend and Jean-Claude stood on the brakes. '*Merde!*'

Ahead of them, a convoy of German trucks and armoured cars was drawn up on the side of the road. The soldiers had left the vehicles and were lounging on the verge, smoking and chatting. So far, they showed no sign of having noticed the van.

'Don't stop!' Christine said quickly. 'If you do, it will look suspicious. Drive on past them. After all, this is just a harmless-looking butcher's van. If anyone asks, you've just been out delivering orders.'

Jean-Claude glanced sideways at her, his face pale, but he nodded and let in the clutch. The van drove slowly past the convoy and none of the men gave it more than a second glance. Just ahead of them was a T-junction, and on the corner there was a garage. As they passed it they saw why the convoy had halted; a staff car was drawn up on the forecourt and a sweating mechanic was struggling with one of the wheels, while a German officer paced around and a corporal, presumably his driver, stood watching.

'*Merde!*' said Jean-Claude again. 'That's the place where my friend works. Now we're stuck.' He drove round the corner and stopped the van out of sight of the convoy. 'What do we do now? Wait until they go?'

'It'll look suspicious if we just sit here,' Christine said. 'Can't you just drive into the garage and pretend you've come to check the oil or something?'

The Frenchman shook his head vehemently. 'I dare not show my face in there. I'm the right age for the STO. I was supposed to go. If they question me I've had it.'

'You were supposed to go for STO? How did you get out of it?'

'The morning we were supposed to assemble at the station, I scarpered and went to the *Maquis*. That's why I can't risk being asked to show my papers.'

'I see.' Christine was thinking hard. 'I can see why it's a problem for any man your age. But they wouldn't question a woman. I could walk in on some pretext. The way I'm dressed,' she glanced down at her grease-stained dungarees, 'they would probably think I worked there.'

'You can't!' Jean-Claude protested. 'It's too dangerous.'

'I don't see why. I bet the *Boche* wouldn't even notice me. What's your friend's name?'

'Laurent. But he won't know you. Why should he trust you? You could be a collaborator, spying for the Germans.'

'You're right. I need some kind of signal, some kind of code word, that would tell him I must have come from you. Think! Is there anything you used to do or say at school that only you and he would know about?'

Jean-Claude frowned. Then his face cleared. 'There were three of us, who were always together. We called ourselves the Three Musketeers. I was Athos, Laurent was Aramis.'

'Who was Porthos?'

'That was Albert.'

'What happened to him?'

'He was called up for STO the same time as me — but he went. I tried to persuade him to come with me, but he was too scared.'

'Why wasn't Laurent called up?'

'Medical grounds. He had polio when he was a kid and it left him with a weak leg. Are you definitely set on trying this?'

'Yes. Why not?'

'OK. You'll probably find Laurent in the workshop. Say that his friend Athos sends greetings to Aramis. Then he'll know you must come from me.'

'Right.' Christine opened the door. 'Wait for me for half an hour. If I'm not back by then get back to the *Maquis* and tell Gregoire or Cyrano what has happened.' She looked at her companion's face, creased with worry, and smiled. 'Don't look like that. I'll be fine.'

She walked back to the corner. The convoy was still waiting. Her heart was pounding and she felt that her hands were beginning to shake. To still them, she thrust them into the pockets of her dungarees, pouted her lips and forced herself to whistle. *Auprès de ma blonde* . . . The tune wavered, then gained strength as she sauntered across the road and onto the garage forecourt. The officer was now haranguing the unfortunate mechanic, who was having difficulty removing the wheel with its flat tyre. None of them looked at Christine. At the rear of the forecourt, she could see the open door of a workshop and hear the sound of someone using a file. She walked in and a slight young man straightened up from the workbench and peered at her.

'Yes?'

'Your friend Athos sends his greetings to Aramis.'

He gave a gasp, quickly suppressed. 'You have come from Jean-Claude?'

'Yes.'

'Then you are . . . you are . . .' he left the sentence unfinished, staring at her in confusion.

'It doesn't matter,' she said. 'We need your help. Can you supply me with a new set of these?'

She produced the old points from her pocket and held them out. Laurent took them and examined them.

'Wait a moment, please, Madame . . . Mademoiselle . . .' he stammered into silence again and disappeared into a storeroom.

Christine waited, biting her lip. Outside, she heard the mechanic give an exclamation of triumph and guessed he had finally succeeded in freeing the recalcitrant wheel. It occurred to her to wonder if there was a telephone in the storeroom and if even now Laurent was ringing someone to inform on her. He returned at last and held out a packet.

'These are the right ones. I knew we had some somewhere. You need them for . . . ?'

'For a car that won't start, obviously.' She smiled at him. 'Thank you. Your friend will be very grateful.'

'Give him my best wishes.'

'I will. Goodbye — and thanks again.'

As she crossed the forecourt, the mechanic was tightening the last nut on the replacement wheel. The officer glanced at her, then walked out into the road and shouted an order. She heard the clatter of boots as the men climbed back into their trucks. The driver revved the engine of the staff car and the officer jumped in and the whole convoy moved off. Christine watched them go and then moved over to where the mechanic was packing up his tools.

'Dirty *Boche*! What are they doing here?'

The mechanic spat expressively.

'God knows! But it looks as if they're planning to stay. The officer was agitating because he was supposed to meet the advanced party at the camp site half an hour ago.'

'Camp site! You mean they're going to make camp somewhere near Montsauche?'

'Looks like it, damn them! But what can we do?' He squinted at her suspiciously. 'Anyway, who are you? I've never seen you round here before.'

'Oh, I'm just visiting. My uncle needed some new points for his Citroen. I'd better get back. He'll be waiting. *Au revoir!*' She gave a quick wave and hurried away to where Jean-Claude was parked.

'Thank God!' he exclaimed as she climbed into the van. 'I was beginning to think the *Boche* had taken you with them.'

'No. They didn't even notice me. But we'd better get back. The mechanic who changed the wheel thinks they are here to stay. Gregoire needs to know.'

Back at the *Maquis* camp in the woods above the town, they found Luke pacing the area in a ferment of anxiety.

'Where the hell have you been? I've been worried out of my mind.'

She looked at his face and felt suddenly contrite.

'I'm sorry. You weren't around to tell and I had to make up my mind quickly. We've been to get these from Jean-Claude's friend at the garage.'

'You've been into Montsauche? Are you mad?'

Cyrano had seen her arrive and joined them.

'You could have told me, Chris. I was here and I've been worried, too. You really shouldn't go off without telling someone.'

Christine scuffed the dead leaves with her toe. She regretted worrying her brother but being told off by Cyrano, even as gently as that, really hurt.

'I'm sorry.' She looked up. 'But I've got some really important news. The Germans are in Montsauche.'

'What? Are you sure?'

As quickly as she could, she related what had happened.

Jean-Claude, who had stood by silent until then, said, 'She was brilliant! I was too scared to go into the garage, but she didn't turn a hair.'

Cyrano looked at her and shook his head. 'Chris, I don't know what to say. You shouldn't take risks like that but . . . you really are an amazing girl! Well done!'

Luke was looking at her with an expression she could not quite read.

'My God, Sis. Don't put the wind up me like that again
. . . Please!'

Gregoire was still absent but Cyrano sent the young man
with the motorcycle to fetch him from the *Maquis Vincent*.
He listened to her story in silence and when she had finished,
he nodded briefly.

'OK. You've got some useful equipment and brought
back some important intelligence. But in future you refer
all such expeditions to me or Cyrano before you set out.
Understood?'

'Yes, Gregoire.'

He smiled. 'Cheer up. You've shown initiative and a
cool head. Luke, you should be proud of her.'

CHAPTER 17

Three days passed without further excitement, then Gregoire called them together and spread out a map.

'This is our next objective. Luke, you and Christine will be particularly interested in this. Those gunboats you saw being hauled out at Auxerre — you were quite right that they are heading for the Saône. But it's a long, cross-country route from Auxerre to Chalon and I've just received some very interesting intelligence. Between Arcy-sur-Cure and Voutenay-sur-Cure, there is a road tunnel and apparently it is too narrow for those huge vessels to go through. So they have had to divert along the valley of the Yonne to Mailly, and then cut across to rejoin the main road at Voutenay.'

'Just a minute,' Xavier interjected. 'That's in the *Maquis Jean*'s neck of the woods.'

'It's through them that I heard about this,' Gregoire said. 'In order to get through the village of Avigny, the Huns had to demolish several houses, including the bar. The owners' son was so incensed that he took himself off to the *Maquis* to tell them what was going on. Jean doesn't have the necessary equipment or expertise to do anything useful, so he passed the word to me.'

'So what have you got in mind?' Xavier asked.

'Look here at the map. Just before reaching Voutenay, the road passes through the Bois de Mailly. It is thickly forested on both sides — perfect for an ambush.'

'Marvellous!' Xavier said. 'We can blow them all to kingdom come.'

'Not quite, I'm afraid. The convoy will be very heavily guarded and we should be very foolish to try a pitched battle and we don't have enough explosive to be sure of causing real damage. What we can do is bring them to a halt and then call in the heavy mob, in the shape of the RAF.' He paused and regarded the bemused expressions on the faces of the men around him with a grin. 'Cyrano and I have been hatching a little plot. He has already been on to London and they have agreed to have planes standing by. By my reckoning, the distance from the airfields on the south coast of England to Voutenay is roughly three hundred miles. A Mosquito fighter/bomber can cruise at 300 mph easily, more if necessary. From Avigny to Voutenay is eight kilometres and my informant tells me that the convoys can only average about five kilometres per hour. So this is the plan: we create some kind of obstacle that will stop them before they get into Voutenay. As soon as a convoy passes through Avigny, the boy from the bar will telephone Father Martin, the curé at Montsauche. Cyrano will be set up ready to transmit from the church tower and at his signal, the Mossies will be scrambled. If everything goes according to plan, they should arrive just about the time the convoy reaches our barricade. It won't be easy for the pilots to spot it under all that tree cover, but I can talk them in with the S-phone. Any questions?'

'Won't it be dangerous for Cyrano to transmit from the church, now the Germans are in Montsauche?'

The men turned to look at Christine with expressions of irritation, but Gregoire nodded. 'It's not ideal, but as far as we can ascertain, the *Boche* do not have radio detection vehicles in the area at the moment. And the message will be very short. Just a single code word.'

'When is all this going to happen?' Xavier asked.

'I'm told one convoy goes through every day, so we'll plan for the day after tomorrow. We'll need to reconnoitre the area to decide the best approach, so I plan to leave tomorrow morning. It will take several hours to get there. I'll take four of your men, Xavier, plus Jules and Fernand,' with a nod towards his two inseparable bodyguards.

'Only four!' Xavier exclaimed. 'Surely you need more men than that.'

'Not for what I have in mind. So can I have four volunteers?'

Hands went up all round the group. Luke put his up too, in a desperate effort to attract the leader's attention. Gregoire looked around and indicated four men, then just as Luke was about to drop his hand in defeat, he said, 'All right. You can come along, too, Luke.' Overriding the murmur of disappointment from the rest he went on, 'There are two more important jobs. We have been promised another *parachutage* but we need to find a more convenient DZ; somewhere we can get transport in to remove the containers instead of having to open them and carry back the contents piecemeal. Xavier, can you and some of your men scout for somewhere suitable? You know what's needed, a reasonably open area, not too close to any villages but accessible by some form of wheeled transport.' Xavier nodded. 'And finally,' Gregoire went on, 'we need someone to go down and check out the situation in Montsauche. Are the Germans still there and in what strength and for what purpose? Do we have any informants in the town, Xavier?'

'Plenty,' Xavier replied. 'It's just a matter of contacting them.'

Christine raised her hand eagerly. 'I could do that.'

Gregoire shook his head. 'No, you have taken enough risks already.'

'But I've been thinking,' she hurried on before he could turn to other things. 'Xavier's men can't show their faces while the Germans are there, because any young men who have not been sent on STO are liable to be stopped and questioned. But that wouldn't apply to a woman, or a girl. I could walk around town without anyone taking any notice at all.'

He looked at her with a frown. 'Well, you have a point . . . but you would need to look . . . to blend in with the locals. Local girls don't dress like that.'

'No, I know. If I could get hold of a skirt somehow . . .'

'I'm sure that can be arranged,' Cyrano said.

'I don't want to wear stuff belonging to that girl at the Beau Rivage,' Christine said hastily. Then, when they both looked at her in surprise, she added, 'They wouldn't fit. She's much bigger than I am.'

'I wasn't thinking of her,' Cyrano said. 'You remember I told you I was trying to arrange some private pupils for music lessons? Well, one of them is the daughter of Madame de Labrier, who owns the *château* at Lantilly. Her name is Colette and I'd guess she is about the same size as you. They are already supporters, so I'm sure they would be prepared to help.'

'Oh, right,' Christine said, embarrassed by her outburst. 'That sounds fine.'

'I could take her over this afternoon,' Cyrano suggested. 'Now my ankle is strong enough for me to drive, I want to get to know the area better. I can drop Christine outside Montsauche on the way back and then pick her up again.'

'OK. But no heroics, Christine, understand? Xavier will tell you whom to contact. It shouldn't be difficult to find someone who can tell us what we need to know. Everyone will have been asking the same questions. Then you come straight back here. OK?'

'OK.' Christine sat back.

As the meeting broke up, Luke drew her aside. 'Chris, I wish you wouldn't.'

'Wouldn't what?'

'Volunteer yourself for jobs like that.'

'You've just volunteered yourself for something much more dangerous,' she pointed out.

'I know, but . . .'

'But what?'

'I feel responsible. Well, I am responsible.'

'We're responsible for each other,' she said, with sudden warmth. 'But that doesn't mean we can sit back and let other people do all the dangerous things. And don't tell me it's different because I'm a girl. It's being a girl that makes it less dangerous. You do see that, don't you?'

He sighed. 'I suppose so. But do take care.'

'I could say the same to you. We must both be as careful as we can, under the circumstances.'

The sabotage contingent set off the following morning in two cars. Gregoire led the way in the Mercedes, with Luke, and his two bodyguards, and the four men he had chosen followed in the most serviceable of the two Peugeots. Loaded into the boots of the two vehicles, was a quantity of plastic explosive and a selection of connecting wires and time pencils. Luke was uncomfortably aware that if they were to be stopped and searched, there was no chance that they could pass themselves off as innocent farmers. They headed north, along forest tracks or narrow lanes until they saw the great cathedral of Vézelay towering above them on its hilltop. Here, they had to cross the main road to Avallon, which was in regular use by German patrols. Gregoire stopped the car and went forward on foot. He stood for a moment, peering in either direction, then at his signal Fernand accelerated forward and slowed just enough for Gregoire to jump aboard.

'Turn right! We've got a kilometre to cover before we can turn off again. Put your foot down!'

At top speed, the Mercedes roared along the road. Looking back, Luke saw the Peugeot struggling to keep up. Mercifully, the road was deserted, but he felt as if he was holding his breath until they swerved left into a narrow lane no wider than a cart track and, with a whine of gears the Peugeot swung in behind them.

In the woods outside the tiny village of Blannay, they were flagged down by three bearded men, who identified themselves as Jean and two of his *Maquis*.

'A convoy went through just after dawn today,' Jean told them. 'They seem to keep to a pretty regular schedule and we know there is another one on its way, so you can expect it about the same time tomorrow.'

'Ideal!' said Gregoire. 'Jump in. You can show us the way.'

A few miles further on, they found themselves looking down on a narrow road winding through the forest. They left the cars parked in the shelter of the trees, guarded by two of Jean's men, and worked along the hillside from one vantage point to another while Gregoire studied the road through his field glasses.

'That's our best bet,' he said eventually. 'See that line of tall poplars where the road leaves the forest? If we can bring them down it will take the *Boche* quite a long time to clear them all.' He glanced at his watch. 'There's nothing more we can do now until dark. We may as well go back to the cars and relax for a while. We shan't get much sleep tonight.'

Several miles to the south, Cyrano, with Christine sitting beside him, drove up to the front of the *château* of Lentilly. It was typical of its type, with an elegant grey stone facade topped by pointed towers at each end, surrounded by a moat and set in a formal garden, which now showed signs of neglect.

'M. de Labrier was killed in the fighting before France capitulated,' Cyrano explained. 'Madame has never forgiven the Vichy government for giving in and rendering his sacrifice useless. That's why she is a fervent supporter of the Resistance. Come along, I'll introduce you.'

They found Madame de Labrier in a salon decorated with silk wallpaper and Louis Quinze furniture, but she herself presented a much more down-to-earth image, dressed in rather shabby tweeds and carrying a pair of secateurs.

'M. Cyrano! We were not expecting you. Forgive my appearance. I was busy pruning the roses. Have you come to give Colette a lesson?'

'No, Madame. We have come to ask for your assistance.'

Without going into details about Christine's background, he explained that she had been forced to leave her own clothes behind and was in need of the loan of something more suitable than her current attire. 'I think Colette is very much the same build as she is,' he concluded. 'I wondered if she might be able to help.'

'Of course!' was the immediate response. 'I will call her. I'm sure we can find something that will do very well.'

At her mother's summons, a slim, dark-haired girl appeared from the garden and Christine was introduced. When the problem was explained to her she caught hold of her hand.

'You poor thing! It must be horrible to lose everything like that. Come upstairs. I'm sure I've got things that will fit you perfectly.'

In her bedroom, she pulled open a wardrobe.

'I haven't got anything very up-to-date, I'm afraid. With clothes rationing, it's impossible to keep up with fashion. But you're welcome to anything you like.'

'I don't need anything fashionable,' Christine said. 'I just want to look . . . well, ordinary. So no one will notice me.'

'Oh?' Colette looked puzzled for a moment. Then she said, 'Of course. You're with the *Maquis*. I should have realized when Cyrano brought you here. How brave of you! Well, let's see what we can find.'

It was obvious that before the war and the advent of clothes rationing, Colette had acquired an extensive wardrobe and she pulled out garment after garment, laying them out on the bed for Christine to examine. It took a little persuasion to make her understand that most of her offerings were too good, too expensive looking, to serve the purpose; but eventually they settled on a simple blue pinafore dress with a white blouse and a grey and green plaid skirt with a dark green blouse. She put on the dress and Colette exclaimed:

'Oh, it suits you! You look better in it than I ever did. Now, what about shoes? It's too warm for those boots now.'

Christine's feet were larger than hers, but a search produced a well-worn pair of sandals that could be adjusted to fit; and Colette insisted on providing her with underclothes and ankle socks as well. Eventually, feeling unusually self-conscious, she made her way downstairs to where Cyrano was waiting with Mme de Labrier. She saw his eyes widen as she appeared.

'Well, look at you! You look great!' He took her hand and spun her round, laughing, and she found herself responding with the kind of girlish giggles she would have despised in anyone else.

In the hall on the way out, she had a sudden thought.

'Madame, do you have a shopping basket I could borrow?'

The basket was quickly forthcoming and with it, a small handbag.

'You must have something to carry your money in, and your papers and your ration card,' Madame pointed out.

Christine transferred the items from the pockets of her dungarees and, on reflection, left her penknife and the other bits and pieces she had carried with her since she left home where they were. They hardly fitted with the new image she wanted to present, and there was always the possibility of being searched.

Back in the car, Cyrano said, 'Do you have any money? If you are going to go shopping you will need some.'

'Not much,' she confessed, and he reached into a pocket and handed her ten francs.

As they approached the outskirts of Montsauche, they were suddenly confronted by a German road block.

Cyrano said quickly, 'You have your papers, don't you? If they ask why you are here, you are visiting Mme de Labrier. Make out she's a relative of some kind.'

A bored soldier took their identity cards and glanced from the photographs on them to their faces.

'Where have you come from?' he enquired in heavily accented French.

'From the *château* of Lantilly.'

'What was your business there?'

'I am a music teacher. I was giving a piano lesson to the daughter of Mme de Labrier, the *châtelaine*.'

'Where are you going?'

'I am going to Duns-les-Places to see another of my pupils. Mademoiselle here is going shopping in Montsauche, so I offered her a lift.'

The soldier transferred his attention to Christine.

'You don't come from these parts. What are you doing here?'

'I'm visiting Mme de Labrier. She is my godmother.'

He handed back their documents without comment and waved them on. Neither of them spoke for a moment.

Then she said, 'Well, that seemed to work OK.'

'Yes,' Cyrano agreed, 'but it tells us something. The men of the *Maquis* can't drive around the area with impunity any longer. They will either need a very good cover story or someone will have to scout ahead to check for road blocks.'

He dropped her at the edge of the town, saying, 'I'll be back to pick you up in an hour. Try not to be late.'

Christine took her shopping basket and strolled as casually as she could manage down the main street of the old town. The swastika flew over the Town Hall and German soldiers were everywhere. Sentries stood on guard outside the entrance and an armoured car was parked opposite. Other soldiers, off duty, were sitting at the pavement cafés or strolling through the streets. She joined the queue outside the butcher's shop, trying to eavesdrop on the conversations of the other women waiting. There were plenty of grumbles about the presence of the Germans, but no concrete information.

When she reached the head of the queue, she bought the small piece of *boudin noir* to which her ration card entitled her, and said quietly, 'Xavier sends his greetings.'

She saw his expression change and he glanced quickly around the shop.

'Give my regards to Xavier and tell him it is not convenient for him to visit at this time.'

'I'll tell him,' she promised and turned away, feeling she had learned nothing she did not already know.

At a café round the corner, she ordered a lemonade and when the proprietor served her she repeated the mantra she had been given. 'Xavier sends his greetings.'

This time the reaction was more helpful.

'You come from Xavier?'

'Yes. He has sent me to find out what is going on.'

'We're overrun with *Boche*, that's what.'

'I can see that. Do you have any idea why they are here?'

'They are looking for the *Maquis*. Already they have interrogated the mayor and all the members of the council. They are threatening reprisals if the *Maquis* commit any more acts of what they call terrorism.'

'Will anyone tell them what they want to know?'

'Never.' He raised his eyebrows and his hands in a gesture of innocent puzzlement. '*Maquis*? What *Maquis*? We know nothing about any *Maquis*.'

'Have they said how long they are staying?'

'Who knows? Maybe they will decide they've hit a dead end and move on. But for God's sake tell Xavier to keep his head down for a bit. We don't need him making the buggers angry.'

'One more thing. Have you seen any radio detector vans about? They would have big aerials on top.'

The man shrugged. 'Never seen anything like that around here.'

She finished her drink and paid, and set off to explore the rest of the town. On a street corner, two German soldiers were lounging against the wall, smoking. As she approached, two young women attempted to pass them but with one coordinated movement they blocked the pavement. Christine heard them saying something. She could not tell what it was but the reaction of the two women gave her a pretty good clue. They both ducked their heads, stepped aside and scurried off down the road. As she drew nearer, the men performed the same manoeuvre and one, the older of the two, said, in execrable French:

'*Bonjour, mam'selle. Voulez-vous coucher avec moi?*' and gave vent to a bray of laughter, like a schoolboy passing on a dirty joke. Christine guessed it was probably the only French phrase he knew.

Instead of side-stepping and ignoring him, she gave him a level stare and said, 'Give me one good reason why I should want to sleep with a brute like you.'

He gawped at her and it was obvious that he had not understood. Not so his companion, who addressed her in good French.

'Please excuse my friend, Mademoiselle. He has no manners. But we are not all brutes. Some of us are actually quite human, and we long for a bit of feminine company. Would there be any point in my asking if I can buy you a drink?'

Her first reaction was to say that she would never dream of fraternising with the enemy, but she looked at his face and something made her pause. He was very young, younger than Luke probably, and something in his eyes told her that he was lonely and probably frightened. Besides which, it occurred to her that this might be useful.

'Not today,' she said. 'But I have the afternoon off on Saturday. I might be able to meet you then. If you're still here, that is.'

His lips parted in surprise. He looked like a child who has been given an unexpected present.

'Oh, we'll be here, no doubt about that. Next Saturday? That would be wonderful! Oh, my name is Franz, by the way.'

'I can't promise,' she hedged. 'But you can wait for me here next Saturday, if you like.'

Across the street, two older women glared at her and one of them hissed 'Whore!'

Christine ignored them.

'I have to go now,' she said, and the two men stepped aside without demur.

'Till Saturday!' the one called Franz called after her. She hurried on without looking back. Her mind was whirling. Did she really intend to meet him? Was it even possible? And what purpose would it serve? But at least she had one piece of information: the Germans would be in Montsauche at least until the end of the week.

The afternoon was warm, and normally it would have been pleasant to lounge in the shade, but none of them felt able to rest. Gregoire got the explosives out of the boot and carefully made up a series of charges. Then they moved the cars to a position closer to their objective. From that point, it was necessary to proceed on foot. As the sun went down, they ate the provisions they had brought with them and Gregoire distributed the equipment among the men.

'What do you want me to take?' Luke asked.

'Nothing,' was the reply. 'Your job is to stay here and guard the vehicles. We don't want to get back and find someone has gone off with them.'

'No! Let me come with you. Please! Can't someone else stay on guard?'

Gregoire looked at him severely. 'I allowed you to join in on the understanding that you would obey orders without question. Remember? I've given you an order. That's the end of it.' He paused and went on more gently, 'Someone has to keep an eye on the cars. This job shouldn't take much more than an hour, but don't worry if it turns out to be more like two.' He looked at his watch. 'It's coming up to ten o'clock. We should be back by midnight at the latest. If we're not here by dawn, take one of the cars and get back to the Bois de Montsauche and tell Xavier. You can drive, can't you?'

'Oh yes,' Luke said. He had driven a car belonging to a neighbour a couple of times, but he was by no means sure that he could drive either of the vehicles they had come in — even supposing he could find his way back to the *Maquis* camp.

'Right.' Gregoire picked up his pack. 'Let's move. See you later, Luke.'

There was no more to be said. Bitterly disappointed, Luke watched the others move off into the growing darkness. Initially, he could hear the occasional crunch of pebbles underfoot or the rustle of fallen leaves, but soon those sounds faded and he was completely alone. He moved a short distance away from the cars and found a dip in the ground screened by bracken from which he could look down onto the pale ribbon of road. There was no sign of movement, but with the curfew in place that was to be expected.

Time passed with frustrating slowness and he found himself checking his watch every ten minutes. Now that his ears were attuned to the night-time sounds of the forest, he could hear faint rustles and snufflings; an owl hooted somewhere nearby and made him jump and then, even more disturbing though further off, came the blood-chilling scream of a vixen on heat. Then silence fell again.

Luke was getting chilled and cramped, and his eyes were beginning to feel heavy. He shifted his position. The last thing he wanted was for Gregoire to get back and find him asleep at his post. He looked at his watch again. Five minutes to eleven. The others should be back soon.

Suddenly all drowsiness was banished and he literally felt the muscles behind his ears twitch. Far away, down on the road, he could hear an engine. He craned forward. Round a bend away to his right, an open car appeared, heading towards Voutenay: the area where Gregoire and the others were operating. Even in the moonlight, there was no mistaking who the vehicle belonged to. He could see the light reflecting faintly off the helmets of four German soldiers, and the outline of a gun of some sort.

For a moment, Luke's head spun. If the car continued on its way, it might catch Gregoire and his men in the act of laying the explosives. They would hear it coming, of course, but would they be able to conceal themselves and their equipment in time? Could he do something to stop it? He raised his rifle and drew back the bolt. He could perhaps take out one or two of the enemy, if he was lucky, but the others would come after him and he was not sure he could hold them off for long. And they would summon reinforcements; dogs, too, probably.

Then he had an inspiration. He rested the rifle on the rim of the bank and took careful aim. He remembered what he had learned when his father had taken him pigeon shooting before the war. That was with a shotgun, of course, but the principal of shooting a moving object was the same. Estimate speed and distance and fire a little ahead of the target. He aimed, held his breath and squeezed the trigger.

He saw the car swerve and skid to a standstill, its front nearside tyre flattened, and let out a silent whoop of triumph. The four men jumped out and he could hear them swearing, their voices carrying clearly on the night air, as they examined the damage. None of them looked in his direction. As he had hoped, the sound of the bursting tyre had masked the crack of the rifle. Then, somewhat belatedly, two of them took up defensive positions with their Schmeisser automatics at the ready, while the other two changed the wheel.

Luke looked at his watch again. 11.15pm. Gregoire and his men must have finished their work by now surely, and be on their way back. The Germans were working very efficiently. It would not take them long to get the new wheel on. What should he do if they were ready to move off and Gregoire was still not back? If he tried another shot, they would undoubtedly return fire and his rifle was no match for their automatic weapons.

The wheel was on, but to Luke's relief, the Germans leaned against the bonnet and lit up cigarettes, obviously convinced that they were in no danger. He was concentrating so fiercely on them that he did not hear the noise of his companions returning until Gregoire dropped into the hollow beside him. He swung round in a panic, bringing his rifle to bear at short range, but Gregoire pushed the barrel aside.

'Easy! It's only me. Fine sentry you are! I could have made off with one of the cars by now.'

'I was watching them!' Luke explained defensively. 'I was afraid they were going to get started again and catch you in the act.'

'They might well have done,' Gregoire agreed. 'What stopped them? A puncture? That was a bit of luck.'

Luke removed his rifle from the other man's grasp and directed it towards the Germans on the road. 'It wasn't a puncture.'

'What?' Gregoire leaned closer and stared into his face. 'Are you telling me you shot the tyre out on a moving vehicle?'

'It was a fluke,' Luke mumbled, disconcerted by the intense examination.

'A fluke?' Gregoire sat back with a low chuckle and slapped him on the shoulder. 'It was bloody good shooting, that's what it was! Forget what I said just now. You've done a good job.' He squirmed back out of the hollow. 'Come on. Let's get going.'

'Did you get the explosives in place?' Luke asked.

Gregoire nodded. 'They're on five-hour time pencils, so they should go off,' he consulted his watch, 'just before dawn.'

'Oh,' Luke said. 'I was hoping they might go up just as the Germans were going through.'

'No, we don't want that. If the ambush is going to work, the obstruction has to come as a surprise. Hopefully, our Jerry friends will be safely in their barracks and none the wiser when the balloon goes up.' He swung himself into the driving seat of the lead car and turned over his shoulder to the two men in the rear seat. 'Meet our new sharp-shooter. I bet neither of you could hit a target the size and speed of an elephant, let alone a single tyre on a moving vehicle.'

As they drove back along the forest tracks, Luke had the satisfaction of hearing his feat described to an appreciative audience, with the knowledge that it would be all round the camp by morning. He was just beginning to doze off when the car came to a halt.

'With any luck,' Gregoire said, getting out, 'we should get a grandstand view of the fireworks from here.'

214

They were parked on a ridge and the ground fell away from them in the direction of the road. Gregoire looked at his watch.

'OK. There's nothing we can do now but wait for dawn.'

The night seemed interminable. Luke dozed and woke and dozed again. He was jerked into wakefulness by a voice.

'Listen!'

Luke scrambled out of the car and stretched. Gregoire and the rest were huddled together, all their heads turned towards the west. For a moment, he could hear nothing, then he became aware of a low throb, the sound of heavy engines a long way off.

'They're coming!' one of the men said. 'Why haven't the explosives gone off?'

Gregoire looked at his watch. 'Any minute now. But at this length of delay, those time pencils are notoriously unreliable.'

Luke looked to the east, where the first streaks of light were gilding some low cloud.

'The convoy has made better time than we expected,' Gregoire said. 'Let's hope the message got through to the RAF as planned.'

As he spoke, there was a flash from somewhere below them and then a low rumble; then in rapid succession, a series of other flashes, followed by the boom of explosions. The men around Luke gave a cheer and Gregoire turned to them with a grin of satisfaction.

'Well done, chaps! That should hold the *Boche* up for quite a while.'

All the time, the growl of the engines had grown louder and soon they could see the convoy winding its way through the trees.

'*Mon Dieu!*' someone exclaimed. 'That is not a boat. It's a ship!'

'Where are the planes?' someone else asked anxiously.

'They'll be here,' Gregoire promised.

Below them, there was sound of brakes being engaged and gears grinding. Then, there were shouts and they saw men jumping out of the escorting armoured cars and throwing themselves flat beside the road, rifles at the ready.

'They are expecting a *Maquis* ambush,' Gregoire said with a chuckle. 'They're in for a nasty surprise.'

In tense silence, they watched the activity on the road. There was a sound of sawing and one of the tractors hauling the boat was uncoupled and brought forward.

'It won't take them long to clear the road with that,' Fernand muttered.

Gregoire was holding the S-phone transceiver to his ear. Suddenly it crackled into life and a voice spoke through the static.

'Foxhunter to Hound. Are you receiving me? Over.'

'They're here!' Gregoire said. 'Hound to Foxhunter, receiving you loud and clear. Please state your position. Over.'

There followed a rapid exchange of map co-ordinates and estimated distances, then quite suddenly the planes appeared, three of them, flying so low that they seemed to be skimming the tree tops.

'Foxhunter to Hound. I have visual on the target. Going in for the kill. Over.'

They watched as the planes changed formation into line astern and swooped over the road. There was a crackle of machine-gun fire and rifle fire in return, and then three loud explosions.

'Bullseye!' came the voice over the S-phone.

The planes pulled up and circled, and then came in for a second run. This time, the watchers could see the tracer bullets striking the escorting vehicles in the convoy and one of the tractors burst into flames.

'Foxhunter to Hound. Job done. Turning for home now. Over.'

'Hound to Foxhunter. Bloody good show! Well done. Give our love to Blighty. Out.'

They stood in silence until the planes had disappeared, then Gregoire yawned. 'Come on chaps. This may not be very healthy neighbourhood once the Huns get over their surprise. Time to head for home.'

CHAPTER 18

Luke slept most of the way home and it was not until he had devoured the meal that Jacques had waiting for them, that he went to look for his sister. He found her kneeling by the pool below the spring, scrubbing at her dungarees with a piece of soap. With her back to him, it took him a moment to recognize the dark-haired girl in the green blouse.

'Chris?' he said, with a hint of doubt.

She looked up sharply and got to her feet.

'Ah-ha! The hero of the hour! Good afternoon.'

'Don't know what you mean,' he mumbled.

She laughed. 'Yes, you do. The story of your sharp-shooting is all round the camp. Well done, *chéri*.'

'It really was just luck,' he protested. 'I see you got some proper clothes at last.'

'It's like wearing a uniform, really,' she said. 'I need it to blend in. But I still don't feel right in a skirt.'

'Well, you look right,' he told her. 'In fact you look very nice.'

'Well!' she said. 'That's a first! I can't remember you ever paying me a compliment before.'

He grinned. 'Well, don't start expecting it to happen regularly.' Then he added seriously, 'Did you go into town?'

'Yes, and it's full of Jerries.' She told him briefly what she had found out, omitting the encounter with the young German. She had told no one about that, so far.

Over the days that followed, changes began to occur in the camp. The *Maquis* numbers were swollen by young men from all around the area, escaping the STO and more importantly, they were joined by two ex-army officers who had decided to throw in their lot with the Resistance. Their arrival caused some discord in the camp as they, not unnaturally, felt that they were better qualified to lead than Xavier, the blacksmith.

Christine and Luke were aware of several tense conferences at which Gregoire was acting as mediator before the issue was resolved. Xavier remained the leader of the group but accepted the two newcomers as advisers on military matters. The men were organized into sections of ten, each with a leader, and training became much more intense.

One day, Gergoire arrived in the camp with a stranger, who he introduced as Dr Martel.

'The doctor has left his practice in Orleans to throw in his lot with us,' he told them. 'He will be setting up a hospital for all the *Maquis* groups in the area at the Château de Vermot. I have requested a drop of medical supplies and he is looking for volunteers among the local women to act as nurses.'

Xavier had found a new, more accessible, dropping zone, as Gregoire had requested, in the woods not far from the village of Quarré les Tombes, so called because of the strange sarcophagi in its churchyard. One night, there was a *parachutage* which provided them with heavier and more sophisticated weapons. A local farmer lent a cart and a team of oxen to carry the containers to the camp, where the contents were unloaded and the containers themselves put to use as storage, while the parachute silk was cut up and distributed to be made into sleeping bags. Many of the members of the group had worked in the timber industry, and soon solidly built log huts began to replace the makeshift tents and shelters. Gregoire was well on the way to achieving his aim of transforming a rag-tag collection of undisciplined amateurs into a useful fighting force.

With the German presence in the area and the frequent patrols and road blocks, it became much more difficult to obtain food supplies. There were still outlying farms which would provide eggs and milk, and sometimes a ham or a chicken or two, or even a sheep; but Christine found herself making regular trips into Montsauche or some of the other small towns, armed with forged ration cards, to collect essential items. She could not be seen carrying the quantities required for so many people, so she often shopped in two or three different villages, lugging her loaded basket to pre-arranged rendezvous where Cyrano would pick her up.

She did not keep her appointment with Franz. It was not that she was afraid that he intended her any harm; but the reaction of the two women who had called her a whore held her back. She had heard how suspected collaborators were treated and she did not want to risk the same fate for herself.

A day or two after the *parachutage*, she returned to the camp with disturbing news.

'The *Boche* know about the *parachutage*. They descended on Quarré in force and arrested the mayor and his deputy. They are threatening reprisals if the locals don't tell them where to find us.'

Gregoire shook his head grimly. 'I'm afraid there is nothing we can do about that. We shall just have to hope the villagers remain loyal, but I fear for the consequences for them.'

'But they haven't done anything wrong,' Christine said in distress. 'We can't let them suffer.'

'What can we do to prevent it?' he asked. 'Any form of resistance is going to provoke reprisals. The alternative is to give the Germans free run over the whole country. I'm sorry Christine, but these are the grim facts of war. Sometimes innocent people have to be sacrificed for the greater good.'

One day Gregoire took Christine and Luke aside, his face serious.

'Christine, I want to make a suggestion to you, but please bear in mind that it is only a suggestion. You are not obliged to agree to it.'

She looked at him with some trepidation.

'What is it?'

'Have you ever heard the term "*femme de liaison*"?'

Her anxiety increased. There was something in the phrase that suggested immorality.

'No.'

He smiled briefly. 'It's not what you are thinking. In areas where the *Maquis* operate, they often employ local women and girls as messengers. They are people who are part of the local community and who can move around without inviting suspicion. In that way they can observe what the enemy is doing, where there are road blocks, where there are movements of troops that might suggest an attack, that kind of thing, and then feed that information back to the *Maquis*. In that way they perform an invaluable service.'

'But isn't that what I have been doing?' she asked.

'Indeed it is. What I am suggesting is an extension of that. At the moment, you rely on Cyrano to take you into Montsauche or wherever and he already takes enough risks. The explanation that he just happened to be giving you a lift worked well once, but if he was stopped again with you in the car, it would look suspicious. No, hear me out!' This to Cyrano, who was listening and seemed about to protest. 'Also, you do not have an address or an adequate cover story to explain your presence in the area. As I said, the ideal "*femme de liaison*" is an embedded part of the local community.' He paused and looked into her face. 'What I am going to ask you to do will not be easy for you. I know that. I am suggesting that you take up residence at the Beau Rivage. Madame Bolu is prepared to employ you as a waitress and general help, so that if you are questioned, you can give a credible account of yourself. She will also send you on various errands — she will be able to concoct reasons for them — which will enable you to move around the area, keeping your eyes and ears open as you go. So, that's the idea. What do you think?'

'You mean I wouldn't live here, in the camp, anymore?'

'Yes. I know that isn't easy to accept. But I'm sure you will be made very welcome at the Beau Rivage. I think Jeanette Bolu must be about the same age as you. Perhaps it would be nice for you to have some feminine company.'

Christine lowered her eyes. The last person whose company she wanted was the girl who had flirted so openly with Cyrano, among others.

Luke cut in. 'No! I don't like the idea at all. Chris and I should stick together.'

'But you are happy to go off on missions and leave her here,' Gregoire pointed out.

'That's different. She's safe here.'

'But she already goes down into the villages on her own. If she was stopped and questioned, she might have difficulty explaining herself. This way, I am giving her a cover story that should convince the *Boche* that she is genuine.'

'What about the story she told before, about being Mme de Labrier's god-daughter?'

'She would still need to be staying there and Lentilly is not sufficiently central. She would have to make long trips on bicycle to report.'

'So I should come back here to report,' she said hopefully.

Gregoire shook his head. 'No. One of the principles of running a successful circuit is that none of the members should have direct contact with any others. That's another reason why I don't want you to have to rely on Cyrano. We will set up what we call a "dead drop", a place where you can leave a message, which he can pick up on the way to or from his pupils' houses.'

'So I wouldn't see . . . any of you?' There was a quaver in her voice that she tried unsuccessfully to repress.

'There are places we could meet,' Cyrano said. He turned to Gregoire, who was shaking his head. 'We would need to do that if Christine had anything important to report. There isn't time to teach her an elaborate code. What we need is a simple message that conveys the fact that she has some information and gives a time and place for a meeting.'

'Where would you suggest?' Gregoire asked.

'I already go to practise the organ in two different churches. Duns-Les-Places on Tuesday evenings and Montsauche on Fridays. All Chris would need to do is leave a message saying something along the lines of "meet me on Tuesday" and I would be there. Nobody would think there was anything suspicious about a young girl going to church. And if by any chance someone else read the message, it would just seem like some kind of lovers' tryst.'

Gregoire nodded thoughtfully.

'Yes, that sounds pretty foolproof. OK. What do you think, Christine?'

'I'll do it!' She did not pause to consider the full implications. The idea of secret meetings with Cyrano, even if the romantic implications were fictional, was too tempting to resist.

'No!' Luke said again. 'It's too risky. If something happened to her we wouldn't know. We might not find out for days.'

'OK. Here's an idea,' Gregoire said. 'Suppose we agree that every day Christine will leave a sign of some sort in the dead drop. It could be something as simple as a scrap of paper with that day's date on it. Cyrano will check the drop daily. That way you will have the reassurance that she is still safe. And there's something else.' He took a piece of paper from his pocket and handed it to Christine. 'Memorize this phone number and then burn the paper. If you should ever feel that you are in danger, or if you simply don't feel you can carry on any longer, for whatever reason, ring that number and someone will come and get you. Just say, "I want to come home". Does that help to allay your fears, Luke?'

'I suppose so,' he said unwillingly.

'Christine?'

'Yes. Don't worry about me. I'll be fine.' She turned to Cyrano. 'There's just one thing. Could you ask the BBC to broadcast another message? I know Maman will be worrying. Just ask them to say: "Michou's pups are still safe".'

Next day, Cyrano drove her down into the valley. He took her first to a ruined building at the side of the road between Montsauche and Duns. It had once, she imagined, been home to a shepherd or a forester but the roof had fallen in and the interior was deep in nettles and smelled of urine and animal dung.

'Sorry about the pong,' he said. 'It's the sort of place people find handy if they're caught short, which is why no one would ask too many questions if they saw you or me coming out. Now, look.' He reached up to a small space between the wall and what remained of a rafter and withdrew a tobacco tin. 'If you have a message for me, or if you are just leaving the date as we agreed, put it in here. I will come by every afternoon to check.'

'What sort of messages?' she queried. 'I mean apart from the one saying I need to meet you.'

'You know the kind of information we need. Are the *Boche* searching a particular area, or are there checkpoints on certain roads? And I may need to ask you to find out specific things, like is it safe for a mission to set out along a particular route.'

'But we can't just put that sort of thing in words anyone could understand,' she objected.

'No, we need to have some kind of code. I was thinking, if the message about meeting is going to sound like a clandestine love affair, why don't we pursue that idea. For example, if I want to know if the road to Marigny is safe I could leave a note saying: "I have to go to Marigny. Can you meet me there?"'

'And if it isn't I could reply: "I can't get away to meet you. Father is watching me."'

'Yes, that's good. "Father" could be our code word for the Germans. So "Father has gone to Planchez" would mean the *Boche* are there.'

She looked at him and saw that his eyes were sparkling. Was it amusement, or delight at their combined ingenuity — or something else? All she knew was that they were sharing a joke.

She grinned back at him. 'Yes, that's good.'

He drove her next to the church at Duns-les-Places.

'The *curé* here is a supporter. He holds confession every Monday and Thursday evenings. If you need to get an urgent message to me tell him in the confessional. He will make sure I get it.'

Finally, he drove her to the Beau Rivage, where Madame Bolu was waiting.

'Come in, *chérie*! It's good to see you again. Jeanette has been asking what has happened to you. She's quite excited at the idea that you are going to stay for a while.'

Jeanette came in from the kitchen.

'*Salut*, Christine! Oh, I like you in that dress! I felt so sorry for you in those horrible dungarees. Doesn't she look smart, Maman?'

'Take Christine upstairs and show her her room,' her mother said. 'But don't be too long. I need you to help serve the lunch. You can show Christine what to do.' She smiled at her. 'You may as well start to learn the job. We need you to be convincing. Are you staying to eat with us, M. Cyrano?'

Cyrano shook his head. 'No, Madame. Thank you for the invitation, but I have to get on.' He turned to Christine and took her hand. 'Are you quite clear about everything?'

She nodded, her throat suddenly tight.

'Good luck, then. I'm sure we'll be meeting again very soon. Goodbye, Madame. Thank you for your help. France will be grateful.'

With a smile and a squeeze of her hand, he was gone, and she found herself abruptly cut off from everything that had become familiar over the last weeks. It was much harder than she had imagined it would be.

Jeanette led her up to the private apartments on the top floor and opened a door.

'This is your room. I wasn't sure if you would have all your own things, so I've laid out a nightdress and there are some undies in the drawer. The bathroom is next door and I've put a toothbrush and some soap on the shelf. Is there anything else you need?'

Christine hesitated. It was almost a month since she had left home and there was one necessity that was becoming ever more pressing.

'Some S.T.s,' she mumbled.

'Oh, that's no problem. I've got some in my room. I'll fetch them.'

Left alone, Christine looked round the room. It was prettily decorated, with floral wallpaper and a patchwork quilt in pastel colours, and there was a vase of fresh flowers on the dressing table. She glanced into the bathroom; a large fluffy towel was hanging on the rail.

She felt a lump in her throat. Until now she had not been homesick. Life on the boat and in the camp had been so different that home had seemed to belong to another life. Now, she was vividly reminded of her own room, with its familiar comforts, and her mother's voice calling her to come and eat.

She washed her hands and splashed her face with cold water and by the time Jeanette returned, she had recovered herself.

In the Bois de Montsauche, the *Maquis Xavier* was continuing its reorganization. With the arrival of enemy troops in the area, security had become a priority. Xavier set up guard posts at the beginning of all the tracks leading up to the camp, which were manned night and day on a regular rota. Gregoire showed them how to set up trip wires on the narrower paths, attached to small explosive charges which would go off and alert them to the presence of intruders; but these had to be abandoned after a few days since they were regularly set off by the wild animals that inhabited the forest. After the whole camp had been jolted awake and leapt to arms in the middle of the night two or three times, it was decided that the explosives should only be connected up if there was an imminent threat of attack.

Training continued, with the help of the two regular officers and the acquisition of more heavy weapons, partly from another *parachutage* and partly as a result of an ambush on the road to Château-Chinon. Luke found himself learning to use both a Bren gun and the German Schmeisser.

Gregoire's main objective was still the sabotage of German lines of communication and to this end, he selected a small group for more intensive training in the use of explosives and Luke was delighted to be one of those chosen. Their first objective was the railway between Decize and Auxerre at Tamnay, where the line branched towards Château-Chinon. They set out late one afternoon, intending to reach their target around midnight. There were seven of them, in two vehicles; Jean-Claude's butcher's van and a pick-up truck with a Bren gun mounted in the back. Luke, to his great pleasure, was put in charge of the Bren. They took the minor road through Ouroux and on towards Montigny.

Coming to the edge of the forest they were brought up short by a barricade of tree trunks across the road. Luke swung the Bren round to cover it, while rifle barrels appeared from the car windows; but to their relief a voice hailed them in French.

'*Qui-vive?*'

'*Maquis!*' Gregoire shouted back, and half a dozen friendly faces appeared over the barrier. They had run into the edge of territory controlled by a new group; this was the *Maquis Socrate* and they were soon introduced to its leader, a good-looking young man who was delighted to make the acquaintance of the 'famous' Gregoire.

'Not too famous, I hope,' Gregoire murmured.

Bottles of wine appeared from somewhere, and they all drank to victory and 'death to the *Boche*', and then the barrier was dismantled and they were on their way again.

The next hazard was the level crossing, where the line to Château-Chinon crossed the road just outside Chougny.

It was dark by this time and the barriers were down. There were lights showing through the cracks in the blinds at the window of the crossing-keeper's house, but there was no way of knowing what the man's attitude would be to two vehicles breaking the curfew for no good reason. It was possible also, that he was not alone. The Germans had conscripted a number of men known as *Gardesvoies*, whose job it was to patrol the lines watching for signs of sabotage. It was likely that they had no more sympathy with the Nazis than the *Maquis*, but threatened with draconian punishment if anything went wrong on their stretch of line they could not be relied upon to cooperate. There might even be German guards manning the crossing, and with the van packed with explosives they could not afford to be stopped and searched.

Alphonse, one of the older men, got out of the truck and went to knock on the door. They heard him call, '*Ouvrez la barrière, s'il vous plaît.*'

There was a tense pause, then the door opened and Luke heard a low-voiced exchange between the two men. Finally, the heavy wooden barrier creaked up. Gregoire let in the clutch and Alphonse jumped aboard as they bumped across the lines, with the van close behind.

They stopped eventually just outside Tamnay and gathered around Gregoire for a final briefing.

'I will take Jean-Claude and Pierre with me. Our target will be the engine turntable just outside the station. Alphonse, you and Francois deal with the points where the lines diverge. Luke and Raoul, I want you to work your way down the line a hundred yards or so towards Decize. Alphonse and I will set our time pencils for a one-hour delay but I want you Luke, to fit yours with pressel switches. Once the damage has been done to the points, the first thing to come down the line will be an engine pulling trucks carrying repair equipment. Your charges will take care of that and make it even longer before the track can be made usable again. Understood?' There was a murmur of agreement. 'OK. Rendezvous back here at 01.00 hours.'

Luke collected what he needed from the van and he and Raoul loaded it into rucksacks and set off along the tracks. Raoul was one of the recent recruits, who had been co-opted on to the explosives team because he had been apprenticed to an electrician and pronounced himself adept at all kinds of wiring jobs. This was his first operation and Luke noticed that as they walked, he was glancing apprehensively around him. Twice he stopped abruptly and whispered 'What was that?'

Luke, listening, could hear nothing but the normal night-time sounds, but his companion's behaviour worried him. It was plain that he was extremely frightened. Luke considered his own emotions; he was excited, keyed-up to a point of extreme tension, but he was not scared. There seemed to be nothing to be afraid of at that moment.

As soon as they were clear of the station, Raoul said, 'This will do, won't it?'

Luke looked around. There seemed to be no reason to go further. He lowered his rucksack.

'OK. You start on that side. I'll do this.'

He began to unpack his gear, then stopped and looked up. Raoul was standing stock still, as if paralysed by fear.

Luke said, 'Come on, Raoul! The quicker we work, the sooner we can get out of here.'

The other man cast frantic glances to one side and then the other.

'It's my guts!' he whispered. 'I can't . . . I need . . . Sorry!' And with that, he made a dive for the side of the track, slithered down the embankment and disappeared among some bushes.

Luke stayed completely still for several minutes, listening for any sound that might suggest that Raoul's hasty departure had raised the alarm, but the night remained quiet. It was clear that Raoul had no intention of reappearing, so Luke set to work grimly. He had twice as much to do now, and enough time had been wasted. It crossed his mind that Raoul might be a traitor who had deliberately infiltrated the group, and might even now be alerting the local *Milice* to what was going on; but he had no grounds for assuming that, so he told himself that the sooner he got the job done, the less chance there was of being apprehended.

He crouched beside the track, withdrew a lump of *plastique* from his rucksack and began to wedge it between the sleeper ties and the rail. Once this was complete, he took out a fog signal and attached it to the rail. This was a small explosive charge which would be detonated by the wheels of the engine. Its original purpose was to warn drivers that there was some hazard ahead, but in this case it would be linked to a length of Cordtex, which would set off the larger explosive charge under the rails. He had almost completed the work when he heard the faint crunch of approaching footsteps.

'Raoul?' he called softly.

There was no response and the footsteps came closer. Luke jumped to his feet and grabbed his rifle.

'Who's there. Stop, or I fire!'

The steps halted and a voice from the darkness said, 'Take it easy. I'm on your side. I don't mean any harm.'

'Come here, where I can see you.' Luke's hands were shaking and he hoped that his voice did not betray his fear.

The newcomer walked forward and in the light of his torch, which lay on the rails where he had been working, Luke made out a solidly built figure wearing the armband of the *Gardes-voies*.

Luke said, 'There's nothing for you to do here. Push off, before you get your head blown off. My colleague will have you covered.'

There was a soft chuckle. 'No he won't. I heard him crashing down the embankment and when I last saw him he was skedaddling back towards the town as fast as his legs would carry him. That's what alerted me to your presence. Look, I meant it when I said I'm on your side.'

'Oh yes? That's why you're wearing that armband, I suppose.'

'This? You don't think I'd really work for those bastards, do you? I'm a railwayman. I work in the marshalling yard at Decize. I belong to the union and we are all one hundred per cent behind the Resistance. We've no quarrel with you fellows blowing holes in the tracks, we just don't fancy going up with them. So we patrol the tracks to keep an eye on what you are up to. Forewarned is forearmed. Right?'

'I see your point,' Luke said dubiously. 'OK. You've seen what I'm doing. Now you can make yourself scarce.'

The stranger looked down at the track.

'Fog signals, eh? So you are not just aiming to blow up the track. Has it occurred to you that the first train through here in the morning will be packed with civilians going to work?'

'No, it won't,' Luke said. 'It'll be a repair train going to make good the damage further up.'

The man glanced over his shoulder. 'Ah. So you're not working alone. Now I get the picture. A repair train? OK, fair enough. But you do realize that you're not laying that in the best place?'

'What do you mean?'

'You're not local, are you?'

'No.'

'I thought not. If you were, you'd know that about 200 yards further on the railway crosses the River Trait. Set your charges there and with any luck the engine and the trucks it is pulling will end up in the river. Have you got any more of that stuff?'

Raoul's discarded rucksack lay where he had dropped it. 'Yes,' Luke said.

'Come on then. I'll show you.'

The man picked up the rucksack and started down the track with it. Luke followed, his rifle at the ready. It was possible he was being led into an ambush, but his instinct told him otherwise. He remembered that some of the other *Maquisards* had told him that the railwaymen were supporters who could be relied on. After a short distance, the embankment fell away and he realized that they were on a bridge with the river below them. His companion walked to the middle of the bridge and stopped.

'Here should do nicely. You get busy. I'll keep watch.'

Luke looked around him. The rails gleamed faintly in the moonlight along the length of the bridge. There was nowhere to hide there and to either side there was only the void. It was a very unlikely place for an ambush. He took the rucksack from the other man and crouched down to insert the plastic explosive. His hands were cold and still shaking slightly and it seemed to take a long time to connect up the charge and the detonator. In the middle of doing it a sudden thought caused him to freeze.

'What?' the railwayman asked.

'I've just thought. The driver of the repair train will be a Frenchman, won't he? And his fireman?'

'I wondered if you'd thought about that.' A pause, then in a softer tone. 'Don't you worry about that, lad. I told you why I'm doing this job. I know all the drivers back at the depot. I'll find out who is going to drive the repair train and warn him. He and his mate can bail out over there, before the start of the bridge, and the engine will keep going under its own steam. You won't have them on your conscience.'

Luke looked up at him gratefully. 'Thanks. I'm glad you came along.' He finished connecting the charge and stood up. His watch told him that he had twenty minutes to get back to the rendezvous. 'I'd better get going.'

'Me, too.' The man stuck out his hand. '*Bonne chance, mon ami!*'

'Good luck to you, too,' Luke replied. He shouldered the two now empty rucksacks and turned to walk away. After a few paces, he looked back. It was still possible that the stranger was only waiting for him to leave before dismantling his work; or that he intended to head straight for the nearest phone to alert the authorities. But he was striding away along the track, in no apparent hurry. Luke calculated mentally; in less than an hour, the time pencils attached to the other charges would go off. So even if the man intended to betray the whereabouts of the one on the bridge, there was no chance that the others would be found before they exploded. He could only hurry back and hope that everything would go according to plan.

He set off as quickly as possible, keeping below the top of the embankment so that he did not present a target against the faint light from the sky. At the point where he had laid the first charge, he stopped and called softly, 'Raoul?'

There was no response. He called again, twice, then went on. The railwayman had said he saw Raoul heading for the town, but perhaps he was only making a detour in order to get back to the rendezvous. If not, the rest of the group could be in the hands of the Gestapo by now, but there had been no shooting and he did not believe that they could have been rounded up without at least one bullet being fired. Nevertheless, it was sensible to approach carefully. Heart thumping, he climbed the fence beside the track and edged his way up to the point on the road where they had left the vehicles. To his intense relief, a shadowy group of figures was standing near them. He drew breath and whistled softly, the musical phrase that they used as a recognition signal. Gregoire's voice came quietly from the group.

'Luke? Come on. Where the hell have you been? We began to think you'd got lost. Where's Raoul?'

Luke lifted his shoulders. 'I don't know. He got into a blue funk and ran off, just as we were about to start laying the charges. I thought he might have come back here.'

'*Merde!* No, we haven't seen him. Did you manage to lay the charges anyway?'

'Yes, but . . .'

'But what? No, never mind. Tell me later. If that little swine Raoul has gone rushing off to tell the authorities, they could be on us at any moment. Into the cars, everyone. Let's get out of here.'

The men scrambled back into the two vehicles and a minute later they were heading for the comforting shelter of the forest. As before, when they were well away, Gregoire stopped at a vantage point where they could look back into the valley.

'Any minute now,' he said, looking at his watch.

As he spoke there, was a bright flash and the roar of an explosion.

'That's the turntable,' he said, with grim satisfaction.

The big explosion was followed by a series of smaller ones.

'There go the points,' said Alphonse.

'I wish we could see mine go up,' Luke said wistfully.

Gregoire squeezed his arm. 'Never mind. I'll make sure someone goes to check tomorrow and I'll let you know the result. You were going to say something about it. You did set the charges correctly?'

'Yes, I'm pretty sure about that,' Luke said. 'It was where I set them that I wanted to tell you.' As briefly as possible, he described his encounter with the railway guard and the advice he had given him.

'Of course!' Gregoire said when he finished. 'I should have thought of that.'

When they got back to the camp, Luke's euphoria gave way to a sense of emptiness. When he had returned from previous missions, Christine had always been there to welcome him and ply him with questions; now she was gone. They had parted that afternoon in an offhand manner that was partly the product of English restraint, but largely due to Luke's disapproval of her decision and her determination to go ahead. Now he felt he had been ungenerous and wished he had given her a warmer send off.

Next day, Gregoire arrived back from one of his unexplained absences and slapped him on the shoulder.

'Total success! The bridge collapsed and the engine and two trucks ended up in the river. It will take Jerry days to repair the railway. So well done!'

CHAPTER 19

As the days passed, Christine settled into her new life at the *Beau Rivage*. Mme Bolu only required her to work in the evenings, when dinner had to be prepared and served to the little group of permanent residents, so she was free during the day. Jean-Claude dropped off her bike on the second evening, so from then on she spent most of her time cycling around the area. Madame played her part with enthusiasm, inventing errands that would take her to different places, as required by her new duties.

Every morning, she was careful to leave a note with that day's date and her initial in the tobacco tin in the ruined building and sometimes there would be a slip of paper waiting for her: *'Can we meet in Brassy tomorrow?'; 'I have to go to Ouroux. Can you meet me there?'*

Then she would set off on her bike to the place in question, watching out for German checkpoints on the way, and enquiring locally if there had been any signs of enemy activity. Sometimes the answering note which she left in the tin read: *'I could meet you tomorrow in the place you suggested'*. In that case, she usually heard via local gossip that there had been a *Maquis* ambush on the road there, or an electricity sub-station had been blown up or pylons blown down. Sometimes her note read: '*Can't meet you as arranged. Father is watching.*' Then she knew that she had stopped her friends walking into a trap.

It was hard work, cycling around the Morvan hills, where no road seemed to run flat for more than a few hundred metres. But there were rewards, apart from knowing she was doing a useful job. Often she would emerge from a long uphill ride through thick forest to find herself on an open ridge, with wide views in every direction, with the undulating landscape of woodland and pasture stretching away towards Burgundy to the east and the valley of the Yonne to the west. She grew to love the little towns, with their strange names and their grey stone houses clustering around churches that seemed too big for the local population. And she came to admire the people for their dogged devotion to their land and their animals and their stoical acceptance of the troubles brought upon them by the activities of the *Maquis*. German reprisals were becoming more and more frequent and she heard that the mayor of Quarré les Tombes had been shot, and several houses in the village burned down, in an effort to terrify the populace into revealing the whereabouts of the *Maquis* camps. As far as she could ascertain, no one had come forward with any information.

Her relocation to the *Beau Rivage* had other, unexpected, benefits. She had been prepared to dislike Jeanette intensely but instead she had found a friend. Transferred from an English girls' school to a French Lycée at the age of twelve, she had found it hard to settle and with her tomboy attitude, she had been regarded as an oddity and had never made any close friends. She realized that her initial appearance at the hotel, filthy and unkempt, was enough to put off the fastidious Jeanette; but when she returned, more conventionally dressed, the other girl was delighted to find someone of her own age as a companion.

She was not the only person whose attitude changed. On the first evening when she was being introduced to work behind the bar, Adrienne de Montfort came over and gazed at her.

'Why, it's the little boy/girl who was here the other week! But, *chérie*, you are so pretty! Why do you try to hide yourself?'

'I don't,' Christine protested. 'Those were the only clothes I had.'

'And what are you doing here?'

'I'm working, Madame. I have a job here now.'

'You're right, Madame,' Jeanette put in. 'I keep telling her she could be really stunning if she took a bit more trouble.'

'*Bien sûr*! A little powder, a touch of lipstick — and something must be done with that hair. What do you say, Jeanette? Shall we take her in hand? Shall we transform this chrysalis into a lovely butterfly?'

So it was that, closeted with Jeanette in the older woman's bedroom, Christine was given access to her precious hoarded supply of cosmetics and learned how to apply them. And for the first time in her life, she was prepared to listen and learn. Her hair, which she had always worn as short as a boy's, had grown since she left home and with some trepidation, she allowed Jeanette to wind it in curl papers and restyle it in waves round her face. Afterwards, looking at herself in the mirror for the first time, with her face powdered and her lips reddened, she was disconcerted to find herself beautiful.

The proof of the transformation came a few days later. She was serving behind the bar when the door opened to admit Gregoire with Cyrano and Luke and a group of *Maquisards*. Their visits to the hotel had become rarer since the Germans arrived in Montsauche, but it was an act of defiance; one that proclaimed their domination of the area. Unsurprisingly, it made the permanent residents uncomfortable and the two groups would sit on opposite sides of the room, ignoring each other except for occasional suspicious glances. The only person who ever acknowledged the presence of the rebels was Adrienne de Montfort, who seemed to take delight in the disapproval of her fellow guests.

On this occasion, Christine's first reaction was one of delight at seeing her brother and her friends, quickly followed by anxiety at the risk they were taking.

Gregoire strode across to the bar, his face breaking into a grin.

'Christine, I hardly recognized you! Your brother was worried about you, so we decided we had better bring him down to let him see that you are all right. There you are, Luke. You see? She's quite safe — and flourishing, by the look of it.'

Christine felt herself blushing. She looked at her brother. He was frowning and smiling at the same time and his voice when he spoke was oddly husky.

'Hello, Chris. You OK?'

'Yes. I'm fine. You?'

'Yes, thanks.'

Gregoire turned to the *Maquis* leader beside him.

'There, you see, Xavier? How eloquently we British express our affection for each other!' He looked back at Christine. 'Beers all round, if you would be so good, Mademoiselle.'

It was only then that she allowed herself to look at Cyrano. He was standing a little back from the others, but as they moved away to find a table he came closer.

'Chris, you look gorgeous! What have you done to yourself?'

She ducked her head. 'Oh, it's just a bit of face powder.'

'No, it's more than that,' he said. 'Gregoire's right. It's a transformation! Here, let me give you a hand.'

He helped her carry the beers over to the others, and there was no doubting the impression her new appearance made. Once she would have been embarrassed, but now she found herself enjoying the attention. It was only Luke's attitude that she was uncertain of. He kept casting sidelong glances at her and she could not decide whether he approved or not.

Next morning she met Adrienne in the foyer and was surprised to see that she was dressed very simply and wearing hardly any make-up.

'You wonder where I am going, dressed like this?' Adrienne said. 'I will tell you. Watching you and your friends last night, I was suddenly ashamed. I decided I must do

238

something useful. I hear that there is a doctor at the Château Vermont who needs nurses. I have a little experience in that direction, so I am going to volunteer.'

The *Maquis Xavier* had an unexpected addition to its numbers that day. Four of the men who had been keeping watch on the road below the camp came in with a prisoner. He was a German despatch rider who had been knocked off his motorbike by a tripwire stretched across the road, and had suffered a broken arm. The four men were very proud of their trophy, hoping that the despatches he was carrying would provide useful intelligence about German intentions. The despatch case turned out to be empty except for blank sheets, the messages it contained having been delivered, but the prisoner, whose name was Hans, professed himself delighted at having been captured and willing to offer whatever help he could to the *Maquis*.

He was a soft spoken, intelligent man and when Gregoire interrogated him, his explanation was simple and shocking.

'I hate the Nazis. You see, there are two categories of people whom they regard as being virtually subhuman, inferior beings who should be exterminated. One is the Jews and the other is homosexuals. I have the misfortune — if misfortune it is — to belong to the second category. So far, I have succeeded in hiding the fact, but I know of many friends who have been arrested and sent to the camps; camps from which, we are beginning to realize, no one ever returns. I am convinced that it would only be a matter of time before someone denounced me and I suffered the same fate. So you see, I have good reason to hate the Nazis as much, perhaps more, than you do. If I can do anything to hasten their downfall, I am happy to do it. But if you feel you cannot trust me enough for that, I shall still be better off as a prisoner of the French than as a soldier in the Wehrmacht.'

Xavier grunted sceptically and muttered to Gregoire, 'What makes him think we have the facilities here to keep prisoners?'

'What would you do with him, then?' Gregoire asked.

'Shoot the bastard!' was the reply.

'Not while I have anything to do with it!' Gregoire said. 'We don't shoot prisoners. Anyway, I think he could be useful. I'll take responsibility for him and if it turns out he can't be trusted, I might have to turn him over to you. But until then, he is to be treated in a civilised manner. Understood?'

So Hans was sent to the *Maquis* hospital, where his arm was set, and then he was returned to the camp. For a while, two of the men were sent to keep watch on him and at night he was handcuffed to his bunk, but it did not take long for everyone to be convinced that what he had told them was genuine. By day, he was prepared to help with any menial chores that his arm permitted and in the evenings his conversation made a welcome addition for Gregoire and Cyrano to the limited preoccupations of the *Maquisards*. Soon, he was accepted as just another member of the group.

Pedalling up the long hill from Montsauche towards Dun, Christine rounded a curve to find herself facing a German checkpoint. It was not an unusual occurrence and she had a ready-made excuse. Madame Bolu had sent her to deliver some plums from the orchard around the hotel to an old friend. What made her pulse suddenly race, was the face of the young soldier manning the barrier. It was Franz, the boy who had tried to make a date with her. It was clear that he had recognized her.

'I waited,' he said, as he handed back her papers. 'That Saturday afternoon. I waited a long time for you.'

'I'm sorry,' she responded breathlessly. 'I couldn't get away. I had to work.'

'Work? What at?'

'I'm a waitress at the B*eau Rivage* hotel, down by the lake.'

'I've seen it. It looks a nice spot.'

'Yes, it is.'

'Maybe I'll come down there one evening when I'm off duty, to see you.'

Christine's heart thudded faster. She could not have him walking into the bar, maybe bringing his friends with him. Suppose Gregoire and the others decided to call in again. At all costs, she must scotch that suggestion.

'No, please don't do that!' she begged. 'My employers wouldn't approve of me fraternising with . . . with one of you.'

'OK. Where can we meet, then?'

Her thoughts were racing. If she refused to give him another rendezvous, he might take it into his head to come to the hotel after all. And at the back of her mind was the thought that this young soldier could be a useful source of information, if she played her cards right. It was a high-risk strategy, but the only one she could think of at that moment.

'All right. Listen. The grounds of the hotel run right down to the edge of the lake. The trees are quite thick there. We could meet there and no one would see us.'

His face lit up and she saw the friendly boy beneath the uniform.

'Tonight? Can I come tonight?'

'Yes, all right. But it will only be for a few minutes, or I might be missed. Nine o'clock?'

'I'll be there!'

As she cycled away, she could not decide whether she had made a clever move or taken a foolhardy risk.

They met as arranged and walked by the lake shore. He was polite and almost pathetically grateful.

'You have no idea how awful it is to have no other company than soldiers,' he said. 'Most of them are ignorant oafs who can't talk about anything but women or football.'

They exchanged stories about their homes and their childhoods, which involved Christine in some rapid improvisation. To her relief, most of the time he was happy to do the talking. When she said that she had to go in before she was missed, he clicked his heels and kissed her hand and she found herself thinking that if circumstances had been different, it would have been quite nice to have him as a boyfriend.

Three days later, four German officers walked into the bar of the *Beau Rivage* and demanded champagne. Christine's first instinct was to refuse to serve them, but Madame Bolu was there and she greeted them as she would have done any other customer and sent her scurrying down to the cellar for the wine. As she searched among the bottles, Christine's thoughts were in turmoil. Suppose Gregoire and the others chose that evening to call in? There would be no passing them off as regular customers. For one thing, it was after curfew; and for another they always carried rifles, wherever they went. One glance would be enough to identify them as *Maquis* and the only possible outcome would be a firefight. She wondered desperately if there was any way she could get a message to her friends but she could think of none. All she could do was lurk as near to the door as possible, straining her ears for the sound of an approaching vehicle, until Madame Bolu reprimanded her sharply for failing to attend to her duties.

As she returned to her place behind the bar, the proprietress hissed into her ear, 'Do you want to make them suspicious? Anyone with half an eye could see that you are terrified that someone else is going to come through that door. The best thing we can do is behave normally. Let them see we have nothing to hide.'

Immediately after breakfast next morning, Christine cycled off to the derelict cottage. She had already written the note, which she hid in the tobacco tin.

'Must see you tonight. Meet in the usual place.' She could simply have written a note telling him not to come to the hotel any more, but she felt it needed more explanation. At least, that was the excuse she gave herself.

'The usual place' was the church in Montsauche, where she knew Cyrano practised the organ every Friday. When she arrived, he was already there and the notes of *Jesu Joy of Man's Desiring* were filling the space below the high vaulted-roof. Apart from the organist, the church was empty. Christine slipped into a pew halfway down the nave and waited. There was a quivering knot of anticipation in her stomach and she took herself mentally to task. *Anybody would think there was something to be afraid of. What's the matter with you?*

She shut her eyes and let the music flow through her, a steady stream of perfect notes supported by the deep base of the melody. The organ fell silent and she felt her pulse quicken. A moment later Cyrano slid into the seat beside her.

'*Salut*, Chris! Is something wrong?' He spoke softly, but she could hear the concern in his voice.

'No! No, I'm fine, if that's what you mean. But I have to warn you about something. You must tell Gregoire and the others not to come to the hotel again. Last night four German officers turned up. I was terrified that you or some of the *Maquisards* might walk in.'

'Thanks for the warning. That could have been disastrous. You've done a good job there. Do you think they'll be back?'

'I don't know. But they seemed to enjoy themselves. They ordered champagne and of course Mme Bolu had to make them welcome.'

'Yes, of course.' He sighed ruefully. 'Oh well, that's an end to our little evenings out. I shall miss them.'

'I suppose,' she said hesitantly, 'there are other hotels around the lake.'

'True, but none where we can be sure of a welcome. And anyway, they don't offer the added attraction of such a pretty barmaid.'

She looked at him, wondering if he meant Jeanette, but he met her eyes with a mischievous grin that told her otherwise.

'I shall miss seeing you,' she murmured, 'and Luke of course.' The implications of what had happened had sunk in for the first time and her voice shook.

He reached out and took her hand. 'It's a rotten shame, but you're not completely cut off. I'm always here, or up at Duns, on the days I told you, if you need me.'

She nodded dumbly and he went on, 'You're shivering! Are you sure you're all right? If you're not well I could take you to see Dr Martell at the *château*.'

'No, I'm fine, really. Just a bit cold. I forgot how chilly these places always are.'

It had been a hot day and she was wearing the pinafore dress without a blouse underneath, leaving her arms and shoulders bare. He slipped off the tweed jacket, which he wore as if it was some kind of protective covering, and put it round her shoulders. She huddled into it and felt again the quiver at the base of her stomach.

He touched her forehead, as if checking for fever.

'You are such a brave kid! It must be very hard, being all on your own.'

'I'm not really. Mme Bolu and Jeanette are very kind and at least . . .' she strove for a lighter tone, 'at least I get a hot bath once a week.'

'Well,' he smiled back at her, 'that's a luxury we don't all have.' He looked at his watch. 'We need to go, or we shall both be caught out after curfew. Oh, wait a minute! I almost forgot. I've got some news for you. You remember those German gun boats you saw being hauled out of the canal?'

'Of course I do.'

'I had a message last night. Not one of them got as far as the Med.'

'What happened to them?'

'I don't have any details. I imagine they were bombed en route. Anyway, the High Command wish to pass on their thanks for the intelligence, so there you are. Your own unique contribution to the war effort.'

Under the borrowed jacket, Christine hugged herself joyfully. 'That's wonderful! Thank you, Cyrano.'

'Don't thank me. It's all down to you and Luke. Now, was there anything else you needed to tell me?'

'No, it was just about the *Boche* in the hotel.'

'Well, thanks again for the warning.' He got up and she followed him to the door. 'You go first. It's better if we aren't seen leaving together. Can I have my jacket back?'

'Yes, of course. Sorry.' She took it off, reluctant to lose the comforting warmth and the even more comforting sense of closeness to him.

He squeezed her hand briefly. 'Take care.'

'And you.'

She rode away with a tightness in her throat, but at the same time a sense that something good had happened, something important, and the news about the gunboats was only part of it.

The next time Franz appeared in the hotel grounds she accused him.

'Did you tell your officers about this place?'

He gaped at her. 'What do you mean?'

'Four of them turned up the other night, out of the blue. Was that because you told them about it?'

'Don't be stupid! Why would I want officers showing up here? I'm not supposed to be fraternising any more than you are. Anyway, you don't think I have that sort of conversation with the officers, do you?'

She was contrite. 'Sorry, I didn't think. It was just the coincidence, that's all.'

It took him a few minutes to get over his annoyance, but before long they fell back into the comfortable mood of their previous encounter.

When it was time for him to go he said, 'May I kiss you?'

She had been dreading this. She wondered if he would not come back again if she refused, and if it would matter if he did not. It was not as if she had got any useful information out of him. But she found she was reluctant to hurt his feelings.

'All right.'

His lips were dry, slightly rough, and when she felt the tip of his tongue between them she drew back quickly.

'Good night, Franz.'

He did not seem unduly put out. 'Can I come again, next time I'm off duty?'

'Yes, if you want to.'

He clicked his heels and saluted. 'Goodnight, Christine.'

Several days passed and then she saw him waiting for her by the lake. He greeted her as usual but she sensed at once that something was wrong.

'What is it, Franz? You seem a bit fed up.'

'Oh,' he skimmed a stone into the smooth water. 'Don't take any notice of me. I'm in a bad mood, that's all.'

'Why? Has something happened?'

'Happened? Nothing happens here. I don't know what we're here for. Do you know what I have spent my day doing?'

'What?'

'Counting pigs! That's what. It's not what I imagined myself doing when I joined up.'

'Counting pigs! Why?'

'Orders. The captain's had us all going round to every farm in the commune, making a record of what livestock they have.'

'For what reason?'

'Because the beasts are being requisitioned. They have got to bring them all into Montsauche so they can be shipped off to Germany.'

'All of them? You mean, you are taking away all their animals?'

'Every last one. That's why we were ordered to count them. "Don't rely on what the farmers tell you," the captain said. "You can bet if they say they have four pigs there will be half a dozen more hidden away somewhere. So you check, and count them yourselves."'

'When is this going to happen?'

'On Saturday. The farmers are being told they must bring them to market. But it won't be a market, as they think of it.'

'But what are these poor people going to do if you take their animals?' Christine asked. 'What are they going to eat?'

He threw another stone, his expression mulish. 'The same rations as everyone else, I suppose. The captain reckons the farmers are feeding the *Maquis*. He says it serves them right to lose their animals and he's hoping it'll turn them against the rebels and make them more keen to cooperate when we ask for information.'

'It won't!' Christine said sharply, and then moderating her tone, 'I mean, I should think it will have the opposite effect. They will hate you all even more.'

He looked at her. 'Do they hate us?'

'You are occupying their country. Of course they do.'

He sighed and turned away. 'We're told we are fighting for the Fatherland, and all the animals are going to feed our mothers and sisters back home. But I don't know . . . It isn't the way I thought it would be.'

'It's wrong, all of it,' she said more gently. 'Look at us. We're friends — or we could be, if circumstances were different. Why should we fight each other?'

He took hold of her hands. 'Why indeed?'

This time, his kiss was more forceful and she could not prevent him from pushing his tongue into her mouth. It was the first time she had been kissed like that and the idea revolted her; but at the same time it woke some deep-seated response that suggested if only it had been someone else, she would feel differently.

She gave little thought to this aspect of the encounter, however. What mattered now was to pass on this information. As soon as Franz left, she gave her mind to the problem. It was Wednesday. Cyrano would not be at organ practice until Friday and that would not give enough time for any plans to be made. She did not know what the *Maquis* could do to prevent what was intended, but she was certain they would wish to do something. Then she remembered something else Cyrano had told her; the priest at Duns-les-Places was a supporter and he held confession every Thursday afternoon.

Christine arrived at the church in Duns out of breath from the long ride uphill and glad this time of the coolness of the interior. It was a very long time since she had been to confession. She and Luke had been baptised into the Catholic Church at the behest of her mother's family, though Isabelle herself was not a regular attender. An English upbringing and a strictly C of E girls' independent school had given Christine a different perspective, and when the family returned to France she had found the Catholic emphasis on hell and repentance inimical. As a result she was now more or less agnostic. Nevertheless, she was familiar enough with the rituals of the church not to look out of place.

Three or four women were waiting in the pews, and Christine found a place a short distance away, drew her scarf over her head and knelt. For once, she found herself praying in earnest. She prayed for her mother, waiting for news at the Cave des Volcans, and for Luke, taking she knew-not-what risks with the *Maquis*, and for the farmers and their families who were about to lose their livelihoods.

When all the others had gone, she slipped into the confessional and knelt. The ritual question came from the other side of the screen.

'When was your last confession?'

Christine drew a deep breath. However little she believed in the rite, it seemed wrong to circumvent it like this.

'Father, I haven't come to confess. I have an urgent message for Xavier.'

'For Xavier?' The tone of voice from beyond the screen was different. 'What message, child?'

'You must tell him that the Germans are going to take all the animals from the farms round about and send them to Germany. The farmers have been told to bring them to market in Montsauche on Saturday.'

'All the animals?'

'Yes, every one. Soldiers have been sent to count them, so they know how many there should be.'

'Merciful God! How are these people supposed to live?'

'I don't know, Father. That is why the Germans must be stopped. The *Maquis* must do something.'

'It's hard to know what they can do. But I shall get a message to Xavier. Have no fear of that. You have done well to tell me. Now, God bless you. Go in peace.'

CHAPTER 20

The next morning, a young lad, one of the altar boys from the church at Duns, arrived on his bicycle at the guard post on the track leading up to the *Maquis Xavier*. Thanks to equipment dropped in a recent *parachutage*, the camp was now provided with field telephones and within minutes, Xavier and one of his lieutenants arrived to hear what the boy had to say. An urgent message was sent to summon Gregoire from his base at the *Maquis Vincent* and he arrived, bringing Vincent with him. Half an hour later, a council of war was assembled around the table in the hut which had now become Xavier's HQ.

'We can't do anything in Montsauche,' Gregoire said. 'It would inevitably result in a firefight and innocent civilians would be caught up in it. I think we can safely assume that the beasts will be transported in cattle trucks to the railway at Château-Chinon, for onward transfer. So the only chance would be to ambush the convoy on its way there. Let's have a look at the map.'

'They will be bound to take the main road,' Xavier said. 'But it's not ideal for an ambush.'

'Agreed,' Gregoire nodded. 'Any suggestions?'

'We need to divert the convoy onto a minor road,' said Vincent. 'Here, for example, on the road up to Chevigny.'

'We could block the main road, I suppose,' Xavier said dubiously. 'But there are *Boche* patrols going up and down it all the time. The blockage would soon be reported and cleared.'

'Suppose we could convince the officer in charge of the convoy that the road was blocked, or unsafe in some way,' Gregoire suggested.

'How?' Xavier asked.

'Your German despatch rider!' Vincent exclaimed. 'Could he be trusted to deliver a despatch telling the officer in charge that the main road was unsafe and he must take a diversion?'

'Possibly,' Gregoire said thoughtfully. 'It would be asking a lot, but he has said he would be willing to do anything.'

'There's one snag to that,' Xavier put in. 'You've all forgotten that he has a broken arm. He can't ride his motorbike like that.'

'Then we need a substitute,' Vincent said. 'We have his uniform and his bike. We need a volunteer who is roughly the same size and can pass as a German.'

'And can speak the language, presumably,' Xavier said scathingly. 'Oh, there's plenty of men here who fill that description.'

'Need he actually speak?' Gregoire asked. 'I'm just thinking aloud. If a man in the correct uniform was to ride up to the officer in charge, salute in the proper way, hand over the despatch and then turn his bike around and roar off down the road, do you think the officer would smell a rat? Even if he did, our man would be well away, and then the officer would have to decide whether the message was genuine or not. And if he chose to disregard it, he could be heading straight into danger. There was spare paper in Hans's bag with the right insignia and he could compose the message and write it out. It would look genuine.'

'Then all we need,' Vincent said, 'is a man to deliver it. Someone who looks like a German.'

'Well, you can count my lads out,' Xavier said. 'There's not one of them who looks right. How about your men, Vincent?'

'No one comes to mind.'

'There is one person I can think of,' Gregoire said slowly. 'Tall, fair, blue-eyed . . .'

Cyrano had listened in silence to the discussion. Now he broke in.

'Gregoire, you're not thinking of Luke, are you? You can't!'

'Why not?' Xavier asked. 'He volunteered to join us and said he would do anything he was asked to do. He's the ideal man for the job.'

'But he's just a kid!' Cyrano protested.

'He's eighteen,' Gregoire said. 'If he was back in the UK, he would have been called up. He would probably have been flying Spitfires by now. Xavier's right; he volunteered to do whatever was required.'

'You can't order him to do something like this,' Cyrano said.

'Of course not. We have been talking about a volunteer, haven't we? But we can at least put the idea to him.'

'And that's your idea of "volunteering" is it?'

'I'll make it clear that he is at liberty to refuse. Alphonse, see if you can find Luke and bring him here.'

Alphonse did not have far to seek. Luke was lurking nearby, tormented with anxiety at the thought that the sudden crisis conference might have something to do with Christine. When he was summoned, his worst fears were confirmed. He entered the hut nerving himself for bad news.

'You wanted me, Gregoire?'

'Yes. There's a job to be done and I think you are better suited to it than anyone else. But I want you to be clear, you are not obliged to agree. This is a job for a volunteer.'

Luke's gasp of relief was audible. 'A job? Oh, that's all right. I thought . . .'

'What?'

'I thought something might have happened to my sister.'

'You need not worry about Christine,' Cyrano said. 'We know she was at the church in Duns yesterday, because she sent us a message through the curé there. I think we can assume she is all right.'

'Thank God! Sorry, Gregoire. You were saying . . . ?'

When Gregoire had explained what they had in mind, Luke's first reaction was, 'But I don't speak German.'

'We've thought of that. Hans can coach you with the few words you will need. The idea is for you to ride up to the head of the convoy, salute and hand over the letter, which Hans will write, and then scarper at full speed. You can ride a motorbike, can you?'

'No. Well, I've never tried.'

'Fernand can teach you. It isn't difficult. Will you give it a try?'

Luke took a deep breath. 'When is all this supposed to happen?'

'Tomorrow.'

The next twenty-four hours were the most crowded of Luke's life. Hans was summoned and was happy to agree to compose the necessary directive. While he set to work, Luke had his first lesson on the motorbike the German had been riding when he was captured. Then, Hans drilled him into the correct behaviour and made him repeat over and over the necessary words, until his accent was as near perfect as he could make it. Then, it was back to the motorbike again and then to what Cyrano facetiously called a 'costume fitting' in the German's uniform. They were much the same height, but Hans was bigger in the waist. A belt fixed that problem but the boots were more difficult; Hans's feet were smaller than Luke's and the boots pinched his toes, but there was no way around that. He consoled himself with the thought that at least he would not have to walk far in them.

Meanwhile, Gregoire was busy with Xavier and Vincent planning the ambush. A spot was chosen on the way up to Chevigny where the trees grew close to the narrow road. A barricade would be built just beyond it, with a one of the Bren guns mounted on it, and two other Brens would be positioned to cover the rear of the convoy.

'I don't want anyone getting back to Montsauche to alert the rest of the garrison,' Gregoire said.

In between, the members of the two *Maquis* would line the road on either side, armed with rifles, grenades, and captured Schmeisser automatics.

'There's one thing we've all forgotten about,' Cyrano pointed out. 'If this all goes to plan we are going to find ourselves left with several truckloads of assorted farm animals. How are we going to return them to their rightful owners?'

'*Mon Dieu!*' Gregoire exclaimed. 'You're right. It hadn't occurred to me. We can't take them back to Montsauche and anyway, there's no way we can turn big vehicles around in that narrow lane.'

'We could take them on to Chevigny and tell the farmers to collect them from there,' Xavier suggested. 'How they get them back to their farms will be up to them.'

'That seems to be the only answer,' Gregoire agreed. 'That's a job for Christine. She must meet with the farmers as they bring their beasts to town and explain the idea. Can you get a message to her, Cyrano?'

Cyrano looked at his watch. 'She'll have checked her dead drop by now. I'll have to call in at the hotel. After all, there's no reason why I shouldn't drop in for a beer on my way to my next piano lesson.'

When Cyrano walked into the bar at the *Beau Rivage*, Christine's first reaction was a mixture of delight and anxiety. Something must have gone wrong for him to set aside the normal protocols. His smile as he came over and ordered a beer reassured her, though she found herself glancing uneasily round the bar to see who was watching. Three of the usual residents were playing cards on the far side of the room but they merely glanced up and then returned to their game. Cyrano leaned across the bar seductively.

'I think I'll take my drink outside. Could you bring me out a sandwich of some sort? Anything will do.'

When she came into the garden with a hastily constructed baguette with a morsel of cheese, he was sitting with his face raised to the sun, giving every impression of relaxation.

'Sit down a minute. I need to talk to you.'

Anyone watching would have thought he was just chatting up a pretty girl, as he explained the plan for the following day, omitting any reference to the part Luke was to play.

'So what you need to do,' he concluded, 'is mingle with the crowd and get the message round to all the farmers to go to Chevigny. But tell them to wait for about an hour and for God's sake impress on them not to all set off together, or the *Boche* may smell a rat. Can you manage that?'

'I don't see why not,' she replied. 'But I want to know how it all goes, afterwards. Can you meet me? I'll be dying to hear the news.'

He smiled. 'OK. I'll come to the church, about six. Meet me there.'

The streets of Montsauche were clogged with animals. Flocks of sheep and goats, with dogs at their heels, trotted bleating along narrow lanes; slow-moving herds of cattle plodded down the main road, udders swinging; horse-drawn trailers full of pigs followed. All converged on a field at the edge of the town, where cattle trucks were drawn up in readiness.

As each farmer arrived with his beasts, they were counted and checked off against a list and then directed into one of the trucks. Very soon angry voices were raised above the background of lowing and bleating.

'We were told to bring them to market. What payment are you offering?'

'You can't just take our animals! What are we supposed to live on?'

The answers were always the same.

'Your beasts are needed to feed the Fatherland. They are being requisitioned by the authority of the government in Vichy.'

Men swore and shouted, women wept.

'Please! Leave me at least one milk cow. I have small children. They need the milk.'

'You should have thought of that before you fed those bandits up in the hills.'

Some of the farmers tried to turn back and take their animals home, but they met a line of soldiers with bayonets fixed. A cordon had been drawn around the field and there was no escape.

Christine threaded her way between the furious men and the distraught women, plucking at sleeves, trying to get someone to listen to her; but they were too angry to pay attention to a slip of a girl. Desperately she sought for a familiar face and finally found a man she remembered from an earlier expedition.

'Monsieur! Do you remember me? I came with Jean-Claude. I have a message from Xavier.'

'Xavier?' His lip curled. 'I don't want to hear about him. If we hadn't helped the *Maquis*, we wouldn't be in this mess now.'

'But that's the message,' she said urgently. 'You helped the *Maquis*, now they will help you. If you go to Chevigny in an hour from now your animals will be returned to you.'

He stared at her. 'Returned, how? You mean the *Maquis* intend to ambush the convoy? Is it true?'

'It's true. You must help me spread the word. Everyone is to go to Chevigny, but not all at once. The *Boche* mustn't suspect.'

'It will never work.'

'It will! You must have faith. Tell the others.'

The cattle trucks were loaded and the men and their wives began to turn away, defeated. Christine and her new ally went from one group to another and slowly, a few at a time, they left the town and set off, along forest paths unknown to the occupiers, towards Chevigny.

Luke, in the uniform of a German despatch rider, stood beside Hans' motorbike in the narrow lane leading from the main road towards the village of Chevigny. Gregoire and Hans were with him and beyond them, concealed in the trees on either side of the lane, were all the men of the *Maquis*

Xavier and the *Maquis Vincent*. Luke's mouth was parched and he felt sick, but there was no turning back now.

Gregoire was holding a walkie-talkie radio.

'Jules is waiting a mile up the main road. As soon as the head of the convoy passes him, he will let me know. That will be your cue. All you have to do is ride up to the officer in charge and hand over the letter. Then come back up here, ride as far as the barricade, then get yourself and the bike off the road out of sight. The rest is up to us.'

'You remember the words I taught you?' Hans asked. 'Repeat them for me.'

Luke spoke the German phrase, which had been going round in his head all night and Hans nodded.

'Very good!'

'Oh, in case you're worried,' Gregoire said, 'I have told the men that the first German they see will be you, and they are not to shoot you.'

'Thanks for that,' Luke muttered. The danger of being shot by his own side was something that had not occurred to him.

The radio in Gregoire's hand crackled.

'They are coming,' said a disembodied voice.

'Understood. Over and out.' Gregoire put his hand on Luke's shoulder. 'Go! Good luck!'

Luke mounted the bike, kicked the engine into life, and rode out of the lane and into the main road. As he rounded the first bend, he saw the convoy coming towards him. There were two motorcycle outriders at the front, then a jeep, which he guessed was carrying the officer in charge. As he rode towards them, he expected to be challenged at any moment, but the outriders did not seem surprised by his sudden appearance. The jeep slowed to a standstill and he passed it, then swung round in a circle to come alongside it facing the direction of his escape. Heart pounding, he dismounted, came to attention and gave the Nazi salute.

'*Heil Hitler!*' Then the phrase he had learned from Hans. 'A message from the Colonel, Herr Major.' He held out the envelope and as soon as the officer had taken it he jumped back onto the bike and gunned the engine.

As he roared away towards the turning to Chevigny, his spine crawled with the anticipation of a bullet but there was no attempt to stop him. He rounded the corner and glanced behind him in time to see the head of the convoy following in his tracks. There was no sign of Gregoire or Hans now, of course. They would be hidden somewhere in the trees. He rode on, catching great gulps of air, until he came in sight of the barricade. There was a narrow track into the woods just before it; that was where he intended to leave the road and hide.

As he approached, he let out a whoop of triumph and raised his arms in a gesture of victory. Then the bike seemed to explode beneath him and he was hurtling through the air and into oblivion.

Gregoire, perched in the branches of a tree above the road, saw Luke go past. He waited until the last vehicle of the convoy and the troop carrier which brought up the rear were beneath him, then he fired a Verey pistol. As the flare rose into the sky, a cacophony of shots broke out. The Bren gun positioned below him chattered, and several men in the troop carrier screamed and fell. The rest vaulted out onto the road and flung themselves flat, firing blind into the trees. All along the road, rifles cracked and three hundred yards further on, the Bren on the barricade opened up. A random shot blew off the catch that held the door at the back of one of the cattle trucks and a stream of terrified sheep and goats poured down the road and disappeared into the forest.

For five minutes, chaos reigned and then the firing stopped as suddenly as it had begun. There was a moment of eerie silence and then a cheer rose from the trees and the men of the *Maquis* broke cover. A blood-drenched face appeared from the troop carrier, followed by the muzzle of a rifle, and a shot rang out. One of the *Maquis* cried out and fell to his knees. Xavier shouted an order, there was another shot and the face disappeared. Xavier and six of his men began to work their way along the convoy, peering into the cabs of the trucks and searching the ditches. Occasionally another shot was fired.

Cyrano was standing with Gregoire at a vantage point a little above the road.

'They are shooting the wounded!' he exclaimed, aghast.

Gregoire shrugged grimly. 'What do you expect? We have no facilities for keeping prisoners.'

At length, the firing ceased and Xavier joined them, grinning broadly.

'We showed them, yes?'

'Oh yes, we showed them,' Gregoire returned, unsmiling. 'Come on, let's get these trucks up to Chevigny.'

As they approached the village, they found the street lined with cheering men and women. The trucks were drawn up in the square and then the process began of returning the animals in them to their rightful owners.

It was no easy task. Many of them were not marked with any kind of brand, each farmer relying on recognizing his own beasts. Inevitably, disputes broke out and it took all Gregoire's abilities as a diplomat to resolve them. And there was still the question of the whereabouts of the sheep and goats that had escaped during the fight.

The day was drawing to a close by the time all the farmers had departed with their flocks and herds. It was only then that someone had the time to say:

'Where's Luke?'

The men were called together and a roll call taken. Three had been killed in the firing, and five others wounded, but Luke was not there and apparently no one had seen him. Vincent's men seemed puzzled.

'Who is he?' one asked. 'What does he look like?'

'You must have seen him,' Gregoire said. 'He rode right past you on his motorbike, just before the convoy reached us.'

A stocky peasant boy seemed to wake from a daydream.

'Oh, you mean the German despatch rider? I shot him.'

'You shot him! What do you mean? Did you hit him?'

The boy lifted his shoulders. 'I dunno. I might have hit the bike instead. He crashed into the ditch.'

Gregoire turned furiously to Vincent.

'I told you to warn your men! You were supposed to tell them that the despatch rider was one of ours and was not to be harmed.'

Vincent shrugged. 'I told them, but that one there . . .' he indicated the peasant boy, 'he is stupid. Half the time he doesn't take in anything he is told.'

'So a brave young man gets shot!' Gregoire ground out. 'Well, we'll take that up later. Right now, we need everyone back to the site of the ambush to search. And let's pray the *Boche* haven't got there before us.'

His prayers were not answered. Before they reached the section of the lane where the ambush had taken place, they could hear the noise of engines and shouted commands. Gregoire stopped and raised his hand to halt the men behind him.

'Too late! They must have raised the alarm at Château-Chinon when the convoy failed to arrive, and it wouldn't take a search party long to find the remains. There's nothing more we can do. If Luke's alive, he's a prisoner by now.'

Cyrano clenched his hands so that the nails dug into his palms.

'We should never have let him do it!'

Gregoire turned on him. 'He took no more risk than any of the others. Three men are dead! If Vincent had made sure all his men understood . . .' He stopped and softened his tone. 'I'm sorry, Cyrano. I know you feel a special responsibility for the two of them.' He hesitated. 'Christine will have to be told.'

'I know,' Cyrano said dully.

'Can you arrange a meeting?'

'Yes, I . . .' He looked at his watch. 'Christ! I'm supposed to be seeing her now, at the church! She'll be waiting.'

'Do you want me to come and talk to her? It is my responsibility, in the long run.'

'No.' Cyrano took a long breath. 'No, I'll do it. You need to get the men back to camp. I'll see you there later.'

When Cyrano entered the church, Christine was waiting for him. Before he could speak, she hurried to him, her face alight with excitement.

'I've heard! It was a great success. Some men came into the bar at the hotel, talking about it. Of course, I didn't let on I knew anything about it, but they were laughing, saying it was one in the eye for the *Boche*. So all the farmers have got their animals back. I'm so glad!' Something in his face stopped her. 'What's wrong? What's happened?'

He took both her hands in his. 'Chris, it's bad news, I'm afraid.'

'Luke?' She felt as if she had suddenly lost the ability to breathe.

'He's missing. We don't know what happened exactly. It's possible he's been taken prisoner.'

'How?' The words were choking her. 'How could it happen?'

'Come and sit down.' He led her to a pew and sat beside her. As briefly as he could, he explained the deception they had played and Luke's crucial part in it. 'He didn't have to accept the idea, but he agreed, and he must have played his part perfectly because the convoy followed him into the side road, just as planned. It was one of our own men, well, one of Vincent's men. He'd been told the man dressed as a despatch rider was one of ours, but it seems he didn't take it in. He . . . took a pot shot at him. That's all we know. By the time we realized Luke was missing, the Germans were searching the area. There was nothing we could do.'

Christine sat frozen, her hands clenched in front of her.

'If . . . if he's a prisoner, how will we know?'

'We'll . . . we'll make enquiries. Gregoire has contacts. Word will get out, somehow.'

'They will know, won't they — the Germans. They will realize he must be with the *Maquis*. They will interrogate him.' Her voice cracked.

Cyrano gripped her hand. 'If he's being held locally we will find out and somehow, somehow we will get him out!'

She shook her head. 'You won't be able to. Perhaps . . . perhaps it would be better if he was killed outright.'

He put his arm round her. 'Oh, my dear child! I wish I could say something comforting. I blame myself. If it wasn't for me, neither of you would be here.'

'That's not true. We came of our own accord. It isn't your fault.' Her voice was toneless but he could feel her shaking.

'You mustn't give up hope. He may just have been wounded. The *Boche* may not have found him. He could be hiding out, waiting for dark. Tomorrow we will search the area again. Nothing is certain, yet.'

She looked at him and nodded dumbly.

'Do you want to come back with me? Back to the camp?'

She shook her head. Somewhere at the back of her mind, through the numbness of shock, a plan was forming: Gregoire might have his contacts; so did she.

She stood up. 'I need to get back. It's almost curfew.'

He rose too and took her by the shoulders. 'Chris? Are you all right? Why don't you come back with me?'

'I'm OK,' she muttered. 'I'll be all right.'

'Then meet me here again tomorrow night. I need to know you're OK. And there may be news.'

She nodded. 'Yes, that's a good idea.'

He looked at her, dry-eyed, pale as death, resolute. He took her in his arms and for a moment she nestled against him. Then she drew back.

'Must go now. Curfew. 'Night.'

The door opened and closed behind her.

Isabelle was washing dishes in the kitchen at Cave des Volcans and humming softly. As the summer weeks had passed, the burden of anxiety seemed to have lifted from her. There had been another message on the BBC, telling her that 'Michou's pups' were still safe. She had no idea where they were, or whether they had reached England or not; but all that mattered was that someone was obviously looking after them. There had been no further requests from the local *Maquis* for her to store arms or explosives, and her father had finally reconciled himself to the presence of the two Germans in the house.

She turned her head as she heard her two lodgers coming in. As she dried her hands, there was a tap on the door to the kitchen and Hoffmann appeared, followed by Schulz. Something in the Leutnant's face told her that something had changed.

She smiled at him. 'Good evening. How are you today?'

He smiled back. 'Better than usual, Madame. I have good news. From tomorrow you will be relieved of the intrusion into your privacy.'

'What do you mean?' She frowned. 'Are you being posted away again.'

'Yes, but this time it is not for active duty. The powers that be have finally come to the conclusion that I am not much use to them as a fighting soldier. I have been given a desk job in Berlin.'

She caught her breath. 'Oh, my dear boy, I am so glad! Glad for you, that is. You will be out of danger. And you, Fritz? Will you be going with the Leutnant?'

'Oh yes, Madame. Where he goes, I go.'

'Did you say from tomorrow? That is very sudden.'

'That is the way the army works, Madame. Those most concerned are always the last to know.'

She felt a sudden sense of loss. 'I shall miss you, both of you.'

'You are very kind to say so. And we shall miss your generous hospitality. Living here has been a bright interlude in this horrible war.'

For a moment no one said anything. Then Isabelle turned aside to take a bottle from the cupboard under the dresser.

'We must have a glass of wine, to celebrate your release. Sit, please.' She set glasses on the table and drew the cork. 'This is one of our best wines. I have been keeping it for a special occasion.'

She poured the wine and sat opposite her two uninvited guests.

'What shall we drink to?'

'To a time when we can meet as friends, not as people divided by the stupidity of war.'

'I shall always think of you as friends, war or no war.'

'Then let us drink to the end of the war. To peace.'

'Yes, let's drink to that!'

The three glasses met and touched. 'Peace!'

'Peace!'

'Peace!'

CHAPTER 21

Luke regained consciousness to a sense of total dislocation. A moment ago, he had been sitting by the campfire, listening to Cyrano playing his flute, and now he was lying somewhere cold and extremely uncomfortable with no recollection of how he had got there. Boots rattled on stone not far away from his head, and a German voice barked an order. Luke had started to struggle into a sitting position but at the sound he dropped back. Had the Germans overrun the camp? Why could he not remember any fighting? He began to lever himself up again. A shaft of pain stabbed up his left arm and he passed out.

Next time he came to, everything was quiet. He opened his eyes and saw that he was lying in some kind of ditch, overhung with brambles and ferns, through which he could see the last streaks of sunset in the sky. Or was it the first streaks of dawn? He ought to get up. There was something he had to do; words he had to remember.

He lifted his head and was seized by a wave of nausea. He twisted on to his side and vomited. Slowly, the memory of the last twenty-four hours reassembled itself; he had ridden the motorbike, delivered the letter. It had all gone according to plan; but now he was here with a throbbing head and an excruciating pain in his arm. He still had no idea how that had happened. Gregoire must be looking for him, he reasoned. He must find him and report.

Gritting his teeth, he hauled himself out of the ditch and staggered out onto the road. Opposite him, was the burned-out remains of a jeep and to one side, the tree trunks that had been used to build the barricade. The verges on either side of the road were churned up by vehicle tracks. But there was no sign of human beings, either dead or alive. Luke turned downhill and began to walk.

'*Hände hoch!*' The words were German but the voice was young, almost childlike.

Luke turned slowly, raising his right arm. His left hung by his side and any attempt to lift it sent pain shooting through him. A boy of about twelve, in rough peasant dress, was facing him. In one hand he held a German pistol and in the other the end of a rope, to which were attached two goats.

Luke attempted a smile. 'It's all right. I'm French, like you.'

'Liar! You're a filthy *Boche*.' He raised his voice. 'Papa! Come here! Come and see what I've found.'

A man appeared from the trees, leading three more goats. 'Have you got them all?' He stopped short and stared. 'What's this?'

'He must have been hiding. I saw him coming out of the forest.'

'Look, you don't understand!' Luke said. 'I'm French. I'm with the *Maquis*. I've been wounded somehow. Can you help me please?'

'Oh yes!' the man said. 'How come you're in German uniform then? If you expect me to swallow that story you must think I'm stupid.'

'But it's true! I'm in disguise . . .'

'What shall we do with him, Papa?' the boy asked. 'Shall I shoot him?'

His father frowned, obviously at a loss. 'No, no. We can't do that, not in cold blood. We'll take him with us, give

265

ourselves time to think. Give me that.' He reached for the pistol.

'But Papa . . .' the boy protested.

'I said give it here!' He snatched the gun and jerked it at Luke. 'Move! Not that way! Up!'

Luke's head was swimming and he thought he was going to be sick again. Argument seemed useless, so he turned and began to plod up the road, the farmer and the boy close behind him. How he stayed on his feet for the kilometre or so between there and the farm, he did not know. Every step made him feel as if his head was going to split open and set the nerves in his broken arm jangling. Finally, he found himself outside a darkened building.

'What shall we do with him?' the boy asked.

'Lock him up with the goats until morning. Then we'll decide the best thing to do.'

'I tell you I'm with the *Maquis*,' Luke croaked. 'Contact Xavier. He'll vouch for me.'

A door was opened in what appeared to be a shed of some sort. 'Get in there! Move!'

'Water, please! At least give me a drink of water!' His pleas fell on deaf ears. He was thrust through a low door into a noisome darkness. He tripped on something, fell and lost consciousness again.

Christine hardly slept at all. After leaving Cyrano the night before, she had cycled back to the hotel as if she was doing it in her sleep. She had said nothing to Mme Bolu or Jeanette. They were not *Maquis* after all and the less they knew the better, or so she told herself. The truth was that some instinct told her that once she talked about Luke, she would have to confront the reality that he might be dead.

She went through the motions of her job behind the bar and in the dining room, and when people asked her if she was all right, she told them she had a headache. As soon as she could, she escaped to her room, but there was no respite.

One thought churned over and over in her mind: she had to find out if her brother had been taken prisoner.

She could not eat at breakfast. The bread tasted even more like sawdust than usual and the ersatz coffee turned her stomach. Mme Bolu wanted her to go back to bed, but she insisted on going into Montsauche. There, she searched the streets for German soldiers, someone who might be able to get a message to Franz. If she could find him, she felt sure he would tell her if any prisoners had been taken. But today there were none drinking in the cafés or loitering on street corners. All leave, it seemed, had been cancelled.

At last she saw a solitary figure sitting at a table outside the café owned by the man who was one of her regular contacts. He was a young officer, and she recognized him as one of the men who had started to frequent the bar in the *Beau Rivage*. She had always found him polite and she knew he spoke a little French.

She slipped into the café by the back door and found the proprietor pouring a glass of beer.

'Is that for the German officer?'

'Yes. Why?'

'Let me take it to him. I want an excuse to talk to him.'

When she set the beer on the table, the officer looked up with a puzzled frown.

'Hello. You're the girl from the hotel, aren't you? Do you work here as well?'

'I'm just helping out,' Christine said. She hesitated, her mind working overtime. She couldn't come straight out with her question, as she might have done with Franz, but there must be a way to introduce the subject. She said, 'Can I talk to you for a moment?'

'What about?'

'It's difficult. I heard there was some fighting yesterday.'

His expression was bitter. 'A massacre, not a fair fight. Your so-called freedom fighters ambushed a convoy. But what has it got to do with you?'

'I'm worried. You see, I've got a friend — a German soldier. We've been . . . well, seeing each other.'

His eyebrows went up. 'I thought your people took a dim view of that kind of fraternisation.'

'Yes, they do. That's why I've kept it secret. But now — I keep wondering if he might have been caught up in the fighting yesterday.'

'What's his name?'

'Franz — Franz Weber.'

He frowned. 'Weber? I'm sorry. I'm afraid it's bad news. Weber was one of the men escorting the convoy. There were no survivors.'

Christine gasped. Her shock was genuine. It was a development that had never crossed her mind.

The officer looked at her.

'If you are going to tell me that he's got you into trouble, I'm afraid there's nothing I can do about it.'

She felt herself blush. 'No! No, it's nothing like that. I just wanted to know . . . I suppose he could have been taken prisoner?'

'No chance! The *Maquis* don't take prisoners.'

'Did you . . . did you catch any of them?'

'Not yet. By the time we found the convoy, they were long gone. But we will find them, and when we do . . .' He broke off and looked at her, his eyes narrowing. 'You ask too many questions. What are you after, really?'

'Nothing!' She felt panic rising in her throat. 'I just wanted to know about Franz, that's all. I'm sorry.' She looked behind her into the café. 'I'd better get on. The boss will be wondering what I'm doing.'

She hurried back into the shop and slipped out by the back door. A few minutes later, she was cycling back towards the hotel.

She could not decide whether what she felt was relief or greater anguish. The spectre of her brother in enemy hands, being interrogated and perhaps tortured was banished, but the necessary corollary was that he was probably dead. It was possible, she told herself, that Cyrano was right and he might be hiding out somewhere, but she could not see any reason why he should be; and she refused to allow herself to hope.

For Luke, the hours of the night passed with excruciating slowness. He drifted in and out of consciousness; the pain was so bad that it made his whole body shake and once he heard a high pitched whine, which he did not recognize immediately as his own voice. Eventually, light began to show through the cracks in the wooden walls and he heard the family moving about outside. He shouted, begging to be let out, but no one came. Then, the door opened and the boy, Louis, called the goats out, but he had the pistol in one hand.

'Stay back! Don't move or I'll shoot you!'

Luke remembered how the boy had wanted to shoot him the night before, and anyway he was not at all sure that his legs would carry him if he tried to escape, so he stayed where he was.

After another long wait, he heard a vehicle drive up to the farm and then a familiar voice called, 'Hey, Gaspard! Got a minute? I need to talk to you.'

Luke wriggled over to the barred door and began to kick at it with all his strength.

'Jean-Claude! It's me! Luke! I'm in here. Tell them to let me out!'

There was a confused babble of voices, then the door was flung open and Jean-Claude leaned in.

'Luke! What the hell are you doing there? We've been searching all over for you. There's no need to hide.'

'Not hiding!' Luke managed to say. 'Kidnapped by these people!'

Christine arrived at the church that evening with a sickening sense of foreboding. Cyrano would have news, and she thought she knew what that news would be. He was waiting for her just inside the door and before he could speak, she said, 'He's not a prisoner. The *Boche* didn't take any prisoners.'

269

Cyrano came to her and took her by the shoulders. He was smiling. 'It's all right. We've found him. You needn't worry anymore.'

She stared at him, gulping for air. Then, she threw her arms round his neck and burst into tears. 'Oh, Cyrano, thank you! Thank you!'

He held her tightly and said, half laughing, 'You don't have to thank me. I'm just the messenger.' Then, as she continued to weep, 'Come on. It's all right. There's nothing to cry for now.'

She swallowed and sniffed and lifted her face to look at him.

'Sorry. It's stupid, isn't it? I didn't cry yesterday, I couldn't. Now I can't seem to stop.'

'It's shock,' he said. 'It does funny things to people.' He fished in a pocket and produced a handkerchief and dabbed at her wet cheeks. 'Here. It's not all that clean, I'm afraid. The laundry service isn't up to much around here.'

She took the handkerchief and blew her nose. 'And he's all right, really?'

'Yes. He's injured, but it's not serious — a broken wrist and concussion. He's been taken to the *château*, and Dr Martell says he should be up and about in a few days.'

'Do you know what happened to him?'

'He doesn't remember anything about it, but we found the bike when we went to search this morning and it looks as if the bullet aimed at him hit the bike instead. He was probably pitched over the handlebars into the ditch. It's just lucky the *Boche* didn't stumble across him while they were collecting their own dead.'

'So where has he been?'

He smiled grimly. 'It seems a local farmer found him when he was looking for his goats and thought he was a German. When Jean-Claude went to the farm to ask if they knew anything, he found Luke shut up in the goats' pen.'

'Oh, poor Luke!' In spite of herself she giggled, then added, sobering again, 'When can I see him?'

'Tomorrow. It's too near curfew now. I'll take you. Meet me at the ruined cottage at ten. OK?'

'Yes. Oh, Cyrano, I can't believe it! I've been so worried.'

'I know.' He frowned suddenly. 'When you came in, you said you knew he wasn't a prisoner. How did you know?'

'I went and asked, this morning.'

'You did what?'

'It's all right. I didn't give anything away. I said I was looking for news about a German boy I've been seeing.'

'What do you mean? What boy?'

'One of the soldiers. His name's Franz — it was. He died in the ambush.'

'You've been conducting some kind of relationship with a German soldier?'

'Oh, it's not like that. I mean, it wasn't real. He asked me to meet him and I said yes, because I thought it might be a useful way to get information. He's the one who told me about the requisitioning of the animals.'

'Where did you meet?'

'In the grounds of the hotel, down by the lake. I mean,' she looked up at him and then away, suddenly uncomfortable, 'we just talked, that's all. He was quite sweet really. I feel sorry he got killed in the ambush.'

Cyrano sighed. 'Oh, Chris! Don't you realize what a risk you were taking? Meeting him secretly, and then going asking after him. Who did you ask?'

'One of the officers. One that comes to the hotel sometimes. He was having a drink at the Cheval Blanc.'

'So he knows where you work. Are you sure he didn't suspect anything?'

'I . . . I don't think so.'

'Look, I think you should come back to the camp with me. You've been out on your own long enough.'

'No! No, I'm fine, really. I want to go on being useful.'

He looked at her for a long moment. 'I'm going to discuss this with Gregoire. I shall tell him I think we should pull you out.'

'Please don't!'

He reached out and touched her face, brushing back a strand of damp hair. 'I worry about you. If anything happened to you, I'd never forgive myself.'

She looked up into his eyes; kind, blue eyes, full of concern, and she thought suddenly: he is going to kiss me. At last, he's going to kiss me. She lifted her face to his and half closed her eyes.

But Cyrano turned away and went to fetch his music case. When he came back, his tone was different.

'You'd better get going. I don't want you out after curfew, on top of everything else. Come on.'

He went to the door and opened it for her. She paused a moment beside him.

'See you tomorrow?'

'Yes. Ten o'clock. Ride carefully.'

Cycling home, she put aside her momentary disappointment. Luke was safe, that was the important thing. And perhaps Cyrano was shy, or perhaps he felt it would be unprofessional to start a relationship. He was attracted to her, she felt sure of that. Sooner or later, it would happen. She would make it happen.

Cyrano was waiting for her when she arrived at the ruined cottage, with her hair waved and her face carefully made-up, and within half an hour they were in the hallway of the *château* which had been given over for use as a *Maquis* hospital. Dr Martell met them on the stairs.

'He's doing well, but I want him kept quiet for the next few days. There is a possibility of a fractured skull. He needs to lie still and rest, until we can be sure that there is no serious damage. I've put him in a private room so that he is not disturbed.'

Luke was lying almost flat. His forearm was in a cast and the flesh around one eye was bruised and yellow. Christine hurried over to the bed and bent to kiss his cheek.

'Oh, darling, I'm so thankful you're all right! You poor thing! How are you feeling?'

'Not too bad. Better than this time yesterday.' He managed a smile. 'That's the first time you've called me darling.'

'Well, don't get used to it. And don't make a habit of taking risks like that. Maman would never forgive me if she knew what you were doing.'

'Talk about pots and kettles! Are you all right? I'm sorry I gave you a scare.'

'More than a scare! I've never been so frightened in my life. But Cyrano has been wonderful. He looks after me.' She gave the older man a brilliant smile as he came to the other side of the bed.

'I would, if she'd let me,' he said. 'But she's a very determined girl, your sister.'

'You don't have to tell me,' Luke said. 'Pig headed, is the word I'd use. Anyway, thanks for trying. By the way, what's happened to those people who held me prisoner?'

'Gregoire went to see them yesterday. I don't think they'll make the same mistake again. And the idiot who took a pot shot at you has been disciplined by Vincent. Thank God he's not as good a shot as you are.'

'I suppose I've been lucky, really.' He shifted restlessly. 'I don't suppose you've got cigarette?'

'Here.' Cyrano produced a packet. 'Want me to light one for you?'

'Please.'

Cyrano lit the cigarette and put it between Luke's lips. Then he laid the packet down on the bedside table. 'There are only a couple left in there. I'll go and see if I can rustle up any more. I'll be back to collect you in a while, Chris.'

When he had gone, Christine clicked her tongue disapprovingly. 'You never used to smoke.'

'Well, I do now. And you never used to wear lipstick.'

She felt herself blush. 'It's what I wear for working at the hotel.'

'You're not at the hotel now. I bet you put it on for Cyrano's benefit.'

'Well, why shouldn't I? Don't you like me like this?'

He looked at her. 'Actually, it suits you. And the way you've got your hair. I'm just not sure it's . . . well, appropriate.'

'I don't know what you mean.'

He shifted uncomfortably and she said, 'Would you like another pillow?'

'Not allowed, unfortunately. Martell says I have to lie flat for at least three days. I even have to be spoon-fed and drink from a cup shaped like a teapot. It's humiliating.'

She leaned over and stroked his hair. 'Poor thing! But you must do as you're told. You've got to get well again.'

'I'm OK. I keep telling them that.'

'Well, you will be back on your feet soon. Try to be patient.'

'Hey, guess who is here, working as a nurse.'

Christine smiled. 'Adrienne. I know. I think she was suddenly inspired to "do her bit". Is she any good?'

'Yes, actually. She's very gentle, and she doesn't seem to mind doing all the . . . you know, all the less pleasant things that nurses have to do.'

'Good for her.'

There was a silence. After a moment he said, 'You like Cyrano, don't you?'

'Of course I do. So do you, don't you?'

'It's not the same.'

'I don't know what you're getting at.'

'Yes, you do.' He reached for her hand. 'Chris, he's years older than you.'

'So what?'

'Well, just don't . . . don't expect anything.'

'Oh, shut up, Luke. Just mind your own business.'

Cyrano returned.

'I'm sorry, Luke. It seems the hospital has run out of cigarettes. But I know there are plenty at the camp. Some of our lads held up a delivery last week, so we've got supplies for the next month, at least. I'll bring you some this afternoon.'

He returned as promised, with two packets of cigarettes. After the usual exchange of pleasantries, they both fell silent, until Luke said, 'Cyrano, I want to ask you something.'

'Ask away.'

'Is anything going on between you and Chris?'

'What!' Cyrano stared at him. 'I can't imagine what you're driving at.'

'You know what I mean.'

'I do not! What do you take me for? She's just a kid.'

'Not any more. Haven't you noticed how she's changed lately?'

'She's certainly grown up a lot over the last few months. But that happens, doesn't it?'

'It's more than that. She never wore make-up or bothered about her hair. And it's all for your benefit.'

'No, it isn't. It's being with Jeanette at the hotel. She's taught her all that.'

'You can't teach Chris anything she doesn't want to know. Haven't you noticed the way she is around you?'

'Well, a little bit of harmless flirting. She's trying out her wings.'

'That may be all it is to you. Don't you realize she's in love with you?'

'Oh, well. An adolescent crush . . . Look, I'm fond of Chris. I'm fond of both of you. But that's as far as it goes.'

'I don't think she sees it that way.'

'You mean she's expecting . . . something different? An affair?'

'Something more permanent, I should imagine.'

Cyrano ran his hand through his hair.

'Oh, my God! What a fool I've been! What a blind, stupid fool! I never dreamed . . . For God's sake, I'm ten years older than she is, at least.'

'I think she doesn't see that as a problem.'

He sighed deeply. 'Poor kid! I would never have willingly hurt her. You do know that, don't you?'

'I believe you. The question is, what do we do about it now? I don't want to see my sister's heart broken.'

'Of course you don't. Nor do I. She's such a great kid! Brave and intelligent — and beautiful, too. I'll have to explain, somehow.'

'Let her down gently, won't you?'

'Yes, of course. I'll do my best.'

'You won't tell her I've said anything, will you?'

'No, no. I think . . . I think it will be better if she doesn't realize that I've guessed how she feels. I'll try to keep it as low key as possible . . . just give her the hint that, well, that we can never be more than friends.'

'I think that sounds the best way.'

Cyrano got up. 'I'd better get back. Is there anything else you need?'

'No, I'm OK. Thanks for the cigarettes.'

Cyrano hesitated, looking down at Luke. 'No hard feelings?'

'No, of course not.' Luke offered his hand and Cyrano took it in a firm grasp.

When Cyrano had gone, Luke fidgeted uncomfortably. The day was very hot and although he was naked under a single sheet, he could feel sweat pricking and itching in his armpits and his groin. He longed to get up and join the other men for a dip in the cool waters of the spring, back at the camp. The door opened to admit Adrienne carrying a bowl and a bundle of clean linen.

'There, now your visitor has gone I expect you would like a nice wash. It's very hot today.'

'Yes, it is. I wish I could get up and have a bath.'

'*Pauvre petit!* Well, we must do our best to make you comfortable.'

She squeezed out a sponge and bathed his face with cool water. Close to, he could smell her perfume. She was not wearing make-up and her luxuriant blonde hair was captured in a pleat at the back of her head, but her skin was smooth and the lashes round her deep blue eyes were thick and darker than her hair. He took all this in as she leaned over him, and then his eyes moved to the hint of cleavage in the open V of her overall, and the outline of her breasts. She finished washing his face and moved down to his neck and then his shoulders. When she took hold of the sheet to pull it back he grabbed it.

'No, please!'

She looked at him with her head slightly on one side.

'What are you worried about? You think I haven't seen a naked man before?'

'No, it's just . . .' He floundered into silence.

She smiled. 'What have you got to be shy about? You are a beautiful young man. You will feel so much better afterwards.'

She drew the sheet back to his feet and in spite of all his efforts at control, his penis reared up in response. She looked from it to his face and said softly, 'I think you are an innocent. You have never made love to a woman. Am I right?'

He nodded, too ashamed to speak.

'Then we shall put that right at once.' She leaned down and kissed him on the mouth, and at the same time her fingers undid the buttons of her overall, and he saw that beneath it she too, was naked. '*Chéri*,' she murmured, 'there is nothing for you to worry about. This is a once only event and there will be no consequences, no obligation, for either of us. Think of it as part of your education.'

Afterwards she washed him all over and even changed the sheets on the bed. 'So, roll over on your right side for me. That's right. Now back the other way. There, isn't that better?'

'You're very good at this,' he said, then, blushing, 'I mean the nursing bit.'

'At all of it, I hope. No, don't look like that. I know what you mean. When I was a girl, my mother was very ill. I learned then how to look after her.'

'Oh, I'm sorry.'

'It was a long time ago now.'

He stretched. His body felt smooth and relaxed, as never before.

'When you said this was a once only . . .'

'I meant it.' She stroked his cheek with cool fingers. 'Soon you will find a girl to love and she will love you. Do not tell her where you learned to make love so well. Let her think it is her beauty that has inspired you.'

'I shall never forget this,' he said huskily. 'I shall always be grateful.'

She bent and kissed him on the forehead. 'And I shall remember, too, with great pleasure. Now, I must go. There is still work to do. But not such enjoyable work, I think.'

She winked at him, picked up her bowl and the dirty linen and left.

Next morning, Christine found a note in the tobacco tin: 'Meet me this evening. Usual place.'

She did her hair and make-up with special care, and sought out Adrienne, who had just come back from the hospital.

'Could you possibly let me have a dab of that perfume you wear?'

'Oh ho!' the older woman exclaimed. 'You have a date tonight. Who is he?'

'I can't tell you. Not yet.'

'Well, here. Help yourself. Not too much, now. You don't want to scare the poor boy off. There, let me look at you. Very good! He is a lucky young man, whoever he is.'

Christine arrived at the church earlier than the appointed time, but Cyrano was already there, playing the organ. The music was something she did not recognize, something slow and meditative. It took the edge off her mood of eager anticipation. The organ fell silent and a nervous quiver ran through her body. A moment later he was sitting beside her.

'Hello. How are you this evening?'

'OK. You?'

'I'm fine, thanks.'

'How are things up at the camp?'

'Busy. The *Boche* are getting more active. They attacked the *Maquis Socrate* two days ago and he and his men had to beat a quick retreat and find a new base. Then yesterday, four of our lads were out on a foraging expedition and they ran slap into a German ambush and had to shoot their way out. Fortunately, I think the *Boche* were just as surprised as they were and they got away with only minor wounds. What's the mood like in the town?'

'A bit subdued. People are glad that the farmers have their animals back, but they are beginning to talk about reprisals.'

'I'm afraid that will come. But if we worried about that, we'd have to give up and go home. But there's good news from the real war. Monty's forces have landed in Italy and the Italians have asked for an armistice.'

'Oh, that's wonderful!'

'Yes, it should shorten the war by months. Our armies can march straight through Italy and attack the Germans from the south — what Churchill calls "the soft underbelly" of Europe. Oh, and another thing. You remember I told you, none of those gunboats you told us about ever reached the Med? The RAF finished them off on the Saône. Apparently, Winnie sent his personal congratulations.'

'That's fantastic news!' She looked at him and felt a glow of pride. Then a new thought dimmed it. 'Do you think the war might all be over by Christmas?'

'I hesitate to pin too many hopes on that. We seem to have heard it all before. But you never know. The Russians are making headway in the north. Maybe Hitler will see the game's up and sue for peace.'

She hesitated. 'It's an awful thing to say, but part of me hopes he won't. I don't want it to be all over before I have a chance to join in.'

'You've done your bit, far more than most other girls. What you need, what we all need now, is a chance to get back to our normal lives. Oh, speaking of that, there's something

I want to show you.' He reached into a pocket and drew out an envelope. 'We had another *parachutage* — well, you know about that because you recced the location for us. There were letters from home, as usual. But there has been so much going on I nearly forgot about these.' He paused. 'We're not supposed to tell anyone about our personal lives, back home. But I want to show you these.'

He took out two photographs and handed them to her. In the first, she saw a pretty, fair-haired woman with a small girl on her knee; in the second picture the child was alone, squinting at the camera and waving. Christine turned the photographs over, but there was nothing written on the back.

'My wife, Susan,' he said. 'And that's our daughter, Caroline. She was four last month.'

For a moment, Christine was unable to speak. She cleared her throat but her voice came out as a whisper. 'I didn't know you were married.'

'No. As I said, we're not supposed to talk about our private lives. The idea is, we should be so immersed in our cover story that we almost become different people; but it doesn't work like that. Not for me, anyway.'

'You miss them?'

'Very much. Caroline was only three when I last saw her, and they change so quickly at that age.'

She handed the pictures back and muttered gruffly, 'Thanks. Thanks for showing me.'

'I wanted you to know,' he said quietly.

For a moment neither of them spoke. Then he reached over and took her hand. 'You OK?'

'Yes, 'course. Why shouldn't I be?'

'You know,' he said, 'I think you and Luke should be thinking about going on with your journey, if it can be managed. You've both done excellent work here but you could be so much more useful back in England. I don't believe there is much chance of the war being over quickly and there is a lot you could do to help the war effort — both of you.'

'In a munitions factory,' she said bitterly.

'No. You haven't forgotten that address I gave you, have you?'

'No.'

'Believe me, you would be welcomed with open arms there. I'll make sure they know what you've done out here. And you would get so much out of it, too. New skills to learn, new people to meet. There's a big, exciting world out there, Chris, full of new experiences and new challenges. You would have such a lot to look forward to.'

She looked at him for a moment, a look that pierced his heart; then she stood up.

'I'd better get back. It'll be curfew soon.'

He walked to the door with her.

'Ride carefully. You know I worry about you. I couldn't bear to see you hurt.'

She lowered her head and pulled the heavy door open. ''Night, Cyrano.'

He would have been horrified if he could have watched her riding back to the hotel. Blinded by unshed tears, she raced through the darkening lanes, heedless of traffic or possible German checkpoints. Reaching the hotel unscathed, she locked herself in her room and when Jeanette called her to start work in the dining room, she shouted back that she was unwell and could not come.

Three days later the newly installed telephone rang in the command hut at the *Maquis Xavier*. Cyrano, who was busy encoding a message, answered it.

'It's me, Pierre. I've got a message for those two youngsters I sent up to you, back in April.'

CHAPTER 22

Christine continued to check the messages in the tobacco tin in the ruined cottage and leave the dated slip of paper that assured Cyrano she was still safe. She knew that failure to do so would precipitate a chain of events whose outcome she could not predict.

There were no missions for her, and she spent her days aimlessly cycling round the lanes. Twice she was stopped by German patrols and when asked where she was going she shrugged and muttered, 'Just out for a ride,' and they let her go. Then one morning there was a note in the tobacco tin:

'Time to come home. Pack your things. I'll pick you up at twelve.'

She went back to the hotel in a mutinous mood. She felt that she was being removed from her post, that she had been judged too immature, too emotional for the job. It seemed like the ultimate failure. When she told Mme Bolu and Jeanette that she was leaving, they wanted to know why, and she could give them no explanation.

Jeanette hugged her. 'I'll miss you so much! It's been like having a sister.'

'I'll miss you, too,' she replied and realized to her surprise that she meant it.

'Perhaps it is only temporary,' Madame said. 'You will be welcome to come back, at any time.'

At twelve she was waiting, with her few belongings packed into the old rucksack. Cyrano drove up and tied her bicycle onto the roof of the old Citroen. She thanked Madame for her hospitality, kissed Jeanette and got into the car.

'Don't look like that,' Cyrano said. 'You're not in trouble or anything. It's good news.'

At the camp she found Luke waiting. His arm was in a sling and there was still the faint remains of bruising round his eyes, but otherwise he looked his old self. He put his good arm round her and gave her a hug.

'How are you, Sis?'

'I'm OK. You look better.'

'Yes, good as new — well, almost.' He studied her face and noted that it was bare of make-up and her hair was dragged back into a plait.

'How long have you been out of hospital?'

'Only since yesterday. Gregoire wants to see us for some reason. Come on, we'd better not keep him waiting.'

Gregoire was sitting behind the table in the command hut with Xavier. Cyrano followed them in, and took his place beside the others.

'Sit down, both of you,' Gregoire said. 'Don't look so worried. You're not in trouble. There's been a development. We had a message via Pierre at the pharmacy from your friend Rollo.'

'Rollo!' Luke said. 'Rollo was in Corbigny?'

'No, I think it was a written note, delivered by a third party. But this is the gist of it. The *Madeleine* — that's his father's boat, isn't it? — is en route to Longvie. That's just east of Dijon. There's a big airfield there, so I guess they are delivering supplies of some sort. If you can meet them there, they think they may be able to get you to Montbéliard.' He paused and looked from one to the other. 'It's risky. There is bound to be tight security around the airfield, but we think you should take the opportunity while it's offered. You have both become very valuable members of the *Maquis* over the last few months and we shall be sorry to lose you, but I don't have the right to keep you here. Your parents expect you to go back to England and it's right that we should do all we can to make that possible. Do you agree?'

Luke looked at his sister. Her face was pale and set and her eyes were fixed on the ground. He thought he had never seen her so downcast and it hurt him to know that he was in part responsible. Cyrano had not told him what had passed between them, except to say 'I think Christine understands the situation now.' It had to be done, he told himself, and now it was up to him to try to heal the wound. Left to himself, he would have been happy to throw in his lot with the *Maquis* for the duration of the war, but he knew that would be irresponsible.

'I think Gregoire's right, Chris,' he said. 'We should go.'

She lifted her eyes and shrugged. 'Yes, I suppose you're right.'

'How do we get to Longvie?' he asked. 'Do we cycle?'

'I think we can do better for you than that, after all you've done,' Gregoire said. 'I've had a word with some of my contacts in the other *Maquis* and they've agreed to help out. Be ready tomorrow morning and you should be there by the evening.'

At first light, Luke shouldered his rucksack and let himself out of the log cabin that served as dormitory for himself and half a dozen men of the *Maquis*. The morning was damp, with low cloud hanging in the tops of the trees, and as he walked across the clearing, something crunched under his boot. Looking down, he saw it was a freshly fallen sweet chestnut, the prickly green case broken open to show the nut inside. He stooped and picked it up as a kind of talisman.

Cyrano joined him, looking strained, and soon the other members of the *Maquis* tumbled out of their huts and came to say goodbye. Fat Jacques brought him a mug of coffee and pressed a loaf of bread and some goat's cheese into his hand.

'Where's Christine?' Cyrano asked.

'Here she comes,' Luke said, seeing her approaching from the direction of the spring. She had discarded her skirt and was wearing a pair of corduroy trousers that must have been borrowed from one of the smaller men. Even so, she had had to cinch them in with a belt and turn up the bottoms. The baggy sweater she had been given by Marie at the beginning of their journey completed the outfit. Luke's heart gave a lurch at the sight of her, remembering the pretty, smiling girl who had come to visit him in hospital.

Cyrano said, 'Give us a few minutes, Luke.' He touched Christine on the arm and drew her aside a short distance.

They looked at each other.

He said quietly, 'Christine, I think I have hurt you. I didn't mean to and I'm very, very sorry. I hope you know I never intended anything of the sort.'

She looked into his eyes. 'I know. I was being silly. I see that now. You mustn't blame yourself.'

'I do,' he said. 'But there's nothing I can do about it now. I'm very, very fond of you. You know that. But I love you like a sister, like Luke does. I hope, when the war is over, if . . . if I'm still around . . . that we can be friends.'

'I should like that,' she answered huskily. 'Very much.'

'Good. Now, you haven't forgotten that address I gave you?'

'64 Baker Street and ask for Mrs Bingham,' she repeated.

'And tell her that you know Morse and can use a Morse key,' he said.

She managed a smile. 'I'll tell her.'

He reached into his pocket. 'There's something I should like you to have. A little keepsake. Here.' It was a gold signet ring. 'It's French, so it won't compromise you if you should happen to be searched. That's why I was allowed to bring it with me. It was given to me by my professor when I left the Conservatoire.'

'But it must be precious to you,' she protested. 'I can't take it.'

'Yes, you can. I never wear it. I'd like you to have it.'

'If you're sure . . .'

'I'm sure.' He put the ring into her hand and closed her fingers over it.

The Mercedes drove into the compound with Gregoire at the wheel and his two bodyguards riding pillion as usual. It was followed by a jeep containing four men, and with a Bren gun mounted at the rear.

'Come on,' Gregoire called. 'Time to get going.'

Cyrano took hold of Christine's hands and kissed her on both cheeks.

'*Au revoir, chérie*. We'll meet again when all this is over.'

Tears were choking her but she managed to whisper, 'Goodbye, dear Cyrano.' Then as a sudden thought struck her. 'I shan't know how to find you. I don't even know your real name.'

'Don't worry,' he said. 'Phyllis Bingham will know how to contact me. Off you go, now. Good luck.'

The men gathered round them. Xavier kissed them both on both cheeks; the others shook their hands and slapped Luke on the back. Cyrano took him by the shoulders.

'I think we're both French enough to do this, don't you?' he said, and embraced him.

Amid a chorus of '*Au revoir, bonne chance!*' they climbed into the back of the Mercedes. One of the bodyguards squeezed in beside them and the other got into the front beside Gregoire. With the jeep going ahead, they bounced down the rough track leading to the road. Luke twisted in his seat, waving until the last minute; but Christine kept her eyes down, gripping the signet ring so tightly that it left an imprint on her palm.

They drove east, across country, keeping to the minor roads. Whenever they had to cross a major route, Gregoire ordered them to stop and wait, while he went forward with one of his men to check the area for German roadblocks. Once, a convoy of enemy vehicles passed within forty metres of the junction where they were standing, but paid no attention to them.

As they approached Saumur, they were waved down by a girl on a bicycle. After a brief exchange of passwords with Gregoire, she led them by back roads around the town, where a German garrison had taken up residence. At Pouilly, they crossed the main road leading south to Chalon then, as they entered the forest above the valley of the Ouche, they were brought to an abrupt standstill by a barrier of tree trunks, and saw that they were being covered by a dozen automatic weapons. Gregoire got out and three men, all heavily armed, appeared from the trees beside the road. Gregoire conferred briefly with the leader, a tall man with a heavy dark beard, and then he opened the rear door of the Mercedes.

'This is where we part company, I'm afraid. From here, you will be the responsibility of the *Maquis Valmy*. This is Renard, the leader. He will see you safely to Longvie.'

They climbed out and shook hands with the tall man, and then there was only time for brief handclasps with Gregoire and mutual wishes of '*Bonne chance!*' before they were led away round the barrier. There, a pick-up truck was waiting with six men carrying Schmeisser automatics in the back.

Renard indicated that they should get into the cab and climbed in behind the wheel. By contrast with Gregoire's cautious approach, it seemed he preferred to rely on speed and the element of surprise and they careered along the forest tracks and down into the Côte d'Or, catching glimpses of signposts to towns whose names had been a familiar background to their childhoods; Clos de Vougeot; Nuits St Georges; Aloxe Corton.

Crossing the main road from Dijon to Beaune, they almost ran into another German convoy, but Renard put his foot down and roared across the path of the leading vehicle, while his men jeered and shouted obscenities at its occupants. Apparently, the convoy's escort had more important things to do than pursue a solitary maverick, and no one followed them as they plunged into the woods again.

It was almost sunset when they reached their destination. In the village of Ouges, on the banks of the Canal de Bourgogne, Renard stopped the truck.

'The airfield is on the other side of the canal. The basin where the barges unload is about half a kilometre north of here, but the *Boche* probably patrol the towpath. Wait until dark, and then go carefully. Good luck!'

They were hardly out of the cab, before he was reversing to turn around and a minute later he and his men had disappeared in the direction from which they had come.

'Well, he wasn't going to hang about, was he,' Luke remarked.

Christine shrugged. 'Let's hope Rollo and his father are here somewhere. Otherwise we're on our own.'

Luke picked up his rucksack. 'It'll look suspicious if we hang about here. We'd better find somewhere to hide out until dark.'

They took refuge in the church porch and ate the last of their provisions, watching the darkness draw in. It was a damp night and mist lay low over the canal.

'We're in luck,' Luke murmured as they set off. 'There's less chance of being spotted.'

On the far side of the canal, they could just make out the high fence surrounding the airfield but the towpath seemed deserted, until Luke came to a sudden halt.

'Down here!' he whispered, dragging his sister into the ditch that ran alongside the path.

They were just in time. Two German guards passed within a few feet of them, talking together in low voices. When they were well away, Luke straightened up and pulled Christine with him. 'Come on. It can't be far now.'

A few minutes later, they came to the point where the path skirted a wide basin. Several barges were moored there and they crept from one to another, searching for the *Madeleine*.

'Here she is!' Christine whispered. 'Thank heaven!'

She stepped aboard and tapped softly at the door of the cabin. For a moment, there was no response, then the door opened and Rollo stood outlined against the light from inside.

'It's you! You made it! *Salut*! It's good to see you. Come in! Quickly.'

As the door closed behind them, Pasquier got up from the table.

'Well, so you're still here! I thought you'd be long gone over the frontier by now — or else in prison. Sit down, then. Rollo, bring some glasses.'

When they had drunk each other's health, Luke said, 'What brought you here? I thought the *Boche* had commandeered the *Madeleine*.'

'So they have,' Rollo said. 'We've been all over the place since you left, up to the Seine, back to Paris, then Auxerre again. But then we were ordered to bring some crates of replacement parts for the airfield here and I thought if you could get here there was a chance we could help you on your way.'

'Does that mean you are going to Montbéliard?' Christine asked.

Pasquier shook his head. 'I'm afraid not. We're ordered back to Auxerre. But we shall start by going down to Saint-Jean-de-Losne to see if we can pick up a cargo going that way. That's the junction with the Saône. There's a big depot there and it's a meeting place for barges from all over the country. It's very likely that we shall be able to find someone going up the Doubs who will take you.'

Christine bit her lip; this was a disappointment. For a few moments, she had felt safe, on familiar ground. Now everything was uncertain again.

Rollo was saying, 'So what have you been doing all these months? What happened to your arm, Luke?'

'It's a long story,' Luke said and Pasquier got to his feet. 'In that case, it can keep until morning. We have to make an early start. You know where you sleep. Goodnight.'

As the sun rose next day, the *Madeleine* slipped her moorings and chugged south. By noon, the next day they were in Saint-Jean-de-Losne, which was, as Pasquier had predicted, crowded with boats from all over France. As they threaded their way through the throng, greetings were shouted from deck to deck and it was obvious that they were among a close community of friends. As soon as they were moored, Pasquier left them and it was evening before he returned, slightly drunk and very pleased with himself.

'It's all settled. Ton-ton will take you to Montbéliard.'

'Ton-ton?' Luke queried and Rollo laughed.

'His real name is Antoine, but he's always called Ton-ton. He's some kind of second cousin. It's like that here. Almost everyone is related in some way. Ton-ton's all right. You'll be safe with him.'

They were introduced to their new host the following morning. Antoine was a younger man, thick-set and with a mop of curly reddish hair. With him on the barge were his wife Josie, and their 3-year-old son. When Luke tried to thank them for offering their help, Ton-ton brushed his words aside with a brief '*Il n'y a pas de quoi, mon brave,*' and Josie smiled shyly and asked if they had had breakfast. Pasquier and Roland had come with them, but Antoine was ready to cast off and there was time only for a quick handshake and repeated thanks, before the bows swung out into the current and the two were left waving on the quay.

The *Alouette*, as their new temporary home was called, threaded her way through the throng of boats and out onto the broad reaches of the Saône. Here, she turned north-east for a short distance before turning right to join the Canal du Rhône au Rhin. At the pretty town of Dole, where scarlet geraniums in window boxes overhanging the canal seemed to signal defiance, both to the austerity of war and the coming winter, the canal met the River Doubs. After the comparative calm of the canal, they found themselves buffeted by a fierce current.

'The river is in flood,' Ton-ton shouted above the noise of the water. 'It's always bad at this time of year. We must hope that the locks are not under water and impassable.'

At Besancon, where the grim medieval castle loomed above them on its crag, a swastika flag fluttering from its battlements, they entered a tunnel carved out of the rock.

'The river makes a loop round the town,' Ton-ton explained. 'This saves us three kilometres.'

They came at last, late one afternoon, to the big industrial city of Montbéliard, its factories and huge car plants a stark contrast to the pretty countryside they had passed through. As they entered the suburbs, Antoine cut the engine and drew the barge into the side of the canal.

'The *Boche* will probably be waiting for us when we get to the wharves. You'd better nip off here.'

There was another sudden parting, another rapid exchange of handclasps, and then they were on the bank, with their rucksacks containing their few possessions at their feet, and the *Alouette* was already pulling away.

They stood watching her for a few moments as she dwindled into the shadows, then Luke picked up his rucksack and said, 'Come on. I'm not sure where we are, but it must be a fair way to the city centre. It'll be dark soon.'

They had been to the city many times before to visit their godfather, but they had always arrived by train and this area down by the canal was unknown territory. They set out along back streets, unsure of the best route.

'The castle makes a good landmark,' Christine pointed out, indicating the conical towers rising above the surrounding trees on a hilltop. 'Uncle Marcel's shop is in the Rue du Château, so it must be that way.'

By the time they found themselves in the right street, the sun had set. Luke caught hold of his sister's hand and smiled at her. He was already imagining a warm welcome, a comfortable chair, and hopefully something to eat.

'Nearly there! Uncle Marcel is in for a big surprise.'

They hurried along the road, ignored by passers-by hastening home before the beginning of the curfew. When they reached the shop, the shutters were down.

'He's closed, of course,' Luke said. 'We'll try the door to the flat.'

He led the way into the alley that ran alongside the shop and rang the bell at a side door. They waited, but there was

291

no sign of movement inside. Christine craned her neck to look up at the windows, but with strict blackout orders in force, no chink of light could be seen from any of the houses around. Luke rang again, and then knocked loudly. The ensuing silence left them in no doubt.

'He's not there,' Christine said.

'Perhaps he's gone to visit friends, or made a last minute dash to the shops,' Luke suggested.

'He'll have to be quick, then,' she replied, 'or he'll be caught by the curfew, unless . . .'

'Unless he's staying the night somewhere,' Luke finished for her.

'I suppose he could have gone up to the chalet,' she said.

'It's a bit early in the season. And there won't be any skiing, will there?'

'He might just have felt like getting away for a few days. We could try telephoning.'

'The trouble with that is, I've no idea where the nearest phone box is. If we're caught wandering about after curfew looking for one, we'll be in trouble.'

Christine shivered. The day had been clear and sunny, but at this altitude, the nights were already cold. She had put on her good coat, the one she had been wearing when they left home, but she still felt chilled.

'We can't stand around here all night.'

'No, that's true,' her brother agreed, 'but what else do you suggest? We dare not try to check into a hotel. They would be bound to ask for our papers.'

Christine thought. 'We're not far from the railway station, if I remember rightly. Perhaps we could shelter in a waiting room overnight.'

'It's an idea,' Luke agreed. 'Anyway, there's no point in standing here. Let's give it a try.'

The station, to their dismay, was dark and silent, the entrance closed by a heavy gate.

'So much for that idea,' Luke said. 'Now what?'

'Goodness knows.' Christine peered despondently along the platform. Then she said, 'See those goods trains in the sidings over there? If we could get into one of the box cars, that would give us shelter and hide us till morning.'

'Maybe,' Luke said. 'But there's no way of getting to them from here.'

'Perhaps from the other side of the tracks?' she suggested. 'There's some kind of embankment under the trees. Maybe there's a way down?'

'OK. Let's try,' her brother agreed, without much confidence. 'At least if there isn't, we can hide up among the trees till the curfew is lifted.'

They made their way back to where a level crossing gave access to the far side of the rails. The moon was rising, huge and amber-coloured, and above them, the fairy-tale turrets of the castle glimmered in its light. A narrow road led around the bottom of the hill, between the woods and the railway embankment, but it was bounded by a tall fence of wire mesh. They trailed along it, hoping for a way in but finding none.

Christine stopped suddenly. 'Luke, look down there, on those flat-bed wagons. Aren't those tanks?'

Luke peered down. A long line of wagons each bore an identical shrouded shape, but the barrel of a gun protruding from each made identification easy. 'Yes, you're right.'

'I bet they're destined for the south,' Christine said. 'Now that Italy has capitulated, the Germans must be desperate to reinforce their defences down there.'

Luke sighed wistfully. 'If only we had some *plastique* and a few detonators.'

'If only,' she agreed. 'Unfortunately, that's not among the things I carry in my coat pockets.'

It was the nearest she had come to making a joke since they left the Morvan and Luke gave her arm a squeeze. 'Never mind. Come on.'

They walked on, until Christine stopped again. 'Hang on a minute.' She went back a few steps and bent to examine the fence. 'Look here! The fence has been cut. It doesn't show unless you happen to be looking, but there's a flap here, like a small gateway.'

Luke squatted beside her. 'You're right. I bet it's the work of the Resistance. Maybe they are planning some sabotage.'

'Good for them!' she responded. 'Meanwhile, here's our way in.'

'Chris . . .' he said doubtfully, but she was already tugging the flap of wire open and wriggling through it. After a moment's hesitation, he followed, pulling the wire back into position so that the gap would be almost invisible to the casual eye.

They slid down the embankment and found their progress checked by a heap of sand, some sacks of cement, and other builders' materials. Picking their way through them, they came alongside the train carrying the tanks. When they reached the engine, Christine stopped.

'There must be a way of disabling one of these monsters,' she murmured. 'If it was a car it would be easy — cut the brake cables, drain the oil . . .'

'Well, it's not a car,' Luke said. 'Come on.'

She seemed not to hear him.

'Oil . . . These wheels must need lubrication, and this crank shaft that drives them.' She squatted down, peering at the wheels of the engine. 'Look here. These little cup-shaped things on top of the block that connects the rods . . . I wonder . . .' She ran a finger around the top of one of the brass cylinders and sniffed it. 'That's oil, all right. If one could introduce some kind of abrasive, that would do the trick. Do the tops of these come off?' She twisted one experimentally. 'Yes! They do!'

Luke looked around him uneasily. He had a feeling that someone must be watching.

'Leave it alone, Chris. Let's get out of sight.'

She straightened up. 'Sand! Of course. Come on.'

'Where are you going?'

'To get some sand. Come on!'

They found a bucket left behind by the builders, shovelled in some sand and lugged it back to where the engine stood. Christine unscrewed the top of one of the containers and trickled sand into it.

'I'll do this side. You do the other. If I'm right, once the engine gets up to speed the bearings will overheat and then the whole thing will come to a grinding halt.'

'Bloody hell!' he grumbled. 'The things you have me doing!' But he went round to the far side of the engine as she had told him to.

He rejoined her just as she was screwing on the last cap. 'There. That should do it.'

As she stood up, there was a shout and floodlights came on along the footbridge which crossed the lines, illuminating the whole yard as brightly as a stage set. Luke grabbed her by the wrist.

'Run! Come on!'

Bent low in the shelter of the line of trucks, they ran back the way they had come. Behind them, Luke could hear running feet and then two gunshots, but the bullets were not, it seemed, aimed at them. The pile of sand served as a marker and they scrabbled up the embankment on all fours to the hole in the fence. As he wriggled through, pulling Christine after him, Luke just had time to register the fact that the flap of wire was not as neatly replaced as he had left it. Then something hit him on the back of the head.

Luke came round to darkness and a sense of movement. He was being jolted around on a hard surface; he was in the back of a truck — again. The thought was comforting. They were being taken back to the *Maquis* camp.

From nearby he heard his sister's voice. 'Luke? Luke! Are you all right?'

'Mmm. Think so. Don't worry. It will be all right. Cyrano will vouch for us.'

'Cyrano's miles away. We're not going back to the camp. We were in the rail yard. Try to remember.'

'Railway yard? Oh God! Yes. What happened?'

'I don't know. Suddenly all the lights came on and we had to run for it, and then someone grabbed me from behind. I think they must have hit you.'

'Where are we?'

'In the back of a truck.' She gave a small giggle, which verged on hysteria. 'Talk about déjà-vu!'

'Who's got us? Do you know?'

'No. No one spoke. But it must be the Germans. They must have been mounting some sort of surveillance. I think . . . I'm afraid . . .' her voice shook. 'I think it must be the Gestapo.'

He said nothing, struggling through the fog in his brain to take in the implications of what she had said.

Christine went on, 'Listen! If they question us, we must stick to the same story. We're refugees, looking for somewhere to shelter for the night. We were looking for our godfather but he wasn't there. The closer we stick to the truth, the easier it will be. Have you got that?'

'Mmm,' he mumbled. 'Got it.'

The truck came to a standstill and rough hands dragged them both out and pushed them down stone steps to the door of a cellar. Inside, blinking in the light of an unshaded electric bulb, they saw their captors for the first time. Four men, dressed in black and wearing black ski masks. There was a wooden table with some upright chairs round it. One of the men pulled out two chairs and said gruffly, 'Sit!'

The strong hands gripping their arms left them no option but to obey. An inner door opened and another man appeared. He was wearing a civilian suit, his light hair was cropped close to his head and he had cold blue eyes above hollow cheeks. He perched himself on the edge of the table in front of them and barked something in German at Luke.

'I'm sorry. I don't speak German,' Luke replied.

The man's lip curled in disbelief. 'Oh, I think you do. But we will continue in French if you prefer. Who are you working for?'

'What? I don't understand.' Luke's voice was still slurred from the effects of the blow.

The man leaned forward and jabbed a finger into his chest. 'Don't try that with me. I want some answers, and I don't mind what I have to do to get them. Understand? Now, who sent you to that rail yard?'

'Leave him alone!' Christine broke in. 'He's only half conscious, thanks to your thugs. We didn't mean any harm. We're just a couple of refugees looking for somewhere to sleep.'

'Oh yes? And you just happened to choose a spot exactly where an act of sabotage was about to take place.'

'Sabotage? We don't know anything about sabotage.'

He twisted towards her. 'Don't you start! There's nothing wrong with your head. You know exactly what I'm talking about. Someone sent you to spy on what was happening and to raise the alarm. I want to know who it was.'

'What do you mean, spy? We didn't raise an alarm.'

He raised a hand as if he was going to strike her. Then he sat back.

'Very well. Let's start again. Name?'

The question was directed at Luke. 'Luke Beauchamps.'

'And I'm his sister, Christine.'

Their interrogator raised a sceptical eyebrow. 'Sister, eh? Papers!'

She fumbled in her pocket and produced her identity card. He scrutinized it and then turned to Luke with the same demand.

Luke shook his head. 'Haven't got them.'

'Our house was bombed, by the Allies,' Christine said. 'We lost everything. That's why we are refugees. We are looking for our godfather. He lives in Montbéliard, but he wasn't at home. That's why we needed to find somewhere to sleep.'

'And you just happened to know how to get into the rail yard.'

'No, we didn't! We just happened to spot the place where the wire had been cut.'

He laughed with what sounded like genuine amusement.

'Oh, you're good! I'll give you that. Quite an accomplished little actress.' Then, deadly serious again, 'You are a liar. You are a filthy collaborator in the pay of the Germans. Now, tell me who you are working for.'

'But I don't understand. You are German. If we were working for you, you would know about it.'

'German? Are you out of your mind? Why would we try to blow up our own train?'

'You were trying to blow it up?'

'As if you didn't know! And thanks to you and your brother here — if he is your brother and not a *Boche* spy — two of my men are dead or prisoners and that load of tanks will be on its way to the Front tomorrow.'

'No it won't! It won't get very far. We've seen to that.'

'You? You expect me to believe that you two were trying to sabotage that train yourselves?'

'Yes.'

'With your bare hands, I suppose.' He grabbed her wrist and sniffed her hand. 'You haven't been anywhere near explosive.'

'No. We didn't have any *plastique* so we put sand in the oil pots.'

He stared at her in silence for a moment. Then he said, in a different tone, 'This godfather you are looking for. What's his name?'

'Lemaître. Marcel Lemaître.'

He looked from one to another, frowning, then turned to one of his men.

'Fetch the *patron*. I think we'd better let him deal with this. Put them in the other room till he gets here.'

They were hustled into the inner room and the door was slammed shut behind them. Without speaking they turned to each other and clung together for a long moment.

Then Luke said, 'You were marvellous. I couldn't think straight.'

'I just said the first thing that came into my head,' she replied. 'Are you all right?'

'More or less. My head aches.'

'Poor you. Come over here and sit down.'

There was another table and more chairs in the room and they sat facing each other, their hands clasped.

'I think it's going to be all right,' Christine said. 'I think they are Resistance. We're all on the same side.'

'As long as we can convince them of that,' Luke said. 'They obviously blame us for the operation going wrong.'

'But it wasn't anything we did. The Germans must have been expecting them.'

'And they think we were the ones who gave the game away. I hope we can persuade this *patron*, whoever he is, that it wasn't us.'

They sat in silence after that, until the door was opened and the man in civilian clothes said, 'Come on out. The boss wants to see you.'

A man was standing in the middle of the room; a tall man with fair hair and a neat beard. For a second no one spoke.

Then Christine said, 'Papa?'

They were sitting around a table in a mountain hut. A fire of pine logs was burning in the grate and the air was filled with a resinous scent that reminded Luke of Christmas. On the table were the remains of a breakfast of ham and eggs and real coffee, smuggled over the border from Switzerland. Luke, with interruptions from Christine, had just finished telling the story of their journey and their many adventures.

Marcel Lemaitre, whose chalet they were in, shook his head in amazement. 'What a saga! You both deserve a medal.'

'I rather think,' Roger Beecham said, with a smile, 'that their mother would say they both deserve to be smacked and sent to bed without their supper.' He leaned across the table and took hold of a hand of each of his children. 'My dears, I can't tell you how proud I am of both of you. But if I had

had any inkling of what was going on I should not have had a moment's peace. Thank God you were able to give your mother some reassurance.'

'That was Cyrano's doing,' Christine said. 'He sent the messages for us.' Neither of them had mentioned her infatuation with the English radio operator, but she was beginning to find that she could speak of him without so much pain.

'Yes, a good chap, Cyrano,' her father said. 'And a brilliant pianist.'

'I thought the flute was his main instrument,' Christine said.

Her father laughed. 'Yes, I believe it is. It just so happens that company slang for a radio operator is a pianist. You can see why.'

'Oh, I see! I suppose it is a bit like playing an instrument. Cyrano taught me to use a Morse key, and I know all the Morse alphabet.'

'Do you indeed!' He looked at her fondly. 'You've grown up so much. When I left home you were just a little girl, and now look at you.'

'You should see her in a skirt and lipstick,' Luke said with a grin.

'A skirt and lipstick? Chris? Surely not!'

'I had to. It was a sort of uniform, when I was working behind the bar.'

'Dear God! Working behind a bar and wearing lipstick. Whatever would your mother say?'

'She'd approve. She was always on at me to make myself look more attractive.'

Luke cut in, 'You actually know Cyrano? And Gregoire?'

'Yes. I trained with them both.'

'So that's why they asked what you looked like,' Christine said. 'When I told them you looked like Luke, I think they recognized you, but of course they didn't say anything.'

'We did wonder if you might have volunteered for the same thing,' Luke said. 'But why weren't you sent to the Auvergne, where you had contacts?'

'Precisely for that reason. Too many people would have recognized me. But when the top brass found out I knew this area well they suggested I should come here. I was pretty sure I'd be able to recruit Marcel, but when I arrived I discovered he was already running his own circuit, so we were able to join forces.'

'Who was the man who questioned us, before you arrived?'

'Laurent. He's one of our best men, which is why I put him in charge of the operation last night. I hope he wasn't too rough on you.'

'No, he behaved pretty well, considering. I'm really sorry if we got in the way, but it wasn't intentional.'

'I know that. It was just an unfortunate coincidence. Someone must have tipped off the Germans and we shall have to find out who, but that's for another day. At least, if Chris's scheme works out, the train won't get far.' He looked at her teasingly but with a kind of wonder. 'Who would have thought that your interest in all things mechanical could be put to such good use?'

In spite of herself, Christine yawned and her father got up.

'Bedtime! None of us has had any sleep tonight. Tomorrow Marcel will take you over the border, but for now you both need a good rest.'

They set off soon after dawn, in borrowed boots and warm ski jackets. Roger came with them on the first leg of the journey, but at the top of a ridge he stopped.

'This is where I have to leave you, I'm afraid. There are things I have to attend to down there in Montbéliard. Marcel will see you safe across the border and his contacts there will get you to the British Consul. As you are both technically minors, there shouldn't be any difficulty about getting you sent back to England. Don't tell your grandparents that you've seen me. As far as they know I'm in Canada, training their pilots.'

'We won't say anything,' Luke promised. 'But I wish you'd let me stay here with you and join the circuit. Chris would be all right on her own from here.'

'Not possible, Luke. You know that. Anyway, you told me last night you want to join the RAF and fly Spitfires. You'll be much more useful doing that.' He reached out and drew them both to him. 'I'm so proud of you both and I can't wait for the war to be over, so I can come home and get to know this brave young man and this lovely girl that my children have grown into. Take care of yourselves and please, don't be any more heroic than you absolutely have to!'

He kissed them both and turned away down the mountain path. They stood watching him until Marcel said, 'Now we must go. We have a long walk in front of us.'

A week later, Isabelle was crouching over the radio in her kitchen. Her two German lodgers had gone and no one else had taken their places, so she felt safe in bringing the set indoors. The news was not good; instead of being able to march through Italy almost unimpeded, the Allies were facing determined opposition from the German army. There was bitter fighting. When the bulletin ended, she only half listened to the *messages personnels*. It was so long since there had been any news.

Then it came: Michou's pups are safely back in their proper kennel and the old dog who sired them sends his love.

THE END

ACKNOWLEDGEMENTS

The author wishes to thank the following people:

Tony Davis for the original idea and for sharing his expertise in all things related to the French canal network.

M. Philippe Bernard, ex-lock-keeper at Augy n°79V.S for information about the use of canals during World War II.

My husband David for his unstinting help and support, particularly in matters relating to computers.

ALSO BY HILARY GREEN

STANDALONE NOVELS
OPERATION KINGFISHER
TWICE ROYAL LADY
APHRODITE'S ISLAND

Thank you for reading this book.

If you enjoyed it please leave feedback on Amazon or Goodreads, and if there is anything we missed or you have a question about, then please get in touch. We appreciate you choosing our book.

Founded in 2014 in Shoreditch, London, we at Joffe Books pride ourselves on our history of innovative publishing. We were thrilled to be shortlisted for Independent Publisher of the Year at the British Book Awards.

www.joffebooks.com

We're very grateful to eagle-eyed readers who take the time to contact us. Please send any errors you find to corrections@joffebooks.com. We'll get them fixed ASAP.